A MERRY LITTLE CHRISTMAS

Julia Williams has always made up stories in her head, and until recently she thought everyone else did too. She grew up in London, one of eight children, including a twin sister. She was a children's editor at Scholastic for several years before going freelance after the birth of her second child. It was then she decided to try her hand at writing. The result, her debut novel, *Pastures New*, was a bestseller and has sold across Europe.

To find out more about Julia go to her website at www.juliawilliamsauthor.com, visit her blog at www.maniacmum.blogspot.com or follow Julia on Twitter @JCCWilliams.

By the same author:

A Merry Little Christmas

JULIA WILLIAMS

AVON

AVON
A division of HarperCollins*Publishers*
77–85 Fulham Palace Road,
London W6 8JB

www.harpercollins.co.uk

A Paperback Original 2012

1

Copyright © Julia Williams 2012

Julia Williams asserts the moral right to
be identified as the author of this work

A catalogue record for this book is
available from the British Library

ISBN-13: 978-1-84756-089-6

Set in Minion Pro by Palimpsest Book Production Limited
Falkirk, Stirlingshire

Printed and bound in Great Britain by
Clays Ltd, St Ives plc

For my gorgeous girls: Katie, Alex, Christine and Steph
And in loving memory of Rosemarie Williams

Prologue

The last rays of a winter's sunset sent streaks of orange and pink across the white fields. Dusk was settling as a motorbike roared its way through the snowy countryside. Large groups of birds took to the air as it sped past, and flocks of sheep ran wildly round in circles. The sound of the engine echoed down the country lanes, disturbing the chilly peace. The leather-clad rider wore a black jacket with a flaming sword emblazoned on his back which, along with his gold and orange helmet, made him resemble a modern day knight. As the rider stopped at the top of the hill overlooking Hope Christmas, he took off his helmet and stared down into the town. The Christmas lights were still twinkling in the High Street. The lamps from the houses down below gave the place a cosy homely feel, as if the whole town were drawing a collective sigh.

The rider flexed his hands, and smiled; the words, *Dux*, on one set of knuckles and *Michael* on the other, just visible underneath his fingerless gloves. He was good looking, with a dark complexion, devastating cheekbones, curly dark hair which tickled the collar of his jacket, and piercing blue eyes.

'So Hope Christmas, long time no see,' he muttered. 'Uncle Ralph was right, it's a beautiful little place. I shall look forward to renewing my acquaintance with you.'

He put his helmet back on, revved the engine, and roared

down the road and into town, noting the quaint little shops; the antiques market, flower stall, the bookshop and market square where a Christmas tree stood proudly in the centre. The town was deserted, with only one or two brave souls prepared to come out on such a cold night. One of them, a pensioner tootling along on a mobile buggy, stopped to say hello.

'Well, Michael Nicholas, as I live and breathe. Your uncle said you might be coming. It's good to see you after all these years.'

'And you, Miss Woods,' Michael smiled a devilishly handsome smile. 'It's been far too long.'

'Will you be staying a while?' she asked.

Michael looked around him. 'That, I think depends on who needs me,' he said.

'I think you'll find there's always a need,' said Miss Woods.

'Then yes, I think I'll be here a while,' said Michael, his smile crinkling up to his blue eyes.

'I look forward to it,' said Miss Woods. 'Happy Christmas.'

'And to you,' said Michael, before climbing back on his bike and speeding off to Hopesay Manor.

It was good to be back.

New Year

Cat Tinsall unwound the fairy lights from her suddenly bereft Christmas tree, then carefully placed them in the Santa sack which was bulging with the rest of the Christmas decorations. She sat back on her heels and looked out of the large patio door onto her frozen garden, where a lonely looking robin pecked at the crumbs on the bird table. It was a grey cold day, the sort that sapped your soul in early January. She sighed and tried not to feel too bereft herself. Even the Shropshire hills (the view of which was one of the reasons they'd bought this old converted farmhouse when they'd moved up to Hope Christmas four years earlier) were shrouded in grey gloom.

Christmas, her favourite time of the year, was over once more. The bright shiny new year, which had beckoned so enticingly at Pippa's New Year's bash through a happy haze of mulled wine and champagne, now seemed less so; reality being grey and drab in comparison. Noel was already back at work, groaning as he'd left in the dark to look at a project the other side of Birmingham, where he'd be meeting Michael Nicholas, Ralph Nicholas' nephew, for the first time. The kids were at school (Mel to mock-GCSEs for which Cat had seen no evidence of any revision over the holidays), and Cat herself had a pile of proofs to tackle for her new cookbook, *Cat's Country Kitchen*. They'd been guiltily shoved aside in a pre-Christmas planning frenzy, but she knew she could ignore them no longer. She looked at the picture of herself on the front cover – thanks to the power of Photoshop, looking more glamorous and slimmer then she felt right now. No doubt it would add fuel to the tabloids' 'Top Kitchen Totty' moniker that had haunted her since the launch of her first book, *Cat's Kitchen Secrets*, three years earlier.

All in all it had been a good Christmas, Cat thought as she carried the Santa sack up the creaking stairs of their old country cottage, to put back up in the loft later. Even Mel's moodiness had done little to put a spanner in the works. It was weird how a previously model daughter had morphed into the teenager from hell over the last year. From having once enjoyed a close relationship with her daughter, Cat felt constantly baffled by Mel now. Noel was always telling her she needed to relax and not force the issue so much, but she couldn't help wanting to find out what was going on in her daughter's head – while realising that the more she pushed, the further Mel retreated from her.

It was just that now, with her mum's dementia having taken her away from them forever, Cat wanted that closeness with Mel even more. One of the most heart-wrenching sights this Christmas had been seeing Louise looking so bewildered as she sat down to join them for Christmas dinner. It still gave Cat such a pang to see her mother like this; to see her refer to Mel as 'Catherine', and watch her wander in to help with the turkey, stirred by some memory of Christmases long ago, then stand around with an air of uncertainty saying, 'This isn't my kitchen.' None of this behaviour was unusual, but somehow it was always worse seeing her mother away from the home, where for the most part there could be at least a pretence that things were quite

4

well. Cat knew she should be used to it by now. But she was not, and probably never would be.

The trouble was, every time she saw her mother, she remembered what they'd had, what they'd lost. It had just been her and Louise throughout Cat's childhood, a two-woman united team, and Cat had always assumed she would share that same easy closeness forever – and when she had children of her own, replicate it with her own daughters. Mel was proving her wrong about that on a daily basis. Cat tried to think of any major moments of rebellion in her childhood, but there hadn't been any. There had been no need. She loved her mum, knew how hard Louise had to work, and had no intention of making her life harder than it already was. Whereas Mel . . . Cat sighed. Where had she gone wrong with Mel? Maybe it was, as Noel seemed to think, that her daughter was jealous of the attention James had garnered as her cooking companion.

The TV company who'd produced her original series, *Cat's Kitchen Secrets* four years ago, had pounced on James when they spotted how often he was in the background helping her out. With his cute (then) ten-year-old goofy grin, cheeky manner and angelic good looks, they'd realised he was ideal TV fodder. Mel, a gawky twelve-year-old, was far too self-conscious to appear on the TV, even though she'd been given the option to.

None of them could have predicted what a success James would have been. Now fourteen, he was relaxed in front of the camera, and having been a natural cook from an early age, had always showed far more interest in helping her in the kitchen than his sisters. The girls enjoyed baking but couldn't be bothered to cook a meal, whereas James was developing his own creative ability to cook up tasty food. Although to be fair, his menus did include a lot of pizza

5

and nachos. Consequently, a TV series of his own aimed at kids was in the offing, and he was already (with Cat's help) writing his second book, *James' Top Tips for Hungry Teens*.

Cat had tried really hard to ensure that the attention hadn't gone to his head. Luckily James was a down to earth sort, just as happy kicking a football about with her friend Pippa's sons, Nathan and George, as lording it in front of the TV cameras. And as for writing cookery books, that was clearly far too much effort, so Cat was writing most of it for him. Cat tried to make up for the attention James was getting by focusing as much on the other things the girls did, like Paige's singing or Ruby's dancing, and so far they seemed unaffected. Paige was so sure she was going to be on *X Factor*, and aiming at being twelve going on thirty that she couldn't care less, while Ruby was still too young to notice.

Mel, on the other hand was another matter. One by one, she'd dropped the activities she used to enjoy, no longer playing tennis, attending Scouts, or to Cat's great disappointment, playing the piano. Instead she spent far too much time mooching about in nearby Hope Sadler where she worked in a café at the weekends. On top of that, having initially mixed with a crowd of pleasant, hard-working girls when they'd first arrived in Hope Christmas, Mel seemed to have dropped them all to hang out with the rebels of the year. From what little Cat had gleaned, they seemed to mainly spend their time in the local parks, smoking and drinking. Mel always denied joining in, but Cat had long since given up completely trusting her daughter. Something she'd never before imagined could happen.

Cat sighed again and climbed up into the loft with the decorations. Time to get back to reality.

*   *   *

Marianne North drove into the large sweeping farmyard of the home she shared with Gabe, and breathed a huge sigh of relief. Their ancient farmhouse had never looked more welcoming. Gabe had been home for a week already. It was difficult for him to take any time away from the farm, so he'd come back early, while Marianne had ended up stuck at her mum's for pretty much the whole fortnight of Christmas, the longest time she'd spent there since university days. But Mum – feeling cheated that her precious grandchildren had missed their first Christmas at Nana's (Marianne's protestations that three-month-old twin babies were pretty nightmarish to take anywhere had fallen on deaf ears and despite an invitation to Hope Christmas, Mum had resolutely refused) – had been so martyred about how the twins' other granny saw so much more of them that Marianne had had to capitulate and trek down to London this year. Gabe's mother Jean, whom Marianne knew would miss the twins dreadfully, was fortunately immensely generous and said, 'I'll survive without you all. I do get to see the twins a lot more than your mother,' which was true, especially as she looked after them twice a week while Marianne was working. 'I had a demanding mother-in-law and always promised I wouldn't be the same. David and I will have a nice quiet time together alone.'

Marianne had hugged her with gratitude, and they'd had a pre-Christmas lunch with Pippa and Dan and their family the week before the big day. Marianne had then set off two days before Christmas, and Gabe and Steven had joined them on Christmas Day. Poor Steven had been nearly as bored as she and Gabe were. There was precious little for an eleven-year-old boy to do in the drab London suburb where Marianne had grown up, particularly when he knew no one there. Then Gabriel had taken Steven over to his mum, Eve, for a few days. Eve, though in the past an unreliable mother, seemed in recent years to have sorted herself out, even managing to hold down both a good job and a rich boyfriend, Darren. Gabriel was much more relaxed about Steven visiting her now, and this time around Steven had leapt at the chance to go, Marianne noticed, a little sadly. She worried that since the arrival of the twins, Steven had felt left out, and it must be really hard to take on an extra set of grandparents, who, let's face it, weren't *really* interested in him. Though Marianne noticed, gratefully, that Dad had made huge efforts as far as Steven was concerned, but Mum just couldn't help herself from cooing over the twins. You couldn't blame her in a way, she'd waited a long time for grandchildren and then to get two for the price of one . . . Marianne loved her mother dearly, but it was the sort of relationship that benefited from distance – two hundred miles was just about right.

'Hi Gabe, we're home.' Marianne unloaded the car, while the children slept in the back. So much crap for two little people who hadn't reached the age of two yet; nappies, buggies, car seats, toddler seats for sitting at dinner, two travel cots . . . And that was without the presents Mum had insisted on buying – a pram set for Daisy and a toy car for Harry – nothing like clinging to stereotypes – as well as countless soft toys, rattles, shiny things with plastic knobs and buzzers on. Marianne felt sure her parents must be nearly bankrupted by the arrival of their twin grandchildren, but nothing she said would stop her mother from buying stuff for them. ('You can't spoil babies,' she'd trilled when Marianne faintly tried to suggest that maybe it was all a bit much.)

'And it's fab to see you.'

Gabe. Her heart still did that funny little skipping thing when she saw him standing in the farmhouse doorway in a thick knit sweater and jeans, his dark brown hair slightly mussed up where he'd been running his fingers through it, those deep brown sensitive eyes. She loved that wonderful thrill of knowing he was hers.

'God, I've missed you so much,' said Marianne, burying her head in his shoulder as he enveloped her in a warm bear hug. 'Never *ever* let me stay that long with my parents again. Next year they are so coming to us. The twins haven't slept all week. I'm exhausted.'

'Me too,' yawned Gabriel. 'I had a lamb born last night. The mother had gone off in the dark, and it took Steven, me and Patch ages to find her.'

'Did Steven have a good time with Eve?' Marianne felt a pang of guilt. She should have been back in time for Steven to start back at school – she normally was. But her mum had insisted she stay an extra day and come home on Monday. Steven and Gabe had assured her they could cope, but she still felt bad. Since she and Gabriel had got together four years earlier, she'd always been around for the start of term. It didn't feel right staying away. But since having the twins and juggling her career with motherhood, Marianne had got used to a familiar feeling of being torn in two.

'I think so,' something in Gabe's tone stopped her. He looked pensive, the way he used to when they first met, when Eve had left him and he was coping with being a single dad.

'What's Eve done now?' said Marianne.

'You remember that choir school she mentioned back in the autumn?' said Gabe.

'Yes,' said Marianne, remembering a conversation about the impossibility of them affording to send Steven to a fee-paying school, however good his voice was.

'She's persuaded Steven he should try out for it,' said Gabe. 'She's talking about moving up near Middleminster, and having Steven stay with her and Darren at the weekends. That means we're going to be fifty miles away, and they'll be on the doorstep. We'll never see him.'

'What does Steven say?'

'He wants to go,' said Gabriel. 'She's got him so excited about it, and I don't want to bring him back down to earth.'

'But surely we can't afford it,' said Marianne. 'Even if we all pitched in together?'

'There are scholarships apparently,' said Gabriel, running his fingers distractedly through his hair. 'I don't know, Marianne, I know it's a big opportunity. But to be away from us? I don't think I could bear it.'

'Maybe it won't come to anything,' said Marianne. 'After all, he's got to get in first.'

'True,' said Gabriel, 'but he's a clever boy, you said so yourself, and with your help he could do it. And Darren knows the Head of Music there. Eve seems to think he's got a really good chance.'

'Then you can't deny him a shot at it,' said Marianne firmly. 'If that's what he wants to do.'

'I know,' said Gabriel miserably. 'I feel really guilty about this, but I don't want him to go.'

Pippa Holliday slammed down the phone with uncharacteristic anger. 'Of all the small-minded, patronising, bloody useless pieces of—' A clicking to her left reminded her that Lucy was there, so she curtailed the expletive she was going to use and said, 'Oh Luce, it's that social worker.'

Lucy tilted her face to one side and pulled a grumpy face and shook her head.

'No, we don't like her,' said Pippa with a smile. Lucy always managed to make her laugh, even when things were really grim. 'She's being so unhelpful.'

Unhelpful. That was one way of putting it. Yes, Pippa

understood there were cuts. Yes, she also understood that Lucy's case was only one of many that Claire King dealt with daily, and yes probably to Claire-I've-no-idea-how-you-do-it King, Pippa and her family weren't a priority, living as they did in a comfortable house with a reasonably good income, and inconveniently Dan was neither an absentee father nor a wife-beater. Pippa knew she didn't help her case by presenting a calm unhurried manner to the world, but it was the only way she knew of coping with the difficulties life had thrown at her.

From the first catastrophic moment when she and Dan had been told that their precious longed-for baby daughter had cystic fibrosis, and would grow up needing constant care, Pippa had known she would manage, because what other choice was there? Besides, when she, to her everlasting shame, had fallen apart at the news, Dan had been so together, so strong for the two of them, she knew they'd get through it somehow. Without Dan, she doubted she would have been so calm, so capable, so *coping*. So many men in his position might have walked out on them, but Dan loved their daughter with a constant and devoted tenderness that Pippa could only marvel at and be grateful for. His support and love had kept them all afloat, making huge efforts to ensure the boys never missed out on activities because of Lucy; always trying to be there for hospital visits when he could, and running the farm to boot. Dan. Her perfect hero.

And they had coped and managed all this time because eventually, after long years and battles, Pippa had organised respite care for her daughter, giving the rest of the family precious time together. Pippa hated to use the word *normal* – but doing the things that other families took for granted, going for long walks in the country, having a pub lunch without establishing first whether they had disabled access, and having to face out people's stares. People could be so cruel, even in this allegedly enlightened day and age. And now that was all about to be taken away from them, as Claire bloody King had just informed her that due to a tightening of budgets, Lucy might lose her precious respite care.

'It's not definite, but–'

Reading the subtext, Pippa knew Claire thought there were more needy, deserving families than hers. There probably were, but that didn't make it right. Since Lucy had been going to respite care, Pippa had had some precious time for herself. Not a lot, but enough for her to be able to cope with the demands of her beautiful, gorgeous daughter, and feel she was still looking after her boys and husband too. Without that lifeline she felt she might sink.

'I'm sure you'll manage,' said Claire, 'you're so calm. And you have so much support. It will be fine.'

'And what if it's not?' said Pippa frankly. 'Having the respite care is what keeps me calm. Without it I don't know what I'd do.'

She put the phone down in frustration. There was no point taking it out on Claire. The woman was only doing her job. But still. She looked at her precious daughter, sitting in her custom-made wheelchair, sighing to cheer her up – Lucy had an instinct for sniffing out when Pippa was sad and stressed, which was one of the most lovable things about her – and wondered how they would cope. Lucy was nearly ten now and getting bigger all the time. There might come a point when Pippa couldn't lift her or bath her, or do all the little jobs she needed. It was like having a toddler for life. A large overgrown toddler, with hormones. For the first time since that terrible day when Lucy had been born, Pippa really felt overwhelmed. What if, after all she *couldn't* cope? What would they do then?

Part One

Let Your Heart Be Light

January

Chapter One

Marianne was simmering a lamb stew on the Aga, in the homely country kitchen she and Gabriel had recently renovated in oak, while the twins sat in their high chairs banging spoons on the table, giggling away at each other. It was a deep and abiding relief to her that they were so happy in each other's company; they kept themselves usefully occupied when she was busy. It was a wintry Monday afternoon and Gabriel had taken Steven over to have a look around Middleminster. Marianne had thought of coming with them as she wasn't working, but decided that the twins would probably be too distracting, and it might be better for Gabriel to do this with Steven on his own. She also hoped that it might persuade Gabriel that this was really a good idea.

She was just serving the twins' portions into two identical plastic bowls when an animated Steven burst through the door, followed by Gabriel, looking slightly less than thrilled. Marianne was caught afresh with the realisation of how similar father and son were getting. Steven had grown a lot recently and his hair had darkened, and his eyes, though blue, retained something of his father's look about them.

'So what's it like?'

'It was fab, Marianne!' Steven was jumping about with

15

glee. 'They've got a brilliant football pitch and I could get to play cricket too!'

Steven had started playing cricket the previous summer, and been disappointed to learn that the local secondary school hadn't got cricket on the curriculum.

'What about the choir?' laughed Marianne, caught up with his infectious enthusiasm. 'I mean, that's the main reason for going.'

'It was cool, wasn't it, Dad?' Steven's eyes lit up. Unusually for a boy, he loved singing – and had a talent for it too.

'Very cool,' agreed Gabriel, 'but you have to get in first.'

'We'd better get started on those practice tests, hadn't we?' said Marianne, giving Steven a hug. Since the idea of Middleminster had first been mooted in the autumn, she had occasionally run through a past paper with Steven. He was a bright boy, and she saw no reason why he couldn't get in, but he needed more experience of the entrance tests if he were to stand a chance. Marianne looked at Gabe and gave him an encouraging smile. She knew how hard this was for him. On the one hand, he wanted to give his son the best chance he could have, of course he did. But on the other, Gabe had no desire to lose Steven to a choir school fifty miles away, despite Marianne's pointing out it *was* a good opportunity if Steven wanted to take it.

'Mum says Darren knows someone at the school who might be able to help,' said Steven.

'I gathered that,' said Gabe. 'If you're going to get in, I'd rather you did it on your own merits.'

'So you did like it then?' Marianne said as Steven disappeared upstairs to play on his Xbox.

'It's a great school,' admitted Gabe. 'And I could see Steven loved it. Hell, *I* loved it. You should have seen the facilities they have. I think Steven could do well there.'

'That's good isn't it?'

'Yes . . .' Gabriel had a slightly forlorn look on his face. One she hadn't seen in a long time.

'I sense a *but* here,' said Marianne.

'Eleven is very young to be away from us,' said Gabriel. 'I hate the thought of him going away. And if Eve does move up here, we won't even have him every weekend.'

'I know,' said Marianne, 'and I do understand, but if Steven really likes it . . .'

'And he does,' said Gabriel with a rueful smile. 'I'm being selfish.'

'No you're not,' said Marianne giving him a hug. 'You love your son. Which is perfectly natural, and is one of many reasons that I love you. And here's another.'

She handed Gabe Daisy's bowl, and she took Harry's, and together they fed the twins. It was one of the most fun parts of a hectically busy domestic routine, and one which always made her happy and grateful that she'd found Gabriel four years ago, when she'd nearly left Hope Christmas after Luke Nicholas had broken her heart. As she'd hoped, five minutes of making aeroplane noises for the twins cheered Gabriel up no end, and his mood was much lighter by the time they were clearing up.

'Try not to worry about Steven,' Marianne said, lifting Daisy out of her high chair and popping her into the playpen that sat in the corner of the kitchen. 'I know it's hard, but even with a nod from Darren's mate, he's not certain to get in.'

'True,' said Gabe, carrying Harry to join his sister. 'And even Eve admitted we can't afford it if he doesn't get a scholarship.'

'There, you see,' said Marianne, kissing him. 'No need to waste your energy on ifs and buts. It might never happen. Why don't we just enjoy what we have?'

*   *   *

Pippa was baking; her kitchen smelling warm, comforting, and safe. It was her default position when stressed. Plus she was part of the volunteer group who kept the local shop open, stocked and supplied with local produce and home baking. The rate she was going today, the shop was going to be well stocked for weeks. She'd spent all morning making chocolate brownies, blueberry muffins, and scones – all to put off facing up to the unpalatable news that Lucy's social worker, Claire King had given her that morning.

'I'm sorry,' had been Claire's opening gambit, 'but we're all having to cut our budgets for the next financial year, and one of my more unpleasant jobs has been working out which services have to be cut. One of the options we're looking at is reducing our respite care packages. It has to go on level of need, I'm afraid . . .'

The pause spoke volumes.

'And ours isn't great enough,' Pippa said flatly.

'I wouldn't go as far as to say that,' Claire was clearly floundering a bit, 'and I'm not saying this is a definite, or that you'll lose the respite altogether . . .'

'But it's a possibility?' said Pippa.

'I think it's more likely that Lucy will be receiving respite care once a month in the foreseeable future, rather than once a fortnight,' said Claire, 'and rest assured we will be working hard to sort out an alternative for you, but . . .'

But that was no guarantee of help in the long term. Reading between the lines, and given the level of cuts being imposed on social services, it was highly unlikely that Lucy would be having any respite care in a year's time. Pippa was desperately looking round for alternatives, but as far as she could see there were none. She'd written a letter to her MP, Tom Brooker – without much hope of success, given that it was his party implementing the cuts – and was now trying to drum up support from other parents similarly affected. The trouble was, most of them, like her, were worn down by the years and years of fighting a system that at its best could be brilliant, but at its worst was cold, indifferent and cared little for individual sob stories.

Her next port of call was going to be Cat Tinsall. With her media contacts, Cat might be able to help, not just Lucy, but the other kids who got help from the Sunshine Trust. And Cat, Pippa knew, would understand. When Cat had first moved to Hope Christmas just under four years ago, they had instantly bonded over children, cooking and how hard it was being a carer. Cat's mother, Louise, suffered from dementia, and Pippa knew how tough she found it. She empathised with the guilt, the feeling that maybe you could do more, be better, be less selfish.

'Mmm, something smells good. Bad day?' Dan's six-foot frame filled the kitchen. He had a way of dominating a room. He'd come fresh from the outhouse where he scrubbed down after milking the cows, before entering the house. He'd been out since dawn and had come back now to have breakfast. Pippa's heart swelled. However hard life was, she had and always would have Dan. A sudden memory snuck its way into her brain, of her and Dan, lying together in their field at the bottom of the hill on a sunny day, Dan saying quite seriously, 'Love you forever,' when Pippa had only just got round to thinking the 'L' word. Everything was manageable with Dan by her side.

'How did you guess?' asked Pippa, lifting her last batch of scones out of the Aga and putting them on the pine kitchen island in the middle of the kitchen, replacing them with muffins. She took a broom out and swept away the mud Dan had brought in with him.

'You always bake when you're in a bad mood,' said Dan.

'And you always bring mud in from the farm,' she said.

'I did wash up,' protested Dan.

'But you forgot to take your boots off, as usual,' Pippa rolled her eyes at him.

Dan responded by picking up a scone and taking a bite. 'Delicious.'

'Oi, they're not for you,' said Pippa. 'But why don't you sit down and I'll make you a cuppa and a fry-up.'

'No, you sit down,' said Dan, 'and tell me all about it. What's that bloody woman done now?'

'Nothing more than usual,' said Pippa, loving him for so perfectly tuning into her mood. 'She's wrung her hands as much as she can, but the upshot is we still have respite care for the short term, but monthly not fortnightly.'

'Well, that's something at least,' said Dan.

'I know,' said Pippa. 'But it's the long term I'm worried about. What happens if we lose it altogether?'

'We cross that bridge when we come to it,' said Dan, handing his wife a cup of tea.

'Why are you always so positive?' said Pippa. 'Here I am finding problems, and you go round making out it will all be okay.' That was Dan all over, her rock, her strength. He always managed to help her see a way through, when she felt overwhelmed.

'One of us has to be,' said Dan, 'and you do enough worrying for the pair of us. Something will turn up, you'll see.'

'Oh Dan,' said Pippa, suddenly feeling a bit teary. 'Whatever did I do to deserve you?'

'I don't know,' said Dan with a grin, 'but if I'm allowed another one of those scones, you never know, I might even stick around a while.'

Cat was on the set of *Cat's Country Kitchen,* her new TV show which was due to air in the autumn, when her phone buzzed. She'd been busy talking to Len Franklin the director

20

about setting up a shot of her chopping onions for her Shropshire hotpot, which she was meant to be doing without crying. The phone buzzed insistently again. Damn. She thought she'd turned it off. Cat took it out of her pocket and saw, to her dismay, the school phone number. Her heart sank. Now what had Mel done?

'I'm terribly sorry,' she said to Len. She hadn't worked with him before, and found him a little taciturn and unfriendly, so she wasn't quite sure how he'd take the interruption. 'Would you mind if I take this?'

'If you must,' said Len in long-suffering tones. 'But please be quick, we've got a busy schedule and a lot to get through.'

'Thanks,' said Cat, smiling apologetically at the film crew, and wandered to the back of the studio.

'Hullo, Catherine Tinsall here,' she said. 'Sorry to keep you waiting. How may I help?'

She dreaded phone calls from school, which seemed to be happening with monotonous regularity of late.

'Mrs Tinsall?' The crisp tones of Mrs Reynolds, the school secretary, always made her turn to jelly. 'It appears that Melanie is absent from school, and we haven't heard from you. I take it she is ill?'

'Ill? No of course not,' said Cat in bewilderment. 'I saw her off to school myself. Did you send me a text message?'

'Of course,' said Mrs Reynolds.

'Oh,' Cat checked her messages. She'd missed one. 'Yes I did get it. I'm at work, and didn't pick it up. Didn't Mel come in at all?'

'Apparently not,' said Mrs Reynolds frostily. Cat knew it was paranoid, but she always got the impression Mrs Reynolds thought all mothers should stay at home till their children had left school.

'I am so sorry,' said Cat. 'I'll try and find out what's happened and where she is.'

She put the phone down, her heart thumping. Bloody hell. She'd had far too many conversations this year with Mel's form teacher about her bad behaviour, but usually it was about cheeking the teachers, or not working hard enough. She'd even been suspended for a day for being caught smoking. Why on earth would she have skipped school? It was probably because she was due to get her mock results. Mel had been grumpy as hell for the last few days, and judging by how little work she'd done over the Christmas holidays, Cat wasn't expecting miracles. It was the first time Mel had ever bunked off. That is, if she *was* bunking off, and not dead in a ditch somewhere. Oh God, Cat thought, what if something had happened to her?

'Don't even go there, Cat,' she muttered to herself, and rang Mel's mobile. Switched off, of course. She sent a text instead. *You've been rumbled. RING ME, Mum.*

She texted both James and Paige at school, though she knew, technically, they weren't supposed to have their phones on them.

Do you know where Mel is?

No idea. James' response was swift and to the point.

Paige took longer to reply.

Saw her talking to Andy outside school.

Andy who?

Dunno was the helpful response.

Great. Thanks for nothing, Paige.

'Ahem, if we could get on?' Len was tapping his watch, the film crew were looking bored, and Cat was conscious everyone was looking at her.

'Yes, of course, nearly done.' Cat made one last phone call.

'Noel, I'm really sorry to do this, but Mel's bunked off. I've no idea where she is and I was due on camera five

22

minutes ago. Can you deal with it? I assume she's in town somewhere. Possibly with a boy named Andy.'

'Cat–' began Noel.

'I know, I'm sorry,' said Cat, 'I'll get away as soon as I can, I promise.'

'Okay, leave it with me,' said Noel, 'I'll go out on a recce.'

'Thanks,' said Cat. 'I owe you.'

'*Again*,' said Noel, who had, she realised guiltily, been picking up more of the domestic slack than her of late. 'I'll bloody kill her when I find her.'

'Not before I do,' said Cat.

'When we're ready,' interrupted the director, sharply.

'Ready,' said Cat, turning her phone off.

She allowed the make-up girl to touch up her face, and stood in front of the shiny hot plates on which she was about to demonstrate making her twist on a traditional Shropshire stew.

'Hello and welcome to *Cat's Country Kitchen*, where I'll be showing you recipes old and new from Shropshire, the food capital of Great Britain,' she said, trying with all her might to forget about errant daughters and concentrate instead on cooking. After all, that's what she got paid for.

Chapter Two

'And, cut.' Eventually Len was satisfied. It seemed to have taken ages to get the exact shots he'd wanted, and Cat had been itching to get off the premises for the last half hour. As soon as she decently could, Cat made her excuses and, heart hammering, dashed to the door. She switched her phone back on, to one text message from Noel: *Got her*. Thank God for that. Cat felt herself unwind slightly. At least Mel wasn't in danger. But now she knew they were going to have the sort of confrontation Cat always dreaded, with Mel screaming in their faces and her losing her rag. She tried to stay as calm as Noel somehow managed to, but Cat found herself bewildered by their daughter's unreasonable behaviour. Mel had everything she wanted, why did she have to put them through the mill like this?

Noel was always saying she should try and see it from Mel's side more. Mel would no doubt say that she had everything but her mum's time, Cat reflected. Guilt, guilt, guilt. Her default position. They'd left London so Cat could spend more time with the family, so how was it she seemed to spend less? And now there was more guilt, when she discovered Noel had had to leave an important meeting with Ralph Nicholas' nephew, who had just joined the firm. If it had been Ralph, Noel was sure he would have understood, but Michael Nicholas was still an unknown quantity according to Noel, and while he hadn't said anything, Noel had felt awkward about curtailing the meeting to deal with an absconding teenager.

'Next time, it's your shout,' said Noel. 'I can't keep doing this.'

'I know, I know,' said Cat, thinking *well, I can't either*. The trouble was she had been so busy filming over the last few months she had dropped lots of balls into Noel's lap, from dental appointments to meetings with Mel's teachers. She sighed and wished more than ever Louise hadn't become ill. Life in Hope Christmas with Louise on hand to help out would have been perfect.

'So where was she?' asked Cat while rooting around in her bag for her keys.

'I found her in the café,' said Noel. 'They were a bit dim, really. It wasn't hard to track them down.'

'And where's Mel now?' said Cat.

'In her room, sulking,' said Noel.

'Oh joy,' sighed Cat. 'I'll be home soon.'

She got in the car and put her foot down, and soon found herself escaping the gloom of Birmingham's high rises for the snow-capped hills of her adopted county.

'Blue remembered hills indeed,' she murmured, as she drove down the main road towards Hope Christmas, seeing the hills she and Noel loved to walk on looming in the distance. It was a grey winter's day, and shafts of light streamed out underneath the louring clouds, as she sped her way home.

Snow had started to fall as she finally drove into the large gravel driveway in front of their oak-beamed house. Their home in Hope Christmas was so different from their London abode – a converted farmhouse with a fabulous kitchen, its gleaming modern steel apparatus still managing to retain a traditional feel when married to grey flagstones and marble-topped work surfaces; creaking stairs, wooden beams, and a huge wood burning stove in the middle giving it a cosy aspect, particularly on a gloomy January day, like today.

'I'm sorry,' said Cat as she walked through the door, into their lounge, where the fire was already lit and the sweet smell of wood smoke filled the room, 'I just couldn't get away.'

'No worries,' said Noel, looking vaguely up from his laptop. He pushed his glasses up his nose in an absent-minded gesture and smiled in a way that still made her go weak at the knees. 'At least I found her.'

'Did she say why she did it?'

'Nope,' said Noel with a sigh, rifling his fingers through his greying hair. 'I read the riot act, and all that did was produce floods of tears. I couldn't get her to say a word about what she's been up to. So I've just left her to stew on it. Now might be a good time for some softly softly.'

Okay, time to gird her loins. Cat made her way to the top of the house, and to Mel's low-beamed bedroom where she spent a huge amount of time in splendid teenage isola-tion. She disappeared up there for hours, plugged into either her iPod, her phone, or her laptop. (Cat was vaguely aware Mel had an anonymous blog, but she had no idea what it was called and despite her massive curiosity about it, at Noel's suggestion had kept away – 'Give her some space,' Noel was always saying, 'if you read her blog, it will be the equivalent of your mum reading your diary.' Except she'd never written anything worth hiding from her mum in her diary. At fifteen, Louise had known all Cat's secrets.) Mel was only secretive as far as Cat was concerned, hiding anything dodgy on Facebook, and chatting to God knows who on BBM, and for all Cat knew making a bunch of unsuitable friends.

It had been so different when they'd first got to Hope Christmas, four years earlier. Having been bullied at her old school, Mel had been happy to fall in with a bunch of self-confessed geeks, and not felt the need to worry about it. But in the last year Mel had drifted away from them, becoming close to a girl called Karen whose entire raison d'être seemed to be going out and getting as drunk as possible. She hadn't been a very good influence in Cat's opinion – but she didn't dare say so. The more Cat and Noel criticised Karen, the more intransigent Mel got.

'May I come in?' Cat poked her head round the door. Mel was lying on her bed looking moody, listening to her iPod.

'Suppose,' was the ungracious response. 'But if you're going to give me a lecture, it's okay; Dad's already done the third degree. And now I'm like, grounded, forever.'

'Mel, what did you expect?' said Cat, her hackles rising. 'You weren't at school and we were worried about you. You can't just bunk off because you don't feel like going in.'

'I was okay,' said Mel.

'Yes, but we didn't know that,' said Cat trying to keep her voice level. 'And besides, until you're sixteen you have to go to school every day, like it or not.'

Mel just grunted, and shifted awkwardly on the bed.

'So who's this boy then?' said Cat after a pause.

'A mate,' said Mel.

'Does his mum know he's been bunking off, too?'

'He's not at school,' said Mel.

'Christ, how old is he?' Mel was still only fifteen. Cat had visions of her dating a twenty-one-year-old.

'Nineteen,' said Mel sulkily. 'And before you go off on one, he's got a job.'

'So why wasn't he at work?' said Cat.

'Day off,' said Mel.

'And what does he do?'

'Farm labourer,' said Mel. 'He works for Pippa sometimes.'

At least that was something, Cat supposed, making a mental note to quiz Pippa about him later.

'Well, I can't say I'm impressed that you've found yourself a boyfriend who's encouraged you to bunk off,' said Cat. 'Tomorrow, I want you to go into school and write a letter of apology to Mrs Carter. And I shall be taking you into school for the rest of the week to make sure you get there.'

'But, Mum,' wailed Mel. 'I'm not a kid anymore.'

'But Mum, nothing,' said Cat. 'I'll treat you like a grown-up when you learn to behave like one.'

'That's so unfair,' said Mel.

'That's as maybe,' said Cat, 'but it's still what's happening.'

She left Mel still in a strop, no doubt texting the whole world to complain about her lot in life, and made her way downstairs with a heavy heart. Sometimes she felt like her daughter was an alien from another planet. When Mel was little Cat had never imagined that she would ever think it, but life had been so much easier when she was five.

Pippa had just parked on the village square, outside Hope Christmas Community shop – known locally as Vera's (in tribute to Vera Edwards who ran it with her husband Albert) – to deliver her baking, when she saw Marianne's slight form struggling with her double buggy in the doorway. Like a lot of buildings in Hope Christmas, it was quaint and old, but not terribly baby friendly. Pippa put down her boxes of cakes and ran over to help. Marianne smiled her thanks as she pushed the twins into the dark interior of the shop. Her dark curls were held up in a loose ponytail, and her blue eyes looked pale and tired.

'You look done in,' said Pippa, following her in with the cakes.

'I am a bit,' said Marianne. 'The twins are teething and they keep taking it in turns to wake up. Thank God I'm not teaching today. Otherwise I would have been a zombie.'

'Have you time for a coffee?' Vera's was not only a thriving village shop and post office, but it also housed a café run by volunteers which was the hub of the local community. Thanks to their help, Vera had been able to keep her post office going when it was under threat of closure.

'That would be great, thanks,' said Marianne, settling herself down at a creaky table by the window overlooking the village square, which allowed enough room for her to fit the buggy in. Luckily the twins appeared to have dozed off.

'I'll just give the cakes to Vera,' said Pippa, 'back in a minute.'

She went over to the counter, handed over her cakes and ordered their drinks at the same time, before going back to join Marianne.

'How are things?' said Marianne. 'Sorry I haven't seen much of you since I've been back from London. As soon as I'm back in work mode, I don't know what happens to the days. And yet when I'm home with the twins I couldn't tell you what I do all day.'

'I remember that feeling very well,' laughed Pippa. 'The upside of the kids getting bigger is that I do have a bit more time.'

'Oh, and thanks for looking after Gabe when I was away,' added Marianne. 'He and Steven would probably have lived on baked beans if you hadn't fed them every other night.'

'Looking after Gabriel is my default position,' laughed Pippa. 'I've been doing it since he was a baby.'

Though Pippa and Gabriel were cousins, having been brought up on neighbouring farms, they were closer than many siblings. Now that their respective parents had retired,

Pippa and Dan ran one farm, and Gabriel the other, and each helped the other out when they could.

'Have you heard any more about Lucy's respite care?' said Marianne. 'I know you were waiting for a call before I went away.'

Pippa pulled a face. 'She's only going to get monthly help instead of fortnightly, but at least they haven't cancelled it altogether. For the moment the Sunshine Trust is still guaranteeing its respite care, but it's only a matter of time. It's a small independent centre which is mainly funded by charitable donations, and the respite care is funded by Social Services. With all the cuts I can see them pulling the plug.'

'But that's outrageous,' said Marianne. 'What will happen to all those families?'

'I know,' said Pippa. 'It makes me so angry, but what can I do?'

'Can you get together and find some private support?'

'In this day and age?' said Pippa. 'No one has any money. But if the money could be found to support the respite care package, then maybe the Trust can still provide it. I'm thinking of starting a campaign, but I'm not sure it will make any difference.'

'That's not like you,' said Marianne. 'Come on, you're the campaign queen. Look at this place – it wouldn't be here if it weren't for your help.'

Pippa looked around at the busy shop, bursting with produce from local farms – hers included – and the café, packed as it was with a combination of local mums and the occasional brave winter walker. It was true that without Pippa, the campaign to help save Vera's livelihood wouldn't have happened. But that had been four years ago, and there had been a lot of water under the bridge since then.

'I know,' said Pippa. 'But I'm so tired. I've been fighting

and fighting for every scrap of help I can ever since Lucy's been born. I'm not sure I have the energy to fight anymore.'

'Well, let us help you, then,' said Marianne. 'Come on, you can't give up on Lucy now.'

'Your friend's right,' a leather-clad man sitting at the next table suddenly butted in. He was good looking, with dark tousled hair and deep blue eyes, and a captivating voice. Pippa thought she spotted tattoos on his knuckles; not the usual sort you got in Hope Christmas. 'You owe it to your daughter to keep on fighting.'

'And what do you know about it?' Pippa bristled. How dare this stranger tell her what to do?

'More than you'd think,' said the stranger, touching his nose and giving her a wink. He got up to go. 'I'd say nothing's impossible till you've tried it.'

And with that, he was gone.

'Well of all the–' said Pippa in disbelief. 'What business was it of his, the cheeky sod?'

'Maybe,' said Marianne, 'but he did have a point.'

'I suppose,' said Pippa gruffly.

'And did you see how good looking he was?' grinned Marianne. 'Ladies of Hope Christmas, beware! Trouble's coming!'

Pippa laughed. For some reason, she suddenly felt better, as if a burden had been lifted from her shoulders for a while.

'Okay, then,' she said, 'what do you think my plan of action should be?'

'We're off for a stroll up the hill,' said Gabriel brightly, to Steven who was crouched over his Nintendo DS. 'Care to join us?'

'Do I have to?' whined Steven. 'It's cold out there.'

'It will be refreshing and good for you,' said Gabriel. 'We

31

should make the most of the moment. We haven't had many opportunities to get out recently.'

'Come on, Steven,' said Marianne. 'It's been ages since all of us have done anything together.'

'We can't do anything with babies,' grumbled Steven, but Marianne sensed he was weakening. Steven loved his baby siblings, and it was rare for him to moan about them. 'They don't do anything.'

'So, we need you to keep us company,' cajoled Marianne, she was always careful to make sure Steven knew how important he still was, and that the twins hadn't replaced him. 'The twins can't tell us interesting facts they've discovered.'

One of the joys of being in Steven's company was that he had an encyclopaedic brain and could trot out all manner of fascinating information about anything from astronomy to what really happened to the dinosaurs. But more and more of late he had retreated into himself and wouldn't tell them anything.

'Go on,' said Gabriel. 'You never know, you might even enjoy it. Plus Patch needs you too. You could bring your sledge, and take it down the valley if you like.'

'Oh, okay,' muttered Steven, going off to get ready, while Marianne and Gabriel went to wrap the twins up warmly and put them in their backpacks. It took forever to get sorted, but eventually they set off up the lane.

Having the twins with them meant they couldn't take the more difficult paths, so they kept to the lower slopes, which had the advantage of meaning Steven didn't moan quite as much as he might have done if they'd made him climb up the really steep bits.

But Marianne thought wistfully of the walks she used to take before the twins arrived. Then she hadn't thought twice about heading off up to the top, walking on her own among the heather and the sheep for several hours. She wouldn't be without the twins for a minute, but she was taken aback sometimes at the feelings of resentment that sometimes came from nowhere. It seemed to have got worse since she'd gone back to work. She had naively thought she'd just slot back into being a teacher, just the way she had done before. No one had told Marianne that it wasn't that straightforward; no one had prepared her for the feelings of been split in two, feeling she was neither doing the job she loved well, nor wholeheartedly enjoying her babies. She hadn't figured on feeling that resentful about the loss of her freedom when she was pregnant, and she felt guilty for it. And for the first time Marianne appreciated Eve, Gabriel's first wife, who, woefully unsuited as she had been to life as a farmer's wife, had been trapped by being a mother. Marianne loved her country existence, but at times felt stifled by the twins. Thank God for Gabe's mum, Jean. Without her help, Marianne would have gone nuts by now. And she also felt guilty about Steven, aware she was giving him less attention since the twins arrived. No wonder he was stroppy with them.

Only not today. They arrived at the end of the path that led onto a large slope which led them straight back down into the town. Steven whooped when he saw that it had become pretty much like an ice rink. Luckily for Gabe and Marianne there were steps and a banister to hold on to so they could get down safely, while Steven leapt on his sledge and went hurtling down to the bottom of the hill. He was in his element, his face flushed with exertion, his eyes bright and sparkling. Particularly when Pippa's husband Dan showed up with Steven's cousins, Nathan and George.

'That was brill!' he said running over to them, with an enthusiasm they hadn't seen in months. He gave Gabe a hug and ran straight back up the hill with his sledge.

'I feel exhausted just watching him,' said Gabriel with a grin.

'See,' said Marianne squeezing his hand. 'He is still ours. He's just growing up and we need to give him some space.'

'You're probably right,' said Gabe, and together they watched Steven having fun as the sun set on a snow-filled field, while the twins slept cosily in their backpacks behind them.

Being a mum was definitely tough, Marianne thought, and it required huge sacrifices, but moments like this made it all worthwhile.

Chapter Three

'So how exactly can I help?' Cat Tinsall had tucked her tiny frame behind the ancient oak table which had been in Pippa's family for generations, and was nibbling on a muffin and sipping a cup of hot chocolate. 'I have to say, this is the perfect combination on a cold and windy January day. These muffins are delish. Can you give me the recipe?'

'It's only my mum's, which I adapted,' said Pippa.

'The best kind,' grinned Cat. 'Anyway, tell me what's going on.'

One of the things that had endeared Pippa to Cat on first meeting her was her can-do mentality. She was willing to help out at the drop of a hat, and frequently had Nathan and George over, without ever asking for anything in return.

'Well, like I said on the phone, it looks like we're losing Lucy's respite care,' said Pippa. She was sitting opposite Cat, cradling her cup of chocolate, and feeling very gloomy. 'And I'm not sure what to do about it. I want to get a campaign up and running to save the services, but I don't know if it's going to make a difference. After all, everything's being cut at the moment. Who's going to care about one family's small problems . . .'

Her voice trailed off miserably. Pippa was trying to keep positive about it, but she was a realist. The money had run out. Simple as. And Lucy was only one of many many people who needed help.

Cat whistled sympathetically.

'What a nightmare for you,' she said. 'As if things weren't tough enough.'

'Apparently, I'm one of the lucky ones,' said Pippa. 'Other people have it worse. At least I've got Dan, and the boys are really good and helpful. They could easily resent the time it takes to look after Lucy and they don't – or they don't seem to. Of course, I could be in for a whole load of teenage angst, but it hasn't happened yet.'

'Be thankful they're boys,' said Cat. 'James is a dream compared to the girls. Mel's a total nightmare at the moment, and all Paige wants to do is read magazines, wear lots of make-up and listen to rap music with inappropriate lyrics.'

Pippa laughed. 'It's not that bad, surely?'

'Worse,' said Cat. 'I swear Paige speaks a language all of her own. Have you any idea what "bad boy" or "peng" mean?'

Pippa looked understandably blank.

'Me neither. And as for calling me a "swaggerdon", I have no idea what she's on about most of the time.'

'Ah, that I do know,' said Pippa. 'It's from *The Only Way is Essex*. I think it's meant as a compliment.'

Cat laughed, 'Well, you could have fooled me.' She sat back and had another sip of her chocolate. 'I do love your kitchen, it's just the way a farm kitchen should be.'

'What – old and falling down?' chuckled Pippa, taking in the ancient welsh dresser with the soup tureen inherited from her great grandmother, the kitchen range that looked like it came out of the ark, and the worn-out flagstones.

'It has character,' said Cat. 'I like it. Anyway, back to Lucy. Have you had any thoughts about what you can do? I'll help in any way I can.'

'I've written to the local MP,' said Pippa, 'but funnily enough – him being part of the government making the cuts – have had no response, so far. And I'm in the process of sorting out a petition. But what we really need to do is figure a way that the centre Lucy goes to can be self-funded and run at a profit. The basic problem is lack of funds – it needs to be able to keep offering the same services, but Social Services are cutting their budgets, and I'm not sure there are any charities who'd be able to step in.'

'Any of the private care companies shown an interest?'

Pippa pulled a face.

'I don't know if that would help. I'm a bit cynical about these companies. You don't read much good about them in the papers.'

'The one that runs Mum's nursing home seems okay,' said Cat.

'Still,' said Pippa. 'I was thinking of more of a kind of cooperative. If the people who actually benefit from the centre could also be involved, that would be brilliant. But money's a problem . . .'

'Isn't it always,' said Cat.

'So the only thing I can think of for now, is to run a major PR campaign and raise the centre's profile, and find out if there is a way to get it to self fund. But these services are expensive. Dan and I could pay some of the cost towards Lucy's care, but lots of the families who use the centre can't. They need help too.'

Cat thought about it.

'I've always been a bit reluctant to use my mum for the purposes of newspaper articles,' she said carefully, 'but I think everyone who cares for someone else is in the same boat. I'll pitch an article about caring to a few of the mags I write for if you like, and see if I can somehow write a feature about the centre, if you think that would help?'

'Anything would be fantastic,' said Pippa. 'Although I feel a bit shameless, picking my famous friend's brains.'

'I'm hardly that famous,' laughed Cat, 'and besides, we're mates. You and Dan made Noel and I feel so welcome when we came here. I'm happy to help.'

Cat slowly drove into the home where her mother lived on the other side of Hope Sadler. It was a bright modern building, on the edge of an old estate, so every room had a view of the impressive gardens that had one day belonged to a long-forgotten local gentleman. It was a lovely location, and Cat was really grateful for the care her mum had received. The home she'd been in briefly in London hadn't been up to much, and getting Mum up here had assuaged a lot of Cat's guilt about being unable to look after Louise. She knew it wasn't practical, but still, she wished she'd been able to.

Ruby had come with her today. Cat never forced the kids to see Louise but she was grateful that even though they referred to her as 'Mad Gran', they all still loved and accepted Louise the way she was, and came to see her when they could. Even Mel took herself over here on the bus from time to time. As it happened, Ruby was quite happy to prattle on about what she'd been up to, regardless of the fact that Granny didn't have a clue what she was talking about, or could barely remember her name. It made visiting easier.

It was getting harder and harder visiting Mum. For a start there was the sheer loneliness of knowing that she could no longer reach her mother in the way she once had. They had been so close once, and Cat missed her mother's wisdom. Louise would have known how Cat should deal with Mel, and Cat felt all at sea without her support. Noel was much more relaxed about it. He too had been a rebel in his teens and kept telling Cat that Mel would get over it, which was probably true. But, Cat felt a massive failure for not having managed to create the same strong mother and daughter bond she'd enjoyed with Louise before her illness. Guiltily, she felt she'd let Mel down somehow, and the further Mel retreated from her, the less certain Cat was that she would ever get her back.

Their latest row had been about Mel's mock results which, as predicted, were abysmal. Mel's response to being told off was to spend even more hours out of the house, presumably at Karen's, though Cat never knew if she was there, because Mel barely deigned to tell her. Andy's name hadn't been mentioned again, and if Cat tried to broach the subject, Mel clammed up, leaving Cat worrying why her daughter was being so secretive about it. Short of locking her in her room to prevent her going out, Cat didn't know what more she and Noel could do.

Cat and Ruby knocked on Louise's door, and found her sitting in her chair, rocking back and forth slightly, as was her wont.

'Hallo, dear,' said Louise with unseeing eyes. 'How nice of you to come. I'm waiting for my daughter, she'll be here soon.'

'I am your daughter,' said Cat, holding up the picture of the family which she kept by the bed for this express purpose. 'See, here I am, it's Cat. And here's Ruby, your granddaughter.'

'What, this little girl?' said Louise. 'My granddaughter? Well I never.'

'Hallo Granny,' said Ruby, 'I made you a picture.'

Cat could have hugged her for taking it in her stride.

'How lovely. What a kind little girl you are,' said Louise, 'My granddaughter. Amazing.'

Ruby rolled her eyes at Cat, and said, 'Yes, Granny,' before proceeding to rattle off a manic account of her week, which mainly consisted of the fact that Maisie Cordwell was really mean and it was unfair the boys got to play football and the girls didn't.

Towards the end of her visit, Louise asked to go in the lounge.

'I need to see Alfie,' she said. 'We've got a date.'

Cat grinned. One of the few good things to come out of Louise's condition recently had been meeting up with Alfie, a fellow Alzheimer's patient. They could barely remember each other's names, but they seemed to get on like a house on fire.

'Of course you do,' said Cat. 'Here, let's take you down.'

Taking her mum's arm, she gently led her downstairs to the lounge where several of the residents were assembled to hear the piano being played by an equally elderly gentleman.

Alfie, a dapper eighty-year-old, whose tidy appearance belied the vagueness of his mind, came straight up to Louise and pecked her on the cheek.

'Hello me darling,' he said. 'Let me take you on a spin around the room,' and with that he took Louise into his arms, and led her in a waltz, lustily and tunelessly singing 'Daisy Daisy, give me your answer do!', while Louise spun round with him looking pink and flustered. She'd clearly forgotten they were there. Cat grinned. 'Time to go, Ruby,' she said, 'I don't think Granny needs us anymore.' It wasn't all bad. Mum was safe and warm and well cared for. Things could be a lot worse.

Marianne rushed into the staffroom, five minutes late for the staff meeting, conscious that her curly dark hair was rebelliously falling out of the clips which she'd shoved back into them, after Harry pulled them out just before she'd left for work. She was late because Daisy had smeared porridge down her top, necessitating a quick change. In fact she wasn't the only member of staff to arrive after the official time of the meeting's start, but the way Mrs Garratt, the new Head teacher of Hope Christmas Primary School, looked at her, made Marianne feel that she was a real lightweight.

Mrs Garratt had been brought in by the governors as 'a new broom', according to Diana Carew, after the previous incumbent had left under a slight cloud involving missing amounts of money that the bursar couldn't account for, but she seemed keen to sweep everything else clean too.

Marianne's mood didn't get any better when, during the course of the meeting, she had to admit that she wouldn't be able to help on the Year 4 residential trip to the Black Mountains, as it coincided with a week when Jean and David were away, so she had no childcare. Ali Strickland, who had taken over as Year 4 coordinator while Marianne had been on maternity leave, looked smug as she took over and explained to everyone where the trip was taking place, and what the schedule was. She was taking credit for a trip that Marianne had organised the previous year, before she went on maternity leave. She'd left it all ready for Ali just to pick up the pieces, but unfortunately the original date had fallen through, and without telling her, Ali had rebooked for a date Marianne had been unable to attend. Marianne could see from the slightly pursed look on Mrs Garratt's face that her lack of commitment had been noted. Mrs Anderson might have had her hand in the till, but at least she'd understood about family life.

In a way, Marianne couldn't blame Ali. Theirs was a small village school, and there were precious few opportunities for promotion. Marianne had just about managed to negotiate a part-time job share with Jane Sutherland, who'd had a baby the year before her, but Mrs Garratt had made it clear that the situation could be reviewed at any time. Her view was that part-time teachers were not the most effective way of managing staff maternity leave, and Marianne felt conscious that she was under the microscope, the previous five years' worth of dedication she'd given to the school seeming to count for nothing. But, it was money, she was still hanging on by her fingertips, and for now, Marianne had to be content with that.

She became vaguely aware the meeting was winding up. Marianne was so tired, she had not exactly been dozing, but her mind had certainly been elsewhere, so it was with a certain amount of trepidation she heard Mrs Garratt saying, 'So, Marianne, I understand it is normally your job to put on the local nativity. Can we count on you to help the community out again this Christmas?'

Biting back the retort that, if Mrs Garratt was really interested in the community, she would have known that Marianne had put on the nativity as usual only a month ago.

'Er, to be honest, I haven't given it much thought,' said Marianne. 'I've only just got over last year's efforts.'

'I understand,' said Mrs Garratt, 'and I appreciate it's a long way off, but I was just thinking it would be an excellent opportunity for Ali to show us what she's made of. So I thought that perhaps next year, we'll hand it over to her.'

Marianne had in fact been thinking that putting on the nativity was a bit much now she had family commitments, but the idea that something she'd put her heart and soul into over the last few years could just be taken away from her like that was a further kick in the teeth.

Miserably, she went to her classroom, and started

writing up the literacy topics for the day. Once upon a time she'd loved this job, now she was beginning to hate it. What's more, every day she was here was a day away from the twins. She felt like she had the worst of all possible worlds.

Mel

FACEBOOK status Karen. Message me. Urgent!!!
Kaz: What's up babe?
Mel: Andy. ONLY TOLD ME I'M FIT.
Kaz: WOW!!! What about Kelly R thox? :-S
Mel: Kelly who? She's history.
Kaz: You're sure?
Mel: Totes. He thinks I'm hawt!!
Kaz: And you are, babe!
Mel: Meet tomorrow for beef!
Kaz: Laters.
Mel: xxx

Teenage Kicks
Random thoughts of an Anonymous Teen

Saw the Boy today. It's the first time since that whole Dad finding us in the cafe shit. He hasn't been replying to my texts, so it was always going to be AWKWARD. Christ. He must think I'm such a loser. To have a dad like that . . .

So I try to play it cool. I say hi, and pretend I've come in to collect my wages. I sashay slowly up the aisle, hoping he's looking at me.

44

Instead I stack over my new platforms & look like a total douche. I get up feeling an idiot & I want to die.

But then he looks at me and my heart goes all funny and he says, 'Hey babe, I know you like me, but you didn't need to fall at my feet.'

Which isn't true actually. I didn't fall at his feet. I want to die even more, but then I realise he's grinning at me, and so we have a coffee together and he says it's ok that my dad shouted at us.

'It's cool,' he said, 'He's your dad. If I had such a fit daughter I'd probably do the same.'

He thinks I'm fit. I can't believe it. The Boy, who just happens to be the most amazing, gorgeous guy in the whole world, thinks I'm fit. I am going to ignore those rumours going round school that he's been seen out with the Chav Queen. I'm sure she started them anyway, ever since Best Mate told the whole class how I snogged the Boy at her New Year's Eve party. It's me he likes. I know it now.

He's asked me to meet him in town again. After school. I was sooo nervous. I made Best Mate come with me till we saw him. I could barely speak. Best Mate, said there's another rumour about him and a girl who doesn't even go to our school. 'Be careful, babes,' she said. I know she's looking out for me, but I wish she'd shut up. I know the Boy isn't interested in anyone else, cos he told me. Said not to listen to any silly rumours. I'm the only girl for him. Held *my hand and said he loved me. I think I love him too . . . Does it always feel this exhilarating and mad, and miserable and mental? How do you KNOW for sure?*

February

Chapter Four

Marianne came home from work after another depressingly difficult day, feeling shattered and miserable. But her step lightened as she walked into the house and heard the babies gurgling in the kitchen. However crap her day had been, no one could take away the pleasure the twins brought her. She went to open the door, and then she heard voices. Steven was talking to Gabe's mum.

'I really liked Middleminster, Granny,' he said. 'But Dad doesn't want me to go.'

'Of course he does,' said Jean. 'But if you do go there, he's going to miss you.'

'I don't think I'm going to get in anyway,' said Steven gloomily. 'I've been practising with Marianne, and the tests are really difficult.'

'I'm sure you'll do fine,' said Jean, 'and if you don't get in, it's not the end of the world. You can go to Hope Sadler School with your friends.'

'But I don't *want* to go to school with them,' Steven burst out miserably. 'Apart from George, they all take the mickey out of my singing. And it's what I want to do more than *anything*.'

Steven sounded so miserable, Marianne's heart contracted. Poor poor thing. She and Gabe had been so caught up in their worries about losing him they hadn't stopped to consider properly how Steven felt.

Feeling she'd eavesdropped enough, Marianne called out, 'Hi, I'm home,' and entered the kitchen. She really wanted to go and give Steven a hug, but thinking it would be hard to explain without giving away the fact that she'd been listening, just grinned at him instead, and said, 'Good day?'

'It was okay,' he grunted.

'And how have the twins been?'

'Fine,' said Jean, 'no trouble at all. You know how much I love looking after my grandchildren.'

The twins sat in their highchairs smiling at her, their faces covered in dinner.

'You sure about that?' laughed Marianne and went to give each of them a sticky cuddle. It was difficult with two not to feel guilty that she might be favouring one above the other, so cuddles were on a strict rotation. Sometimes she thought she was being a bit bonkers. After all would sixteen-month-olds even notice? But she wanted to be fair.

'Here, let me clean up,' said Marianne, starting to load the twins' dinner plates in the dishwasher. She was glad that when they'd revamped their kitchen she'd persuaded Gabriel to buy both a new dishwasher and washing machine. Both had had their work cut out since the babies had been born.

'Have a cup of tea, first,' said Jean pulling up a kitchen chair. 'I insist. It's a long day that you work.'

'And I couldn't do it without you,' said Marianne, immensely grateful that her mother-in-law provided her with the support to allow her some of her old life at least. She loved the twins dearly, but she also loved her job. She'd thought at first she was lucky to be able to have both, but Mrs Garratt was certainly making it harder to feel like that. Marianne was getting fed up with the snide little comments about pulling her weight. More often than not, she was one of the last to leave work, just to prove a point. Often she wondered if it were worth it.

Ten minutes later, while Marianne and Jean were sitting at the table having a cup of tea, each with a baby on their laps, Gabe walked in cuddling something in his arms. It was a newborn lamb.

'The mother died,' he said. 'Found this little chap in the fields, baaing away. He's nearly frozen to death. Steven, do you want to keep him?'

Steven, who had been assiduously working on one of the test papers, looked at his dad in disdain. 'No, I don't,' he said, 'I think pet lambs are babyish.'

'Steven—' said Jean, but he'd got up and walked out.

Marianne looked at Gabe, wishing she could take the hurt away from his face.

'He'll get over it,' she said. 'He's just trying to find his way at the moment.'

Gabriel didn't say anything, but set about making a home in a cardboard box by the fire for the lamb, while Marianne cleared the rest of the dinner away, and Jean sorted the twins out.

The evening wore away, and by the time Jean had gone home, the twins were settled in bed, the washing-up done, and the lamb comfy in his new home, it was gone eight-thirty and there had been no sign of Steven.

'He's being picked on at school, you know,' said Marianne carefully. Gabriel was so sensitive about the whole choir school thing, she had learnt to tread warily when discussing it, lest he fly off the handle.

'Is he? About what?'

'His singing,' said Marianne. 'I overheard him telling your mum. I can't say I'm surprised really. There are some tough little cookies in Year 6, and Steven's so sensitive. I'm surprised no one's mentioned it to me. That's one of the problems being part time, I'm out of the loop.'

'Oh,' said Gabriel. 'Now I feel even worse, thanks.'

'He just wants you to be happy about his choices,' said Marianne. 'Go up and tell him it's okay. That you're fine about him trying out for choir school.'

'Even if I'm not?' said Gabriel.

'Even if you're not,' said Marianne firmly. 'It's not about us, it's about him. If that's what Steven wants, we should back him all the way.'

Ten minutes later, Gabriel and Steven were downstairs, both wreathed in identical smiles. Marianne warmed at the sight of them. Her two lovely boys, so alike and yet so different. She hated to see them at odds with each other. They were so close normally.

'Can I feed the new lamb?' said Steven.

'Of course,' said Marianne, and sent him to fetch a bottle of milk.

'Well that went well,' said Marianne. 'What on earth did you say to him?' she whispered.

'I said I didn't mind if he goes to that school, so long as I can get us a season ticket for Shrewsbury Wanderers, and come and take him to the football once a month.'

'Bribery will get you everywhere,' laughed Marianne softly.

'Well it worked.' Gabriel nudged her and they watched Steven across the room gently pick the lamb up and give him some milk. Not so grown up after all.

Pippa felt extraordinarily self-conscious. She'd arranged a meeting for all the families in the area affected by the proposed loss of respite services at the Sunshine Trust. She hadn't been sure whether anyone would come – parents of special needs children were often stretched to the hilt. Who had time to fight the system even further? And while she had been involved in numerous campaigns, from helping set up the communal village shop, to fighting for a safe crossing by the children's school, this was different. This was her call. She'd started the ball rolling, and she was going to have to deliver.

Pippa looked around at the hugely expectant faces, all waiting to hear what she had to say. They were relying on her, all these people, to help keep the Sunshine Trust respite services open to give them the lifeline they so desperately needed. It felt like an awesome responsibility. She couldn't bear it if she failed them.

'Hallo, and thanks so much for coming,' she said. 'I know lots of you have come a long way' – Shropshire being a big county, the majority of people who used the respite centre came from far and wide – 'We're here today to set up a campaign to try and protect our services. All of us who use the Sunshine Trust know what a vital resource it is for families to gain much-needed respite. The issue isn't so much about the centre closing, but the withdrawal of the respite care which is funded by local government. We need to find a way of paying for these services by alternative means. So to start with I'd say beg, borrow and steal from everyone you know. If you have links with local businesses, let's see if we can't get them to pledge some help.'

'What about lottery money?' someone said.

'We're applying for a grant,' said Pippa.

'And telethon charities, like Children in Need or Red Nose Day?' said someone else.

'Good idea,' said Pippa, 'but we want this to be sustainable in the long term, so we need to find somebody prepared to fund it, run by sympathetic professionals who know exactly what is required.

'We're also petitioning our local MP, Tom Brooker, but

so far we haven't heard anything back from him. I'd urge you all to write to him yourselves, so he realises the depth of feeling about it. And you'll all be delighted that Cat Tinsall has kindly volunteered to give us some free PR by writing a series of articles highlighting the excellent work of the centre.'

Soon a barrage of suggestions was coming in: some helpful, some not, but by the end of the meeting Pippa felt she'd at least achieved something. It was a start. She wound up, having agreed to create a steering committee which would look into all the feasible suggestions, with a promise they would report back in six weeks.

'How did it go?' Dan hugged her as she came through the door. It felt safe and warm to walk back home into his arms. So long as Dan was there, she felt anything was achievable.

'Okay, I think,' said Pippa. 'Are the boys in bed?'

'Not yet,' said Dan. 'Probably time to winkle them off the Xbox.'

Pippa grinned and went into the lounge to find the boys heavily engrossed in some game that seemed to involve an inordinate amount of shooting. She extricated them from it with difficulty and shooed them up to bed.

She climbed the stairs and checked on Lucy to see if she was asleep, and watched from the doorway as her daughter made her usual alarming snuffly noises in her sleep. Her beautiful daughter. People didn't always see that, pitying her for having a child with such special needs. But they couldn't see her uniqueness, or her inner beauty, or the joy she took in life. They couldn't see how secretly subversive Lucy could be, often sharing jokes with her or Dan via the electronic keyboard they had recently bought for her, which had become her window to the world, or pulling faces when she thought someone was treating her like an idiot. It was hard, so hard sometimes, having a daughter like Lucy – Pippa would be the first to admit that. It was difficult for all families who had special needs children. But what people didn't realise was that along with the struggle came something exceptional and different. Lucy showed her every day how to accept the simple things in life, and to be grateful for everything she had. But she couldn't do it without Dan by her side, or without the help she got from the Sunshine Trust. Which was why it was so important to her. Without it, Pippa knew she wouldn't be able to cope. They had to keep it open at all costs.

Cat woke up feeling lousy. She often did these days. She put it down to middle-aged exhaustion, coupled with being that scourge of the *Daily Mail*, a middle-aged binge drinker. Although of late, she'd been too tired even to manage that.

As Noel was constantly telling her, she did too much, but Cat had never been one to sit still for long, and between the demands of teen and preteen children, her poorly mother, devoted husband and her job, sitting still wasn't always an option. Oh well, at least it kept her thin. Mind you, that didn't stop her having a less than flat stomach, which seemed to bulge slightly more as time went by. When she was in London, she'd kept it down by a rigorous gym routine, but somehow that didn't fit in with a country lifestyle, though regular long walks kept her fit. Now when she looked down at her stomach it seemed to have filled out, sagging more than it used to. If she didn't know any better, she might have thought she was pregnant. But with her periods having become increasingly sporadic over the last year, it was far more likely that she was heading for the menopause and middle-aged spread. Oh joy.

Besides, she and Noel were so knackered most of the time, sex was rarely on the agenda these days. In fact, rather shamefully, she realised that they'd probably not had any since New Year's Eve. Must do better, she muttered to herself. Lack of sex had nearly done for them in London, when she and Noel had been so busy they'd ended up leading parallel lives. The move to Hope Christmas had cemented their marriage; she mustn't let it slip again. Noel meant the world to her. Their relationship had become even stronger since they'd moved up here. Even after all this time, she felt her heart sing when one of them had been away from the other.

Noel was already showered and ready by the time she got down. She kissed him as he went out of the door. Paige was preening herself in the hall mirror.

'You're not allowed make-up at school,' Cat reminded her, before going into the kitchen where James half asleep and yawning, was crouched over his toast and Ruby was chattering away to anyone who would listen (which was nobody) about the excitements of her coming day. Of Mel there was no sign. Great. First row of the day would be getting Mel out of bed. In the past, Cat's response to Mel's laziness had been to make her face the consequences of being late and getting a caution. But since the bunking off incident, Cat had been terrified that left to her own devices, Mel just wouldn't bother going to school. And with the results of her mocks showing them just how much work she needed to do, Cat felt she had to be on her case, however unpopular that made her. But as she had said ruefully to Noel, 'I'm not here to win any popularity contests.'

'Mel, are you up?' Cat gingerly knocked on her daughter's door.

'Humph.' A groan was the only response.

Cat opened the door into a pit. Crikey, it was worse than normal. There was barely a piece of the floor not covered in clothes, clean and dirty, shoes, bags, books and paper.

'Mel, time to get up,' she said, 'NOW!'

'I'm just getting up,' said Mel. 'No need to shout.'

'I'm not shouting,' said Cat between gritted teeth. 'But I will be in a minute. You've got twenty minutes until your bus goes. And by the way, when you get home tonight, I expect to see this pigsty cleaned up.'

'Will you get off my case!' said Mel belligerently.

'If you behave yourself, then yes,' said Cat restraining herself with difficulty. 'Now get up.' She resisted the urge to say, 'or else,' because she knew the response would be 'Or else, what?' The reality was that, short of physical violence, there was very little she could do to make her errant daughter do anything she didn't want to. And they both knew it.

The power was all with kids these days. Cat was sure it had been different when she was young. Then power had *definitely* been with the grown-ups. Just her luck to have been born into the generation which had lost the plot.

She went back downstairs with a sigh, and an automatic, 'Wipe that make-up off your face, Paige,' and receiving a rushed, 'Off now,' from James. And then it was just her and Ruby, still chattering away, Cat guiltily noticed, wondering what exactly she had missed.

Mel eventually appeared looking as mean and moody as her dark eyeliner would allow. There were bags under her eyes, and she'd lost weight. Cat felt a twinge of worry. Maybe there was something wrong and she was handling it badly. All the books said you should listen to your teenagers. Perhaps she didn't do that enough.

'Mel–' she began.

'Oh will you leave me alone,' snarled Mel, grabbing a slice of toast. 'I'm going now!' And with that, she was out of the house, slamming the door in a whirlwind of fury and resentment.

Cat shut her eyes, feeling sick with misery. Another successful morning.

Ruby came over and took her hand. 'Don't worry, Mummy. Mel's like that to all of us. Not just you. It's her hormones.'

'What do you know about hormones?' laughed Cat.

'Paige says I'll get them when I'm grown up and then I'll understand,' said Ruby. 'But Mel has them a lot and that's what makes her grumpy.'

'Right,' said Cat, giving her youngest daughter a hug. At least she had Ruby, sweet, innocent, chatterbox Ruby. How little had she realised just a few short years ago how much tougher parenting was going to get. She should have made the most of it when she had the chance. Cat cleared away the breakfast things, and tried to put the row behind her. Mel would have probably forgotten it by the time she got home. Maybe she'd be in a better mood then. Then again, maybe not.

Chapter Five

Cat got out of the car and walked up to the doorway of an imposing Victorian house, which was the main HQ of the Sunshine Trust. It was a gothic, grim-looking building – but as she went across the threshold and was introduced to Kim Majors, the centre's director, Cat quickly realised that appearances could be deceptive.

'Thank you so much for coming, Mrs Tinsall,' Kim said, holding out her hand. She was a small round, cheerful kind of person, bubbling with goodwill. Cat warmed to her instantly. 'We're so grateful to you for letting us tell our story.'

'Call me Cat, please,' said Cat. 'And it's my pleasure. Pippa Holliday is always singing your praises, and I know what a difference the respite care makes for her and Dan. I'm pleased to be able to help, if I can.'

'Let me show you around,' said Kim.

The house was huge, but felt comfortable and homely. The rooms were brightly lit and cheerful, and Cat was amazed at the general air of fun. There was a games room, where two boys in wheelchairs whizzed back and forth playing table tennis, a soft play area, with younger children enthusiastically hurling themselves about, and several lounges, in which children, some in wheelchairs, some not, were lounging about, chatting or watching TV.

'These are our chillout zones,' said Kim, 'the kids can come and relax here on their own, or when their families come, they have plenty of space for private time. During the week we often arrange recreational pursuits, like games evenings. For a lot of our children, it's about being heard – people look at them as if they are stupid, when it's their bodies which don't work so well, not their minds. That's not true for all of them of course, but it is for the vast majority.'

The tour of the home took over an hour, including showing Cat round some of the more modern buildings where the children who lived here permanently stayed, and an impressive hydrotherapy pool, where Cat witnessed a child with severe muscular dystrophy getting the chance to stretch her muscles and just enjoy the water. Cat was impressed by the range of activities available to the children and could see what a vital resource it was. Kim was an informative guide, who clearly found her job rewarding. She explained that the respite care service had only been in place for a few years.

'You remember the good old days, when the government had so much money sloshing around they could pay for it? Now of course that's no longer the case. And as we're a charity, we're having to work harder and harder for donations. We could really do with a generous benefactor. Unfortunately, as things stand we won't be able to keep the service going if our funding is withdrawn.'

'That would be terrible,' said Cat. 'I'll do my best to drum up interest. I know one or two documentary film makers who might be interested in this kind of thing. I'll sound them out, see if any of them are interested in doing something about this issue.'

'That would be wonderful,' said Kim.

'I can only try,' said Cat. 'I'm so impressed by everything you do here. And really humbled too.'

It was true, Cat reflected, as she got in the car to go home. She did feel humble. Watching the dedicated staff, treating a child with muscular dystrophy in the state-of-the-art hydrotherapy pool; observing a teacher communicate with her class purely through sign language; seeing a nurse gently turn a child who was on permanent ventilation. This place was incredible, and helped so many people. Cat had always been aware how incredibly fortunate she was to have four bright, healthy children, but today she sent a silent prayer of gratitude for her good fortune. Those families, like Pippa's, who needed the Sunshine Trust's help so badly, had so much to contend with. Cat had very little to complain about by comparison. Even with a stroppy teen.

'Hi Pippa. You've been busy again.' Vera opened the door of the village shop with a cheerful smile, as Pippa came in with her latest supply of cakes.

'Well, you know,' said Pippa, grinning. 'I have to do something to keep me out of mischief.'

After a fractious start to the day, involving lost football boots (Nathan), a sudden meltdown about 'forgotten' Maths homework (George) and an unusual strop from Lucy about what she was going to wear that day, Pippa had spent the morning baking. As usual, having the delicious smell of cakes and muffins wafting through the kitchen calmed her nerves, and by the time she had put the finishing touches to her cupcakes, Pippa was in a much better frame of mind.

Her mood was further improved by a couple of emails from interested local businesses whom she'd tentatively approached to see if they would be interested in getting involved in helping Sunshine Trust in some way. It was a small start, but it was something. As she was getting the cakes ready to take to Vera's, Cat rang up to see if she wanted to go for a coffee, as she had some news about a possible TV programme.

'I'm just off to take some cakes to Vera's,' said Pippa, 'meet you in ten.'

Having deposited her wares, Pippa bought a large latte and a toasted teacake and went to sit in a cosy corner of the café, near to the fireplace. A cold miserable February day was made much brighter by coffee and cake, she decided, while she waited for Cat to arrive. The coffee shop was packed with mums and toddlers, and as usual the place gave off a noisy happy vibe. Remembering how close Vera had come to losing her livelihood only a few years before, and how the community had come together to create such a brilliant and lively hub, gave Pippa renewed hope. Nothing was impossible if she put her mind to it.

'Sorry I'm late,' Cat came in shaking rain out of her umbrella. 'I got stuck on a long phone call with my editor.'

'It's okay,' said Pippa, 'I've been having an enjoyable time sitting still and watching the world go by for once. So, what's the score?'

'Well, I've been putting some feelers out, and it's possible the Beeb may be commissioning a series of programmes about cuts in social services and how they affect real people. And they may be looking at one on families who have special needs children. I'm sure they'd love to hear about you and Lucy.'

'I don't want it to be just about me,' protested Pippa. 'There are lots of other families affected too.'

'Yes, but your story is an emotional one,' argued Cat, 'and if it helped get your campaign on the map, it would be worth doing.'

'I suppose so,' said Pippa reluctantly, not quite sure she could see herself as a TV star in the making. 'So long as they concentrate on how we're trying to save the respite services, I don't see what harm it can do.'

'You never know, you might even enjoy it,' said Cat. 'And I bet Lucy would.'

'She'd certainly play up to the cameras,' said Pippa. Lucy was a natural show-off, and Pippa could see her having a ball. 'Thanks so much for doing this for me, Cat. I'm beginning to feel this isn't quite such an uphill task.'

'Have you thought about organising some fundraisers?' said Cat. 'When we were in London, some friends of ours used to organise an annual ball, with a charity auction for a local hospice. It made tons of money.'

'That's a great idea,' said Pippa. 'Perhaps we could do something coming up to Christmas.'

'You could call it a Snow Ball,' said Cat. 'People could have fun while raising money. It's a win-win situation.'

'And I do love an opportunity to get glammed up,' said Pippa, ruefully looking at the battered old Barbour, ragged jumper, jeans and wellies which was her default costume most days. 'Being a farmer's wife means you don't often get the chance to. That's a great idea, Cat.'

Cat smiled. 'Pleased to help,' she said. 'Where would be a good venue do you think?'

'We could let you have Hopesay Manor for free, if you like.' A figure dressed in black leathers who'd been sitting on the other side of the fireplace got up, holding out his hand. Pippa recognised him instantly as the handsome dark stranger who'd offered her advice the last time she'd been in here with Marianne. Suddenly the penny dropped.

'You must be Michael Nicholas,' she said. Everyone knew that Ralph's nephew Michael had come to Hope Christmas to help run the family business while Ralph was away in the Maldives, but Pippa hadn't met him before.

'The very same,' said Michael bowing. 'I hope you don't

mind me interrupting, but I'm a Trustee of the Sunshine Trust, and I'd be happy to help.'

'Thank you,' said Pippa. 'That's an amazingly generous offer.'

'It would be my pleasure,' said Michael, 'nice to meet you, ladies. Cat, I hope Noel is getting used to me hanging around. I think my uncle made a very wise choice in hiring him.'

'He did?' Cat looked as bemused as Pippa felt. 'Glad to hear it.'

'Now if you two ladies will excuse me, I have business to attend to elsewhere,' Michael said, bowing slightly again, before placing his crash helmet on his head, and walking out of the door.

They watched him go into the square, climb on his motorbike and roar off into the dull February day.

'Noel's kept that quiet,' said Cat.

'What?' said Pippa.

'How good looking Michael Nicholas is,' laughed Cat. 'Just as well we're both happily married women.'

'Isn't it just,' said Pippa with a grin. 'Such a shame though . . .'

Marianne ran up the lane in a panic. She'd promised to get home early so she could help Steven go over a couple of practice papers. His exam was less than a week away, and he was getting very nervous. Damn Mrs bloody Garratt. She always seemed to have something urgent to tell Marianne at five-thirty. Before she'd joined the school, although everyone worked hard, and stayed late if they had to, most people left around five p.m. each day. Now you were seen as a slacker if you left before six p.m. Jean was incredibly generous, but Marianne was conscious that it was a long day for her with the twins, and Gabriel couldn't always be guaranteed to be home in time to relieve his mum, so it was up to her to get back as soon as she could. Unfortunately, telling Mrs Garratt she had to get home because of childcare issues cut no ice. Despite having a child of her own, who was allegedly at nursery from seven a.m. to seven p.m., she gave no quarter to Marianne, the implication seeming to be, if I can do it, so can you. The phrase, *work/life balance* was clearly lost on her.

The warmth of the house hit her, as she eventually got in from the cold. And the unwonted exercise had made her a little breathless. She really did need to get out walking a bit more, but what with work, looking after the twins and Steven, there was precious little time for Marianne to get exercising at the moment. It wasn't as if Gabriel didn't help out, it was just that farming was even less forgiving than teaching in sucking up all your time. He seemed to have been working harder than ever recently. There were some days when she'd barely seen him.

As she dumped her bags down and took off her coat and scarf in the hall, she realised she could hear raised voices coming from the lounge.

'Dad, you don't get it!' Steven was standing mutinously shouting at Gabriel, who had one baby in his arms, while the other grabbed his legs, giggling. Marianne's first instinct was to giggle too, he looked so comical, but then she saw the set and angry look on Gabe's face.

'I do get it, Steven, but there's no need to be rude!' said Gabriel. 'I know you've got your exam next week, but Marianne has got a lot on . . .'

'It's okay,' interrupted Marianne, 'I was late back, I'm sorry. I had promised to help,' she said gently.

'I don't want your help!' said Steven raging. 'I know you both want me to fail anyway.' He threw the books he'd been carrying onto the floor, and stormed past Marianne, slamming the door shut behind him, making the whole house quiver.

'What was all that about?' said Marianne, extricating Daisy from Gabriel's legs.

'Steven was having a meltdown,' Gabriel replied, running his hands wearily through his hair.

'Look, he's probably just stressed about the exam,' said Marianne. 'Don't worry about it. I'll get the twins ready for bed, and then I'll go through the papers with him.'

'You don't have to,' said Gabriel.

'I do,' said Marianne, warmly. 'I promised. It's not his fault that Misery Guts Garratt delights in making my life a misery.'

Gabriel kissed Marianne on the top of her head. 'Come on, we'll sort these two out together,' he said. 'Then we'll tackle Steven.'

At least, she had Gabriel's support, Marianne thought, even if she felt she was being pulled in too many directions at once.

Chapter Six

'So, are you all prepared, Steven?' said Marianne with a smile, as she prepared his breakfast while attempting to feed the twins their porridge. With one hand she was stirring scrambled eggs, and the other was shoving porridge into whichever baby had their mouth open at the time. She'd never known the meaning of the phrase multi-tasking until she became a mother.

'How are you feeling?' said Gabriel, giving his son an encouraging smile, as he put some bread in the toaster. Marianne had spent the last few weeks coaching Steven for his exam, and today was the big day.

'Okay,' said Steven. 'My tummy feels a bit funny.'

'That's perfectly normal,' said Marianne. 'Everyone feels like that before tests.'

'And all you can do is your best,' said Gabriel.

'What do you care, you don't even want me to go!' burst out Steven, before hunkering down at the table to eat his breakfast.

Gabriel opened his mouth as if to say something, but Marianne shushed him. 'Ignore it, he's just nervous,' she whispered.

Marianne and Gabriel had both decided to go along with Steven, leaving the twins with Jean. Gabriel was worried that Eve and Darren would be there too.

'They're bound to wind him up, if they come,' he had said to Marianne as they'd gone to bed last night.

'Try not to think about it,' said Marianne, but she knew Gabe was probably right. Eve had 'wind-up' hardwired into her system.

While Jean was looking after the twins, Gabriel's dad, David, was out on the fields of the day. Despite being officially retired, he frequently helped Gabriel and Dan out on the farm when he could.

'Good luck, Steven, I'm sure you won't need it,' said Jean, managing to elicit the first smile from Steven of the day.

They drove pretty much in silence the fifty miles or so to the small cathedral town of Middleminster, each alone with their thoughts. Gabe, Marianne knew, was feeling nervous for his son, but anxious about the future, and guilty for half wishing Steven wouldn't get in.

'I know I should want this for him,' Gabriel had told her the previous night, 'but I hate the thought of him being away from us. I hate the fact that I can't seem to want what's best for him.'

'Whatever will be, will be,' said Marianne. 'Let's just get him through the test first, and hope everything works out for the best.'

She was still hoping that as they eventually arrived at Middleminster. Steven was a clever boy, and had done well in the practice tests she'd done with him. But she didn't know how stiff the competition was, and he was very young. Nerves could let him down on the day.

They entered the school via an impressively long drive, with sweeping views of frosty fields overlooking the pretty medieval town of Middleminster, and pulled up in front of an imposing redbrick Victorian building, where queues of small boys were lining up to go in for the exam.

'Bloody hell,' said Gabriel, looking in dismay at the

numbers. 'I'd no idea there would be so many of them taking the exam.'

Eve, who'd clearly been waiting for them, leapt out of her car with Darren following behind, and ran up to Steven, and gave him a hug.

'Go and knock 'em dead, kid,' she said. 'I know you can do it.'

'See, *someone* will be pleased I get in,' said Steven.

Gabriel said, 'Of course I'll be pleased.'

'So will we be,' said Eve. 'Darren will give you a BlackBerry when you pass.'

Gabriel was about to protest, but Marianne nudged him as they saw the look on Steven's face, so they both said nothing.

'Thanks, Mum,' Steven said, his face lighting up at the sight of her. Marianne felt sad, despite herself. No matter how many years she'd looked after Steven when his mum was unable to – she could never replace Eve. Not that she wanted to, but seeing how happy Steven was to be with his mum, she wondered if it had been right for him to be away from Eve so long, however flaky she was.

Hours passed slowly in the school café, where Marianne and Gabriel felt obliged to make polite conversation with Eve and Darren. Although by the time they'd heard for the zillionth time just how big Darren's Christmas bonus had been, Marianne felt like screaming. She had never met anyone so incredibly self-centred and money orientated in her life. He clearly had no interest in what she and Gabriel did, and she suspected, precious little interest in Steven. Unfair of her or not, Marianne had the distinct impression Darren was only getting so involved to impress Eve, because while the rest of them frequently checked their watches and fretted how Steven was getting on, Darren almost seemed to have forgotten why they were there.

Never had three hours passed so slowly, but eventually it was over, and hundreds of small boys poured out of the examination hall, ready to be reunited with their parents. Marianne spotted Steven in the middle of them, a small pale looking figure with an air of defeat about him. She longed to go and hug him, but knew that would be counter-productive, as Steven was very clear that hugging in public was way too embarrassing for an eleven-year-old.

'How did it go?' asked Gabriel carefully.

'Awful,' said Steven and burst into tears. 'It was really difficult. I'm sure I've failed.'

He looked so miserable that, forgetting her resolution, Marianne automatically gave him a hug.

'I'm sure it's not as bad as all that,' she said. 'Exams often seem worse than they are. Maybe we could go through some of your answers together.'

'I think what Steven needs is to forget all about it,' said Darren.

'I know,' said Eve, 'why don't Darren and I take you out for the afternoon? I'm sure it will all work out. That will be okay, won't it, Gabriel? We'll bring him home for seven.'

'Oh please. Can I?' Steven's face lit up.

Gabriel looked at Marianne helplessly.

'Of course, that's fine.'

'Great,' said Steven. 'Mum, you're the best.'

Hardly glancing back at Gabriel and Marianne, he walked off excitedly with his mum and Darren, talking nineteen to the dozen.

'Great,' said Gabriel heavily as they watched him go. 'Why do I get the feeling we're losing him?'

Marianne gave him a reassuring hug. It was on the tip of her tongue to say *don't be silly*, but looking at how cheerful Steven seemed, it was hard not to dispute Gabriel's gloom. The trouble was, if Steven wanted to spend more time with Eve and Darren, there was very little they could do about it – whether she and Gabriel liked it or not.

Pippa was at home with Lucy, who was having an inset day. It was nice to have Lucy to herself. At the weekends, when the boys were here, Pippa felt conscious that sometimes, in her bid not to let the boys miss out, she didn't spend enough time just being with Lucy. Despite her wheelchair, and her inability to talk directly, Lucy had a lively and vivacious personality, and through her electronic keyboard could convey more than adequately how she felt about things. The keyboard was a fairly new acquisition which had come about at the suggestion of Kim from the Sunshine Trust, and it had transformed their lives. Lucy had always managed to get on with other children, but now, to Pippa's delight, she'd been able to strike up a proper friendship with Ruby, Cat's youngest, who seemed to have a total blindness when it came to Lucy's disability. The two girls shared a similar sense of mischief, and Ruby was often round now at the weekends, which Pippa had to admit made life a lot easier.

You sorted my care out yet? Lucy keyed in, as she over-heard Pippa's long conversation with Claire King about their options (none) should the respite care be taken away altogether.

'What do you think?' Pippa rolled her eyes at her daughter.

Slacker, keyed Lucy, and laughed her head off.

'Cheeky,' said Pippa grinning. Thank God for Lucy's sense of humour. It made the tough bits bearable. 'But I'm working on it, so there. I'm just going to make some phone calls now.'

Talking to Clare King was having the effect of galvanising her into action. Every time Claire put an obstacle in her path, Pippa felt duty bound to clear it away.

She rang up the first of two companies who'd contacted her. It was a medical equipment company, who wanted, 'To give something back,' as the director told her. The second company made some positive noises, but she couldn't get anything more concrete out of them.

'These are difficult times,' the friendly lady on the other end of the phone said, 'so I'm afraid we can't commit at the moment, but keep in touch, and maybe things will be different in a few months' time.'

'Thanks, that's very kind of you,' Pippa said, she gave the thumbs-up to Lucy, who grinned at her. 'I'll do that.'

She put the phone down and high-fived her daughter.

'See, not such a slacker after all,' she said.

Okay. I let you off, typed Lucy.

'You better had,' said Pippa, with a grin, 'I'm working my socks off for you.'

She filed the details of her phone calls away, and made a note of the dates she'd arranged for her meetings on the calendar, before thinking about what to cook for lunch. As if on cue, Dan walked in from a morning's hard graft.

'How are my gorgeous girls today?'

'Ugh, you smell of cows and pigs,' said Pippa, pushing him away in a mock serious way.

'You know you love it really,' said Dan with a grin.

Smelly Dad, typed Lucy, putting on such a pained expression, they all laughed.

At moments like this, Pippa knew they'd be all right. Dan would always be by her side, Lucy was a total joy, the boys were a great support. She was going to fight with every fibre of her being to save the respite care package, but whatever else happened, no one could take her family away from her. Not even Claire King.

* * *

Cat stood in the chemist's irresolute, holding the pregnancy testing kit, checking swiftly that there was no one she knew in there. Hope Christmas was a great place to live, but everyone knew your business before you did.

Should she buy the kit or not? Surely she couldn't be pregnant at her age? Her periods had been erratic for months, but she knew the tell-tale signs, that awful taste in her mouth, the completely debilitating exhaustion, the gentle swelling of her tummy. They hadn't been careful at New Year. It was just possible – if appalling to contemplate. Cat had enjoyed her time as a young mum with babies and toddlers, but she was now enjoying the freedom of having older children. There was no way she wanted to go back to all that.

After hovering around the counter for ten more minutes, during which time the vacant looking teenager behind the counter (whom luckily she didn't know) had started to stare quite pointedly at her, Cat bought the kit. She fled home as fast as possible, feeling vaguely guilty and paranoid someone might have seen her. This was ridiculous. A pregnancy scare at her age. Because that's what it was. A scare. She'd just wasted seven quid because she and Noel had behaved like irresponsible teenagers. She'd laugh about it with him later.

Getting home, Cat found herself putting off the moment. There was no point rushing to take the test, it could wait. Never the most assiduous of housekeepers, she found herself impelled by the urgent need to tidy Ruby's bedroom. Two hours later, knee deep in plastic bags of tat, unfathomable amounts of string, pieces of paper and broken toys, Ruby's room looking better than it had done in months, the floor actually being visible, and the desk under the high sleeper bed being clear, Cat felt she could put the inevitable off no longer.

She went back downstairs, picked up her handbag and walked straight into the bright modern ensuite she and Noel had had installed when they moved in.

Best get it over with. No time like the present. Cat had forgotten how ridiculous it felt to pee on a little white stick, or how very long it felt to wait for the result. She sat on the edge of the bath, staring at the blue and white patterned bathroom tiles, realising that not only did they need a damned good clean, but it was about time she got rid of the spider's webs. Anything to stop herself staring at those two windows. They were both blank every time she peeked anyway. Good. False alarm.

Cat decided that rather than staring at her filthy tiles, she should really do something about cleaning them. Nearly ten minutes had elapsed since she'd taken the test. Time for one last look . . .

Oh God. Oh no . . . Five minutes later Cat was sitting on the edge of the bath, reeling in shock. She looked again at the blue line in the window. *Two* blue lines. One immensely strong. She'd only taken the test to prove to herself how immensely stupid she was being. She couldn't be pregnant. Not at her age. She couldn't possibly be. She felt sick to the pit of her stomach. Ruby was nearly nine; Mel would be off at university in a couple of years, the others following on fast at her heels. Cat's career was going really well, and she and Noel were finally beginning to find some time for themselves occasionally. How could she go right back to the beginning again and have a baby? She'd be ancient by the time the baby went off to college, and Noel would be retired. She knew she was being selfish. But a baby – it would ruin everything.

She turned the test over slowly. But what was the alternative? To get rid of it? Once upon a time, she might have been able to do that, but not now, not after four children, not after seeing the twelve-week scans, and seeing a little person, or hearing the heartbeat, or feeling that silverfish darting movement for the first time. She could no longer kid herself it was a collection of cells, or a blob. To her now, the baby was a future Mel, James, Paige or Ruby. By her calculations she must be at least eight weeks pregnant. By then babies had fingernails. How could she get rid of a blob when it had fingernails? There was no choice.

Bloody hell. Another baby, at her age. A horrible vile thought came into her head. What if there was a problem with it? She'd been lucky before having four healthy children. But she was older now. What if her luck ran out? Cat thought about her visit to the Sunshine Trust. All those children with their complex needs. Cat didn't think she could be as calm or capable as Pippa was in the face of that kind of difficulty. She could barely manage her rowdy family now, how would she and Noel cope if their new baby had special needs? What would it do to the family dynamic? Would that be fair?

Stop! Cat admonished herself. She was letting her imagination run riot. First things first. She was eight weeks pregnant. She needed to tell Noel. She needed to see her GP. And then they would have to take it from there.

Mel

FACEBOOK status Birthday. Woooo!!!

Andy: Happy Birthday, to my legal babe.

Kaz: Happy Birthday to my bezzie xxx

Kyra16: Hey Mel, happy birthday Join the legal club!!!!

Ellie: Happy Birthday to the Melster! You're hot hot hot!!

Fi: Happy birthday, babesxxx

Jen17: Have a great day, Melx

Jake: Happy Birthday Melanie

Mel: Oh I am so hot and gorgeous. But not as hot as Andy.

Mel: Red face. That was my little sis fraping me. Soz.

Kaz: ha ha

Andy: What you don't think I'm hot?

Mel: Andy BBM ME NOW

Mel: Thanks for all the birthday wishes everyone! xxx

Teenage Kicks

My sixteenth birthday. What a let-down.

It's not like I thought it would be at all. Mum and Dad kind of forgot. Well, they got me a present – a laptop since you ask – which would be great but they want me to use it for studying. BORING. And Dad's put some crappy filter on it which means I can't use the internet after a certain time. GREAT.

But today, they were in such a hurry to go to work, they forgot to say happy birthday.

And they won't let me have a party in case I trash the place. It wasn't my fault last year that the Chav Queen found out on FB and came with loads of her mates and got pissed and threw up in the flowerbed.

I did have loads of birthday wishes on BBM and Facebook which was cool. But Best Mate was the only one who remembered to buy me a present.

And as for The Boy. I'd kind of hoped for a bit more. He sent me a text saying, Happy Birthday to my legal babe, then VILE Little Sis put something really embarrassing on my BBM status and we had a chat, but that was it.

Why does he keep doing this to me? Making me feel all churned up and stuff. Is it always going to be like this?

I was thinking about sleeping with him. I kind of hoped we might do it on my 16th. But he hasn't contacted me. Mum always said boys are after one thing. I thought the Boy was different. Maybe I was wrong.

March

Chapter Seven

Marianne was whizzing round the house gathering up toys and discarded toddler cups, while the twins had a late morning nap. It wasn't going to be long before they dropped it altogether, so she was making the most of the time while she could. It always amazed her how much chaos two small children could create in a matter of seconds, and the place would be untidy again as soon as they were up, but she did like to have the occasional point in the day when the lounge was pristine.

Marianne plumped up the faded cushions on the sofa, and moved it out so she could start hoovering. Although she and Gabe had brightened the lounge with a cheerful makeover when she'd moved in, they'd made a deliberate choice not to get a new sofa or carpet when they found out about the twins. Which was just as well, as Marianne had lost count of the number of times they'd been sick and spilt drinks over both.

As she moved the sofa back into position, Marianne glanced once more at the envelope on the mantelpiece, practically burning a hole in it. Addressed to the parents of Steven North, with a postmark from Middleminster, there was no mistaking the letter that could change their lives forever. Marianne was dying to open it, but she and Gabe had promised Steven they would let him do it. She'd been staring at it on and off all morning and the suspense was killing her.

Marianne yawned. Gabe had gone out early for a sheep which was in labour, and although she'd tried to get back to sleep, Harry and Daisy had had other ideas. The biggest downside to having them, she decided, was lack of sleep. Marianne had forgotten what it felt like to be fully rested. Although most of the time the twins slept through the night now, they both seemed to think getting Mummy up at around five-thirty a.m. was essential. Marianne tried to compensate by going to bed earlier, but she found by the time she'd cleared up, sorted out dinner for her and Gabriel, and had a short relaxing half hour in front of the telly, it always seemed to be midnight, and either she or Gabe had fallen asleep on the sofa. Just as well they'd decided to stop at the twins, as they had no chance of ever conceiving again.

She heard the first burbling sounds coming from upstairs which indicated that the twins were waking up. She stopped to listen for a moment as Harry gurgled in his cot, and Daisy responded with a giggle. The sounds never failed to brighten her day. Exhausted and frazzled she might be, but the simple chuckling she heard all day from the twins made her exhaustion more than worthwhile.

Marianne went upstairs to their room to find Harry sitting up, playing with the musical toy attached to his cot, while Daisy was wriggling around in hers, laughing. They'd taken a loan out to convert the attic into a bedroom for Steven, so that later on the twins could have a separate room each, while still enabling them to have a spare room. The nursery was cheerful and fun, with stencils of animals she and Gabe had painted on the wall when she was in the middle of her pregnancy. It had been such a lovely time, the three of them anticipating the birth of the twins.

Marianne sighed a little. She felt life had become a bit more complicated since then.

'Come on you two, lunchtime,' she said. Harry was already trying to climb out of the cot, so she picked him up first and then changed his nappy, by which time Daisy was clamouring to get out. There was certainly never a dull moment with twins.

She took Harry downstairs first, as he was likely to get more grumpy about being left behind, and leaving him in the playpen, went to get Daisy. She'd just settled them down with a few toys when Gabriel came in from the fields, where he'd been working with Dan, for an early lunch.

'Letter's here then,' he said, immediately spotting it on the mantelpiece.

'Yup,' said Marianne.

'Aren't you just the tiniest bit curious?' said Gabriel.

'Of course I am,' said Marianne, as she helped Daisy rebuild a tower that Harry had knocked down.

'Do you think Steven would mind if . . .?'

'Don't even think about it,' said Marianne. 'Steven will kill you if you open it before him.'

'You're right,' said Gabriel, 'but I'm dying to know. Aren't you?'

'Of course I am,' said Marianne. 'It's been driving me nuts all morning. Come on, help me get the twins ready for lunch.'

'We could always steam it open,' said Gabe, as he lifted Daisy into her highchair.

'We so couldn't,' said Marianne, strapping Harry into his.

'Could.'

'Could doesn't mean we should,' said Marianne firmly, going to the fridge to get the toddler-friendly chicken stew she'd made the previous day.

'He'll never know,' said Gabe.

'He might.'

'Oh go on,' said Gabe, helping her fill the bowls with stew, 'you know you're as desperate to know as I am.'

Which is how Marianne found herself hurriedly shoving a bit of bread into each of the twins' hands to keep them going, and turning the kettle on. Gabriel self-consciously held the envelope over the steam, and then carefully opened it.

'Go on then, what does it say?'

For a moment, Gabriel didn't say anything, the colour draining from his face. Then he wordlessly handed her the letter.

'Oh no,' said Marianne. 'He failed.'

'No,' said Gabriel. 'He passed. Steven got in to Middleminster. Now what do we do?'

Cat and Noel sat in the busy waiting room at their GP's surgery, feeling faintly ridiculous. The place was full of old people and young women with small children. Cat felt completely out of place. She shouldn't be here at all.

'Pregnant at my age,' said Cat. 'It's mental.'

'I know it's not part of the game plan,' said Noel, reaching out and holding her hand, 'but I don't mind. In fact, I'm quite pleased in a way. I kind of miss having little ones around.'

'You *are* kidding,' said Cat raising her eyebrows. 'When they were little, you couldn't wait for them to grow up.'

'Ah yes,' said Noel, 'but that was before Mel did.'

Cat laughed.

'Oh dear,' she said. 'All those books we read about taming toddlers, and little did we realise having teenagers would be even worse.'

It was true. Cat had fondly imagined when the children were small, that life would improve as they got older, but while physically things had got much easier, she couldn't claim that parenting had. Cat felt constantly torn by the competing needs of her children. Although Mel's bad behaviour was her major cause for concern, if she wasn't worrying about that it was James' apparent lack of a social life and completely laidback attitude to school, or Paige's desire to reach adulthood without actually passing through puberty. Ruby at least was relatively straightforward, but at times her relentless upbeat chattering could be utterly exhausting. The thought of adding a baby in the mix was making Cat feel weak at the knees. At least Noel seemed positive about it – just as well one of them was.

Cat sighed, thinking about Mel again. She was so hard to talk to these days. Maybe it was her own fault, wanting so badly to be close to her daughter; perhaps she pushed Mel too much.

'Do you think I give Mel enough space?' Cat said to Noel as they sat on the uncomfortable waiting room chairs. Although Noel did get cross when Mel went too far, he seemed to be more tolerant of her than Cat was, and on the rare occasions when Mel did want to talk, she seemed more likely these days to confide in Noel.

Noel laced his fingers round hers, and kissed her.

'I think,' he said, 'you worry too much. Mel is young and rebellious, just like I was. Don't force her to come to you, let her be, and she'll do it in her own time.'

'Easier said than done,' said Cat. She had never been the rebellious type, so Mel baffled her. Although Mel's social life seemed to have dwindled recently. However, if asked whether anything was wrong, Mel's replies were monosyllabic and perfunctory. She seemed to have fallen out with Karen, for which Cat wasn't sorry. As far as she was concerned, Karen was a Bad Influence. The mysterious Andy seemed to have vanished into thin air – presumably the reason for Mel's moodiness. Cat hoped it was nothing more serious than that, but if Mel didn't talk to her, what could she do?

'Catherine Tinsall for Dr Stewart,' the receptionist called over the intercom.

'Here we go,' said Cat, her stomach in knots. 'I feel as daft as a teenager.'

'We can't be the first middle-aged parents she's seen,' said Noel squeezing her hand. 'Come on, let's get it over with.'

Feeling as stupid as a teenager, Cat led the way to Dr Stewart's room.

'I'm almost too embarrassed to tell you why we're here,' said Cat, as they sat down.

'It happens,' said Dr Stewart cheerfully, when Cat revealed her condition, 'particularly at your age.'

'I was just settling in for the menopause,' said Cat, 'I'm too old for babies.'

'Nonsense,' said Dr Stewart. 'Plenty of women go on to have healthy babies at your age.'

'But the risks . . .'

'Are higher for things like Downs, granted,' said Dr Stewart, 'but on the other hand you've had four healthy babies, there's no reason to think you won't produce a fifth. I can always arrange for you to have an amnio and other tests, if you like.'

Cat looked at Noel.

'Doesn't that increase the risk of miscarriage?' she asked.

'It can do,' said Dr Stewart.

'Then, no,' said Cat, suddenly feeling protective towards the blob for the first time. 'I think we'll just take our chances and hope it will be okay.'

'You're sure you want to go through with this then?' said Dr Stewart, 'you still have time to change your mind.'

Cat swallowed hard; it was what she had thought about constantly, ever since she'd found out about the pregnancy.

She'd been scared to mention it to Noel in case he agreed with her.

'Absolutely,' said Noel, he looked puzzled, as if the answer was obvious. 'Why wouldn't we want to have this baby?'

Cat could have kissed him.

'After all, we have four anyway. One more's not going to make that much difference. Besides the others are older now, it won't be the same.'

'Right, in that case, I'll book you into the system and the midwife should call you very soon.'

They got up to go, thanking the doctor for her help.

'Noel, did you really mean that?' Cat asked as they left the surgery.

'Of course I did, you daft mare,' said Noel.

'Because it did cross my mind we could get rid of it,' said Cat. 'I don't know whether I can cope with a baby right now, or whether it's fair on the others.'

'Cat,' said Noel, 'don't even go there. We'll manage, we always do. Besides,' he added, giving her a hug, 'I have faith in your Super Mum abilities.'

'I'm glad someone does,' mumbled Cat, but she was still racked with doubt. Were they really doing the right thing?

Pippa pulled on her Barbour and boots and went out into the yard to feed the pigs. Dan was out in the fields felling trees with Gabriel, and it was a fine clear March afternoon. The crocuses were already out, the daffodils beginning to bloom, and the bluebells in the woods near where Dan and Gabriel were working would be out soon. The welcome sound of baaing newborn lambs and swifts nesting in the barn where they stored the hay were both signs that spring was well and truly here.

For the first time in weeks, Pippa felt herself relax. Life was tough on a farm in the winter, but spring always gave her a renewed sense of purpose and vigour. She was really looking forward to this weekend, as Lucy would be having her fortnightly respite weekend at the Sunshine Trust. Although she and Dan would have to work, farming being 24/7, seven days a week, they'd promised the boys a day out on Sunday, while Marianne and Gabriel were having them for a sleepover tonight so she and Dan could have some precious time alone.

Dan. Pippa shut her eyes and smiled as she thought about her lovely husband. Even after fifteen years of marriage, she had to pinch herself to think how lucky she was to have met him. They'd played together as kids, with Gabriel – she had fond memories of fighting him because he pulled her plaits – and then Dan had gone away, first to school, and then university. So it was a shock to find him again, at a Young Farmers' Ball, all grown up and devastatingly handsome, tall, dark, with a crinkly smile and a great sense of humour. They'd started chatting and never stopped. He walked her home, and somehow, they never got indoors, instead, climbing the hill by her parents' farm and watching the sunrise together, drinking champagne out of plastic cups, sitting on an old picnic blanket, on one of the most magical nights of her life.

It took no time at all to realise how much they had in common. After that, getting together was a foregone conclusion. Pippa had worked out immediately how incredibly kind Dan was, knowing that for her, that was the most important thing. And so it proved. Dan was the best thing that had ever happened to Pippa. Without his love and support, she'd never have coped all these years with Lucy.

As she made her way back into the house, Pippa was aware the phone was ringing rather insistently.

'Hello,' she said, but Gabriel's voice cut her short.

'Pippa, it's Dan. There's been an accident. You'd better come quickly.'

'Oh my God,' said Pippa. She felt sick to her stomach. 'Where are you? What happened?'

'On the big field,' said Gabriel. 'Dan fell out of a tree. An ambulance is on its way.'

Pippa put the phone down and raced out of the house, her heart pounding, and her imagination in overdrive as she ran down to the big field at the far side of the valley. As she got there, an ambulance was bumping its way slowly across the rough track. Two paramedics got out and reached Dan just before she did.

Gabriel was kneeling on the ground next to him, looking white faced.

'Oh,' Pippa held her hand to her mouth. Dan was barely conscious. She moved to go to him, but Gabriel got up, and held her back.

'Let the paramedics do what they have to,' he said.

Minutes passed, and the paramedics didn't seem to be making much headway. Pippa and Gabriel stood watching numbly as they performed chest compressions. This couldn't be happening. Pippa felt in a deep state of shock. How could such a perfect day have gone so drastically wrong?

Eventually, the paramedics pronounced that Dan could be moved. Together, Gabriel and Pippa helped them put Dan on a board, so they could transport him into the ambulance.

'Can I go with him?' said Pippa.

'I think it's probably better you don't,' said the paramedic kindly. 'We'll get him to the hospital safely. You follow with your friend.'

Pippa watched the ambulance leave the field, and then she and Gabe walked in silence back to the farm. She felt utterly numb. Dan was hurt really badly. What if he didn't recover?

Chapter Eight

Marianne had carefully resealed the envelope, and she was pretty sure Steven would never know they'd even opened it, but she was trying hard to compose a 'What wonderful news' kind of face, while simultaneously not giving away that she knew the result already for when he got home from school. The twins were giggling at her efforts. Gabriel in the meantime had miserably gone back to work, and whatever she said, refused to be positive. Feeling miserable herself, Marianne was blowing bubbles with the babies to cheer herself up, ignoring the chaos they were recreating in her newly tidy lounge. She was lying on her back, throwing Harry up in the air and kissing his tummy, feeling an intense joy at the sound of Daisy's giggles, when the phone rang.

'Sorry, sweetie, better answer that,' she said, leaving Harry to toddle after his sister. Shutting the toddler gate behind her, she went to the phone in the hall.

'Gabe?' she said. 'Hi hon-' before he cut her dead.

'Marianne. There's been an accident. Dan's hurt. It's bad.'

'Oh my God,' Marianne felt herself grow cold with shock. 'Does Pippa know?'

'Yes. We're at the hospital now. Pippa's just finding out where they've taken Dan, and asked if you can fetch George from school. She's texted Nathan to tell him to come straight to ours.'

Steven and George normally walked home on their own, while Nathan, in Year 7 came home on the bus. She checked her watch. An hour until home time. Bloody hell, what was she supposed to tell them?

'Of course,' said Marianne, 'anything. What about Lucy?'

'Pippa's mum will wait for her and get her ready to go to the Sunshine Trust,' said Gabriel.

'You'll let me know the minute you know anything, won't you?' said Marianne.

'Of course,' said Gabe, lowering his voice. 'But Marianne, be prepared for the worst. Dan's had a really nasty bang on the head; it doesn't look very good.'

Marianne put the phone down slowly and went back to the twins who were still gurgling away happily, oblivious to the tragedy unfolding in their lives.

Dan. Hurt badly. How awful. Marianne felt sick to the pit of her stomach. Suppose it had been Gabriel, lying there hurt. She'd never heard Gabriel so shaken. She wished she could comfort him. But there was nothing to do but sit and wait for better news.

Half-heartedly she picked up Daisy and started to make funny noises again. Both twins' faces were wreathed with smiles and they clapped their hands delightedly.

The afternoon dragged away, the children's laughter the only thing keeping Marianne going. She tried ringing Gabriel again, but there was no answer.

Eventually, just as she was getting the twins into their buggy ready for the school run, the phone rang once more.

'And– ?' said Marianne. 'What's happening?'

'There's no more news, I'm afraid,' said Gabe. 'No one's telling us anything. We're just waiting for the doctor.'

'Oh God,' said Marianne. 'What are his chances?'

'I don't know,' said Gabriel. 'But they're not looking good.'

* * *

Pippa was sitting in A&E in a total daze. She'd been like it since Gabriel's phone call.

'What happened again?' she said.

'We were working on the tree,' said Gabriel, 'and the branch we were cutting collapsed and took the ladder and Dan down with it. He rolled down the bank and bashed his head.'

It had been terrible watching the paramedics work on Dan. It had taken them so long to move him. That couldn't be a good sign. And then when they'd got here, no one would tell them anything. Pippa had often been here over the years with Lucy and they'd always ended up in the cheerful children's department, where the kind and compassionate staff had treated her for chest complaints, choking incidents and kidney infections. Pippa had sat here so many times, heart in her mouth, wondering what the outcome would be, fearing the worst. And always, always Lucy had pulled through, the crisis averted. Things had got better. But then she'd had Dan with her. And now it was Dan lying there, unconscious to the world.

Gabriel and Pippa approached the casualty desk, where a smart efficient nurse was sitting going through paperwork.

'My cousin's husband was brought in some time ago,' he said. 'Dan Holliday?'

'Ah, yes,' the sister consulted her notes, and then looked at them with compassion. 'I'm very sorry,' she said, 'but he's still in resus.'

'Resus?' croaked Pippa, clutching blindly at Gabriel's arm, as a cold wave of panic washed over her. This couldn't be happening. 'Oh my God, is he going to be okay? Can I see him?'

'I'm afraid you can't right now,' said the nurse kindly. 'But they're doing everything they can to stabilise him.

Why don't you sit in the relatives' room? I'll bring you a cup of tea.'

Numbly, Pippa nodded, her eyes prickling with tears from the kindness of a stranger. She and Gabriel went to sit down to await further news.

'Gabe, what shall I do?' she whispered.

'What do you mean?' said Gabriel.

'If Dan dies,' she said, 'I don't think I'll cope.'

'He's not going to die,' said Gabriel fiercely. 'Put that thought right out of your head.'

'But–'

'But nothing,' said Gabriel. 'You have to stay positive and focused. Dan's a fighter. Everything will be fine.'

'This is a turn-up for the books,' said Pippa through her tears.

'What is?' said Gabe.

'You, looking after me,' said Pippa. 'It's usually the other way round.'

'Then it's about time I repaid the favour,' said Gabriel, giving her a hug. 'You've always been there for me, it's about time I was there for you.'

They fell into silence, each alone with their thoughts.

After what seemed like hours, but Pippa was surprised to find was only twenty minutes, a young, slightly dishevelled doctor came in, looking grave.

Pippa's heart plummeted. Oh God–

'The good news,' said the doctor, introducing himself as Dr Jones, 'is that your husband has stabilised. But there's a lot of trauma to the brain, and some internal bleeding. We think he needs an emergency operation to stop the bleeding. We're taking him to theatre now. It's going to take some time, so I'd advise you to go home, get some things. We'll call you when you're needed.'

'Can I see him?' said Pippa.

'Of course,' said the doctor, 'but be warned, he probably won't know you.'

Pippa followed the doctor into a cubicle, where Dan was lying with tubes, and drips and an oxygen mask.

'Oh, Dan,' she said, taking his hand.

'Got to cut the tree,' he babbled. 'What happened to the tree?'

'Don't worry about that now,' said Pippa. 'You've got to concentrate on getting better, do you hear me? Otherwise I will never ever forgive you.'

'Time to go,' said the doctor, and Pippa followed as the medical team pushed Dan on a stretcher as far as the doors to the operating theatre.

She let go of his hand and watched them wheel him in.

'He's in safe hands,' smiled a friendly nurse. 'We'll do all we can for him.'

Pippa watched her husband disappearing through the double doors, and felt her heart breaking. What if he never came back?

'How come you're here?' said Cat in surprise, to Marianne who was serving behind the café counter at Vera's. 'You don't normally help out do you?'

Cat had come into the village shop for a quick herbal tea and a read through of her page proofs while Ruby had her Saturday morning ballet lesson. There never seemed to be enough time to do tasks like that in the week, and she was looking forward to a quiet five minutes to herself.

'Oh God, haven't you heard?' said Marianne. 'I'm so sorry, we'd have rung you last night, but it was a bit chaotic.'

'Heard what?'

'About Dan. He had an accident yesterday and had to have an emergency operation. He's damaged his brain, but no one knows how badly. Pippa's at the hospital with him now, so I'm covering her shift. I've only done this once or twice before, so I'm glad it's not busy.'

It wasn't quite ten o'clock yet, so Cat was one of the few customers the café had. Marianne didn't take much persuading to join her at one of the tables for a coffee to fill her in.

'I can't believe it,' said Cat, 'such a terrible thing to happen.'

'I know,' said Marianne sipping her coffee gloomily. 'It's so bloody unfair.'

'How are the kids?' said Cat, shivering at the thought of it being her and Noel, and her having to tell the children their dad was in hospital.

'Pippa's parents are with them at the farm, while Dan's mum and dad are at the hospital with Pippa. Luckily Lucy's on a respite weekend, and I don't think the boys have quite grasped how serious it is. I had them last night, and we all tried to play it down as much as possible.'

'How bad is it?'

'It's hard to tell,' said Marianne. 'Gabriel was very gloomy last night, but when I spoke to Pippa this morning, she said the operation had been a success and Dan was talking to her; but it's a brain injury. That's pretty major.'

'What happened?'

'Gabe and Dan were working together on a tree, and a branch collapsed, taking Dan down with it. Gabe's beside himself.'

'Poor Gabe. Poor everybody,' said Cat. 'It certainly puts my problems into perspective.'

'It sure does,' said Marianne with feeling. 'Oh, excuse me . . .'

A customer had wandered in, a small strange looking individual with bottle top glasses, a flat cap, filthy mac, and shirt and trousers which had seen better days. He waddled in a turkey-like manner to the counter – as well he might, considering he was the local celebrity known as Batty Jack, whose turkey farm was county famous. He'd earned his moniker on account of having had bats take over his turkey barns to the extent he'd had to rehouse the turkeys, and was well known in Hope Christmas.

'Have you got a cup of that latte stuff going, my dear?' he said.

'For you, Jack, anything,' said Marianne with a grin.

After serving him, she came back and sat down with Cat.

'I swear that man gets more and more peculiar every time I see him,' said Cat. 'He even walks like a turkey.'

Marianne burst into giggles.

'You're so right. I'd never noticed that before.'

'I'm sorry, we shouldn't be giggling, with everything going on,' said Cat.

'Don't be,' said Marianne, 'I could use the laugh. Anyway, it's not like you don't have problems.'

'True,' said Cat, 'but by comparison, I really don't have much to complain about.'

'So when are you going to tell the children?'

Cat had confided in Marianne the last time they'd met about her unexpected pregnancy. 'Five children,' she'd wailed, 'how on earth am I going to manage?'

'Not sure. We're going to at least wait till the twelve weeks is up. I have no idea how they will take it. Paige and Ruby will probably think it's great, James won't care, and God knows what Mel will say.'

'You never know, she might be pleased.'

Cat pulled a face. 'I really have no idea. She never talks to me at all anymore. It's such a shame. We were really close a couple of years ago. But now she confides in Noel more than she does in me.'

'And what does Noel say?'

'That I should relax more,' admitted Cat. 'He's probably

91

right, but I was such a goody-two-shoes as a kid, I just can't work out where she's coming from. Sometimes I think I gave birth to an alien.'

Marianne laughed again. 'Thanks for that,' she said, 'seeing you has cheered me up. It's been a lousy twenty-four hours.'

'I wish there was something I could do to help,' said Cat.

'I don't think there's anything any of us can do, but wait,' said Marianne. 'And hope that everything will be okay.'

Cat looked at her watch.

'Damn, sorry, I was supposed to get Ruby ten minutes ago. Send everyone my love if you speak to them,' she said, 'especially Pippa.'

'Of course,' said Marianne.

Cat made her way to the village hall where Ruby's lesson was. Bloody hell, poor Pippa and Dan. It really made you think. She resolved to put more effort into renewing her relationship with Mel. Things like this made you realise just how fragile life was. She was lucky to have her children, and she should let Mel know it.

Chapter Nine

Pippa sat by Dan's bedside while he slept. A week she'd been sitting here. A whole week, with the odd breaks in between to go home and check on the children while Dan's parents took over. Mum and Dad were holding the fort at home, while Gabe was doing the work of two on the farm. The boys had been in once to see their dad, but had been so upset, Pippa had thought it better to keep them in their normal routine. It had disturbed Dan, too, who'd cried after they'd gone, then promptly forgot they'd been. Pippa wasn't quite sure which was worse.

She had fallen into a routine of spending most of the day with Dan, because he became agitated when she was away from him, trying to get home for bedtime and be there first thing in the morning, for the boys. So far it seemed to be keeping the boys on an even keel, but she was conscious they were rattled by the disruption in the domestic routine, and worried that she wasn't supporting them enough. But Dan needed her, and that had to come above everything else, even Lucy. Miraculously, the Sunshine Trust had found an emergency fund, so Lucy was staying with them for a couple of weeks till things settled down. Pippa checked in with them every day, and Lucy seemed to be cheerful enough, though Kim said she clearly missed her parents.

A week. How could it only have been a week? How could

93

her whole life have turned itself upside down in such a short space of time? Dan's physical injuries were recovering fast, although his foot was in plaster as he'd broken his ankle in the fall. But his emotional and mental injuries were another matter. The conversations they had were rambling and repetitive. Every day when she saw him, he'd forgotten what had happened, and she'd have to remind him. Every day he wandered in and out of consciousness, sometimes completely unaware that she was there, sometimes wildly enthusiastic and wanting to come home. No one could tell her if he would ever get back to his normal self. And she missed him more than she could say.

Dan stirred in his sleep, and then woke up looking slightly startled.

'Hello beautiful,' he said, a broad grin filling his face.

Pippa grinned back. That was more like Dan. His face was pale and wan, but at least he'd given her a glimpse of the man she knew.

'Hey you,' she said, tears springing to her eyes.

He held her hand and traced a finger down her cheek.

'You're crying,' he said in surprise. He was her old Dan in that instant; kind, caring, compassionate.

'I'm fine,' she said, wiping the tears away, and trying to compose herself.

'Where am I?' said Dan, looking around him very confused, taking in the surroundings of the hospital bed, equipment and hard chairs, as if seeing them for the first time. 'What happened? Why's my leg in plaster?'

He often did this, forgetting that he'd been hurt.

'You've been in an accident,' said Pippa.

'I don't feel great,' said Dan, slowly, as if testing out an idea.

'You're not very well,' said Pippa, 'but you're getting better every day.'

'Oh,' Dan held her hand tight. 'Is that why my head hurts?'

'Yes, you had a nasty bang on it,' said Pippa.

'I did?' said Dan, looking frightened. 'What happened? How long have I been here? I don't remember anything.'

'You fell out of a tree,' she said. 'A week ago.'

'A week, I've been here a week?' Panic was in his eyes now. Pippa stroked his hand. She hated to see him so churned up and miserable, but all she could do was try and soothe his fears.

'It's all right, sweetheart, you're on the mend now,' she said. 'That's the main thing.'

'Where are the kids?' he said. 'I want to see them.'

'They're at school,' said Pippa. 'They send their love and they'll see you soon.'

She'd had this conversation before, and hated it. It seemed to cause Dan physical pain when he remembered the children, and she was almost glad when he forgot about them again.

'You won't leave me, will you?' asked Dan, holding her hand tight. 'I don't want to be alone.'

'I won't leave you,' said Pippa, squeezing his hand. 'You know I'd never do that.'

'Good,' said Dan, 'because I was dreaming you had.'

Pippa kissed his hand by way of reply, and Dan calmer now, laid back on his pillow, shutting his eyes. Soon he was dozing peacefully.

'We'll be okay, Dan,' Pippa whispered fiercely, holding his hand tightly. 'We have to be.'

Dan was a long way from getting better, but maybe, just maybe, she'd been offered a glimmer of hope.

Steven and Gabriel came in from the fields, as Marianne was cooking tea. Steven had been really helpful in the wake of Dan's accident, going out to help Gabriel whenever he could.

In the way of farming kids the world over, he'd been driving a tractor practically since he could walk, and now he was bigger he was getting to be very useful to his dad. Marianne often thought it was a shame that Steven didn't want to go into farming, as sheep rearing came naturally to him, but certainly at the moment, singing was more important. It was a pity that Gabriel couldn't see it quite that way. In the week since Dan's accident, there had been little time to talk about Steven going to Middleminster. Steven's pleasure at getting into the school had been marred by what had happened to Dan, and it had been forgotten about in the general chaos of trying to keep on top of things. But they were going to have to talk about it soon. They had to accept the place or risk losing it.

She was finding it difficult to raise the issue. Not only was Gabe preoccupied with the farm and Dan, his enthusiasm for Steven's achievement had been muted, to say the least. Marianne could see how hurt Steven was that Gabriel hadn't been happier for him, so she had unsuccessfully tried to pass it off as Gabe being busy.

'You could have been more pleased for him,' Marianne had said tentatively to Gabriel the previous night, to which he had shrugged his shoulders, saying, 'But I'm not. And I don't want to talk about it right now.' Marianne knew he was hurting at the thought of losing his son, but it was clear to her that his approach wasn't helping the situation, as it was just making Steven hostile. For all his good points, Gabriel could be very stubborn, and so could Steven. Marianne felt like banging their silly heads together.

Steven shot off straight upstairs without saying a word, no doubt to go straight on the Xbox or play some other violent computer game.

'Well?'

'Well what?' said Gabriel sitting down at the kitchen table.

He looked tired, so Marianne brought him a cup of tea and came over and ruffled his hair.

'Did you find any time to talk about whether we accept the place at Middleminster?'

Marianne had been secretly hoping that spending some bonding father/son time in the fields would help Gabriel see things from Steven's point of view.

'He wants to go. I don't want him to go. What's there to say?'

'I think you should let him,' said Marianne. 'If that's what he wants.'

'This is all bloody Eve's fault,' said Gabriel viciously. 'Putting the idea in his head. It's all right for her to swan in now and cause chaos. It's not as if she's ever been much of a mother to him.'

'Woah.' Marianne had never heard Gabriel express such bitterness to his ex-wife. 'I know things haven't been great in the past, but it's good Eve wants to be involved now, isn't it? For Steven, I mean.'

'I guess,' said Gabriel reluctantly.

'And is it such a bad idea? Steven has such talent. Do you really want to hold him back? Think about what's happened with Dan. We shouldn't pass up a chance like this.'

'You think I'm being selfish?'

'A bit,' said Marianne.

'Thanks for the support,' said Gabe. 'I thought you at least were on my side.'

'I am,' protested Marianne, 'but Steven—'

'Is my son, and he's only eleven years old,' said Gabriel. 'I think I know what's best for him. You're not his mum, and Eve's never been much of a mum to him. It's up to me to decide.'

'But why let him even take the exam then?' Marianne said. 'You've made him think you're okay with it.'

97

Gabe had the grace to look embarrassed.

'To be honest, I didn't think he'd get in,' he said. 'And now with what's happened to Dan, I just can't bear the thought of Steven going away. Life's too short.'

'You're right, life is too short,' Marianne seized on the idea, but she saw a familiar set in his jaw and knew it was hopeless.

'Sorry, Marianne,' said Gabe, 'this is my decision and mine alone.'

Cat was back in front of the cameras, filming the Christmas edition of *Cat's Country Kitchen*. They were filming it early to tie in with the book schedule. It seemed utterly absurd to be decked out in tinsel, slaving over a hot turkey, but it had to be done. She was feeling queasy, and the studio lights were making her feel hot and bothered. She kept fluffing her takes, as she was finding it hard to concentrate, and Les was getting quite irritable with her. A month ago, she would have imagined she was having hot flushes, but now she knew differently. Her body was showing all the tell-tale signs of early pregnancy – the heavy sickness, the swollen and sore breasts; the utter exhaustion. Cat thought she'd felt rough with Ruby, but eight years on, and this was hideous. There was a reason a woman's prime time for giving birth was eighteen. Forty-two felt positively ancient. Cat wasn't at all sure she was ready to go back to nappies after all this time, despite Noel's growing enthusiasm. He was already talking about prams and cots in a way she couldn't recall him doing in the past. He was far more enthusiastic about this baby than she was, but then again, he didn't have to carry it.

Cat's head was really hurting by the time Les called cut. She hadn't dared yet mention to anyone on the production team, that she was pregnant. She had no idea how it would go down. But she had a feeling there might not be a second series of *Cat's Country Kitchen* in the offing. Although, she could probably do a mini-series on feeding new babies if the worst came to the worst. It didn't seem fair. It was all right for the men; Jamie Oliver could just leave Jools to produce away in the baby department while his career wasn't affected a jot. But Cat knew that even if people were still enthusiastic about keeping her on, inevitably her time was going to be more limited than it was now. And the thought of going back to nannies and au pairs again filled her with dread. Oh God, she was having another baby. At her age. It was ridiculous.

'You okay?' Penny, the very lovely production assistant, came up as Cat sat wanly on a chair, concentrating on trying to feel better.

'Fine,' said Cat, then grimaced as she felt a familiar ache in her groin. It felt like period pain, but that wasn't possible.

'You don't look fine,' said Penny. 'You look very pale. Can I get you some water or something?'

'I don't feel all that great,' admitted Cat. 'I might just pop to the loo. I'm sure I'll be better in a minute.'

She got up to leave, and felt a spasm of pain. Something wasn't right. By the time she reached the loos, Cat's body was being racked by the most appalling pain, like the worst contraction she'd ever had. And there was blood. A lot of it. No. No. No. This couldn't be happening. Having just got used to the idea of the blob, she couldn't be losing it. Not now.

'Cat, are you okay?' Penny knocked on the door. 'Sorry to intrude, but I was a bit worried about you.'

'Penny,' she called weakly. 'Can you call an ambulance? I think I'm having a miscarriage.'

Mel

FACEBOOK status)-: Crap
Kaz: wassup babe?
Jen17: You ok?
Ellie?: What's wrong?
Mel: Bad day. Thanks everyone xxx
Mel: Kaz MESSAGE ME Now
Kaz: You ok?
Mel: Andy. I think he's dumped me.
Kaz: No!!! Why???
Mel: We talked about you know.
Kaz: AND???
Mel: I said I wasn't ready yet . . . I thought I was but then . . .
Kaz: You're better off without him, babes
Mel: I knew you'd say that.
Kaz: I'm only trying to help.
Mel: Don't.

Teenage Kicks

The Boy hasn't rung. Or texted. Not since my birthday. He wanted me to have sex, and I said I wasn't ready. I fell out with Best Mate about it.

She says I'm better off without him. But how can I be, when I feel so bad?

And Mum's had a miscarriage. She was really ill for a bit, it was so scary. We didn't even know she was pregnant. Ugh. Mum and Dad. I didn't know they still did it. That's horrible.

I know I've been crap to Mum recently. I feel bad now.

Why is everything so miserable?

I worked at the caff today. And The Boy came in. With a girl. No, not a girl. A woman. She was older than him. And he kissed her on the lips. He didn't see me behind the counter, and I ran in and hid in the kitchen till he'd gone. I can't believe he's doing this to me. I thought he loved me.

I went to see Mad Gran today and told her all about it. I tell her everything. It helps to talk to her, and I know she can't remember or tell anyone. And I have no one else to talk to. My fault. Best Mate's not speaking to me. I'd try and talk to Mum, but she's so upset about the baby, I don't think it's the right time.

Mad Gran's great though. I mean totally bonkers, and she keeps thinking I'm Mum, but she doesn't judge me. She always listens, and seems to understand.

'It will be all right,' she said, and she held my hand.

Part Two

If the Fates Allow

April

Chapter Ten

'Come on, Harry, come on, Daisy, let's see where the Easter Bunny's hidden the eggs.'

As Marianne and Gabriel were having Easter Sunday lunch with Gabriel's parents, they'd decided on an impromptu Easter egg hunt the day before for the twins. Marianne led Harry and Daisy slowly round the garden, looking under plant pots and behind bushes to help them find the eggs ever-so-obviously planted by the Easter Bunny i.e. Gabriel, who was filming the moment for posterity. Steven, who had also helped a little too well in the hiding, was going round picking up the eggs which he'd managed to hide too high up for toddler hands. It was a gorgeous day, the sky a cloudless deep blue and the sun already burning hot.

Daisy and Harry were having a lovely time. With Marianne's help they managed to pick up plenty of eggs, and already had chocolate smeared all over their mouths. They were chattering away in a language all their own.

'They seem so perfectly content with their lot in life, don't they?' said Gabriel, giving Marianne a hug. 'It's as though the rest of the world is superfluous to their needs.'

'As well they might be,' laughed Marianne, when they'd finally finished egg collecting and she let them sit down on a blanket on the grass with all their spoils. 'I cannot think of a nicer way to spend my time, pottering around picking up chocolate eggs while Mummy runs around after me. It must be bliss.'

Gabriel grinned. 'And you're so good at it, isn't she, Steven?'

Steven just grunted. Uh oh. He had been quite cheerful today so far, but whenever Gabriel spoke to him directly, he had given him the cold shoulder.

'Don't put Steven in an awkward position,' said Marianne, 'you know he wants to disagree, and now he can't.'

She flashed him a smile, which had a slightly desperate plea of, 'Don't argue with your dad today,' to which Steven responded with his own smile, meaning 'You know you're my favourite step-mum.'

'Just as well, that,' said Marianne. 'Now if everyone's not too stuffed after lunch and chocolate, shall we go for a quick trot over the meadows to see the lambs, before popping in on Pippa and Dan?'

Dan was finally coming out of hospital today, and Gabriel had promised they'd call in later.

'That's a great idea,' said Gabriel. 'Come on you little monsters,' he plucked one twin each off the rug, 'let's go and see some baa baas.'

'Baa, baa! Baa! Baa!' The twins clapped their hands with glee. They couldn't say much else that was intelligible, so it was fitting that they had learnt to say 'Baa' at least.

'Coming, Steven?' said Marianne, as Gabriel took the twins inside to get them ready.

'Do I have to?' said Steven.

'You might enjoy it,' said Marianne.

'And Dad might start nagging me about choir school,' said Steven. 'Please, I don't want to have another row about it.'

So far over the weekend, there had been several terse exchanges between Steven and Gabriel, and Marianne was

106

loath for them to develop into a huge row. It had been a lovely day so far, and she didn't want it spoiled.

'Okay,' said Marianne, 'I'll give him some excuse. Don't worry, we'll work this all out somehow.'

'Steven not coming with us?' Gabriel looked disappointed as they started off up the lane.

'Couldn't prise him away from the Wii,' lied Marianne. 'At least he's getting some exercise.'

'Oh,' said Gabriel and she could sense his disappointment. She sighed as she followed him up the hill, each of them carrying a twin in a backpack. This choir school problem was definitely not going away. Not for a while yet.

Pippa put the finishing touches on her Welcome Home Cake which, to honour the season, she'd decorated in mini eggs. She and the boys had filled the house with balloons and flags, and they and Lucy had spent the previous evening making a *Welcome Home Dad!* banner; Lucy's contribution being mainly to draw big loopy flowers.

Pippa had no idea of how much Lucy understood of what was going on, but she had been restless and unsettled since Dan had been away. Dan had always been fantastic with Lucy, and among Pippa's other worries was a gnawing anxiety about how things would be when he got back.

Dan was still very dependent on her, both physically and emotionally, though he had seemed more settled and less prone to outbursts in the last week. But he was a long way from better and was going to have to undergo intensive physio to get him back on his feet. For someone as active as Dan to be confined for a time to a wheelchair was going to be hellish for them both. A bonus of having Lucy meant that the house was more than able to accommodate Dan's new needs. They already had a wet room, and Gabriel had helped set up a sofa bed downstairs for Dan. But it was going to be a tricky time for them all.

Dan's parents had gone to the hospital to pick him up, and now she and the children were nervously waiting for them to come back. The boys were excited about seeing their dad again, but also slightly ill at ease. They had both glimpsed the change in Dan when he'd shouted at George in the hospital for no good reason.

'Is Dad going to get better?' said George who'd been licking out the icing bowl. He rubbed his fair hair in a slightly worried way, his blue eyes anxious.

'Yes of course he is,' said Pippa. 'What makes you say that?'

'Just something Matt Pilsdon said, about my dad always being a retard now he's in a wheelchair.'

'The wheelchair is temporary,' said Pippa, trying to control the tears in her voice. Kids could be so cruel. 'It's only until Dad gets walking again properly. Of course he's going to get better, it will just take time. Matt Pilsdon knows nothing about it. You should ignore him.'

A frantic and excited clicking from Lucy, who was sitting in the front room, looking out for Dan, heralded his arrival.

Harriet came in first, carrying Dan's suitcase, followed by Phillip pushing the wheelchair up the ramp (already in place for Lucy).

'Daddy!' The boys ran towards him, bowling each other over in their enthusiasm. Dan acknowledged their hugs with a brief smile, and accepted Pippa's kiss with an unfathomable look.

Lucy clapped her hands when she saw him and gave Dan a beaming smile. Dan gently held her hand and squeezed it tight. The tenderness of his look floored Pippa. It was weeks since she'd seen him look like that. It felt good to know that Dan was still in there, somewhere.

They all settled into the kitchen, the children all talking at once. The first problem came when Pippa realised that Dan's wheelchair was too wide to fit comfortably at the table.

'Oh for God's sake!' Dan was clearly feeling embarrassed, and, Pippa realised with dismay, having two wheelchairs made things difficult, as everyone was having to squeeze past them to get to the table. Instead of being homely and comfortable, the kitchen felt overcrowded and awkward. Dan's dad helped him into a chair instead, and Pippa breathed a sigh of relief as Dan seemed to relax a bit more. He duly admired the cake, the banner, the decorations, and the many cards which had arrived from everyone. So many people had helped Pippa in the last few weeks, she couldn't imagine how she would ever repay them.

Gabriel and Marianne popped in briefly with the children, and Dan made the effort to look pleased, but as it was clear he was flagging, they thoughtfully left.

Harriet glanced at Pippa, then tactfully suggested sorting tea for the children, while Pippa took Dan to bed.

They went into the makeshift bedroom Pippa and Gabe had sorted out in the conservatory. Pippa went to help Dan onto the bed, but he brushed her away crossly.

'I'm not a cripple,' he said, 'I can walk a little.'

'Let me help,' said Pippa.

'No,' he snarled, and then with a determination she'd always known he'd possessed, she watched as he painfully inched his way from the wheelchair to the bed, then tried to get himself undressed.

Every overture of help was rejected, so in the end Pippa said, 'Do you want me to go?' practically in tears, after Dan had bitten her head off for the third time.

'Yes,' said Dan, then swore loudly as he tried and failed again to reach down to undo his shoes.

'Let me,' said Pippa, seeing the pain contorting his face. 'Please.'

Dan didn't say anything, but defeated, let her undress him.

'I'm sorry,' he said suddenly.

'For what?'

'For this. For being such a wreck. I'm no husband to you anymore.'

There were tears in his eyes. Her Dan, who never cracked, who'd always been the strong one.

Smiling brightly, Pippa said, 'Nonsense. You are going to be fine, do you hear? We're going to get you better, so there.'

'How do you know?' Dan looked bleak. 'I feel like I'll never get any better.'

'I just know,' said Pippa. 'Come on, we're going to lick this thing. Now get some rest, and I'll look in on you later.'

But as she shut the door, she leant back against it with a heavy heart. This was just the beginning. How on earth was she going to manage?

'Mummy, Mummy, there's a dead mouse in the playroom! It's really gross!' Ruby came screaming hysterically into the lounge where Cat was ostensibly lying with her feet up. Noel had promised to cook Sunday lunch today, in order to give her a rest. She'd been back home from the hospital for several days, but was still feeling shaky and a little weepy.

Oh God. They'd known mice were getting in somewhere, and Noel had set a succession of traps, but so far the mice had been clever enough to elude them. Cat wasn't particularly frightened of them, but the thought of having to deal with a dead one made her stomach churn.

'Where's your dad?' she said tentatively.

'Arguing with Granny in the kitchen about the Yorkshire puddings,' said Ruby.

Brilliant. Cat might have known that the minute Angela arrived there'd be trouble. She knew Angela only wanted to help, but diplomacy wasn't her strong point and she had a genius for rubbing Noel up the wrong way.

'Okay, Rubes, you and me will deal with the mouse,' said Cat. She went to the understairs cupboard where she kept all her cleaning stuff, and pulled out a pair of rubber gloves and a plastic bag to dispose of the body.

'Mummy, do I have to?' Ruby pulled a face.

'Come on, Ruby,' said Cat, 'I thought you liked gross stuff.'

'I don't like dead mice,' she declared, 'they remind me too much of Hammy.'

'Okay, I'll do it alone,' said Cat. 'Wish me luck.'

Ruby hovered outside the door of the playroom, clearly fascinated as well as repelled by the thought of the mouse.

Cat found it in the corner of the room, behind a toy box. The trap had been so efficient it had bounced a few feet away from where it had been left. Ugh. Not one mouse, but two. Babies. Cat felt like a criminal as she emptied the bodies into the plastic bag, and took it out to the dustbin to dispose of. That must mean there was a mum somewhere with a nest. There could be hundreds of the little buggers.

She felt a shot of pain go through her. Ridiculous to get upset about dead baby mice, but it made her think of the blob, and how it was a blob no more.

The doctors in the hospital had been very kind.

'It's an ectopic,' they'd explained. 'There is really no saving it.'

'We can try again,' Noel said, his eyes filling with tears as he held Cat's hand and squeezed it tight. 'It's okay; this doesn't have to be the end.'

Cat had taken a deep breath, and smiled at him through her own tears. 'I think it does, sweets,' she said. 'We're too old. This wasn't meant to happen. Nature's giving us a warning.' It was at that point, she'd decided to have her tubes tied, to prevent her getting pregnant again. She'd always meant to after Ruby, but somehow there'd never been time.

'Are you sure?' Noel was clearly upset, and she felt badly for him, because he was a great dad, and she could see he had allowed himself to get excited about the prospect of a new baby.

'Sure,' she'd said gently. 'I couldn't go through this again. We've got four healthy wonderful kids. We're very very lucky. I think it's better this way.'

She laced her hands in his, and kissed them, trying to draw strength, not to change her mind. She had never been clearly able to see the blob as a proper baby, more as a hindrance. It was for the best. She knew it was, so why did she feel so terrible?

'What's going on?' Noel appeared at the front door as she came back feeling pathetically teary.

'Nothing,' she said. 'The mousetrap worked.'

'You okay?'

Noel gently took her to him, as she burst into tears on his shoulder.

'It's stupid,' she sobbed. 'Two dead baby mice, and I'm a total mess.'

'No it's not,' said Noel. 'Come and sit down, and I'll make you a cup of tea. It's been a rough few days, and you need to relax.'

'Oh Noel, what would I do without you?' Cat sobbed.

'You'd live I expect,' said Noel, as he sat her down on the sofa, and propped up her cushions. 'Now how do you make Yorkshire puddings again?'

It was only the third time of asking today, so Cat threw a cushion at him. But she felt a little better. Noel had a talent for that. She was lucky to have him. And she would survive.

Chapter Eleven

'Right, I'm off to see Granny,' Cat announced after lunch. 'Anyone coming with me?'

It was over a week since Easter and the children had one day left at home before school started again. Noel had gone back to work reluctantly, anxiously asking her every other minute if she were all right, so that in the end, she'd said, 'Bugger off, you're beginning to annoy me now.' Part of her wanted Noel to stay with her for a few more days, so she could stay in bed and sink back into her heartache, but another part knew that the sooner she was up and out in the world the better it would be.

'I'll come.' To Cat's surprise, Mel seemed quite enthusiastic. It wasn't that she didn't visit Louise, but it had been a long time since she'd come with Cat.

'What?' Mel said.

'Nothing,' said Cat. 'I thought you might have revision or something.'

'I've done my quota for today,' said Mel. 'It's fine.'

Reluctant to quiz her daughter too deeply about just how much the quota was, Cat decided not to look a gift horse in the mouth. Ruby, who was the most likely to accompany her, opted to go and play with her friend Holly instead, while James and Paige both suddenly had homework that needed doing urgently. Funny that.

Mel was quiet on the way to the home, so Cat deliberately kept the chit-chat light and airy. No point creating conflict unnecessarily.

'It's lovely that you want to see Granny,' she said, as they got out of the car and walked up the drive of the home.

'Granny's cool,' said Mel. 'I mean she doesn't remember anything, but she's cool.'

Cat wondered wryly if it were better to be a cool granny with memory loss, or to be a stressed-out mum without. Maybe Mum was better off in some ways.

They found Louise in the lounge, where several of the residents were gathered to have afternoon tea. Alfie wasn't around and Mum was sitting dozing in her chair.

'Hi Mum, how are you?' Cat kissed her mother on the cheek, as Louise woke up looking a bit confused.

'Are you the flower girl?' said Mum.

Flower girl? That was a new one.

'Oh no, it must be you,' Mum held out her hand to Mel, who took it gently and smiled at her granny encouragingly. Cat felt a faint swell of pride and gratitude. It was nice to see something of the old Mel for a change, and know that she still appreciated her granny. Mel had always been close to her grandmother as a small child, and obviously retained that closeness even now, when Louise barely recognised her.

'No, that's Mel, your granddaughter,' said Cat.

'Granddaughter?' Mum frowned. 'Who's the flower girl then? Is it you?'

'Yes, I'm the flower girl,' said Cat, exchanging glances with Mel. Sometimes it was better to go with the flow, or Louise grew more agitated. She held her mother's hand, so fragile, so pale.

'You looked so pretty at the wedding.'

Oh, now Cat got it. Mum was talking about the time she

didn't remember, but she'd seen in photos, when she'd been very tiny and been a flower girl at some long-forgotten relative's wedding. For some reason, Mum must have remembered it. She felt oddly comforted, besides the lump in her throat. Somewhere, deep down, Mum still knew it was her.

'My Cat came to see me,' continued Louise. 'I hope that boy doesn't cause any trouble.'

'What boy?' Cat said, puzzled.

'Oh that silly boy who doesn't realise what a prize he's got,' said Louise. 'Poor Cat. I hope she stays out of trouble.'

'Does she mean you, do you think?' Cat whispered to Mel. Louise did often confuse them.

'No,' said Mel. 'You know what Granny's like, she's probably got muddled.'

'Who are you calling muddled?' said Louise, looking slightly pugnacious.

'No one,' said Mel, and kissed Louise. She had the knack of calming her grandmother down, so soon Louise had forgotten the perceived insult.

She looked around her again, as if surprised to see them. 'Hello. Have you come to visit me?'

'Yes,' said Cat with a smile.

'Sorry, I don't know your names,' Louise said. 'Louise Carpenter. Delighted to meet you.'

'I'm your daughter, Cat,' said Cat, 'and this is Mel, your granddaughter.'

She produced the family photo for the umpteenth time. Louise glanced at it, uncomprehending.

'Oh are you, dear?' she said. 'I thought you were Auntie Lottie. Amazing.'

Auntie Lottie had been Mum's favourite auntie; if she got Cat muddled with her, at least it was a benign thought.

'Yes, I'm Auntie Lottie,' said Cat with a sigh. She so missed

116

her mother. If Louise was still as active and able as she'd been a few short years ago, Cat would have poured out all the misery of her miscarriage and Louise would have dispensed comfort and wisdom. Whereas now . . . Cat felt a familiar agonising ache of loss. This was like watching someone die by slow degrees. She couldn't bear it sometimes. It just felt too hard.

They sat with Louise for about half an hour, the conversation turning in similar concentric circles.

'Has it been raining?'

'Yes it has.'

'Well I never. I won't go out then.'

'Best not.'

'So what do you think of our house?' she said with a sweeping gesture, as if somehow, Louise was responsible for the whole place, before reverting to, 'Has it been raining?' all over again.

They were both beginning to flag, when Louise suddenly announced she was going to find Alfie.

'We're running away to Gretna Green,' she said. 'But shhh, it's a secret.'

'That's marvellous,' said Cat, having visions of them tunnelling out of their rooms and escaping like Colditz prisoners. 'We won't say a word.'

Deciding this was a good moment to escape, they both kissed her on the cheek, and went back to the car.

'Running away to Gretna Green,' said Cat dissolving into fits of giggles when they got to the car, 'that's priceless.'

'It wasn't that funny,' said Mel.

'Maybe not,' said Cat, 'but if I don't laugh, I'll cry and cry. And I know which I'd prefer.'

'Oh Mum,' said Mel, and squeezed her arm tightly. 'I didn't know you felt like that.'

'Not all the time,' admitted Cat, squeezing Mel's arm back.

At least that was something. She and Mel bonding over Louise. There was always a silver lining if you looked hard enough.

Marianne was standing in front of a Year 6 class, on the first day of the summer term, feeling totally spaced out. The twins had come down with a tummy bug and had been up half the night. When she'd eventually dropped off at four-thirty a.m., Gabe had woken her up an hour later to go out to Dan's where he was managing the cows this week, on top of his normal duties. Between Gabriel, his father David and Phillip, Dan's dad, they had developed a pretty efficient system for keeping the farm going, but with the bulk of it falling on Gabriel as the youngest, the strain was beginning to tell. Gabe was short-tempered with both her and Steven, and less involved with the twins than he'd been up until now.

Some days Gabe was gone before she'd got up in the mornings and though he'd come back for tea, as the evenings grew lighter, he'd go straight out again after supper, and come back late. On those days, he was so exhausted, he would fall into bed early, leaving Marianne sitting alone in the lounge, wondering what life was all about. She was the one left running the house, and the children. And she was aware that more than ever, Steven was feeling left out and neglected by his dad. It wasn't Gabe's fault, as Marianne kept telling Steven, but she could see why, when Steven barely saw his dad, he could feel that Gabe had lost interest – particularly as the school situation was still unresolved.

It was nothing to what Pippa was going through, Marianne knew, but still, she was struggling. And coming in to face a very stroppy hormonal Year 6 group who were thoroughly bored of revising for SATs was the last thing she wanted to have to do.

Marianne didn't normally teach Year 6, but her Year 4 class had gone on the residential course that Marianne had been unable to attend, so she'd been lumbered with Year 6 instead. Which meant she could witness for herself that Matt Pilsdon evidently had a way of getting under Steven's skin. He'd spent most of the morning needling him, and Marianne found herself having to play a very careful game, of not being very fair to Steven, in order to appear to be fair to Matt. If she came down too heavily on him, she knew the mother would be down on her like a ton of bricks, if there was the slightest suggestion that her darling Matt might appear to be in the wrong, or a hint that Steven's stepmother was giving him special treatment. And knowing how wimpy Mrs Garratt could be in the face of complaining parents (a trait that wasn't transferred to the way she treated her staff), Marianne knew she wasn't going to get any support from that quarter.

Luckily, George, who was Steven's great ally, came to the rescue. Marianne observed and chose to ignore several very sparky clashes between George and Matt. She'd already overheard George respond to Matt's 'You're such a loser' comment with a mild, 'No I'm not. I beat you every time we have a race,' which had made Matt apoplectic. She was hoping it wasn't going to lead to fisticuffs in the playground later. The only thing she could think to constructively do was to have a chat with Carrie Matthews, whose class it was, when she came back. Poor Steven, no wonder he was so desperate to go to a different school.

The end of the day didn't come a moment too soon, but much as Marianne wanted to dash off home to see the twins, she had marking to catch up and various administrative tasks to attend to. If she'd even remotely felt like leaving early, she knew it would have caused raised eyebrows, and resulted in a sarcastic comment from Mrs Garratt. As it was, she was the first to leave at six p.m., and although Mrs Garratt smiled sweetly at her on the way out, Marianne could feel the implied criticism. Marianne was beginning to wonder if the job was really worth the aggro.

By the time she got home, exhausted and hungry, Jean had bathed the babies and was getting them ready for bed. Steven as usual was attached like a limpet to his Xbox, and Gabe still hadn't come in from the fields.

'Lambing's started,' said Jean. 'You know he'll be out and about at all hours for a bit.'

'I know,' sighed Marianne. The downside of being married to a farmer was the antisocial hours, and the fact that a ewe in labour couldn't be ignored, whatever else might be happening. With a sigh, she took the children to bed.

When she got downstairs, Jean had already tidied up the kitchen.

'Thanks so much,' said Marianne. 'I don't know what we'd do without you.'

'You know it's my pleasure,' said Jean.

Steven came down, muttered a grunting acknowledgement to Marianne and stuffed his hand into the biscuit barrel.

'Is Matt always like that in class?' said Marianne.

Steven shrugged.

'He's not normally that bad,' he said. 'I think he was playing up because you were there.'

'I'm really sorry if I made it worse,' said Marianne. 'I didn't want him to go running home accusing me of favouritism to his mum.'

'I know,' said Steven. 'It's not your fault. I can handle him.'

'What was all that about?' said Jean, when Steven had retreated back upstairs.

'There's a boy in Steven's class who keeps teasing him,' said Marianne. 'I had to teach them today, and he was very disruptive.' She paused, wondering if Gabriel would thank her for broaching the subject. 'It's one of the reasons I think Steven should go to Middleminster, actually.'

'Ah,' said Jean. 'And Gabriel doesn't agree with you?'

'Not exactly,' admitted Marianne. 'He thinks it's none of my business.'

'And what do you think?'

'I think Gabe should let Steven decide,' said Marianne, 'but he won't listen to me.'

'Hmm. That's Gabriel all over,' said Jean. 'Stubborn as a mule. Always was. I'll have a chat with him, if you like. See what I can do.'

'Brilliant, Dan,' said the physio, as she watched him hobble up and down the lounge in his walking shoe cast. The NHS waiting list for physiotherapy was so long Pippa had paid her to come to the house to help out. 'You're doing really well.'

'Do you think?' said Dan, managing to raise a smile. 'So I should be back up to speed for next year's Monday Muddle then?'

'Without a doubt,' said the physio, a pretty young brunette called Lauren who, despite looking about fifteen, was immensely good at her job. 'You've done brilliantly today, well done.'

It was what Pippa had been saying to him for days. Dan was still hobbling, but had begun using his stick less and less indoors. She grinned to herself slightly. If she'd suggested he was doing well, Dan would have bitten her head off.

'Okay, what's so funny?' said Dan, as the physio left.

'You,' said Pippa. 'Well sometimes you are.'

121

'How so?'

'If I tell you you're doing well, you don't believe a word of it, but all it takes is for a pretty young physio to come in and you hang on to her every word,' teased Pippa.

'Oh,' Dan looked completely stricken. 'Am I so much of a bastard to you?'

'No, no, that's not what I meant,' Pippa reassured him. 'I was just joking. Sorry. Not funny.'

Dan hobbled back to his chair in the lounge. He was still sleeping downstairs, but Pippa was hoping at this rate of progress, he might be back upstairs soon. Then they could all start relaxing a bit, and focusing on things getting better. She knew they were in it for the long haul, all the doctors had warned them as much, but no one had told them how hard it was going to be.

'Do you fancy a cuppa and one of my muffins?' said Pippa. 'I was baking while you were busy breaking world records in hobbling.'

'That would be lovely,' said Dan. 'God. Hobbling. I feel like such a feeble old man. I can't imagine that I'll ever walk properly again.'

'Now stop that,' said Pippa. 'I will have no more negative talk out of you, do you hear? We're going to get you better and that's that. Now eat this and shut up.'

She popped a bit of muffin in his mouth and kissed him on the head.

He grabbed her hand and pulled her down on his lap.

'Pippa, you're the best,' he said, pulling her close to him. 'I know you're right. I'm just so frustrated watching you run around after me.'

'I know,' said Pippa, kissing him softly. 'But we will get through this, and this time next year, we'll be looking back and feeling so lucky we did. You just wait and see.'

Chapter Twelve

Marianne was pushing the twins up the lane to Pippa's. She'd promised to sit with Dan so Pippa could get a break. Marianne was dreading it a little. The couple of times she'd seen Dan since he'd been home, he'd appeared morose and miserable. Pippa wasn't saying much but it was clear she was struggling, although she had said Dan seemed to be getting on better with his walking, which was something.

As it happened, Dan seemed to be having a good day. He was sitting in the lounge watching a rugby match he'd missed in hospital, but happily switched it off when she came in.

'How are you, Dan?' Marianne asked as she settled the twins on the floor with various toys.

'Fine,' said Dan.

'Yeah, and the rest,' said Marianne. 'How are you really?'

Dan didn't say anything for a minute.

'It's okay,' said Marianne. 'I was being too nosy. If you don't want to talk, it's fine.'

'No, you're all right,' said Dan. 'Things are pretty crap to be honest. Pippa's running herself ragged looking after me, and the kids. My walking's improving, but it's slow. And I keep forgetting things, which is really frustrating. I get these blinding headaches, which make me very grumpy. I must be a total pain in the arse to look after. But I can't seem to help it.'

'What have the doctors said?' Marianne asked, getting down on the floor to help Daisy push a toy ambulance round the room, while Harry toddled over to Dan and offered him a fire truck.

'No one really seems to know,' said Dan. 'They keep saying *time will tell*, and I should be patient. But how can I be patient? It's so frustrating watching Dad, Gabriel and David running the farm for me, while Pippa wears herself out. It's not as if she doesn't have enough on her plate.'

'Oh Dan,' said Marianne, 'I know it's hard, but you have to take each day as it comes.'

'Don't patronise me,' said Dan savagely. 'You don't know what it's like. You can't possibly understand.'

'Sorry,' said Marianne. 'You're right. I have no idea what you're going through. So go on, tell me. All I'm saying is don't run before you can walk.'

'I'd be happy with just walking for now,' said Dan.

'Oh God.' Marianne blushed with shame. 'I'm so sorry, I didn't mean–'

'Don't be,' said Dan, the shadow of a grin passing across his face. 'I'm fed up with people tiptoeing around it. It was quite funny actually. And besides, according to my physio I should be up and running in no time at all.'

'Brilliant,' said Marianne. 'It would probably do you good to laugh about it from time to time.'

They sat chatting amiably for a while, Dan clearly enjoying the twins' chattering and toddling about. It was almost possible to forget that Dan had had an accident.

Then Marianne said, 'You know, I think you need to set yourself some goals. I reckon it would help. Rather than sitting here feeling sorry for yourself–'

Dan winced. 'Say it like it is, why don't you?'

'I thought you wanted people to be direct,' retorted Marianne, who had always had a frank and easy relationship with Dan. 'You're quite rightly feeling sorry for yourself, because you think the problems are insurmountable. You should try and see if you can start improving one small thing each day.'

'Like what?'

'How about trying to improve the distance you walk each day?' said Marianne. 'Today the front gate, next week the end of the lane.'

'That's what my physio said I should do,' admitted Dan.

'Well there you are, then,' said Marianne. 'A small victory each day. It's something to aim at, anyway.'

'To little victories,' said Dan, raising his mug of tea.

'Little victories,' echoed Marianne.

Cat pushed her way into the village hall, where, in Pippa's absence, she'd arranged the latest campaign meeting for the Sunshine Trust. The hall was packed. Pippa and Dan were popular in Hope Christmas, and everyone wanted to help. There were Vera and Albert from the post office, Diana Carew, the local but good-hearted busybody, and Miss Woods, who stomped noisily in with her stick, looking as if she wanted to take over the whole thing. Cat had luckily persuaded her that her expertise in logistical planning was going to be invaluable.

Representing Hopesay Manor was Michael Nicholas, Ralph's enigmatic young nephew, resplendent as ever in black leather. He was rather good looking, with longish curly black hair and the most mesmerising blue eyes Cat had ever seen. He was slightly unshaven and looked like a raffish pre-Raphaelite artist. Rumour had it that half the young mums in Hope Christmas were hopelessly in love. Cat couldn't blame them – if she wasn't married herself . . . In fact judging by the way Diana Carew was fawning over him, it wasn't just the young women.

Calling the meeting to order, Cat said, 'As you know, we've had an incredibly generous offer from Michael Nicholas on behalf of Ralph, to let us use Hopesay Manor for our Christmas ball. Not only that, but I've managed to cadge some funding from the firm my husband used to work for, and they've offered to fund a champagne reception. The TV company I work for are pitching an idea for a documentary, which will involve filming the work of the Sunshine Trust and our efforts to help them, which I hope will raise the profile of our campaign.'

'How thrilling,' boomed Diana. 'I wonder who they'll want to film?'

'The people in the home, I imagine,' said Miss Woods, *sotto voce*.

'Today, I'd like to start sorting some jobs out for the ball,' said Cat. 'I need someone to organise the blind auction.'

'We can do that,' said Vera and Albert.

Diana jumped in to organise the auction itself – leaving Cat to smile wryly at the thought of the people being browbeaten to get donations. Cat sighed with relief. She hated asking people for things like that. It needed someone who had no shame and wouldn't take no for an answer. Much better for Diana to do it – and she was revelling in the idea of meeting some proper celebrities. Cat grinned ruefully. Clearly she was too well known in the village to count as a proper celebrity.

By the end of the meeting, Cat had sorted out table decorations, the auction, the blind auction, and had got someone to organise the catering.

'There'll be nothing for me to do,' she said as she put her file away.

'You're clearly well practised at the art of delegation.' Michael appeared by her side as if from nowhere. His warm, all-encompassing smile made her appreciate what the good ladies of Hope Christmas were feeling. He was seriously gorgeous.

'How's your mother?' Michael continued. 'I understand from Noel she's not very well.'

'She's fine – well, as fine as she's ever going to be,' said Cat.

'It must be a huge worry.'

'It is, like watching someone fade away in front of your eyes,' said Cat. 'It's always at the back of my mind. I still wish we could have looked after her at home, but we can't.'

'You can only do so much,' said Michael with ready sympathy. 'I'm sure your mum understands.'

'If she could only remember who I was,' said Cat. 'Sorry, bad joke . . . a black sense of humour helps I find.'

'I bet it does,' said Michael. 'It's a hard row you have to plough, right now, Cat. But it won't last forever.'

'Don't,' said Cat, her eyes shining, 'I don't even want to think about that.'

'Well make the most of the moment, then,' said Michael. 'Your mum isn't the same as she was, but she's still here.'

'That's a very good way of looking at it,' said Cat. 'Thanks.'

She smiled at him, as she packed her things together, and got ready to leave. Nothing had changed, but weirdly, she felt comforted. Michael was right. At least Mum was still here. That was something.

Pippa was struggling to get Lucy into bed. It had started with her having an unusual tantrum. Don't want to go to bed, she'd typed. Want to watch *Britain's Got Talent*. Pippa sighed. Thanks to endless reruns on ITV2, Lucy was able to watch her favourite shows as often as she liked, but it was late and she had school the next day.

'Tomorrow,' she said. 'Come on, it's way past your bed time.'

Won't go, Lucy typed, and folded her arms, going so rigid in her wheelchair that Pippa wasn't able to move her at all.

It was so unlike Lucy. Normally an amenable child, she had been fidgety and restless since Dan had been ill. And she was getting so big. What was once a relatively easy – physically, at least – job was becoming increasingly more difficult. Just before Dan's accident, he'd been helping her more and more, but the recent weeks had left Pippa feeling very alone. Plus the effort of helping Dan in and out of bed as well was taking its toll. She'd ricked her back and consequently felt like an old cripple most days. Nathan, who'd clearly heard her swearing, came in and said, 'Can I help, Mum?'

She hated to ask him. Nathan was still only twelve years old, and more and more of late was adopting the role of man of the house. With his dark hair and blue eyes, he looked increasingly like his dad too.

'Thanks, sweetheart,' she said. 'Can you help me persuade Lucy she needs to go to bed?'

'Sure,' said Nathan. 'Lucy, you need to go to bed.'

Don't want to go, typed Lucy sulkily.

Nathan made a silly face at Lucy who giggled, and typed, Loser, on her pad.

'You're the loser,' said Nathan, tickling her feet which got her giggling. It relaxed Lucy enough for Pippa to be able to lift her out of the wheelchair, while Nathan carried her feet and continued to tickle them, much to Lucy's delight.

They were both laughing so much, Nathan nearly dropped her feet, which made Lucy laugh some more. But it worked. In no time at all, Lucy who'd been getting as fractious as Pippa, was comfortably tucked up in bed.

'Thanks Nathan, you're a great help,' Pippa said, giving

him a hug. He squirmed away, but looked pleased, before disappearing into the lounge to watch TV.

Pippa went into the utility room off the kitchen to sort out laundry. She was dog tired and felt like an automaton. She just longed to climb into bed and go to sleep for a week. But there was always so much to do, and Dan needed help getting into bed too.

Suddenly there was shouting from the lounge and Nathan was running up the stairs in floods of tears, saying, 'I hate him, I hate him,' before slamming the door to his bedroom.

'What on earth's going on?' said Pippa, following him up to his bedroom. She sat down on the bed and gave him a hug.

'It's Dad,' said Nathan. 'He wouldn't let me watch anything I wanted to on TV, and then shouted at me.'

'Oh sweetheart, you know he doesn't mean it,' said Pippa, hugging him close. 'You remember, I explained Daddy's going to take time to get better. It's his injury that makes him behave like that.'

'But what if he doesn't get better?' said Nathan. 'I looked up some stuff about brain injuries on the internet and sometimes people change permanently.'

Bloody internet.

Pippa took a deep breath. 'I don't know,' she said, 'I honestly don't. But we have to hope and believe that he will. In the meantime, try not to get too upset, Dad doesn't mean to be angry with you.'

Having consoled her son, Pippa went downstairs to tackle her husband. She found him sitting with his head in his hands, looking more desolate and lonely than she'd ever seen him.

'What kind of person am I?' he said. 'What am I turning into? My children are afraid of me. You hate me. I don't think I can go on like this any longer.'

'Oh, Dan,' Pippa fell to her knees and flung her arms around his neck. 'That's not true. Of course it isn't. You're not well, but you'll get better. I promise you. We can get through this.'

'Do you really believe that?'

'Of course I do,' said Pippa. 'For better, for worse, remember. You don't get rid of me that easily.'

Dan's answer was to squeeze her hand tightly and hold her in a long embrace. But as she pulled away she noticed a sadness in his eyes. She wasn't sure she'd convinced either him, or herself.

Mel

FACEBOOK status Beef!!!
Kaz: What, what?
Ellie: Good or bad beef
Mel: good xxxooxxx
Ellie: boy?
Mel: Maybe
Kyra16: Spill the goss
Jen17: Hope he's reem
Mel: He sure is
Kaz: NOooooo
Mel: Yessss!!
Kaz: But we said . . .
Mel: No you said . . .
Ellie: ???
Mel: Kaz thinks I'm being stupid.
Kaz: You are.
Jen17: what, why?
Mel: Nothing.
Kaz: BBM PRIVATE CHAT NOW
Ellie: so the beef is?
Mel: tell you later.
Andy: status. SO NOT SINGLE.

I saw the Boy today. Not just from a distance. Actually saw him. He came into the caff when I was working & we talked. Best Mate isn't speaking to me cos I said she should butt out. It's not her business.

He apologised about before. The girl I saw him with is an ex, and really clingy. And he's been busy working. Asked me to give him a second chance. Best Mate laughed when I told her. But she doesn't understand. She's never been in love.

Because I am. In love, I mean. And the Boy told me he loves me too. He bought me a bracelet to say sorry. It's so pretty. We're meeting tonight. I told The Parents I'm at Best Mate's house. I can't face the questions. Mum's been looking at me funny since last time we saw Mad Gran and she started going on about me seeing a boy. Seems Mad Gran does remember some of the things I say. I told Mum that was in the past. The Boy's my secret, and I don't feel like sharing him just yet.

So. That's it. Last night. We finally did it. It wasn't as special or as brilliant as I thought it might be. The Boy said it isn't usually. He was kind though, and I felt so close to him afterwards. I wish we'd been somewhere romantic, not in the back of his pick-up truck. But he said he can't take me home, and he couldn't come to mine. But still, afterwards, it felt special, when he held me close and told me I was the most beautiful girl he'd ever met.

Best Mate is still cross with me. She said I should have gone to the clinic. But I was too embarrassed, and didn't like to ask The Boy about condoms. I mean, how do you have that conversation? Awkward.

Still, we've only done it once. That can't hurt, right?

May

Chapter Thirteen

'Can I have some money?' Mel sauntered casually into the kitchen, where Cat was preparing a salad for the impromptu barbecue that she and Noel had decided to hold, given that it was a sunny afternoon. She was busy experimenting with marinades for the idea she was planning to pitch for next year's *Cat's Country Summer*. The local butcher did a mean line in minty lamb sauce and she'd been after him for ages to share some of his secrets; but somehow when she tried to recreate it, even with her own home grown mint, it never tasted the same.

'What for?' said Cat. 'Didn't Dad give you your allowance? And what about the money you earn from the caff?'

'Spent it on school stuff,' said Mel. 'Which is why you need to pay me back.'

'Such flawless logic,' said Cat. 'What school stuff?'

'Oh, stuff for art,' said Mel vaguely. 'So can I?'

'What do you need it for? And haven't you got revision?' Mel's GCSEs were starting the following week, and while grudgingly Cat had noticed she'd done a lot more work than for her mocks, she was still fretting that Mel hadn't done enough.

'Cinema, and I've done all my revision for today,' said Mel, rolling her eyes.

'Are you sure?' said Cat.

'Sure,' said Mel. 'You know the teachers are always telling us we need to relax too. I will revise tomorrow I promise. Thanks Mum. I love you.'

With that, Mel grabbed the note that Cat had found in her purse and ran off.

'Who are you going with– ?' Cat said to a slammed door.

'How does she do that?' Cat said to Noel who was just getting sausages and burgers out of the freezer.

'Who? Do what?'

'Mel. She's just conned twenty quid out of me, and I have no idea where she's going or who with.'

'She's gone out with Andy,' piped up Paige.

'How do you know? Did Mel tell you?' Unlikely, Cat felt.

'Because Mel's mate Karen's sister Maisie is in my class, and apparently Karen is always moaning to Maisie how Mel never has time for her anymore since she's started going out with Andy.'

'But I thought Andy was history,' said Cat, which was the last version of events Mel had seen fit to furnish her with.

'Oh, that's old news,' said Paige airily. 'Andy changed his mind, and now they're an item.'

'Oh are they?' said Cat. 'I'd really really like to meet this Andy.'

'And breathe,' said Noel coming up behind her and giving her a tickly kiss on the back of her neck. 'She's a teenage girl. We need to give her some privacy.'

'I know,' sighed Cat, wishing she could be as relaxed about things as Noel was. 'I just wish we knew more about him.'

'Well, we don't,' said Noel. 'So let's cross that bridge when we come to it. You know what teenagers are like. He'll be old news in a couple of weeks.'

Cat smiled and returned to her minty lamb sauce, before

moving on to a couscous salad. While she did so Noel got going on the barbecue with help from James. It was funny watching them together. Noel automatically took charge of the barbecue, his only concession to cooking properly, while James subtly took over the hard work of frying sausages and burgers, occasionally saying things like, 'Dad, you know it isn't obligatory to have charcoal with your sausages,' until Noel threatened to ban him from the barbie. It was a sunny afternoon, and they had a pleasant family time in the garden, which was only hampered by Cat's nagging disquiet about Mel. By six p.m., there was no sign of her.

'She went out at one,' said Cat. 'This is getting ridiculous.'

'Phone?' said Noel.

'What do you think?' said Cat. 'She's switched it off.'

'Bugger.'

'I know.'

Noel, she could see, was beginning to get a bit edgy now, so she did a quick ring round those of Mel's friends she actually knew to find out if they'd seen her, but drew a blank. They cleared up the barbie and were in the process of sending Ruby to bed when Mel wandered in two hours later, looking cool and collected and very much as if the cat had got the cream.

'Well?' said Cat.

'Well what?' said Mel.

'Where have you been?' said Cat.

Mel shrugged. 'I told you, at the cinema.'

'For seven hours?' said Noel incredulously.

'So?'

'So, your phone's been switched off, we didn't know where you were, or who with,' said Cat. 'We've been worried sick.'

'Oh will you leave me alone! You never stop nagging,'

said Mel. 'I went out with friends, all right?' and with that she took herself up the stairs, slamming doors behind her.

'That went well,' said Noel.

'Don't,' said Cat. 'Just don't.'

'Marianne, can I talk to you?' Steven came into the play-room, where Marianne was trying to restore order to the chaos left by the twins, while they slept upstairs.

'Of course, sweetheart. What is it?'

'It's about going to Middleminster,' said Steven.

'And?' said Marianne.

'I know Dad doesn't want me to go there, but I really do.'

'I know,' said Marianne, conscious that the letter accepting the place Steven had been given was still sitting on the study table, waiting for Gabriel's signature. There was only a couple of days to go before the deadline. A decision had to be taken.

'It's not just that, it's . . .' his voice trailed off and he looked awkward and miserable.

'Matt Pilsdon?' guessed Marianne.

'He told me that I was gay because I sing,' said Steven. 'I really hate it at our school. Apart from George, I don't have any friends. I'd much rather go to Middleminster. And then . . .'

'. . . there's your mum,' said Marianne.

Steven squirmed.

'I mean, I know you've been more of a mum to me than she has,' he gabbled.

'But she's still your mum.'

'And I would like it if I saw more of her, but I don't want to upset you and Dad.'

'Sweetie, you won't upset me,' said Marianne, 'but your dad is really going to miss you. I'd like to think you might miss us.'

137

'I will,' said Steven, 'it's not that. But – I know Dad would love it if I did, but I don't actually want to be a farmer.'

'Not when you could win *X Factor*,' said Marianne with a grin.

'I'd rather be on *The Choir*,' said Steven. 'We have to say yes soon, or I might lose the place. And I really couldn't bear it if that happened.'

'Then if that's how you really feel, we'll just have to get your dad to understand,' said Marianne.

'Marianne, you're the best,' said Steven giving her a hug.

Marianne was touched. Now he was older, Steven rarely displayed gestures of affection. She loved the fact that he still felt able to do that, and vowed to find a way to get Gabriel to change his mind. He had to see that his son's needs came before their own. He had to.

So when she'd put the twins to bed that evening, and Steven had disappeared into his room, she sat down with Gabriel in the lounge and poured them both a glass of wine.

'You look done in,' she said, as Gabe leant back against the sofa with his eyes shut. Marianne leant back next to him, and cuddled up to him, stroking his hair.

'I am a bit,' he admitted, opening those lovely brown eyes which had swept her off her feet only four short years ago.

'Mmm, that feels nice,' he said sleepily, and Marianne kissed him on the top of his head. They sat for a few moments in contented silence then she said, 'Gabe, I'm not trying to interfere, I'm really not, but about Steven . . .'

Gabriel looked at her warily.

'I know it's difficult . . .'

'. . . but you think I should let him go to Middleminster?'

'Sorry, but yes,' said Marianne. 'Steven's desperate to go there, he hates the thought of going to Hope Sadler Comp, and he wants to see more of his mum. But he's also really afraid of upsetting you. It's tearing the poor kid apart. Can't you see that?'

Gabriel exhaled a deep breath.

'Bugger, bugger, bugger,' he said.

'What's that supposed to mean?'

'You're right of course,' sighed Gabriel. 'You and Mum. She said more or less the same thing to me. I've been so caught up in all this stuff with Dan and Pippa, and working so hard, I've been being selfish. I haven't given enough thought to how Steven feels. If that's what he wants I should let him do it.'

'So I can really go?' Steven, who'd clearly been eavesdropping, came bounding out of the shadows and threw himself into Gabriel's arms. 'Thanks Dad.'

'Oi, you,' said Gabriel, engaging his son in an arm wrestle, 'haven't you heard that no good comes to those who listen at doors?'

'Well that's not true,' said Steven, 'because I've just heard good news.'

'Cheeky,' said Gabe, and tickled him some more.

Marianne sat back with a feeling of satisfaction. It would be hard for both of them to let Steven go, but it was definitely the best thing to do.

Pippa's mum was sitting with Dan, so Pippa had got a rare couple of hours to herself. She had a thousand and one things she could be doing, but she needed some time to herself.

So she'd struck off down the lane past Gabe's house and taken a walk into the valley beyond. After a stormy start, spring was in full swing, and there was a constant sound of baaing lambs and cooing birds, reassuring her that the natural cycle of the year was still going on, even if her own life was in chaos. The sun was high in the sky, and white clouds scudded across it. A perfect day for clearing the cobwebs. She took a deep breath, and set off up the hill.

Her thoughts were churning as she ploughed on. Dan's mobility was improving daily, and he had dispensed with the wheelchair inside the house, which was one small step forward. But his temper had still not improved and the children were becoming very wary of him. Lucy had even flinched on occasion when Dan had raised his voice, something she'd never done before. Dan had seen it too, and Pippa could see how much it had upset him. But he wouldn't talk to her. That, for Pippa, was the worst thing. She and Dan had always shared everything. And now at the darkest point of her life, she felt shut out from his pain. Never had she felt more lost and lonely.

After twenty minutes of hard pounding, she got to the top of the hill, and looked back down at Hope Christmas. It looked so small from up here, all the problems of the individuals who lived there seeming so tiny and insignificant. Even hers, for a moment. The views were magnificent, and never failed to impress her, even though she'd been looking at them all her life. The thing she loved most about them was how they changed depending on the season. Now in early May, the hills were dotted with lambs among the deep green bushes, and lush green grass. She sat down in the heather for a rest and took it all in.

'If only I could stay up here and get away from it all forever,' she said out loud.

'They do say that when you're at the end of your rope you should tie another knot and hang on.' A stranger in black appeared as if by magic, and plonked himself beside her. Oh, not such a stranger. Belatedly Pippa realised she was staring into the compelling blue eyes of Michael Nicholas.

'I'm sorry?' Pippa was slightly taken aback. She didn't know Michael that well.

'The darkest hour is before the dawn,' said Michael. 'Things can only get better.'

'Have you any more clichés up your sleeve?' said Pippa. 'And how do you know what's going on in my life?'

'I don't,' said Michael. 'You just looked as though you had the cares of the world on your shoulders, and I wanted to help.'

'That's very kind of you,' said Pippa. 'I'm not sure anyone can help. I just have to pull myself together and get on with it.'

'And that's your special gift of course.'

'What is?' said Pippa slightly startled.

'Managing,' said Michael. 'I'm sure you will, but don't forget to look after yourself too.'

'That's what my mum's always telling me,' said Pippa.

'Your mum is right,' said Michael. He got up to go. 'Things will get better, you'll see.'

'I don't think anything's going to change in a hurry,' she said.

Nevertheless, as she set off over the hill, she was humming to herself. Maybe nobody else could help, but Michael was right. Things could hardly get any worse than they were, so the only way forward was for them to get better. It was a thought worth holding on to.

Chapter Fourteen

'How are the plans for the ball progressing?' Marianne had popped in to see Cat on the off chance that she had a free moment. She often felt lonely during the day, when it was just her and the kids at home, and Cat had declared herself more than happy to down tools and stop for a coffee when asked.

It was a lovely warm day for early May, so they sat in Cat's gorgeous country cottage garden. The flower beds were a jumble of forget-me-nots, michaelmas daisies, grape hyacinths and alyssum, while the pots on Cat's patio were tumbling over with lobelia, busy lizzies, and geraniums. At the far end of the garden, Cat had her vegetable plot, with newly erected bean poles and potatoes already sprouting. Cat had dug out a load of plastic toys from the shed at the bottom of the garden, and the twins were happily pottering about with them. Cat had found them a plastic watering can, and they seemed to be quite content pouring water into a bucket.

'Getting there I think,' she said. 'Thanks to Michael Nicholas we don't have to worry about a venue, and we've got some pledges for the auction, but Noel's old company who were sponsoring the champagne reception has pulled out – there isn't quite the money for these things as there used to be.'

'Do people really need a champagne reception?' said Marianne.

'Probably not,' said Cat, 'but the tickets aren't cheap. I hate not giving value for money.'

'What about your celebrity contacts?'

'I don't have that many,' laughed Cat, 'everyone thinks just because I'm on the telly sometimes I'm bosom buddies with all manner of people. But I've got Diana Carew working on a list I got from my producer. She's getting on quite well I understand. Honestly, that woman has no shame. I believe she may even have wangled a signed pair of Calvin Kleins from Beckham's manager.

'Other than that, everything else seems to be okay. I've managed to get some free crackers and other table decorations from the Hopesay Arms Hotel, left over from last year. The manager's granddaughter spends time at the Sunshine Trust and he was happy to help.

'What with that, and writing mince pie recipes and Wassail cups for my Christmas book, I've got Christmas on the brain,' continued Cat. 'I always find it really weird to be thinking about Christmas when the sun's out. Much as I love the festive season, it feels all wrong.'

'Tell me about it,' said Marianne. 'My mum has already asked me what we're planning to do for Christmas, which is a first, even for her.'

'Even my mother-in-law doesn't start asking till July,' grinned Cat. 'What did you tell her?'

'Oh nothing for now,' said Marianne, 'I couldn't face the row. All I really want to do is hide away with Gabe and the children, but I doubt that will be an option. Still it's a long way off; anything could happen.'

Cat sighed and looked pensive. She was still looking very pale and wan. She'd lost a lot of weight too.

'You okay?'

'Sort of,' she said. 'It's silly really. I can't stop thinking about the baby. It would have been about three months at Christmas.'

'That's not silly,' said Marianne, reaching over and squeezing her hand, 'it's only natural.'

'I suppose so,' said Cat, 'but I feel guilty too. I wasn't even sure I wanted this baby. Lord knows I wasn't ready for another one at my age, but . . .'

'Now it's gone?'

'. . . I can't help thinking about what might have been,' admitted Cat. 'It would have been lovely to have had a new baby at Christmas. Really magical. Especially as it would have been our last.'

'Are you sure?' joshed Marianne. 'Have you forgotten the lack of sleep?'

'Well, I never sleep much at Christmas anyway,' said Cat, 'I'm always so busy.'

'Couldn't you have tried again?' said Marianne.

'No,' said Cat. 'The baby wasn't planned, and we lost it. Noel and I have had long discussions about it. It wasn't meant to be. Some things just aren't. So I've had my tubes tied. It's for the best. Realistically, I don't think I could cope with teen hormones *and* the baby blues. That would be a pretty lethal combination. I think Mother Nature was trying to tell me something.'

'Maybe she was,' said Marianne. 'I'm sorry.'

'It's okay,' said Cat. 'I'll get over it. And it's not like I'm not busy enough with the other four. I'll be so glad when Mel's GCSEs are over.'

'How's it going with Mel?' asked Marianne who, looking at the twins getting happily wet, couldn't imagine either of them ever being old enough to exhibit any sign of teenage angst.

'She appears to be working for her exams, which is

something,' said Cat, 'but she's very secretive. I just can't get through to her.'

'What about the boyfriend?'

'God knows,' said Cat, 'she never discusses him. I don't even officially know he exists. I've no idea what she's getting up to. It's a real worry.'

'She'll get over it,' said Marianne. 'It's probably just a phase and she'll grow out of it.'

'I do hope so,' said Cat with feeling. 'It's been a very very long phase.'

'Let's go out for the day.' Pippa had decided it was time to be more proactive. She and Dan had spent far too much time indoors since his accident. Plus Dan had told her what Marianne had said to him about having small goals, so she tried to help him by making plans each day, even if it was only getting him to walk around the living room without his crutches. His mobility was getting so much better. The shock of what had happened was beginning to wear off, but she was worried that Dan might be sliding into depression. She felt it was important she tried to get him reconnected with the outside world.

Dan was grumpy about it.

'I can't even walk up the lane,' he said.

'Well, you haven't tried,' said Pippa. 'Come on, what was it you were saying after Marianne came the other week? You were going to aim at little victories?'

Dan had the grace to look a little shamefaced.

'Sorry, you're right,' he said.

'Good,' said Pippa. 'Because I was thinking a blow on the top of the hills and a pub lunch at the Springer Arms would do us both good. I'll drive. Go on. The kids are at school and once you're fit again, you'll have to work. When was the last time you took me out to lunch?'

That elicited a small smile.

'Better,' said Pippa. 'Let's get cracking.'

It took longer than she thought it would to get out of the door. Dan needed the loo, it was fiddly getting his coat and shoes on, and even with crutches, his walking was still painfully slow.

Getting in the car was also a struggle. Their Land Rover was high, and she didn't have the strength to push Dan up into it. Luckily Gabe turned up at an opportune moment, and with a lot of heaving, a 'Come on, you lazy sod, put your back into it' and an undignified push in the back, they managed.

Luckily that lightened the mood, as Dan saw the funny side.

'I hope you treat your pregnant ewes with more respect,' he said as Gabriel helped Pippa manoeuvre him into position properly.

'At least they don't moan so much,' quipped Gabe, and Pippa was relieved that Gabe's gentle teasing had helped put Dan into a better frame of mind.

And then they were away. Finally driving on the main road out of Hope Christmas, for the first time since the accident.

The sun was out, so Pippa wound down the windows, turned up the music and for a few moments, as they drove past sun-drenched fields of cows and sheep and wound their way to the top of the hills, she could almost forget anything was wrong.

'Penny for 'em?' Dan looked across at her, as she belted out the words of *It's Raining Men* as loud as she could.

'Thinking that this is just like old times,' she said, 'before the kids came along.'

'I need to find a patch of heather to have my wicked

146

way with you,' grinned Dan, as they reached the top of the hill.

Pippa was touched. Dan's memories had been sporadic since the accident. But he remembered that; a tender moment early in their courtship, when they'd played hooky from their respective farm duties and spent a happy Sunday on the hillside, using the heather as cover for their frolics. Afterwards they'd gone to the pub, and held hands, and she'd known then that he was worth hanging on to. It had been a blissful day, and the fact that Dan still remembered it too gave her hope.

'Shall I pull over?' quipped Pippa, but then Dan's face darkened.

'That was then; this is now.'

They sat in silence for the remainder of the journey, and when they got to the pub, Dan stiffly slid out of the Land Rover, eschewing her offers of help. He limped slowly and painfully on his crutches to the pub entrance, and Pippa followed him, full of heartache. How could she help him, when he blanked her out?

In silence they chose a table outside, where the sun shone down and they could watch the birds wheeling high in the sky, and look over towards the Welsh hills in the distance. It should have been idyllic.

'It will be better, Dan,' said Pippa, leaning over and taking his hand, 'I do believe that. Look how much progress you've made already.'

Dan flinched at the contact, and she turned away, hurt, but then he said, 'I'm sorry, I'm so sorry.' She looked up to see tears in his eyes.

'Don't be,' said Pippa, 'it's not your fault. It's just sodding, awful, bad luck.'

'But look at me,' said Dan, 'I'm a bloody wreck. I'm useless to you and the kids.'

'This won't last forever,' said Pippa, holding his hands firmly in hers. She hated seeing him like this. It made her want to hold him tight and protect him forever. 'Come on, the physio's pleased with your progress, and so should you be. You listen to me, Dan Holliday, you just stop feeling sorry for yourself. We will get through this, just like we do everything. Together, do you hear? Little victories, remember?'

'Oh Pippa,' said Dan, leaning over to stroke her cheek, 'what did I do to deserve you?'

Pippa blinked away her tears, and grinned as hard as she could. Dan needed her to be strong, not pathetically weak.

'I don't know,' said Pippa, 'but as long as you don't forget it.'

'I won't,' said Dan, looking at her with such gratitude in his eyes she wanted to hug him again. 'I promise you I won't.'

The sun climbed higher in an azure blue sky, there was the constant sound of bleating sheep, and she could make out the distant hum of the traffic. Life didn't get any better than this at the moment, and for once, Pippa felt herself hope for a better future.

Marianne had put the twins to bed and was pottering around in the kitchen, feeling slightly anxious. It was getting late, and Gabe wasn't yet in. True, in the summer the nature of his work precluded early homecomings, but he was breaking his back all hours to help Dan and Pippa out. He wasn't alone of course. Pippa's dad Jim, Gabe's dad and uncle were all on hand, but Gabe was the one on-site all the time. And he was younger and knew the ropes. Plus he was incredibly conscientious, so would always go the extra mile.

Marianne had known all this when she married him of

course, and she knew why he was helping out now. But whereas before she'd have been out there with him, since the twins' arrival she couldn't. Steven regarded her with affection, of course he did, but he was an eleven-year-old boy. If he wasn't out on the fields with Gabe, he was upstairs on his Xbox, and was hardly great company. Marianne couldn't help it, she felt lonely. All she wanted of an evening, once the children were in bed, was the opportunity to snuggle up to Gabe with a glass of wine. Was that so much to ask?

She felt slightly guilty for feeling it, but she was starting to feel resentful. It was no one's fault, and she knew in similar circumstances Pippa and Dan would help her out too, but she couldn't help it. The bottom line was, without Dan's accident, Marianne would be seeing more of Gabe. She wanted her husband, and that's what she wasn't getting at the moment.

Marianne sat down to a solitary dinner in front of the TV. Steven came down at nine to say good night, and the twins woke once for milk, before settling back down again. Marianne was just thinking about going to bed, when Gabriel walked in. Trying to muster a sympathetic, *you must have had a rotten day* kind of smile, she said, 'Oh poor you. You must be starving. There's a curry in the oven.'

'Oh,' Gabriel looked conscience stricken.

'Oh what?'

'I've already eaten.'

'How come?'

'I went back to Dan and Pippa's to give them a progress report, and Pippa gave me supper. Didn't I tell you?'

'No, Gabe, you did not,' said Marianne between gritted teeth.

'I'm so sorry,' said Gabriel. 'I stopped to have a beer, and Pippa had cooked lasagne . . .'

149

'And it didn't occur to you to pick up the phone to let me know?' snapped Marianne. She hadn't meant to snap, but she was tired and fed up of being alone.

'I forgot,' said Gabriel looking sheepish.

'Well thanks for nothing, Gabriel,' said Marianne. She'd heard the apology, but she couldn't quite bring herself to accept it.

'Look, I'm sorry,' said Gabriel. 'It's been a long day. I'm knackered. I don't need this right now.'

'Neither do I,' said Marianne, staring at him in dismay. 'I just need you. Is that too much to ask?'

'So do Pippa and Dan,' said Gabriel. 'I thought that you, of all people would understand that. I'm done in. I'm going to bed.'

'Gabe–' began Marianne, but he'd stormed off up to bed, leaving her alone over a glass of wine, wondering what the hell had just happened.

Chapter Fifteen

Pippa pushed her way into the village store, feeling happier than she had for a long time. She'd been baking for England over the last few days, and for the first time in ages had time to bring cakes to the café. It felt good to be doing something normal for a change. Dan seemed to have cheered up since their lunch date, and day by day they could both see the progress he was making. He was beginning to take a more constructive interest in the farm and the previous evening had insisted on Gabe getting more help.

'You can't expect to carry on the way you have been,' he said. 'You've been fantastic, but you need a break too.'

'Chance would be a fine thing,' snorted Gabe. 'There's so much to do.'

'Dan's right,' Pippa had said. 'Go on, you and Marianne can't have been out for months. Take a day off, and we'll get cover, so you two can spend some time together.'

Gabe had looked pleased at the prospect, and Pippa had been glad she'd suggested it. They'd had so much support from him and Marianne over the last couple of months and she didn't want to take them for granted.

'Oh, lovely,' Vera said as she walked in. 'A new supply of cakes. We've been missing yours. The lady we brought in to cover isn't a patch on you.'

'Thanks,' said Pippa. 'I've really enjoyed having the time

to do them. The last few months have been manic to say the least.'

'How are things?' Vera asked sympathetically.

'Getting better,' said Pippa. 'Progress is slow, which is frustrating for Dan, but we're getting there.'

The door opened, and Marianne came in pushing the twins in their double buggy. She looked exhausted.

'Bad night?' said Pippa sympathetically.

'Let's just say I didn't get a lot of sleep,' Marianne's response was uncharacteristically terse.

'Oh you poor thing,' said Pippa. 'Are they teething?'

'Just a bit,' said Marianne. She looked pale and tired and a little bit sad.

'Marianne, is everything okay?' said Pippa. It was definitely not like Marianne to be this abrupt.

'Yes, fine. Why wouldn't it be?' retorted Marianne. 'Sorry, I can't stand here chatting. I've just come in for nappies, and then I've got to go home and play the farmer's wife. You know what it's like. Always so much to do.'

'Marianne—' began Pippa, but stopped. Oh lord, perhaps this was her and Dan's fault, Gabriel had been round their house a lot of late. 'Is there anything I can do?'

'Not really,' said Marianne. 'Make sure my husband gets home on time, once in a while.' She sighed.

'Marianne, I'm so sorry about last night,' said Pippa slightly flustered, it suddenly dawning on her why Marianne was cross. 'Gabriel said he'd told you he'd be late.'

'Well, he didn't,' said Marianne abruptly but then she softened. 'Look, I know you've got a lot on your plate, but Gabriel's worn out helping you out. And I hardly see anything of him at the moment. Forgive me, I'm being grumpy about it.'

'Oh Marianne, I'm really sorry,' said Pippa. 'You're the last person I want to upset.'

'It's okay,' said Marianne with a tired grin. 'I'm just tired and fed up. I'll get over it.'

'Well, at least let me buy you a coffee and muffin to make up,' said Pippa.

'Now *that* is a great idea,' said Marianne, 'housework can wait.'

Cat was sitting at home going through the final proofs of her Christmas book, wincing at little errors which it was now too late to put right, when the phone rang. It was Susan Challoner, the matron from her mum's nursing home.

'I'm terribly sorry to trouble you,' she said, 'but your mother has had a little fall. I don't want to worry you but she's on her way to A&E.'

Cat's heart plummeted.

'How? Why? What happened?' she said.

'We're not sure,' Susan admitted. 'One of the staff found her on the floor. It's possible she had a TIA.'

'Sorry, what does that mean?' Cat felt she should know, but somehow she didn't.

'It may be that she's had a slight stroke,' Susan said. 'It's very common in her age group.'

Cat went into a tailspin. Things had been stable with Mum for such a long time, she'd almost started to kid herself that the situation wouldn't deteriorate further. But now it had. She checked her watch. Only midday. She rang Noel, who wasn't picking up his voicemail, to ask if he could get Ruby from school. The others made their way home on the bus. She'd text them later when she knew more. There was no point worrying them unnecessarily, particularly Paige, who had a tendency for melodrama.

Twenty minutes later, Cat found herself in the smart new A&E at her local hospital. She queued patiently at reception, while the ward clerks booked in patients with broken toes, arms, and mysterious gut pains. It seemed to take forever before she was seen to.

'Hello, may I help?' The receptionist barely looked at her.

'It's my mother,' said Cat, her voice coming out in a high-pitched squeak, 'I think she's been admitted.'

'And her name?'

'Louise Carpenter,' said Cat.

'Ah, yes,' said the woman, 'just go through that door on the left, and they'll tell you where she is.'

Cat wandered through into the main area of A&E. Contrary to expectations fuelled by years of watching *ER* and *Casualty*, the staff all seemed unhurried and calm, and if anything, almost bored. She thought about the last time she'd been here, admitted as a patient, terrified and in pain. She shuddered at the memory. But this wasn't about her. She needed to find out how Mum was.

Cat approached the desk, as always in these places, feeling intimidated and out of her depth. Something about medical officialdom did that to her, which was quite ridiculous when you thought about it. They were only people after all. Eventually a nurse looked up from behind a big shiny new desk and pointed her in the direction of bed seven. The curtains were drawn around the bed, and Cat gingerly popped her head in.

Louise was sitting up in bed with a big bruise on her forehead, looking pale and bewildered, while a doctor with an east European accent was shouting, as if to a simpleton, 'Mrs Carpenter, can you tell me what happened?'

'I doubt that very much,' said Cat, 'didn't anyone tell you she has Alzheimer's? She probably doesn't understand what you are saying.'

'Ah, no,' said the doctor, looking somewhat relieved, 'and you are?'

'Her daughter,' said Cat, going over to Louise and holding her hand. 'It's okay, Mum, it's me, Cat.'

'Cat?' Louise looked bewildered. 'Where am I? What happened?'

'It's okay, Mum, you've had a little fall,' said Cat. She tied up the hospital gown that someone had carelessly thrown over her mother's shoulders, to give Louise some more dignity, and went through Mum's medical history with the doctor before they were left alone, for what seemed like forever.

Eventually a young nurse came over to check Louise's blood pressure and temperature. She thoughtfully organised a bed pan for Louise, which impressed Cat, as her previous requests for one had fallen on deaf ears. The nurse was kind and efficient and seemed instinctively to understand how to handle Louise. Cat could have hugged her.

'My granny had Alzheimer's,' she said by way of explanation. 'It's a rotten disease isn't it?'

'Yup,' said Cat, 'it certainly is.'

For the next two hours, Cat sat holding Louise's hand as she rambled in and out of consciousness, and intermittently remembered she was in pain. Staff meandered about the place, patients were admitted, sat around and were either discharged or moved on to a ward, but to Cat it felt for all the world like they'd been forgotten. She only popped out briefly to update Noel and speak to the children, who luckily hadn't picked up on the potential seriousness of the situation. Mel, for once in a helpful mood, had offered to make tea.

As the afternoon wore on the place was filling up, and the evening shift took over. Eventually Cat went over to the desk and said, 'Excuse me, do you know what's happening with Louise Carpenter? Only the doctor said he was going to come back with some results?'

'Louise Carpenter?' The nurse looked blank, and then at her notes. 'Oh, she's still here?' Then accusingly at Cat, 'We're going to need that bed soon.'

Great, as if she wanted her mum to be stuck on a trolley in casualty.

'I'll get the doctor to look at her straight away.'

'Straight away' proved to be another half an hour. A different doctor arrived, who also seemed incapable of communicating any information clearly, and who proclaimed that though Louise probably hadn't done much damage, it would be advisable to keep her overnight to assess her condition.

Another hour elapsed before a bed was available, during which time Cat again updated Noel. 'I think I'm going to be stuck here forever,' she said, but eventually a jolly porter appeared out of nowhere. 'Come on darlin',' he said to Louise, 'let's get you upstairs and comfortable.' His cheery manner put Louise at her ease, and she was even laughing as he pushed her up to the ward, with Cat following behind, clutching a plastic bag full of Louise's paltry belongings.

When she got up there, Cat felt overwhelmed with confusion as there was a general air of chaos and Louise was left waiting for ages to be put to bed properly. It was difficult to know who to ask for help, because every time she flagged down a passing nurse, she was told, 'Sorry, not my patient.' Quite which nurses *were* allocated to Louise was a mystery. By the time Noel came to join her, having fed the children and left Mel babysitting, Cat felt at the end of her tether. Mum was so frail and weak, and needed kindness and compassion, which seemed demonstrably lacking. When a nurse eventually arrived, she barely spoke to Louise, and made no concession to her illness, getting her into bed with a rough efficiency. At least she was settled, so Cat felt she and Noel could leave. As they walked back to the car, Cat's heart felt heavy. 'I don't know, Noel,' she said. 'We don't have any choice, but I'd rather leave her anywhere but here.'

Noel squeezed her hand, and said, 'It's all right, Cat. It's only a night. She'll be fine.'

But as Cat turned back to look up at the brightly lit ward where her mother lay – she hoped not *too* frightened and confused – she wasn't at all sure that Noel was right.

'Do you think you'll be able to run the village nativity this year? Only I can see you've got a lot on your plate, and I have so many ideas.' Marianne's heart sank as Diana Carew's huge breasts hove into view.

'Er, it's a bit early to think of it yet don't you think?' said Marianne. 'And I'm helping out with the charity ball already, so . . .'

'It's never too early to start planning,' boomed Diana, 'fail to plan and plan to fail. It was raised at the last Parish Council meeting.' Diana was on nearly every committee in town. She'd probably raised the matter herself.

'Well to be honest, I haven't given it much thought yet,' said Marianne, thinking no one in Hope Christmas would ever forgive her if she gave the planning of the nativity back over to Diana. 'But Mrs Garratt has been suggesting Ali Strickland takes over.'

Marianne had loved organising the nativity since she'd been in Hope Christmas, but the last two years juggling it with the twins had been challenging, to say the least. By this Christmas the twins would be into all sorts of mischief. And quite frankly Marianne didn't have the energy. Yet the thought of Ali Strickland doing it instead of her filled her with dread. She'd suggest that Diana took it over again, but had a feeling no one in the village would forgive her if she did. Diana's tediously long nativities had been the bane of Hope Christmas till Marianne had arrived. She was likely to lose all the friends she'd made since she got here, if she handed the reins back to Diana.

'Well don't leave it too late,' boomed Diana. 'We've got to make sure things get done, otherwise where would we be?'

'Where indeed?' said Marianne with a grin.

She pushed the twins up the High Street, revelling in the warm spring sunshine. On days like this, she'd never choose to live anywhere else. The birds in the hedgerows, the sun in the sky, the sheep baaing on the hillsides, the sound of the babbling brook. She loved the town, with its pretty little shops, the antique market, the butcher's where Gabriel sold his sheep, the friendly baker's which sold the best bread in the world. Above all she loved the bookshop with its knowledgeable staff and huge display of interesting books – so much more personable and friendly than the chain store bookshop at home in London. Hope Christmas felt like and was her natural home. She'd felt it the moment she came here four years ago. So why was she now feeling so discontented? It was something to do with a feeling of having lost her way a bit. She didn't quite know whether she was supposed to be a mum, a teacher or a farmer's wife. And at the moment the farmer's wife bit was the least enjoyable of her occupations. It would help if she occasionally saw her farmer.

She heard the roar of a motorbike and heard someone say, 'You shouldn't be so hard on him you know.' There, resplendent in leather, sat Michael Nicholas. Her heart gave a sudden little flip – she couldn't help but be reminded of Michael's cousin, Luke, who was the reason she'd come to Hope Christmas in the first place. Stop it, she said to herself, you're a married woman.

'Sorry?'

'Gabe,' said Michael. 'He's got a lot to deal with.'

'I know,' said Marianne, thinking, Well this is a bizarre conversation, how can he possibly know all this? 'I just feel like he's forgotten me.'

'Then you need to remind him you're here,' said Michael.

'And how do I do that?' said Marianne, feeling faintly absurd.

'That, my dear, is up to you,' said Michael, the twinkle of his deep blue eyes reminding her of his uncle, Ralph. Then, putting his helmet on, and revving the motor on the engine, he roared off into the distance, leaving Marianne slightly open mouthed.

Mel

FACEBOOK status Fuck, fuck fuck.
Kaz: wassup?
Jen17: You ok babes?
Ellie: What?
Kaz: Mel???
Kyra16: Tell me!!!
Kaz: Mel?
Mel: Kaz?
Kaz: You can't just leave it like that. BBM ME NOW
Jen17: Everything ok?
Mel: Fine. Panicking for no reason.
Jen17: You sure?
Mel: Yeah. All good.

Teenage Kicks

Oh my god. Oh my god. I'm late. I'm never late. I can't be pregnant. We've only done it twice. And I haven't seen him this week because of my exams.

Best Mate says I should get a test. But oh God. How do I do that? I can't buy it here. Someone will see me.

While The Parents went to the hospital to see Mad Gran, Best Mate and I went out to Boots. I felt so stupid. I'm only a day late. Maybe I'm overreacting.

I was too worried to bring the test home with me. So we went into a café and sat till they started looking at us like we should get out. In the end Best Mate had to practically shove me into the loo. Then I did the peeing on the stick thing. Gross.

   But, guess what? I'm not pregnant. False alarm. There was just one blue line. I'm so relieved. We must be more careful in future. I'll make The Boy wear a condom next time.

June

Chapter Sixteen

Marianne had bathed the twins early, so they were ready for bed, clean and cosy in their babygros, smelling of lemons and baby, a smell she loved with a passion. Steven had gone to a friend's for a sleepover, because it was half term, and Marianne had decided it was time to take matters into her own hands and give Gabe a lovely relaxing evening.

It was a gorgeous summer evening, so Marianne laced some fairy lights around the patio outside the conservatory door. The geraniums, petunias and fuchsias in the pots she'd recently planted, brightened the whole place up, and the scent of wisteria was heavy in the air. In the hedgerow a mother bird was calling to her babies. No doubt they'd soon be trying to fly.

Marianne laid out their little wrought iron table, with a vase of flowers gathered from the garden and a candle smelling of sandalwood, which she'd purchased from the village shop. There was a lady who lived up the road in Hope Sadler who sold both homemade candles and soaps, and Marianne was always buying her produce.

She opened a bottle of wine and went back to the oven, where she'd prepared garlic mushrooms as a starter and salmon steaks following one of Cat's recipes. Marianne hadn't been much of a cook till she got married and was daily grateful for Cat's no-nonsense cookery books, which had helped her out of many a hole. The food smelt delicious.

'What's all this in aid of?' Gabe came in from the outhouse where he sluiced down after a day on the fields.

'Just thought I'd make the most of Steven being away for the night and the twins being in bed,' said Marianne. 'We haven't had much time to ourselves recently, what with one thing and another.'

'True,' said Gabe. 'Sorry, it's my fault. I've been so worried about Pippa and Dan.'

'I know,' said Marianne, 'and I do understand that. But . . .'

'You feel a bit neglected?'

'Sounds pathetic when you say it like that,' admitted Marianne.

'Not at all,' Gabe kissed her lightly on the lips. 'I shouldn't take you for granted. You're my second chance and I know how very very lucky I am.'

He held her tight for a few minutes.

'Ugh, you still smell of cow,' said Marianne, 'go and have a shower.'

'Yes, ma'am,' said Gabe. 'You wouldn't care to join me?'

'Maybe when you're properly clean,' said Marianne, laughing.

Half an hour later, they were sitting in the garden sharing a glass of wine and watching the bats flit through the sky.

'That was delicious,' said Gabe, taking her hand. '*Now* can I persuade you to take that shower?'

'I thought you'd never ask,' said Marianne flirtatiously. This was great. Just like old times. *Nothing* could ruin the evening now.

Just then the phone rang.

'Great timing,' muttered Marianne, before picking up to find her mother on the other end of the line.

'Hi, Mum,' said Marianne rather ungraciously, wishing her mother had chosen any other moment to call. 'What can I do for you?'

'Sorry,' she mouthed at Gabriel.

'Well, it's about Christmas,' began Mum. Not again.

'Mum, it's June,' said Marianne. 'I refuse to have this conversation in June.'

'Well, we're thinking of going away in January, so we wanted to know that you were coming before we booked.'

Oh that was good. Even by Mum's devious standards.

'Who said anything about us coming to you?' said Marianne, feeling direct action was called for.

'We assumed – well it's so cold in Shropshire at Christmas,' said Mum. 'Much better for the twins to be somewhere warm.'

'We do have heating up here, you know,' said Marianne. 'Anyway. Like I said, we haven't even thought about Christmas yet.'

'Well, if you could think about it and just let me know?'

'Of course,' promised Marianne, and put the phone down, resisting the urge to slam it.

'Christmas – in June?' said Gabriel. 'Bloody hell.'

'My thoughts exactly,' said Marianne. 'Damn. I really really don't want to go to London again. Not after last year.'

'Invite them up here,' said Gabriel.

'I doubt they'll come,' said Marianne. Her mother had a well-known aversion to the countryside.

'Okay then,' said Gabriel, 'let's tell everyone we're staying put and anyone who wants to come is welcome.'

'Do you want me to live beyond my next birthday?' said Marianne with a grin. 'Now where were we . . .'

At that moment, a wail came from one of the twins.

'Ignore it,' said Gabriel.

Marianne tried. For about two minutes. Then the other twin started off too.

'No rest for the wicked,' she said, with a sigh.

'I'll do it if you like,' said Gabe.

'No. You've had a busy day,' said Marianne, kissing him on the top of the head. She didn't feel resentful when he offered to help. 'Don't go away, though, because I promise I will be back.'

'Do you think there's something wrong with Mel?' Noel asked Cat, as they drove over to the hospital to see Louise. A night in a hospital bed had turned into a week, during which time Louise had picked up a chest infection. She was barely eating, was more confused than ever, and seemed to Cat to be diminishing before her eyes. How could someone go into hospital and end up being more ill than when they were admitted? It didn't seem right. So far, despite trying to talk to the staff, who all seemed either busy or indifferent, Cat had come no nearer to finding out the cause of her mother's illness – the tests were 'inconclusive' – and she had yet to actually track down a consultant who might have an idea of what was actually wrong with her.

'What, more than usual?' said Cat. 'Maybe she's actually stressing about her exams.'

'I think it's a bit more than that,' said Noel. 'I don't know. She just seems really down. And she looks pale.'

Cat felt guilty. Since Noel had spent more time working at home, he seemed to be more on the ball with the kids than she did. And she'd been so busy and worried about Mum, she hadn't picked that up at all.

'It might just be she's spending too many late nights chatting on BBM,' said Cat. 'We really should make a point of taking her phone off her before bed.'

165

'It might be,' said Noel, looking unconvinced. 'I think she seems really unhappy.'

'Oh God,' said Cat. 'I feel terrible now. I should have noticed.'

'Don't,' said Noel. 'You've had so much on your plate. And I may be wrong. After all, don't I have the emotional intelligence of a gnat?'

Cat laughed. It's what she'd said to Noel once in the middle of a fierce argument. And it wasn't true.

'I'll try and have a chat to her when we get home,' she said. 'But you know what she's like, she never tells me anything important.'

Cat knew she should be trying to take Mel in hand. Her attitude to everything over the past few months had been appalling, but right now Cat simply didn't have the energy. Louise being ill had taken over everything. She was conscious that she wasn't being a good enough mum, but she couldn't worry about that now.

Cat felt bad for thinking it, but she'd rather do anything else than chat with her daughter. Conversations with Mel usually ended up one way, with Mel getting cross, walking out of the room and slamming doors. Lots of doors.

They got onto the ward, and went into the side room, where Louise was. To Cat's surprise and shock, the bed was empty and stripped down. Louise had gone.

'What– ?' said Cat, a cold clutch of fear grabbing her heart. Surely if something had happened, the hospital would have *said*. Wouldn't they? Or maybe not.

'Erm – excuse me,' Cat said to the uninterested looking staff at the desk, 'my mother, Louise Carpenter – where is she?'

'Louise? Louise . . . Oh yes. She was discharged at lunchtime,' said the nurse. 'Didn't anyone tell you?'

'No, they didn't,' said Cat through gritted teeth. 'Can you

please explain to me a) how that happened, and b) she was suddenly well enough to go home, when yesterday, she could barely stand?'

'She responded well to the antibiotics overnight,' said the nurse, 'so the consultant didn't see any point in keeping her. I'm sorry you weren't informed. We dealt directly with the nursing home.'

'Didn't want to bother, more like,' muttered Cat. 'Thanks for your help.'

She and Noel headed back to the car and on to the home, where they found Louise in her own room, at least wearing her own nightie. She was still coughing and looked pale, but there was a slight improvement from the previous day.

'I just can't believe they sent her back,' said Cat to Susan Challoner.

'Sadly, I can,' she said. 'Sometimes the state people are sent back to us in is quite dreadful. Don't you worry, we'll look after her.'

'Thanks,' said Cat.

Having established there was no more they could do for Louise, and encountering Alfie in the corridor with a bunch of flowers heading her way, Cat and Noel headed home, where they found World War III raging, as Paige had accidentally 'borrowed' Mel's straighteners, and Mel was letting her have it in no uncertain terms. Meanwhile Ruby was wailing because she'd caught her finger in the mousetrap, and James was teasing her that there was a rat living under the stairs. It took a while to quieten Ruby's wails, and get James to apologise to her, and Paige to Mel, but eventually things calmed down. Mel meanwhile had disappeared grumpily into her bedroom, so Cat gave it ten minutes before deciding to risk a chat. It was unlike Mel to be so mean to Paige. She usually reserved her fury for Cat and Noel.

Cat gingerly knocked on the door.

'May I come in?'

'I suppose.'

Mel was lying sulkily on her bed, flicking half-heartedly through a history text book.

'How's the revision going?'

Mel shrugged. She did look pale. There were dark circles under her eyes and she looked thin and washed out.

'Are you okay, sweetie?' said Cat. 'Only you seem really unhappy at the moment.'

Mel shrugged, again, but she still looked miserable.

'Is it Granny? She was much better today, you know, and she's back at home.'

'She's never going to be properly better though, is she?' Mel looked bleak.

'True,' said Cat, 'but at least she's not in that hospital anymore. I know it's tough, with Granny, and I'm sorry I haven't been around much.'

'No it's okay,' said Mel, 'I understand. I'm fine. Just busy.'

'And you're sure there's nothing wrong?'

'Nothing,' said Mel.

'You could tell me you know, if there were,' said Cat.

'There isn't, Mum, honestly.' Mel picked up her history book and started looking at it. Cat hovered for a minute, before Mel looked up at her. 'History GCSE, first thing Monday morning? I need to revise.'

Shut out. Again.

'Oh, right,' said Cat, nonplussed. 'Far be it from me to come between you and your exams.'

'Well if you want me to fail . . .' said Mel grouchily.

'It was a joke,' said Cat, retreating with a familiar sense of failure. One day she'd get this parenting thing right. One day . . .

* * *

Pippa was humming cheerfully in the kitchen, baking bread while listening to the radio. She danced around the kitchen, making Lucy, who was jigging along in her wheelchair, giggle happily. You look silly, Lucy typed.

'So do you,' said Pippa and stuck her tongue out, making Lucy laugh.

The sun was shining and Dan had actually gone out to work on the fields with Gabe. He was off his crutches, and still limping a bit, but the improvement was vast. The boys were at cricket, Noel, who helped out with the boys' squad, having kindly volunteered to take them. For once Pippa felt a real sense of contentment.

The letter box flapped open, and she heard the mail dropping through. She wandered out to get it. There were several letters, mainly bills. Great. Thank God for Dan's sickness insurance, which had helped them through the last few months. If she'd had to worry about money on top of everything else, Pippa thought she might go off her head. The last letter was from the council: Social Services. Pippa looked at it with dread. Everything had gone quiet on the Sunshine Trust front, and she'd been hoping that nothing more would come of Lucy's losing her respite care package. Burying her head in the sand of course. All the talk on the news for weeks had been about cuts to social services. She'd been grasping at short straws. She opened the letter and read:

Dear Mrs Holliday,
We regret to inform you that owing to budgetary restrictions for the coming financial year, it will no longer be possible to fund your daughter's respite care package. This is not a decision we have taken lightly, but . . .

'. . . there are more deserving cases, blah, blah, bloody blah.'

Pippa crumpled up the letter and threw it in the bin, her good mood evaporating in an instant. In the past she would have gone to Dan and they'd have raged together and worked out a game plan. But Dan, though much better, needed her support and couldn't be relied on to give her his. It made Pippa feel lonely to think how much she'd lost since Dan's accident. His ready empathy and calmness had gone – she hoped not forever – but it meant she could no longer rely on him, not the way she once had.

'Come on Pippa,' she muttered, 'time to man up.'

She looked at Lucy who was still clucking and dancing along to the music. Her beautiful daughter deserved all the help and care she needed. And Pippa was going to do her damnedest to make sure she got it.

Chapter Seventeen

'So what are we going to do?' said Cat, at the start of the hastily convened meeting at Pippa's house.

'But what can we really do?' said Mary Chambers, a small pale pinched woman, who looked as though the weight of the world was on her shoulders. 'No one's taken any notice of the things we've done up until now.'

'Plenty,' said Pippa decisively. 'Cat's already had several articles in various magazines about the work the Sunshine Trust does, which have helped raise our profile.'

Cat nodded.

'It took a while for people to be interested,' she said, 'but the issue's quite topical now. I am still holding out hope for a TV programme, but these things take time.'

'Next, we're going to have a protest meeting at the centre itself. I've finally got hold of Tom Brooker, our beloved local MP, and it turns out he's against the cuts too, despite the party line. He's even threatened to come along. The local TV bods are interested in covering it, so I'm hoping we can generate a wider story that people can tap into.'

'But what will it achieve?' said Mary. 'We can't save the centre with a PR campaign.'

'True,' said Pippa, 'but I'm still trying to find extra funding. Where there's a will, there's a way. I've been speaking to Michael Nicholas about that, and he was telling me about a company he works with which likes to invest in social and ethical issues. I'm going to follow that up, and see if they can help.

'I've also set up a petition on the House of Commons website, and I'd urge you all to tweet it, put it on Facebook. Whatever it takes. We all need the Sunshine Trust, and I'm damned if they're going to take that away from us.'

'Too true,' piped up Jeanie Martin, a mother of two severely autistic children. 'If we all get involved, I'm sure we can save the respite care.'

Pippa smiled. It felt good to be doing something. Better than sitting feeling sorry for herself and waiting for the axe to fall.

Dan came limping in from the fields. He looked tired – he was still not back to working at full pace – and not best pleased to see the kitchen overrun with Pippa's friends.

'Any chance of a cuppa?' he said.

'Sure,' said Pippa.

'What are all these people doing here?' whispered Dan as she went to the kettle.

'I told you, Dan. We're having a meeting about the Sunshine Trust.' One of the side effects of the accident was Dan feeling wary around large groups of people, which is why she had let him know this morning exactly how many people were coming and why.

'Did you?' Dan looked perplexed and rubbed his head. And she felt an overwhelming sense of pity for him. His short-term memory still troubled him sometimes. It must be infuriating.

She went to take his hand, but he shrugged her off.

'Will they be here long?' he said.

'They're just going actually,' said Pippa, stung. Dan had always welcomed their friends into his home. She tried to

172

remind herself it was part of his condition, but it was hard, when all she wanted to do was go back to normal.

'Good,' said Dan, taking his tea out into the yard. 'And you know you're wasting your time, don't you? No one's got any money. Lucy's losing her respite care, and there's nothing we can do about it.'

Pippa looked at Dan in dismay. She'd thought he'd take an interest in the campaign. In the past, she could have relied on his instant support. But now it seemed he'd gone the other way. He still cared about what happened to Lucy, but didn't seem to think they could change anything.

The old Dan would never have been so bleak. It looked like they still had a long long way to go.

'Look Mum, I'm really sorry, but we just won't be able to come to you for Christmas this year. It was so stressful with the children last year, and I think they need to wake up in their own house on Christmas Day. We'd love it if you could join us of course . . .'

Marianne was sitting in the lounge on the phone to her mum again, while the twins played in their playpen. She'd decided to take the bull by the horns, and state her case about Christmas firmly. It had seemed like a good idea when she'd suggested it to Gabriel the night before, but it wasn't going well. There was a deafening silence on the other end of the phone. She might have guessed. Marianne knew her mum wouldn't – couldn't – bear to give up the baton.

'You might enjoy a year off from cooking the turkey,' Marianne's voice trailed off. What was she thinking? Her mother would be dead before she'd ever contemplate not buying a turkey for four that could feed ten.

'Well there's always Matthew,' said her mother tetchily. 'I'm sure he won't let me down. And if Marcus is at a loose end, I'm sure he wouldn't mind joining us, so your dad and I aren't on our own.'

Sorry? thought Marianne silently, staggered at her mother's blissful lack of self-awareness. Matt felt the pressure of family Christmases even more than she did, particularly since he'd returned from his foreign travels and shacked up with his boyfriend Marcus, which suddenly put his lack of serious girlfriends into perspective. Of course, Mum had no idea of the true state of affairs, referring to Marcus as Matthew's 'friend' if asked. It was totally beyond her to imagine that two men living together might be doing something other than flat sharing, particularly if one was her son. As far as she was concerned, Marcus was helping Matt with the mortgage by paying him rent, having no idea at all that Marcus' name was actually on the mortgage. Neither had it dawned on her that her son's house was unnaturally tidy, with an interior design to die for, for the full-blooded single heterosexual she fondly imagined him to be. Good old Mum, stuck in the dark ages.

Marianne gave up and turned the conversation to other matters before hanging up. It wasn't as though they weren't going to have variations of this discussion at least a dozen times before December. But at least she'd sowed the seed. Maybe by then, Mum would be telling everyone that Marianne had stayed in Shropshire at her suggestion. 'So much less stressful for everyone.' Marianne sighed. Gabe's mum never put any pressure on them. She really wished her mother could accept that her daughter was grown up with a life of her own.

'Huh, some chance,' she said to the twins, who were sitting happily giggling away to each other. She wondered idly what was going on their minds. They seemed to be able to communicate with one another instantly, and were it not for the fact they needed feeding and changing sometimes she thought they'd survive perfectly well without her. One day they'd probably be moaning that she was putting pressure on them to come home for Christmas. She hoped not.

It was a blustery summer's day, and she had the choice of sitting at home and attempting to tidy her pigsty of a house while the twins got under her feet, or taking them to the park and hoping that she could wear them out, so they'd go to sleep for long enough so she could tidy up. The park won. No contest really.

. . . so since the last time we spoke I've been hard it, slaving in my kitchen, preparing for the Christmas edition of Cat's Country Kitchen, *which is imaginatively entitled* Cat's Country Christmas. *Well, when I say my kitchen, I assume you all know that it's – shock horror – not really my kitchen, but a specially designed one set up in a studio, but I can assure you all the delicious recipes you will be seeing on the programme will definitely have been tried out chez Tinsall before they go out on air! . . .*

Cat was updating her blog, something she rarely did now, to let people know that her new book, *Cat's Country Kitchen,* would soon be available, whilst regaling her readers with little snippets about how the latest filming for her Christmas special *Cat's Country Christmas* was going, and pointing out to Mrs J in Worcester, that Yes, she *did* in fact know meringues were made with egg whites and not egg yolks, but it was an unfortunate typo, which would be corrected on the next reprint of her last cookery book. While she had accidentally typed yolk instead of white (and, yes, everyone including Cat had missed it) the rest of the recipe did describe how the yolks needed to be separated off, so only an idiot would have actually whipped the yolks together. Maybe they'd made an interesting soufflé instead.

Mel was at home, upstairs in her room. Allegedly revising, but judging by the thumping music coming from upstairs, precious little study was going on.

Cat got out her latest batch of recipes to start typing up, but was getting increasingly distracted by the dulcet tones of Tinie Tempah. God knows how Mel worked with that racket. She certainly couldn't. Taking a deep breath, she went upstairs, to knock on Mel's door. There was no reply, so Cat tentatively poked her head around the door, to find her daughter in floods of tears.

'Oh, Mel, sweetheart, whatever's the matter?' Any irritation dissipated immediately.

Mel looked up slightly horrified to see her mum, and switched off her phone, where she'd clearly been having a heated text exchange.

'Mum, you could knock,' Mel was still pugnacious, still full of attitude, even if she looked as though the world was ending.

'I did,' said Cat, 'but your music, which I was coming to ask you to turn down, was so loud you didn't hear me.'

She sat down on the edge of the bed. 'Now come on, hon, what's wrong? You look dreadful.'

It was true, Mel looked awful. Her hair was lack lustre, her eyes were red-rimmed from crying and her face looked paler than ever.

'Is it a boy?'

'No, of course not,' Mel poured such scorn on her rebuttal, Cat couldn't help thinking she was protesting too much.

'What about Andy?'

'History,' said Mel. 'And I wouldn't waste my time crying over him.'

Okay. So it was a boy, partly. Whatever Mel said, Andy had clearly got under her skin. But going along with it, Cat pretended that Mel's problems came from another source.

'So what then?' said Cat. 'Is it your exams? Because you know, it's not the end of the world if you fail. Dad and I want you to do well, of course we do, but you can always resit if you have to.'

'It's not my exams,' said Mel.

'What is it?'

'Oh everything,' said Mel, looking miserable. 'Leaving school, and my mates, and Granny being ill. It feels as if everything's changing and I hate it.'

Cat drew an inner sigh of relief. She could remember experiencing that anxious feeling of things and life moving on herself. If that was all that was wrong with Mel, she had been worrying about nothing.

'Oh sweetie, I hadn't realised you were so upset about Granny,' said Cat.

'Of course I am,' said Mel. 'Do you – do you think she's going to die?'

Cat paused for a moment. The thought was never far from her own mind.

'I don't know,' she said honestly. 'Sometimes, yes, but then Granny's very strong. I don't think she'll give up without a fight.'

'Oh.' Mel looked so bereft, Cat hugged her like she used to when Mel was little. Back then it had been easy to promise she could make everything better. Now things were different. But for once, Cat was relieved to notice, Mel responded to her hug. Even big girls needed their mum sometimes, it seemed.

Chapter Eighteen

'It looks like it's going to be a glorious day, today,' Marianne said to Gabriel over breakfast. The sun had come up early, and courtesy of the twins, she had witnessed a gorgeous sunrise over the valley. There had been so few days like this of late, it seemed a waste not to make the most of it.

'Shall we have a barbie? Get Pippa, Dan, Noel and Cat over with the kids? We can get the paddling pool out and they can all splash about.'

'Great idea,' said Gabriel. 'I'll be out all morning, and might have to go back out around six, but I can probably escape for the afternoon. I'm sure Dad can come over if necessary.'

'Good, I'll ring round everyone.'

Gabe went off to work and Steven mooched along after him. Steven had spent more time with Gabriel recently, Marianne was pleased to note. She wondered if the reality that Steven would be leaving home in September was beginning to hit him. Whatever the reason, Marianne was glad. Gabriel and Steven had always had a strong bond, and she would have hated to see it broken.

'What can I bring?' was Cat's immediate offer, when Marianne called to invite her to the barbecue.

'Nothing,' she said. 'You deserve a day off cooking. Just bring yourselves and some booze.'

'We'll all come, except Mel probably,' said Cat. 'She's a law unto herself these days. Are you sure I can't bring anything? I'm happy to. I hate going anywhere empty handed.'

'Oh go on, if you must,' said Marianne. 'You could bring your couscous salad. It's really delicious and I haven't got a hope in hell of making it like that.'

Pippa sounded frazzled when she rang.

'Sorry, Lucy's meant to be having respite this weekend, but they cancelled at the last minute,' she said, 'but yes, we'd love to come. Can I bring anything?'

'No,' said Marianne firmly. 'You bring yourselves. I think you've enough on your plate without cooking for us. Have a day off.'

'If you insist,' said Pippa.

'I absolutely do,' said Marianne.

She got busy the minute the twins had gone down for their nap, making salads and preparing kebabs. She dug out homemade burgers and sausages from the fridge – living on a farm certainly had its uses. Though Gabe specialised in sheep, he often took meat from Dan to make up into sausages and burgers. Even Marianne had got adept at the sausage making machine, something she could never have envisaged in her former life.

By the time Gabe and Steven came back at lunchtime, she had everything ready.

'Okay, get yourself cleaned up,' she said 'and you can take over.'

'A barbecue being a man's job you mean?'

'Of course,' said Marianne, 'while it's my job to sit in the sunshine drinking Pimms.'

Gabe came round and gave her a hug.

'As you should, my darling, as you should.'

'Ugh,' said Steven as Gabriel kissed Marianne lightly on

the lips. Marianne laughed and sent them both upstairs to get changed as she started clearing up the kitchen. It being such a fine day, she had the doors open, and the sun was streaming in, along with the sounds of the country. The twins were cheerfully banging their spoons on their high chairs, and Marianne felt a huge swell of contentment. However tough life might seem at times, she was very very blessed.

'Hope we're not too early.' The entire Tinsall clan were standing on the doorstep. It was an overwhelming sight for anyone, thought Cat, especially now they were bigger. James had really shot up in the last few months, exchanging his angelic looks for lanky teen boyhood, though luckily for him, minus the spots. Paige was more appropriately dressed for clubbing and Ruby was jumping up and down with excitement like a yo-yo, while Mel slouched sulkily behind. It was a brave person who let them all in, and Cat was always grateful to anyone who invited the whole family.

'Not at all,' said Marianne. 'Come on through.'

Mel slouched behind, hands in pockets, wearing a hideously baggy t-shirt and cut-off jeans, listening to something on her iPod; the epitome of the surly teen. Her hair was unbrushed, and unlike Paige who was coated in the stuff, she was wearing no make-up. Cat really wished she'd make more of herself. It was as though she couldn't be bothered at the moment, which wasn't like Mel at all. Up until relatively recently, she'd never gone out of the house with a hair out of place.

Paige and Ruby had brought their swimming costumes, and were soon having a water fight with Steven. As soon as Pippa's lot arrived, they joined in too, leaving James to abandon his too-cool-for-school pose. Soon he was chasing his screaming sisters round the garden, while Lucy and Mel remained with the adults, Lucy clicking her pleasure, seeing all the fun. Did she ever feel left out? Cat wondered. It was so hard to tell. Then Ruby came running up. 'Lucy, do you want me to push you down there, with the others?' Cat could have hugged her, for her thoughtful behaviour.

Will I get wet? typed Lucy.

'Yes!' said Ruby. 'It's no fun otherwise.'

If I have to, typed Lucy, but she was giggling, and she was quickly having a whale of a time with Ruby and Paige, who made sure she didn't feel left out.

Mel was texting her mates and looking bored, but eventually, either driven away by the boredom of adult conversation, or having run out of gossip, she too succumbed to the water fight going on.

'This is great,' said Cat, sitting back and sipping her Pimms. 'Oh for more days of the Great British Summer like this.'

'But not so many that the crops don't grow,' grinned Pippa.

'Yes, I forgot about that,' said Cat. 'I'm a townie at heart, I can't help it. Are you sure the boys don't need any help?'

The boys were huddled self-importantly over the barbie, sipping beer and discussing the relative merits of the sausages.

'I think they're doing just fine,' said Marianne. 'Just relax for five minutes. It's not often you don't have to cook.'

'True,' said Cat, thinking it was nice to feel lazy and carefree for a change.

'Grub's up.' Gabe came towards them, brandishing a plate of burgers. As if by magic, wet children appeared at the table, and the first batch of burgers had gone before anyone could pause for breath.

'Any of you planning to have a burger?' said Gabriel with a grin.

'It's okay, I can live without,' said Cat.

'No worries, we have more,' said Gabriel. 'But who's for kebabs?'

Gabe and Marianne had produced a whole selection of lamb, pork and prawn kebabs.

'Prawns, yum,' said Mel, perking up.

After the children had demolished pretty much everything Gabe had cooked, he produced another plate of food, including steaks.

'I saved the best for us,' he said.

'Quite right too,' said Marianne.

It was an absolutely fabulous day. Cat was enjoying herself, particularly as she wasn't in charge of the catering, and was on her third Pimms, when her phone vibrated. She took her phone out of her pocket and checked her missed calls. Oh lord, it was the care home.

'Cat, it's Susan from the home,' the matron said, and Cat felt herself go to jelly. Something was wrong.

'Yes?' said Cat, her heart sinking.

'I'm really sorry to have to tell you, but your mother's been taken ill again. She's on her way to hospital now.'

Cat sat back. Sod it, she'd had a drink, and so had Noel.

'Shit,' she said, after she'd rung off. 'Mum's been taken ill again and I can't drive. I've had too much to drink. Noel, what have you had?'

'Oh bugger,' said Noel, 'this is my third pint.'

'It's okay,' said Cat, 'I'll ring for a taxi.'

'I can drive you,' offered Dan. 'I'm not drinking.'

'Thanks,' said Cat. 'That's really good of you. Are you sure?'

'Happy to help,' said Dan.

'Noel, do you want to stay here?' said Cat. 'I'll ring you from the hospital.'

Just then Mel came running up the garden.

'I feel sick,' she said, and dashed indoors towards the loo.

Oh great, that was all Cat needed. She started to follow Mel indoors, but Marianne stopped her.

'You need to be with your mum,' she said.

'But Mel–' said Cat.

'Will be fine,' said Marianne. 'Don't worry about Mel, we'll sort her out, won't we Noel?'

'Of course,' said Noel. He gave Cat a hug and a kiss. 'Go and look after your mum, we'll manage.'

Cat felt an overwhelming sense of gratitude.

'Are you sure?' She still felt torn.

'Yes,' said Marianne, 'now go!'

Cat followed Dan out of Marianne's garden, down the lane to where his car was parked, without saying a word. Her head was churning. Mum, back in hospital again. How long for this time?

Pippa and Marianne spent half an hour calming Mel down. She'd thrown up even more violently when she'd heard her granny was ill. She looked so weak and pale, Marianne wondered if she were coming down with something really nasty.

'Sorry, Marianne. I didn't mean to spoil your party,' she said.

'You haven't,' said Marianne. 'Are you sure you're okay now?'

'I think so,' said Mel, 'but I feel a bit queasy still.'

'Do you want to go home and have a lie down?'

'Yes, I think I probably do,' said Mel. 'Dad, is it okay if I go home?'

'Are you sure you're feeling okay?' Noel said, giving his daughter a hug.

'I'm fine, Dad, really. I feel better already. The walk will do me good. I think it must have been the prawns.'

'Sorry,' said Gabriel, 'I hope they don't affect anyone else.'

Pippa would have happily gone home, if she hadn't thought Gabriel and Marianne would be upset. She wasn't at all happy that Dan had elected to drive. Getting back in the car had been one of his targets, but he'd not been back driving long, and she still felt anxious about it. The hospital was a good half an hour away, along winding country lanes; what if he lost it on a bend? Or got a blinding headache on the way back and got confused and lost? Stop it, stop it! Pippa told herself off sternly. At this rate she'd give herself a heart attack.

The sun was starting to dip down in the sky by the time Dan came back. The afternoon's sunny promise had faded into a cooler evening, and grey clouds were beginning to scud across the sky. A heaviness had descended in the atmosphere, promising a hint of thunder. And the mood of the party was sombre too, everyone aware that Cat's mum might be very poorly indeed.

'How are things?' said Pippa getting up to greet him.

'I don't know,' said Dan. 'Cat asked to be dropped off, so I left her at the entrance of A&E,' he replied.

'Oh Dan, didn't you even go in with her?' Pippa said without thinking, her dismay all the greater, because she knew in the past that she'd never have had to ask Dan.

'That's all the thanks I get?' Dan blazed out of nowhere. 'If you hadn't downed so much Pimms you could have taken her yourself,' he continued, his voice full of rage.

'Dan—' began Pippa, kicking herself that she'd set him off in front of everyone else.

'Don't bloody Dan me,' said Dan. 'I do a mate a good turn and all you can do is nag me. You're so damned demanding. If it's not help with Lucy, it's fighting a long battle for her respite care. I'm done with it all, do you hear?'

Dan strode off out of the garden, but suddenly stopped. Lucy was sitting looking at him in distress.

'Oh bollocks. Lucy–' He looked as if someone had shot him through the heart, then turned on his heel and left.

'Oh bugger,' said Pippa, her voice cracking. This was the worst tantrum Dan had had yet. What on earth were they going to do?

Mel

FACEBOOK status Sooo tired. One exam left. Yay.
Jen17: u out Sat?
Mel: What's happening?
Jen17: End of exams party. Jake's from 8.
Mel: Cool
Kaz: Shut up losers. I don't finish till next week
Jen 17: Soz. Can you come anyway?
Kaz: Sure. Who wants to sleepover?
Ellie: Yeah
Jen17: I can, Mel, wbu?
Mel: Will check with parents . . . Mad Gran still ill.
Jen17: Oh soz.
Mel: S'OK. She's my indestructible granny.
Jen17: :)
Mel: Soooo tired. I just want to sleeeeeep . . .
Kaz: Me too. Then partayyy!
Mel: Sounds good to mexxxoooxxx

Teenage Kicks

This is supposed to be the best time of my life, no? School days? End of exams? Why does everything feel so shit?

Went for sleepover at Best Mate's after end of GCSE party. Shit night. Loser boys trying it on. I just wanted to see the Boy. So I got really drunk on vodka, and was really sick in the flower bed. Lucky I didn't go home. Mum not happy, when I got back at 1pm the next day. Was supposed to be babysitting so she could go to see Mad Gran. Oops.

The Boy isn't returning my texts. Every time I ring him his phone is switched off. Why is he doing this? I really want to see him. I really miss him.

I don't know why he doesn't call.

I even went looking for him at work, to see if he was there. I think I'm turning into a stalker.

Mum keeps asking what's wrong so I said I was upset about Mad Gran. I don't want her to know the truth.

I feel really weird too. I've been sick twice recently. I started to worry I might be pregnant after all. But then my period came, so that's ok. I just feel tired. Maybe it's stress. I don't know.

I just wish The Boy would call. Then I'd feel so much better.

Part Three

We Will Be Together

July

Chapter Nineteen

The sun was shining as Cat headed off to the hospital at lunchtime, before going off to pick Ruby up from school. She had got used to this as part of her daily routine over the last couple of weeks. It turned out Louise had had a serious stroke, and for a couple of days things had looked touch and go. Now though, she was on the mend – she was responding well to therapy, or so the nurses said – but Cat couldn't see much difference. It felt instead as if her mother was shrinking, fading away before her eyes. She looked paler, thinner, and her remarks were even more rambling and incoherent than ever. Sometimes Cat felt like she couldn't bear it.

It was silly really to feel it so keenly. Cat had spent the last four years mourning the loss of the mother she'd once known, but this was different. Up until now, she'd felt that all that was left was a shell of her mother – an imposter in her mother's clothing. And sadly, she'd got used to that. But at least Louise was still *there*.

But now Louise was physically declining too, and Cat felt like she was losing her all over again. With a jolt, Cat realised she was facing up to the reality of her mother's death, something she'd put off thinking about over the last few years. Weirdly, she'd got in the way of thinking Louise would remain in a constant state, herself, but not herself;

191

sometimes recognising Cat, sometimes not. But now, she'd sunk even lower than Cat had thought possible. Memories of how her mum used to be were fading fast. Cat wondered if she'd ever remember her properly again.

Cat arrived on the ward to discover as usual, Mum's food was sitting cold and unpalatable in front of her, while she dozed in a chair. There was only one other patient in the opposite bed, an elderly lady by the name of Josie, who was still lying horizontally. There was no way she could eat her meal without sitting up, and it looked like no one had made the effort to try and feed her or Louise. Cat sighed,

'Would you like me to raise the bed, Josie?' Cat said.

'It's all right, love,' said Josie, 'I don't fancy this muck anyway.'

'I've got some food for Mum, if you'd like to share it?' offered Cat.

Josie grinned, 'No thanks. Funny thing, you lose your appetite in here.'

She was so stoical, Cat could have wept for her.

'At least let me fill your water jug for you,' said Cat. As usual, someone had thoughtfully placed the water jugs as far away from the patients as possible. It was as though they didn't want people to get better.

Once she'd sorted Josie out, she got herself a chair and sat down till Mum woke up. She got out the bread and cheese she'd brought with her, knowing that Louise would refuse the cold food once she woke up. And who could blame her?

After five minutes, Louise started to stir. She opened her eyes and smiled at Cat, in a slightly confused way.

'Hi, Mum,' Cat said, leaning over to give her mother a kiss.

Louise's eyes lit up, and she held Cat's hand tightly.

'Lovely to see you,' she said with a slight slur to her voice, one of the hangovers from her stroke. 'Are you enjoying your holidays here? Have you been to this hotel before?'

Cat smiled through her tears. If only her mother was staying in a five star hotel. If only they both were. In the weeks Louise had been in hospital, she had variously imagined she was in a train station, at the seaside, or bizarrely, in the carpet cleaning factory where she had once worked.

'I wonder who you think I am today,' murmured Cat. She pressed her lips to her mum's skinny fingers. 'It's me, Cat, remember? Please remember.'

She should be used to this by now, should accept that that was the way it was, but it was so hard, her own mother not knowing who she was.

'Cat, it can't be my Cat, she came last week. She's having a baby you know. Isn't that lovely? She didn't say, I could just tell.'

'Oh Mum,' said Cat, 'I've had my four babies already. See, remember?' She pointed out a picture of the children taken with Louise in their back garden the previous summer, which she'd brought in the first day Mum was admitted. 'See, there's Mel, and James and that's Paige and Ruby.'

'Well fancy that,' said Louise. 'Such lovely children, who are they?'

'They're your grandchildren,' said Cat despairingly.

'My grandchildren?' said Louise, a big smile crossing her face. 'How lovely.'

Pippa came in from milking the cows with Andy Pilsdon, whom Dan had recently employed full time. She wasn't over-enamoured by Andy, who seemed to like flirting a little too much for her tastes, and felt slightly awkward as she was old enough to be his mother. Still, he was a hard worker, and beggars couldn't be choosers.

Pippa was exhausted, filthy and hot. All she wanted was

to slump down with a cup of tea, watch some mind-dumbing daytime TV, and stop thinking. But she couldn't. She had dinner to prepare, baking to do, a phone call to make to Richard La Fontaine, the contact Michael Nicholas had given her concerning funding and a meeting at Lucy's school to talk about her future, as she would be moving to senior school in the next couple of years. There were two possible choices to make, one involving Lucy at residential school thirty miles away, the other with a day school, much nearer, but with few guarantees of a place.

In the past, Pippa would have automatically discounted the residential home as being not at all what they would have wanted. But now . . . With Dan the way he was, she was no longer sure. For the first time since Lucy's birth, she could no longer rely on Dan, and she wasn't sure how much more she could take.

She came into the kitchen to find Dan slumped in a chair, looking gloomily out of the window. At least he was up. Since his outburst at Marianne's barbecue, Dan seemed to have gone into a mental decline. Physically he was improving daily, but mentally, he seemed to have given up. He'd stopped working on the farm, refused Pippa's desperate pleas to see a doctor, and spent hours online playing violent war games. She had no idea what was happening to him, but she felt like she was losing her lovely gentle husband. She'd even talked to their GP about it. Lindsey Perry, who'd been at school with both Pippa and Dan, had been the family GP since Pippa had first become pregnant, and was very understanding.

'It does sound like Dan's getting depressed,' she said. 'And I can really understand why, given what you've both been through. But unless he comes to see me, there's not a lot I can do. Has he got a hospital appointment coming up?'

'I'm holding out for that,' Pippa had admitted.

'See how that goes, and if there's no improvement, I'll try and pop in to see him,' said Lindsey. 'I'll pretend it's you I've come to see.'

'Thanks,' said Pippa, feeling simultaneously grateful for Lindsey's support and guilty that she was going behind Dan's back. It was so frustrating. Dan had seemed to be getting better, but now he was so much worse again.

'Hi,' she said carefully, to see Dan hunched over the laptop as usual. She was never quite sure what mood she was going to find him in these days.

A shrug and a grunt were all the response she got.

'Cup of tea?' she said, hoping that was a neutral enough comment.

Another shrug, which she took as a yes.

'What are you up to?' she asked gently.

'Yes, I'm online, before you have a go,' was the belligerent response.

'I was only asking,' said Pippa, between gritted teeth.

There was no response to that, so she made the tea and went upstairs to shower before getting on with the evening meal.

'What are you doing that for now?' said Dan.

'Because I won't have time later,' said Pippa.

'Well make time,' said Dan. 'I never see you, you're always busy.'

'Because there's always a lot to do,' said Pippa, trying to keep her voice level, and ignoring the comment bubbling up, 'and because you never do anything.'

'Oh, right, if you'd rather do stuff, than spend time with me . . .' She hated this man who'd stolen her Dan. This wasn't the man she'd married and loved for so long. He looked like a disgruntled child, and suddenly something snapped inside Pippa.

'For God's sake, grow up, Dan! I know you've been

through a lot, I know it's difficult, but have you ever once in the last few months, given any thought to me? I'm holding our family together by the skin of my teeth, and you're not helping at all. And I'm sick of it. I'm sick of everything. And most of all, I'm sick of you.' She caught her breath, shocked at the words that just escaped her mouth.

'How dare you say that?' Dan erupted. 'After all I've done for you and this family. And at the first time of trouble you bail out on me.'

'That's not fair, and you know it,' said Pippa. 'I've supported you through all of this. But your mood swings, your irritation with the children, your refusal to get help. I can't bloody do it for you.'

'Then don't bloody bother.' Dan leapt up from the table and lunged towards her, and for one terrible moment she thought he was going to hit her. But just as suddenly he slumped down, head in his hands.

'Oh God,' he said, 'what's happening to us? To me?'

He looked up, tears streaming down his face.

'I don't know,' said Pippa, her heart melting at the sight of her Dan breaking down in front of her, 'but we'll get through it together, like always.'

She hugged him fiercely, holding him like a talisman against the nasty thought that had weaselled into her brain. What if this time they didn't? What would they do then?

'I can't believe this is the last one of these I'll do for Steven.' Marianne settled down with the twins on a picnic blanket next to Cat in the school's sports field, as they sat down to watch the Hope Christmas school annual sports day. It not being a working day for her, Marianne had been let off taking part, and could be a mum for the day. The twins were playing happily on the blanket, and were just beginning to toddle about, but still content for now to trip over each other and her, and not wander off too far.

'I can't believe the summer we're having,' said Marianne, 'I'm even getting a tan.'

'Could do with some rain soon though,' said Pippa joining them. 'Have I missed anything yet?'

'Not really,' said Marianne. 'Apart from Mrs Garratt pulling two Year 3 boys apart who'd got in a punch-up.'

'Really?'

'Nah. Sadly nothing so exciting,' said Marianne. 'It's the usual dull non-competitive affair.'

In the interests of not upsetting anyone at all, ever, Mrs Garratt had instituted a non-competitive sports day, insisting it was the taking part that counted and points didn't matter. So although there were races, no one actually won. A point of view that Steven and George, who were fiercely competitive with one another, found utterly ridiculous.

'I'd better go and watch events,' said Cat. 'I think Ruby might be running in the next race. If you can call it running. She's the slowest kid in the class, poor thing.' Pippa and Marianne smiled at her sympathetically.

She got up and wandered over to the race track where ten little girls were limbering up.

'You okay?' Marianne glanced at Pippa, who looked tired and pale.

'Not really,' said Pippa, with a faint smile. 'But I'll manage, I expect.'

'Dan?' said Marianne.

'Dan, Lucy, what the hell we do next,' said Pippa. 'You know everyone's always said, "Pippa, how do you cope? You're so calm, how do you do it?" Well, the only reason I've managed to stay so sodding calm is because Dan's always been my back up, and over the last few years having

Lucy in respite has been a godsend. And now . . . Dan just hasn't been the same since his accident, and I can't rely on him anymore. I'm losing him and I might lose the respite. It feels as though my whole world is collapsing and I don't know what to do.'

Her voice trembled a little, and Marianne gave her a hug.

'Oh Pippa,' she said, feeling utterly inadequate. 'I don't know what to say. Can we do anything to help?'

'No,' said Pippa looking bleak, 'I really don't think there's anything anyone can do.' She looked completely defeated.

'Come on, this isn't like you,' said Marianne, 'where's your fighting spirit?'

'Gone AWOL,' said Pippa. 'I really mean it, something's got to give.'

Cat came back to join them, looking slightly stunned. 'Bloody hell, Ruby came second. Who'd have thunk.'

She sat down and glanced at Pippa. 'You okay?' she asked.

'Not really,' said Pippa with a weak smile, 'I've just been bending Marianne's ear about it.'

'I know what you need,' said Marianne with a glint in her eye.

'And what's that?' said Pippa.

'A girls' night out,' said Marianne. 'I think we could all do with one, you most of all.'

'Great idea,' said Cat. 'Come on, Pippa.'

'But what about the children, and Dan . . .' said Pippa.

'We'll get Gabriel to come and keep Dan company, and Mel can babysit for Marianne,' said Cat. 'See? Sorted.'

'Well, then,' said Pippa, looking a little more cheerful. 'You're on.'

Chapter Twenty

'Now don't tell me we don't all feel better for this?' said Cat, bringing three huge cocktails to the table. 'I know it's hardly London nightlife, but we can pretend.'

They had come out to a small trendy wine bar called The Well, which had recently opened up in nearby Adlington, a small village ten miles up the road from Hope Christmas. It had had rave reviews in the local press and, sick of slumming it in the Hopesay Arms, Cat had suggested they try it out for a change. The décor was simple but inviting, and there were cosy little nooks, discreetly lit. Cat liked it. It managed to be welcoming, but feel quite sophisticated at the same time.

'Pretend away,' said Pippa, enjoying her first sip of a screwdriver in more years than she could remember. 'You're right, this is what we all need.'

'And Gabe's agreed to get the twins up in the morning,' said Marianne, 'bliss!'

'Funny how you forget that,' said Cat. 'Time was, when I could kill for a lie in, and now I can have one, I always seem to wake up ridiculously early.'

'You should try being a farmer's wife,' said Pippa. 'Cows are even more unforgiving than babies.'

'True,' said Marianne. 'I'm glad Gabe has sheep to look after. At least they don't need milking.'

'Well, your last attempt to help with the cows wasn't exactly successful was it?' laughed Pippa. 'I seem to remember you got the cows stuck in the wrong bit of the pen, and half the milk spilt out on the yard.' This was doing her good. She couldn't remember when she'd last laughed so freely.

'True. You can take the girl out of the town, but you can't take the town out of the girl,' laughed Marianne. 'I am *so* not cut out to be a farmer's wife. I wonder how Gabe puts up with me sometimes.'

'Can I get you ladies a drink?' Michael Nicholas sat down in front of them, as casually sexy as ever. He wasn't wearing his leather jacket today, but a black t-shirt, tucked into tight jeans. On his broad arms, Pippa could make out a tattoo of a sword, with the word *Invicibilis* on them.

Pippa's heart did a little jump. He always seemed to come out of nowhere. And he really was very good looking. Stop it, she told herself, you're a married woman . . . whose husband is being somewhat less than attentive, said the devil on her shoulder.

'Erm, I don't know about that,' said Pippa.

'Oh, go on,' said Michael, 'it's on the house. Didn't you know I owned this bar?'

'No, can't say I did,' said Pippa.

'Me neither,' said Cat. 'I thought you were busy working on the estate with Noel.'

'Oh I have fingers in all sorts of pies,' said Michael with a teasing grin.

'Such as?' Pippa grinned back. He was really very intriguing, and fun.

'Apart from the work I do for my uncle on the estate,' said Michael, 'I've been investing in all sorts of small businesses since I've been here. There's a new greengrocer's opening up soon, and I thought the town could do with its own retro music shop. Selling only vinyl, natch.'

'That would be great,' said Pippa. 'Dan still has most of his old vinyl, but I know there are things he'd like to get hold of again.'

She tried not to think about the records they'd bought each other when they were first dating. It took her back to a better, more innocent time, and she didn't want to be reminded of that tonight.

'I have my own band, The Dark Angels,' said Michael.

'You do?' said Cat, never one to miss an opportunity. 'Why didn't you say? You could play at the Snow Ball. That would be brilliant, wouldn't it, girls?'

'You haven't heard us yet,' laughed Michael, 'but I'd be delighted.'

Pippa sat back and relaxed. She hadn't had so much fun or laughed so much in ages.

'You're clearly a man of many talents,' said Pippa teasing him.

'Who also knows a great many useful things,' he replied.

'Such as?'

Michael tapped his nose, and looked askance to a quiet corner of the bar, where a familiar face was holding a tête-à-tête with a pretty blonde.

'Isn't that . . .?' Marianne asked.

'Tom Brooker, our local, very married MP,' said Cat. 'Yes it is, but I don't think his wife is a blonde . . .'

'What a coincidence,' said Michael with a wink. 'Didn't you want to discuss something with him, Pippa?'

'Well I did,' said Pippa. 'He's supposed to be coming to our protest, but he hasn't been answering my calls. I was thinking of door-stepping him at his local surgery.'

'No time like the present,' said Michael. 'I *don't* believe he'll wish his wife to know he's – er – otherwise occupied.'

'But that's blackmail,' said Pippa outraged. 'I thought you were one of the good guys.'

'On the side of the angels,' said Michael, getting up to go. 'I prefer to think of it more as leverage . . .'

He winked at them, before exiting to go and chat to the barmen.

'Well should we?' said Pippa. 'It does seem like a good opportunity.'

'Leave it to me,' said Cat. 'I'm a journalist, don't forget. He will really really regret meeting me.'

Feeling less bold than her words suggested, Cat made her way into the far corner, where Tom Brooker looked as though he'd got way past first base with his lady friend. Just as well he wasn't quite on the ministerial ladder yet, otherwise some of the tabloids would probably be sniffing round him. Which left the ground clear for her . . .

'Hello, it's Tom Brooker, right?' She slid down next to him, and tried to hide her glee at his discomfiture.

'Do you mind?' he said. 'I'm having a private moment.'

I'll bet you are, thought Cat.

'I won't take up more than a moment of your time,' said Cat with a winning smile. 'Cat Tinsall – you may have heard of me? *Cat's Country Kitchen*? No? Here's my card. Only, I'm raising awareness on behalf of the Sunshine Trust. It needs your help. I believe you have several constituents who rely on the services it offers. The thing is, that thanks to your government, people like my friend over there won't be getting the help they need anymore. It would make a dreadful headline, don't you think? Local MP turns mother away with dire consequences? What did you say your name was?' Cat turned to Tom Brooker's companion.

'Pam Smith,' stammered the girl. 'I'm just his secretary.'

'Of course you are,' said Cat, 'so I know you wouldn't mind being pictured together, enjoying a business meeting in a local wine bar. Busy day was it?'

'Okay,' said Tom Brooker, putting his hands up, 'what is it you want?'

'Cat, that was amazing!' Marianne let them into her house, where she'd promised them a nightcap. A note on the table said, *Hope you had fun, Gone to bed, love you Gxx*

'Oh he still writes you love letters,' teased Cat. 'You've really not been married very long, have you?'

'Sssh, we mustn't wake him,' said Marianne. 'What's everyone having? More wine, or coffee?'

'Can I have a coffee?' said Pippa. 'I should really call it a night soon. I never like being out too late because of Lucy.'

Marianne shot Pippa a look. She wondered if Pippa was secretly worried about Dan's ability to cope. She'd hinted as much on their last conversation, but then shut up, as if she didn't want to talk about it anymore.

'Won't she be asleep?' said Cat.

'She wakes sometimes in the night,' said Pippa. 'I like to be there when she does.'

'Stay for half an hour?' Marianne said.

'Okay,' said Pippa, flinging herself into Marianne's comfy sofa. 'But really no longer.'

They sat down and Cat regaled them one more time with her conversation with Tom Brooker.

'You should have seen his face when I suggested taking a picture of perfect Pam. I *almost* felt sorry for him.'

'And he's really going to come to our demo?' said Marianne. 'That's amazing.'

'Yup, and he's also promised to raise the matter in the House of Commons. It turns out he's not a total bastard. He has concerns about the way the cuts are being implemented, and wants to use the Sunshine Trust as a stick to beat his bosses with.'

'So not entirely altruistic then,' said Pippa.

'Does it matter?' said Cat. 'Now he's coming to the demo, my mate Angie on Shropshire TV is bound to cover it now, plus he's agreed to write an article about the vulnerable in society. I bent his ear about the state of the local hospital too. Turns out his gran was in there, so he totally gets it.'

'Not a bad night's work then,' said Marianne.

'Not at all,' said Pippa. 'And thanks girls, it was just what I needed.'

'Me too,' said Cat. 'Here's to doing this more often.'

'Sounds like a plan,' said Marianne, 'we should put another date in our diaries now. Though it will have to wait till after the holidays, I think.'

'Are you off anywhere nice?' said Cat.

'A caravan in Cornwall with my parents,' Marianne pulled a face. 'Still, it has to be done. What about you?'

'We're not having a proper break this year,' said Cat. 'Too much on. We're having a few days in Eurodisney, for our sins.'

'It's better than nothing,' said Pippa, looking wistful. 'We're staying put.'

'Oh Pippa,' said Marianne, 'I didn't mean to make you miserable. This evening was all about cheering you up.'

'And you have,' said Pippa with a smile. 'Don't worry about me, I'll be fine. But now I've really got to get back.'

She got up to leave, and Cat soon followed her. They all hugged, promising to do it again soon. Marianne watched Pippa wander down the lane, feeling really sad for her friend. One evening out was great, and it lifted the spirits, but it wasn't enough to sort out her problems, that was for sure.

Chapter Twenty-One

'Are you sure you've packed enough?' Gabriel poked his head around the spare room door, where Marianne was sorting and resorting clothes for the umpteenth time. Deep down, she wasn't convinced the twins needed twenty sets of shorts and t-shirts each for a week in Cornwall, but the Perranporth Caravan Park apparently had limited washing facilities, and she knew how quickly the twins got mucky. And of course, it being the end of July in England, there was no guarantee they would get any sun, so she was also having to pack similar pairs of leggings and little fleeces. And as for the number of nappies they needed . . .

'I'd rather take too much than too little,' said Marianne firmly. 'And you know what my mum's like. If she thinks I haven't brought enough clothes, we'll be forced to go shopping for extra. It's going to be bad enough stuck in a caravan with Mum and Dad for a fortnight, without having a compulsory shopping trip thrown in.'

Since she and Gabriel had been married, they'd always spent a week in Cornwall together with Steven, but this year Eve and Darren had asked if they could take him away to Darren's villa in Spain instead. Steven had been so keen on the idea, Gabriel had reluctantly agreed. Just as they'd been in the middle of sorting it out, Marianne's mum had rung up to ask once more about Christmas and, in a moment of either genius or madness – Marianne wasn't sure – she'd said, 'Mum, would you like to come to Cornwall with us this year?' She'd only said it to deflect the conversation away from Christmas, and was really stunned when Mum's response was, 'What a wonderful idea, of course we'd love to come.'

'It does give us the upper hand when I eventually get round to telling them about our Christmas plans,' she said feebly to a horrified Gabriel.

'We also get to spend two weeks in a caravan, with your parents,' Gabriel pointed out.

'Oh God, what have I done?' groaned Marianne. 'All we can do is pray it doesn't rain.'

'At least we'll get some babysitting,' said Gabe, trying to look on the bright side.

'True,' said Marianne. 'Although that only works if the children are well. Don't you remember Mum calling us back from that night out when Daisy threw up?'

'Well, let's make sure we dose them up with Calpol before we go out,' said Gabriel, grinning.

'It won't be that long before Steven will be able to babysit,' said Marianne, as she crammed the last few things into the case and zipped it up. 'Although we'll only be able to benefit at weekends, obviously.'

Gabriel looked sad, and Marianne touched his arm.

'I know,' she said, 'but there are still weekends and holidays. From what I gather from Cat, once your kids hit their teens you hardly see anything of them anyway.'

'I suppose,' said Gabriel. 'But I keep worrying about Eve. Now she's nearer, Steven's going to want to see more of her. It's only natural, I know, but what if he forgets about us? I can't bear the thought of losing him.'

'You won't lose him,' said Marianne, 'don't be daft.'

But she could share his anxiety. Ever since she'd met

Steven as a shy, lost little boy, uncomprehending as to why his mother had left him, Marianne had had a soft spot for her stepson, which over the years had blossomed into a deep and abiding love. She had always felt privileged to be his stepmother, whilst being conscious that Steven had a real mother out there. And now Eve was coming back into Steven's life, and more and more Marianne had to take a step back. While she knew it was the right thing to do, she was also aware that it was harder than she'd imagined it would be. Despite what she'd said to Gabe, she too feared that Steven would be seduced by the money and size of the house that Eve shared with Darren. Maybe once he'd been at his posh school for a while, he'd be too proud to come and see them on the farm. It wasn't likely, but she worried about it, even though she wasn't about to tell Gabriel that.

'Now come on, let's get our stuff sorted, and then the packing's done. I know it's only two weeks away in a caravan park, and I know Mum and Dad will be there, but let's see if we can have the best time possible.' She kissed him on the cheek and he smiled. 'Where would I be without you?'

'Sitting at home feeling sorry for yourself,' said Marianne. 'Now let's get on, so we can go out and enjoy a sunny evening on the patio.'

'Is everyone ready?' Cat shouted up the stairs for the umpteenth time. The car was packed to overflowing, with so many bags stuffed into corners she wasn't sure there'd be room for the children. Noel was impatiently revving the engine, keen to get going.

'Coming!' Ruby and Paige fell excitedly down the stairs. At least they were looking forward to a long weekend at Eurodisney. Mel had put up a very strong argument for staying home alone. 'I can look after myself,' she said. 'It's not like I'll starve. And someone needs to look after Hammy.'

'Over my dead body,' Noel had replied firmly.

'It's okay, Ruby's friend Molly's having Hammy for us, same as always,' said Cat.

'Oh please,' whined Mel. 'I promise I'll behave.'

'And the rest,' said Noel. 'You'll only have wild parties and trash the place.'

James had been noncommittal about the whole thing, but being an amiable sort wasn't actively complaining about going, which was good enough for Cat.

Cat would have liked a proper holiday, but with her and Noel's work commitments, Mum still being ill and having to get back for Mel's exam results, there wasn't an awful lot of time left. At the time of organising this and another long weekend at the end of the summer, camping in Wales, Cat had felt cheesed off wishing they could have a proper holiday. But now, with Louise in hospital, she was relieved. Cat always worried about what would happen when they went away, but this year, she would have felt frantic with guilt for going away for too long. As it was she still felt guilty about disappearing for four days, despite Noel telling her not to worry.

'You've been there for your mum all year,' he said. 'I can't think she'd begrudge you a few days.'

'I know,' said Cat, 'I just feel our lives are on hold.'

'Besides, it's not fair on the kids,' said Noel, 'they deserve a break.'

Torn two ways, Cat's guilt was utterly intensified.

So here they were, setting off for Paris at some ungodly hour, putting up with moaning (Mel), silence (James), over-excitement (Paige), and vomit (Ruby). Sometimes Cat felt it would be easier just to stay at home. And certainly cheaper.

The journey to Paris was tediously long, making Cat wish for the first time in a long while they still lived in London. However, by dint of setting off at three a.m., and going by Eurotunnel for speed's sake, they managed to arrive at their hotel just after lunch, which gave them a good half day to wander around the park.

Cat was absolutely worn out from the travelling, and would have loved nothing more than to collapse in the very comfortable looking bed in the hotel, but Paige and Ruby were having none of it.

'I want to see Mickey Mouse, now!' declared Ruby, suddenly metamorphosing into a ghastly child from a Disney advert.

'Yes, come on, Mum,' said Noel, who was looking equally sleepy, 'where's your enthusiasm?'

So, reluctantly saying goodbye to the comfortable bed, they got back in the car and sped up the motorway for twenty minutes until they arrived at the Eurodisney car park.

Paige was frantically texting her friends, so the whole world now knew the Tinsalls had hit Disney, and Ruby was jumping about so excitedly Noel kept asking her if she needed the loo. Even James was beginning to look vaguely interested as they approached the entrance to the theme park and heard the sound of cheesy music playing. Cat had got them tickets to both the Disney park and film studios, the latter of which James had actually confessed to being interested in. Cat also knew that, having a taste for terrifying fairground rides, he wouldn't be able to resist the scary ones.

'Woah, look at that!' he said, when beholding Space Mountain for the first time. 'I have to have a go on that.'

'Can I go? Can I go?' said Ruby.

Cat took one look at the rollercoaster ride, the sort she normally avoided like the plague, and laughed. 'Sorry sweetie. I'm pretty sure there'll be a height restriction on that one. Dad can go with James. Unless Mel wants to.'

'Ugh, no,' said Mel, who hated scary fairground rides. 'I'd throw up. And I think we've had quite enough puke for one day.'

'It's not my fault I get car sick,' said Ruby. 'I wouldn't if you all let me sit in the front.'

'We did,' said Paige, 'and you were still ill.'

'I can't help it,' said Ruby. 'You should all feel sorry for me.'

In the end, everyone seemed to have a good time, even Mel, who unexpectedly really enjoyed the Indiana Jones ride, and Big Thunder Mountain. Paige also suddenly developed a taste for the scarier rides, so it was with some trepidation that Cat and Noel let her go off with her brother and queue up for Space Mountain.

'I feel sick just looking at it,' Cat said to Noel, as they watched Paige and James join the queue. 'I hope they come back in one piece.'

'God, Mum, it's only a ride,' said Mel laughing for once. 'It's not like they're going to die.'

'Which is why you were brave enough to go on it,' retorted Cat.

Still laughing, they went to queue up for a Buzz Lightyear ride, which involved zapping loads of aliens. Something which Cat and Mel proved to be spectacularly bad at, and Ruby and Noel extremely good.

'What are we meant to be hitting?' wailed Mel after missing all her targets.

'I have no idea,' said Cat, 'just zap whatever moves.'

It was a tactic that proved only partially successful, and they had about a tenth of the final points that Noel and Ruby had accumulated, but Cat didn't care. For the first time in a long time she and Mel were having fun together. It felt fabulous.

'I can't believe you were so bad,' laughed Noel as they waited for the other two to come back.

'I had no idea what I was meant to hit,' giggled Cat. 'That is one of the most stupid games I've ever played.'

James and Paige came bounding over a couple of minutes later.

'That was awesome!' said Paige.

'The best ever,' said James, which was the most they'd got out of him all day. 'I'm ravenous.'

'What, again?' said Cat. Ever since they'd arrived at the park, they seemed to have been on a constant grazing mission. She'd never spent so much money on fast food.

'Is everyone hungry?' said Noel.

'Yes!' came a chorus of replies.

'Tomorrow we bring our own grub,' she said. 'I don't think I can stand another chip.'

'Good,' said James, 'I'll eat yours.'

'The human hoover,' grinned Noel. 'Where do you put it all, and stay so thin? Bet Mel wishes she could be like that.'

'Noel–' said Cat.

'What? What did I say?'

'So you think I'm fat, now,' Mel flared.

'It was a joke,' said Noel. 'Of course I didn't mean–'

'Cos if you are I'll just show you that I don't need junk food at all,' Mel said, ceremoniously dumping the remainder of her chips in the bin, and storming off.

'I'd have eaten them,' said James plaintively.

'Well done, Noel,' said Cat and followed Mel around the corner.

She found her sitting next to a hot dog stand looking genuinely upset.

'Dad doesn't mean it you know,' Cat said, sitting down and putting her arm around Mel. 'He's a bloke. He has no tact. He thought he was being funny.'

'Well, he's not,' said Mel.

'Is everything okay?' said Cat softly. 'Can I help?'

Mel looked a bit misty-eyed.

'Everything's fine, I keep telling you,' she said. 'I'm just cross with Dad for being such an idiot.'

'Are you sure?' said Cat. 'It's just that, generally, you seem a bit unhappy. If you're in some kind of trouble, you can tell me.'

'Look Mum, nothing's wrong,' said Mel. 'I'm not pregnant, I don't do drugs. All right?'

'All right, all right,' said Cat holding her hands up. 'So there's really nothing to worry about?'

'Just a bit stressed out about my exams,' muttered Mel.

'There's always retakes,' said Cat, 'if it's that bad.' Nudging her daughter's knee, 'Although I'm sure it won't be,' she continued.

Mel said nothing.

'I know,' she said, 'how about you and me sneak off for a little girlie shopping trip tomorrow morning and let the others come here? I'm guessing you're feeling a bit too old for Mickey Mouse these days?'

Mel smiled suddenly, reminding Cat how rarely she did it anymore. Cat searched her face anxiously for clues. Was it just exam stress? Or was something else wrong? Mel was so damned cagey these days, it was really hard to tell.

'How's it going?' Phillip came out to take his turn on the combine harvester, as Pippa drove back from the fields with a trailer full of grain.

'Getting there,' she said. 'The boys, Mum and Dad, have been a great help. But it's going to be a late night. I'll be glad when Gabe's back next week.'

Traditionally Pippa and Dan had always looked after Gabe's farm while he was away and vice versa. And normally each couple only took one week's holiday. But this year, aware of how much Gabe had put himself out for her family, and conscious that it had at times been a strain for Marianne, Pippa had insisted that he take a fortnight off.

'We'll manage,' she told him, when he protested. 'Now go on, book that bloody holiday, before I change my mind.'

She hadn't factored in quite what a strain it was, running two farms with barely any support.

'And Dan?'

Pippa shook her head.

'I can't get him interested at all. He's so demotivated. Feels that he's let us all down or something. The neurologist did say there might be a dip in his confidence, but I wasn't expecting this. I mean, I know his injuries still trouble him, and he can't quite do what he did, but physically there's nothing to stop him.'

'Should I have a word?'

'Could you?' said Pippa, feeling overwhelming gratitude towards her father-in-law, of whom she was very fond. 'He doesn't seem to listen to me anymore. The doctor keeps telling me it will take time, but how much time does he need?'

At least they were having a good harvest. After the difficulties they'd had this year, and the price of milk plummeting, a holiday had been out of the question, with or without Dan's accident. Luckily Lucy's school offered a two-week residential holiday in the middle of the summer, and for the boys, helping out with the harvest was a great treat. Pippa wasn't even sure if they'd missed going away.

She returned to the task in hand, unloading the grain into big silos, where it could be threshed. Andy was at least a hard worker, and it was with a quiet sense of achievement that Pippa noted that they were halfway through with the harvest. Luckily the weather was holding out. The brook at the bottom of the lane had run dry. It was strange now

213

to imagine it bursting its banks and flooding the house as it had done a few years previously. To think then she'd thought she had a lot to contend with.

Pippa was gratified to see Dan's mum approaching with tea and cake – and her heart skipped a painful beat as she saw Dan was with her. He seemed to have aged so much in the last few months, she thought, seeing how he held himself hunched and looked so lost and sad. If only she could help him and put things right. If only life were that simple.

'Hey, you came,' she said, giving him a welcoming kiss. 'We've had a good day.' She was careful to choose her words. While she felt triumphant for what they'd achieved, she didn't want him to think she was disappointed with him.

'Great,' Dan managed a small smile.

'The boys have been brilliant,' Pippa continued.

'Dad, I drove the tractor,' boasted George.

'And nearly put it in the ditch,' said Nathan, poking him.

'That's my boys,' said Dan, ruffling their hair in an affectionate gesture Pippa hadn't seen for some time.

'We could do with some help tomorrow?' Pippa said questioningly.

Dan looked pensively across the fields where a golden sunset blazed through a gap in the hills.

'Shepherd's delight,' he said, 'I'll see what I can do.'

He gave a small smile, and Pippa laced her hands round his.

'One step at a time,' she murmured. 'One step at a time.'

Mel

FACEBOOK status EURODISNEY!!!
Jen17: Lucky you!
Ellie: Having fun?
Kaz: Have you had your photo taken with Mickey Mouse yet?
Mel: No. Goofy.
Kaz: That good?
Mel: Worse.
Jen17: Aw I love Eurodisney.
Mel: It would be ok without my family.
Ellie: Why?
Mel: They're the most embarrassing family in the world. Doh.
Jen17: Wish I was there.
Mel: Wish I wasn't
Kaz: Miss you babes.
Mel: Me too. Damn phone dying. Laters.

Teenage Kicks

Is there anything worse than being dragged on a family holiday when you're sixteen? I could have stayed at home. It would have been ok.

It's not like I was going to have wild parties or anything. Not feeling the way I do.

I'm worried. Really worried. No. TERRIFIED. What if I am pregnant? None of my clothes seem to fit. Even Dad mentioned he thinks I'm fat and he never notices anything.

I keep wearing baggy tops and hoping no one will notice. And I feel so sick. All the time.

But how can I be pregnant? I've come on since we've been away. I didn't think you had periods when you were pregnant. But maybe you do. I wish Best Mate was here. She knows stuff like that.

And right now, I really really wish I could talk to Mum about it. But I know she'll be really angry. And worse, disappointed. I don't think I could bear that.

And maybe I'm not pregnant anyway. Maybe I am just getting fat. I'll wait till I get home. Take another test. Tell her then. IF I have to.

August

Chapter Twenty-Two

'So, have you thought about Christmas yet?' Marianne groaned inwardly. It had admittedly taken three days for Mum to work her way up to the subject, but suddenly, here they were. She could have picked a better moment, thought Marianne disgruntledly. They'd actually had a lovely day. It being the first sunny day of the holiday so far, they'd spent the afternoon on the beach, where the twins had happily discovered the pleasures of sand and tipping buckets of water over their heads. And now as they were sitting on the prom eating fish and chips, watching the sun go down while avoiding the seagulls, Mum had to ruin it all.

Marianne and Gabriel exchanged glances.

'Well, the thing is, Mum,' said Marianne, 'we were thinking . . .'

'That you'll come for the whole fortnight like last year? How wonderful,' interjected Mum.

'Erm – no,' said Marianne. 'You see – well really – Christmas can be such a busy time of year for Gabriel, it's actually really difficult for us to get away for any length of time. And you can't really spare me for that long, can you?'

She dug Gabriel in the ribs, to make sure of his response.

'No, I can't,' said Gabriel, completely straight faced. 'It's going to be difficult.'

217

'But you managed all right last year,' said Mum looking puzzled.

'Ah, but he didn't,' said Marianne, seized with a creative spurt. 'He just put on a brave face for me. And it was really tough on Steven too. You know he's very attached to me, and he doesn't see much of his own mother . . .'

A low blow, but one that might hit home. Despite showing scant interest in Steven since her grandchildren had been born, in Marianne's mother's eyes he would remain forever more, 'that poor little boy with the wicked mother'.

'Oh,' Mum began to look a little doubtful – doubtful was definitely good. Marianne gave a discreet thumbs-up sign to Gabriel and he chipped in with, 'And we feel there are so many of us now, it's such a lot of work for you.'

'I don't mind,' began Mum.

'That's not what you said last Christmas,' put in Dad.

'Of course you don't mind,' said Marianne, 'and we really appreciate it, but we thought you deserved to put your feet up this year. Give you more time to play with the twins . . .'

'Now, that's a good idea,' said Dad, and Marianne could have hugged him.

'I suppose that would be nice,' said Mum. She looked so unsure, Marianne hugged her instead.

'We'd really love it if you and Dad came to us instead,' she finished triumphantly.

There was a pause until Marianne's mum tried to assimilate what had just happened.

'Well, I for one think that's an excellent idea,' said Dad. 'I hate carving turkey. I'd much rather someone else did it.'

'Wonderful,' said Gabriel. 'Jenny and Nigel, really we'd love to have you. We thought we'd have open house this year.'

218

'We did?' Marianne looked slightly aghast – that hadn't been part of the plan.

'We'll stay put, but anyone who wants to can come to us.'

'Oh that sounds wonderful,' said Marianne's mum, warming to the idea. By the time she got back home Marianne knew she would be claiming it as her own. 'Shall we let Matthew and Marcus know?'

'Er, yes, I suppose so,' said Marianne weakly. 'The more the merrier.'

Their farmhouse was large, but not *that* large. 'And I know Auntie Mags is going to be on her own this Christmas . . .'

Gabriel was in danger of exploding with laughter, so Marianne tactfully suggested it was time they went back to the caravan to put the twins to bed, while her parents stayed out for a drink.

'Oh my dear God, what have you done?' said Marianne, when they collapsed, giggling hysterically, into their room after the twins had settled down.

'I don't care,' said Gabriel. 'We've got what we wanted. Christmas at home. Our way. The whole bloody family can come for all I care.'

'*You* don't have to do the cooking,' said Marianne throwing a pillow at him.

'But I do carve a mean turkey,' said Gabriel, throwing her such a sexy look, she felt shivers up her spine. 'Now, I think we've thought about other people quite enough for one night. It's time to think about us.'

'If you insist, Mr North,' said Marianne, falling readily into his arms, 'if you *absolutely* insist.'

'Oh my word, would you look at the price of those shoes!' Cat stood in front of a smart shop on the Champs Elysées. She had no intention of buying anything here – her purse not even stretching to a single shoe – but Mel had never been to Paris, and Cat felt duty bound to make it part of her fashion education. Although it was depressing watching smart elegant Parisian women traipsing along in their high heels, while she felt footsore and weary in her flats.

Cat glanced at Mel, looking casually trendy in jeans and baggy Hollister t-shirt, and not for the first time wished she was young again. Mel had made a bit more effort with her appearance today, and didn't look as pale as she had done of late. She was a natural beauty. Cat felt a sudden stab of jealousy, followed immediately by guilt. What kind of a mother was jealous of her daughter? But sometimes, Cat couldn't help but feel a twinge of envy. Mel had it all before her; uni, boyfriends, career, family.

Oh stop, Cat said to herself, stop being such an old grump.

'They are amazing though, aren't they?' said Mel, eyeing up a pair of incredibly high heeled red Jimmy Choos in the window. 'I'd give anything for a pair.'

'Well, get good grades, a good degree, a good job, never have children and maybe one day you'll afford to buy them,' laughed Cat.

'Did you have to?' Mel snapped.

'Have to what?' Cat was bewildered by the sudden change of mood. So far today, she and Mel had had a fun girlie day of the sort they hadn't had in a long while.

'Go on about exams,' grumbled Mel. 'I've got my results when we get back.'

'Oh, those,' said Cat. 'Come on, hon. You've probably done better than you think. And if it *does* turn out to be bad news, there are always retakes. Nothing is impossible. And I know you'll find this hard to believe, but really at your age, you do have plenty of time.'

'Yeah, right,' Mel replied sarcastically.

'Mel, are you sure you're okay?' Once again, she felt Mel was excluding her somehow. Cat couldn't escape a nagging doubt that there was something she was missing.

'For the last time, Mum, nothing's wrong,' said Mel. 'Do stop going on about it. Now come on, where can we go next?'

'Do you fancy a trip to Montmartre?' said Cat. 'It's so romantic. It's one of my favourite spots in Paris. I'll even buy you a really expensive cup of coffee.'

'Sounds great,' said Mel, who having done both French and Art GCSE, had previously expressed an interest in visiting the area to see the artists in action.

An hour later, having ambled happily through the cobbled streets, Cat and Mel found a café where Cat ordered coffee and hot chocolate for Mel. As they sat down, one of the street artists approached them and asked if he could draw their picture.

Cat would normally have said no, but Mel was clearly thrilled to be asked.

'Oh please, Mummy, can we?' Suddenly Cat was transported back ten years ago when those words were enough to pierce the most hardened of parental hearts. She thought of all the times she and Mum had come away together when she was young, and how she treasured the photos they had taken together. An actual portrait would be a special reminder of a lovely day with her daughter.

'Oh go on then,' she said. 'You only live once.'

So they sat, leaning against one another in the afternoon sun, in the shadow of Sacré Coeur, while the artist captured their likeness in a few swift strokes. Just as Cat went to pay, the artist said, 'Et pour la maman,' and swiftly drew a miniature version of the pair of them. Cat tried to pay him extra, but he waved her away, saying, 'La belle maman, la belle fille. C'est charmante.'

Cat rolled up the large version and put it in her rucksack, before tucking the smaller version in her purse.

'What a hoot,' she said. 'See, I told you Montmartre was romantic.'

'That was amazing,' agreed Mel. 'I can't believe he did such a great picture of us.'

'Don't tell Dad how much it cost,' said Cat.

'Your secret's safe with me,' laughed Mel, and Cat sat back feeling relaxed and happy. For the first time in a long while, she felt as though she had her daughter back.

'So how are you finding things, Dan?' Mr Sheen the neurologist looked at him sympathetically and smiled comfortingly at Pippa.

Pippa loved coming in to see Mr Sheen. In the last few months since Dan's accident, he seemed to be the one person who she felt she could utterly rely on for common sense and good advice. He was so calm and unflappable. She felt like she was in a big soothing bath when in his presence. He seemed to wash all her troubles and fears away. And the good thing was Dan usually listened to what Mr Sheen had to say, something he had more or less given up doing with her when it came to his health.

Pippa looked at Dan expectantly. He always looked awkward in Mr Sheen's office. He was so tall and broad shouldered, the uncomfortable plastic NHS chairs were too small for him, and now he was physically better at least, he looked so out of place there.

Pippa had fully expected Dan to gloss over things; in previous visits, he'd always put a brave face and positive spin on any problems they were having. But to her surprise, he blurted out, 'Not that great actually. I mean, I'm fine. Of course I am. But every time I go on the field, I feel sick and dizzy. I get terrible flashbacks and feel rigid with terror.

It's pathetic I know. And it makes me so angry with myself. I'm no bloody use to anyone in this state.'

Oh God. Pippa had had no idea that he was feeling like that. She leant over and held his hand. To her relief, he didn't push her away.

'And when you get angry . . .?' Mr Sheen prompted gently.

'I lash out,' said Dan, looking ashamed. 'At Pippa. At the boys. Christ, even at Lucy. I can't explain it. It's just this . . . this *rage*. It comes out of nowhere. I can't seem to do anything about it. I don't even know what I'm raging about.'

'I see,' said Mr Sheen. 'And Pippa, what do you feel about it?'

'I'd agree with Dan,' Pippa said. 'I didn't know he was getting flashbacks, you didn't say,' she said, turning to Dan, 'but he does get terrible mood swings. He never used to have them, before the accident.'

'Well let me reassure you, that this is perfectly normal,' said Mr Sheen. 'Your brain has been through quite a trauma, and despite your brilliant progress over the last few months, you're not out of the woods yet.'

'And what about the anger I feel?' said Dan.

'It is possible that you've undergone something of a personality change, hence the rages.'

'You mean, this – this could be permanent?' Dan looked horrified.

'It could be,' said Mr Sheen, 'but it might not. I'm going to send you for another MRI scan, just to see if there are any substantive changes. And I think you should go back on the antidepressants you were taking in hospital. I'm also going to suggest you have some counselling for your PTSD.'

'What?' said Pippa. 'I thought only soldiers suffered from post-traumatic stress.'

'Anyone who's been through trauma can suffer from it,' said Mr Sheen. 'Dan here has had a very nasty and unnerving experience. In the first euphoria of him surviving the accident, it's possible none of you took on board the horror of what Dan's been through. I can prescribe some stronger sleeping tablets to help the nightmares, if you like.'

'Thanks,' said Dan. 'That would be great.'

'You've a long way to go, Dan, but you will get there in the end, especially with Pippa's help,' said Mr Sheen. 'Your support is going to be crucial, Pippa, but I'm sure you know that anyway.'

'Of course,' said Pippa, but her heart sank at the thought. Dan needed her, of course he did. But who was going to support *her*?

Chapter Twenty-Three

'So, big day, today,' Noel said cheerfully, as Mel came downstairs uncharacteristically early. Her face looked thin, but Noel was right, she was putting on weight. God, Cat had a sudden worrying thought – despite her denials, could Mel be pregnant? Although Cat knew she'd had her period recently. Maybe it was just too much sitting around since she hadn't been at school that was causing the weight gain. Now wasn't the time to ask; Mel seemed preoccupied and barely responded to Noel. She looked pale and peaky, and actually quite nervous.

'Do you want me to drive you into school?' offered Cat, thinking it might help.

'Nah, it's okay,' said Mel, 'I'm getting the bus with Karen.'

'Resits, resits,' called James from the lounge.

'Not helpful, James,' said Cat.

'What are resits?' asked Ruby.

'What Mel's going to be doing,' said James.

'Yes, but what are they?' asked Ruby.

'Taking exams again, because you've failed them, for retards like Mel who don't do any work,' said James.

'Don't say retard,' said Cat automatically. 'And don't be mean to your sister. That'll be you in two years' time. And from what I've seen so far of your efforts at school, you don't have anything to boast about, buster.'

As far as Cat could tell James would happily go to school and play football all day long, never seemed to have any homework, and managed to somehow produce good grades by the skin of his teeth. But even he would have to learn what hard work was once the GCSE courses started. The trouble was, the success of the latest cookbook had made him think exams weren't all that vital to success. Which was partly true, of course.

'I did work, actually,' said Mel, shooting James a filthy look, but otherwise being uncharacteristically quiet.

'Best of luck, sweetheart,' said Cat giving her a hug. 'Whatever happens, it doesn't matter, Dad and I will support you.'

'Thanks,' said Mel, looking faintly surprised.

'So you're going to be taking her down the dole office happily, are you?' said Noel, after she'd gone.

'I don't think it's *that* bad,' said Cat. 'But what was I meant to say? We know she could have worked harder, so there's no point getting upset about it now. We just need to focus on getting it right next time.'

'It would be better if she hasn't cocked it up in the first place,' said Noel.

'True,' said Cat. 'And maybe we're being unfair on her. Maybe she did more work than we give her credit for. But if she has cocked up, we just have to deal with it.'

The morning seemed to pass excruciatingly slowly. This was worse than waiting for her own exam results, Cat decided. To while away the time, and resist the urge to ring Mel up, she chivvied James into the kitchen, where they got to work on a batch of new recipes for *Jamie's Top Tips for Hungry Teens 2*, the latest project James had been signed up for. James was particularly keen to try out a new curry recipe he'd come up with.

Mel eventually mooched back in, looking just as

moody as when she went out. Great. How bad was it going to be?

'Well? The suspense is killing me,' said Cat. It was on the tip of her tongue to say, you could have *rung*.

'It's not great . . .' said Mel, 'but . . .'

'Okay,' said Cat with a heavy sigh, 'how many retakes?'

'None,' said Mel.

'None? What do you mean none?' said Cat. 'You must have to retake at least one.'

'Gee thanks, Mum,' said Mel. 'I don't need to do any retakes – because I passed them all.'

'What?' Cat let out a whoop of delight. 'Mel, that's fantastic. So what did you get?'

'Three A*s, Four As and Three Bs,' said Mel triumphantly. 'What do you think of that?'

'Bloody amazing is what I think of that,' said Cat, privately breathing a sigh of relief. 'Fantastic news.'

Thank goodness for that. Mel hadn't cocked up her exams. One thing less to worry about. Finally, she had a reason to be proud of her daughter.

Dan was sitting in the lounge with Lucy, who was reading a book, staring out at the view. The lounge looked onto their fields, with the hills in the background. On a day like today, it was glorious to behold. The heather cut dashes of pink and purple on the hills, contrasting with the bright yellow of the broom, and the green fronds of the bracken. And Dan seemed to have the ability to stare out at it for hours. Anything rather than work on his farm. Pippa would have loved to have sat down and stared with him, but she, unfortunately, didn't have that luxury.

Pippa had tried cajoling and pleading, but it was no good. Dan wouldn't be budged. Neither would he contemplate the counselling suggested by Mr Sheen, brushing off

Pippa's suggestion that it might actually be a good idea. The strain of trying to support him, the family and the farm was beginning to tell. She felt in a permanent state of exhaustion, and worse still, she was beginning to resent Dan's attitude. If it hadn't been for Lucy, Pippa might have felt like giving up. Somehow, Lucy always knew how to cheer Pippa up, with a beaming smile or making a sly joke about Dan's laziness, to which he responded with a rueful smile – the only one in the family who could still manage to bring him out of himself. Thankfully, Dan had for the most part retained his special bond with Lucy, and for that Pippa was immensely grateful.

Pippa would have given her right arm to sit down and be waited on, but that wasn't about to happen anytime soon. So she resisted the urge to make a sarcastic comment to Dan and instead started to clear up around him.

Dan made no move to help, or even acknowledge she was there. She sighed with frustration. What on earth could she do to change things? It was all very well for Mr Sheen, telling them both to be patient, but he wasn't living with it, and every day seemed to be getting worse, not better.

'Any chance of a cup of tea?' Dan suddenly said.

'What did your last slave die of?' snapped Pippa.

'There's no need to be so touchy,' said Dan. 'I only asked.'

'And I'm too busy at the moment,' said Pippa. 'It would be really nice if you made me a cup of tea for a change. Or cleared up the mess you've made in here. I know you're ill, Dan, but you could occasionally stir yourself out of that chair and do things for yourself!'

Time out you two! Lucy typed and then clapped her hands – a gesture Pippa used when the boys were fighting.

'Oh,' Dan looked stricken and she automatically felt guilty. 'I'm so sorry, Pippa. I hadn't realised. I'm being a sod again, aren't I?'

Yes, typed Lucy disapprovingly.

'You are a bit,' Pippa said weakly.

Give her a kiss, typed Lucy.

'Right,' said Dan, and pecked Pippa on the cheek. 'I'm sorry. You've been so fantastic. I don't know what I'd do without you. Here, why don't you sit down while I make the tea?'

Pippa was mollified. It was the sort of thing Dan would have automatically done in the past.

'Thanks,' she said, giving him a kiss on the cheek. 'I'm sorry. I'm turning into a bad-tempered old bag. I'm just so tired all the time.'

'No, I should be sorry,' said Dan. 'I don't mean to be a selfish git. Go on, put your feet up for five minutes, and I'll sort the tea.'

That's better, typed Lucy, smiling.

Pippa sank down into the sofa for five minutes and shut her eyes gratefully. In seconds, she was asleep.

'Oh for fuck's sake!'

Pippa came to with a start, as she heard something smash on the floor. Dan was standing in the doorway looking furiously at the contents of the tray he had been holding, which had spilt out all over the floor.

'I can't even manage to bring you a cup of tea,' said Dan. 'I'm worse than useless to you!'

'Dan,' said Pippa in dismay, but he'd stormed out in a fury.

So much for putting your feet up, typed Lucy, and reached out and squeezed her mum's hand.

Pippa smiled ruefully and picked up the mess. At least he'd tried. That was something, she supposed.

'Steven!' Marianne flung her arms around her stepson's neck as soon as he walked in through the door with

Gabriel. He looked tanned and healthy, and she could have sworn he'd grown a couple of inches since he'd been away.

The twins toddled towards him. 'Tevie, Tevie,' they said, holding out their arms. Marianne felt a swell of warmth as Steven bent down and hugged them. It was lovely how well he got on with them, when it could so easily have gone the other way. For a few minutes, they all laughed and hugged one another. It was wonderful to be back together again.

'How was your holiday?'

'It was brill!' said Steven. 'Mum and Darren took me scuba diving. And I went on a jet ski. And climbed a mountain, and swam with dolphins. It was awesome.'

'Sounds it,' laughed Marianne. 'Well it's lovely to have you back. The place hasn't been the same without you.'

'Hasn't it?' Steven smiled shyly at her. 'Only Mum kept saying you must be pleased to have more time with the twins.'

'Oh Steven,' said Gabriel. 'You know that's not true. We'd much rather have you with us all the time. It's been really quiet without you.'

'Do you mean that?'

'Of course we do,' said Marianne, giving him another hug. She looked anxiously at Gabriel. Why did Eve have to say these things? 'Now why don't you come in the kitchen and I'll make you my special ice cream sorbet.'

Marianne's ice cream sorbet was one she'd pinched from one of Cat's recipe books, but adapted to use whatever fruits from the garden came to hand. Knowing how much Steven liked it, today's version featured raspberries, which grew in their garden in abundance.

When Steven had exhausted telling them about the holiday, and shown them the thousand and one photos he'd taken of the same jellyfish, he retired upstairs, ostensibly to unpack, but more likely to be reunited with his Xbox.

'Isn't it great to have him back?' said Marianne. 'I can't stop grinning.'

'Me neither,' said Gabe. 'But honestly. I could bloody kill Eve sometimes. What on earth possessed her to say that to Steven?'

'Well, she was probably looking at things the way she would – to her it would probably be better to have Steven out of the way, if she was in our position,' said Marianne. 'But I agree. Not helpful. Not at all.'

'And with him starting school soon, as well,' said Gabriel. 'The last thing I want is Steven thinking we want to get rid of him.'

'He won't think that,' said Marianne. 'He knows how upset you are about him going.'

'I hope so,' said Gabriel, 'because I'd hate him to think we don't want him. It's the furthest thing from the truth.'

'Try not to worry about it,' said Marianne. 'It's just Eve stirring things up. Steven knows us better than that. I'm certain of it.'

Just then, Steven came downstairs with a pile of dirty clothes for the laundry. Having lived with Gabriel for so long on his own, he was well trained in domestic matters.

'Dad, Marianne, can we watch a DVD and have Domino's pizza tonight?' he said. 'To celebrate me coming home?'

'Of course we can,' said Gabriel, ruffling his hair. 'It's great to have you back.'

'See,' whispered Marianne, giving him a kiss. 'I told you so.'

Chapter Twenty-Four

'Come on, Dan,' Pippa put on her briskest, bossiest voice. It was one she usually employed at the end of boring committee meetings, or to get the children up when necessary. She hated having to use it on Dan. 'It's a lovely day and the kids are back at school next week. We're going to go out. Your dad and Gabe are covering the farm today.'

'Where?'

'Let's go to Ironbridge,' suggested Pippa. 'We haven't been there in ages.'

'Okay,' said Dan, to her surprise, not putting up any resistance. It felt like weeks since she'd got him out of the house. He always made excuses for why he needed to stay in.

It was a clear hot sunny day, and Pippa felt her spirits revive as she drove out of Hope Christmas and onto the road for Ironbridge. The boys were grumbling happily in the back of the car, more for show than anything else. She had the feeling that they were pleased to be going out as a normal family once again. Lucy, who loved being in cars, was giggling with pleasure. Pippa felt a stab of joy go through her. Despite all the difficulties of her life she wouldn't be without Lucy, whose boundless optimism was food for her soul. Other people never understood that, always feeling sorry for her, not understanding that Lucy was an integral part of the family. It helped that the boys were so good. They managed a complicated life with very little fuss and were fiercely protective of their little sister. But then again, Lucy bossed them about as much as she could. It was more of a two-way street than people realised.

Dan seemed quiet, but relatively calm, so Pippa had high hopes of having a really good day for once.

And they did. The boys always enjoyed changing their modern money for old as they entered the old-fashioned bank at the top of the High Street in the Victorian Town. As usual, they spent most of their newfound wealth on the mind-boggling array of sweets in the traditional sweetshop. Even Pippa, whose sweet tooth had definitely disappeared as she'd got older, was tempted by the gobstoppers, liquorice and lollipops on display.

They walked through the town visiting the bakery (where sticky buns were a necessary purchase) and the grocer's, and stopped for a pint in the pub, where an old-fashioned knees-up with slightly inappropriate songs was going on.

'Why is Fanny a funny name?' asked George innocently, when Nathan dissolved into fits.

'Time to go, I think,' said Pippa, and they carried on down the main street, where they watched an impromptu display of Shakespeare from a travelling theatre group and witnessed candles being made at the candle-makers. At the doctor's surgery the boys made Lucy laugh by trying out the antiquated wheelchair in the waiting room.

'I think Lucy's is better,' pronounced George. 'It's got super-duper powers.'

Pippa had to restrain them from racing down the hill with Lucy as they tried to see how fast her wheelchair could actually go.

Eventually they found themselves at the ironworks, where the boys were fascinated with the process of smelting iron into coke, and Dan's interest was also fired up. To Pippa's surprise, he grew quite animated when he started to tell them all about Abraham Darby III who'd built the world's first iron bridge, and explained how it all worked. They rounded off the day in a Tex-Mex place they found on the way home. Dan delighted Lucy by buying her a cowboy hat and putting on silly accents, while the boys stuffed themselves silly with burgers and chips, followed by the largest ice cream Pippa had ever seen.

All in all, it had turned out to be a really great day.

'Feels like old times,' she said, squeezing Dan's hand, as they watched the boys compete to see who could stuff the most ice cream down fastest.

'Yes, it does,' said Dan, squeezing her hand back. 'Thanks Pippa. I know this has been tough on you. You've been brilliant. Better than I deserve.'

'No worries,' said Pippa lightly. 'You'd have done the same for me.'

She sat back, feeling relaxed for a change. Maybe things were looking up at last. She really hoped so.

Marianne and Steven were at the school outfitters, in the most expensive department store in Shrewsbury. She'd left the twins with Jean, so she could fully concentrate on Steven. It was a big deal for him, and she didn't want to be distracted by having to feed the twins or change nappies at inopportune moments.

'Bloody hell,' she said. 'This kit list goes on forever. And it's so expensive. Do you really need it all?'

'We don't have to get it all if it's too much,' said Steven, looking worried.

'No it's fine, sweetie,' said Marianne. 'There's just such a lot of it.'

Steven not only needed PE kit, but a House PE kit, plus gowns for choir, an exorbitantly priced blazer, and trousers which were more expensive than the last pair of designer jeans she'd bought. Thank God for Marks and Spencer's and plain white shirts.

'I thought we'd find you here.'

To Marianne's surprise, Eve and Darren were bearing down on them.

'Sorry,' she was confused. 'What are you two doing here?'

'Well, I did say to Steven that we'd be buying his uniform. Didn't he tell you, silly boy?'

Steven looked so panic-stricken, Marianne immediately wanted to deck Eve and hug him.

'Sorry, Marianne, I forgot to tell you.'

'And I rang the farm and Gabriel's mother told me where to find you. Isn't that nice?' continued Eve, blithely oblivious to any awkwardness. The shop was old-fashioned with narrow aisles. There was barely room for the four of them to stand comfortably.

'Er, yes,' said Marianne faintly.

'And I'm sure that money must be tight for you two right now, what with the twins and everything. So we'll pay for this.'

'I don't think Gabriel would like that,' began Marianne, who was damned sure Gabriel would be furious. Money was tight it was true, but Gabriel had always prided himself on giving Steven everything he needed, and he wouldn't be about to stop now.

'It's fine,' said Marianne. 'We're nearly done here, anyway. Aren't we, Steven?'

She could see Steven squirming. Poor kid. He clearly hadn't known what to do. Even after all this time, Eve still didn't understand how much pressure she put on him.

'We can take over here,' said Eve, 'why don't you strike

out for some retail therapy of your own, while we help Steven sort it all out?'

'I can't do that,' said Marianne, trying to rein in her fury for Steven's sake. This was ridiculous; they were like two fishwives arguing over the same fish. She was so incensed on Gabriel's behalf, for once she was prepared to fight her corner. But then she saw the look on Steven's face. He looked mortified. This wasn't his fault, and he shouldn't have to watch his mum and step-mum slug out the family dynamics in front of him.

'Well, at least let me pay for half,' said Marianne feebly. 'Gabriel will be so cross if I don't.'

'And we could take you out for a lovely lunch,' said Eve. 'It's all right, Marianne, we'll drop him home later on.'

'Is that okay with you, Steven?' said Marianne. She knew it would be. Steven could never resist spending time with his mother, flaky as she was. His loyalty, much like that of his dad's, was one of his most endearing qualities.

'Well, okay,' said Marianne reluctantly. 'But I do mean it about the money. We want to pay for half.'

'Of course,' said Eve, who'd clearly got what she wanted – to do the uniform shop with Steven.

Marianne watched them go and felt bereft. Steven wasn't her son, it wasn't her place, but she felt like she was losing him already. In a week's time he would be away at school, and spending every other weekend with Eve and Darren. From being a constant presence in her life for the last four years, he was suddenly going to be a part-time one. She was only his step-mum, but she was going to miss him badly. And life for her, Gabe and the twins was going to be very very different.

Cat walked in from the shops, where she'd been stocking up for the new school year, into a family meltdown.

'It's my turn on the laptop!' Paige was screaming at the top of her voice at James. 'You've been on it for ages.'

'Just a sec,' James was delighting in teasing his sister by taking forever to respond. 'Nearly done.'

'You said that ages ago.'

'RUBY WILL YOU STOP BEING SUCH AN ANNOYING LITTLE RUNT!' Mel yelled from the top of the stairs. Cat had to concede she had a point, as Ruby was standing on her head singing the *Go Compare* tune tunelessly because she knew it annoyed her siblings.

'Christ, I leave the place for five minutes,' muttered Cat, as she picked her way through the detritus left behind by the children. She'd left just after breakfast, and no one had thought to clear the dishwasher. Someone (probably Ruby) had spilt Cheerios on the floor, and dirty bowls and cups were littered everywhere throughout the house, wherever a child had happened to be sitting at the time.

'Noel!' she called. No response. Noel was probably in the shed, oblivious to all the chaos, doing his carving. Since they'd come to live in Hope Christmas, Noel had started wood carving as a hobby. He found it therapeutic, which was great, and Cat was glad he had a hobby, particularly as the results were so spectacular. Cat was all for it, apart from the mess he made with the wood shavings. But still . . . She wished he wouldn't leave things in *quite* so much chaos.

She found him, as predicted, deeply involved in carving an owl.

'Did you get everything you wanted?' he said.

'Just about,' said Cat. 'I've bought new school shirts and socks and boring stuff like that.'

'Great,' said Noel absentmindedly, but she could tell he wasn't remotely interested. And why would he be? Why would anyone be? Buying shirts and socks and pants was just one more dreary task in among all the other dreary mundane tasks of the domestic side of life.

'That's looking good,' said Cat, 'but were you ever planning to sort the chaos out inside?'

'Oh,' said Noel, 'I told them all to clear up. Haven't they?'

Cat rolled her eyes.

'What do you think?' she said, before going back indoors to marshal the troops. Eventually, after much yelling and many slammed doors, the house was restored to some semblance of order.

'Sorry, Mummy,' said Mel. 'Shall I make lunch?'

'That would be lovely,' said Cat warily. Mel hadn't called her Mummy for ages.

'Do you want a cup of tea?'

'Yes, thanks,' said Cat, wondering what all this was in aid of. She peered at Mel, who looked nervous. Suddenly Cat's heart was in her mouth. She had an inkling that something was badly wrong, her anxiety increasing when Mel asked, 'Mum, can we have a chat?'

'Yes of course, sweetheart,' said Cat, now seriously worried. It was ages since Mel had wanted a chat about anything. 'Just give me a minute–'

The phone rang, and within seconds there was no room for chatting with anyone.

'Mrs Tinsall?'

'Yes,' said Cat.

'This is the sister on the stroke ward. I'm afraid your mother's taken a turn for the worse. You need to come right now.'

'Oh, of course,' Cat felt the shock of it wash over her. This was a phone call she'd been half expecting, and still it came as a surprise. She put the phone down in a daze. Her legs had gone to jelly, and her brain to mush, and she was shaking all over.

'What's the matter?' said Mel looking worried.

'It's Granny. She's got worse suddenly. I have to go.' Cat grabbed a bag and coat as if in a trance. 'Can you get Dad? We need to go to the hospital right now.'

In the end, the whole family came.

'I don't think you should be alone,' Noel had insisted, and the children refused to be left at home. Despite Louise's lack of memory and awareness of who they were, the children all loved her dearly.

'It's probably best if we're all together anyway,' Noel said.

Cat squeezed his arm, unable to say anything. He was right. This was a time for the family to be together.

The journey to the hospital was conducted mainly in silence, apart from Ruby worrying whether she'd left the catch on Hammy's cage.

'I'm sure he'll be fine,' said Cat for the millionth time as they approached the hospital. She was feeling faintly surreal. Worrying about a sodding hamster when her mother was so ill seemed odd, to say the least.

When they entered the ward, Cat's heart dropped to her boots. The sister, a bright breezy sort with kind eyes, who introduced herself as Kathleen, was coming towards them with a look of sympathy which could only mean one thing. No, no, please don't let it be. Cat felt panic rise inside her. This couldn't – mustn't – be happening. And yet somehow it was. She was vaguely aware that Noel was holding her hand tightly as the nurse ushered them into the family room, and sat them down and said, 'I'm so sorry, Mrs Tinsall, but your mother died a few minutes ago.'

'Right. Thank you.'

Cat felt weirdly spaced out and detached, as if all sense of feeling had left her. Mel gasped aloud, and Paige burst into tears. James looked awkward, as if he wanted to be somewhere else and Ruby clearly hadn't got it, as she said, 'Is Granny going to be okay?'

That was the catalyst. A torrent of feeling broke through Cat, and she struggled to hold back the tears as the children all hugged her fiercely.

'Do you want to see her?' asked Kathleen gently.

Cat nodded mutely.

'I'll stay here, with the kids,' said Noel. 'Give you some time.'

Cat kissed him and followed Kathleen to a side ward, where Louise's body lay on a bed. She looked cosy and comfortable in her best nightie, for all the world as if she had just fallen asleep. But her face was pale, and had a slightly waxen look. And her hands, when Cat touched them, were cold. She looked so frail and small.

'I'll leave you to it. Let me know if you need anything,' said Kathleen, drawing the door shut behind her.

Cat approached the bed, and felt her legs buckle as she sat down next to Louise and held her hand. She let out a howl of anguish. Her mother was dead. It was over. She was never going to see her again. Cat had never felt so alone or lost.

A while later, there was a tentative knock at the door, and Mel appeared.

'Dad wanted to see if you were okay,' she said.

'Oh, Mel,' said Cat, tears streaming down her face, as her daughter came over to hug her. She felt a strange sense of peace at the three of them being together, it felt so natural and right.

'Sorry,' Cat said, wiping away her tears. 'Are you okay? Wasn't there something you wanted to tell me?'

'No, Mum,' said Mel. 'It doesn't matter. It can wait.'

Mel

FACEBOOK status Worst day ever)-: RIP Mad Gran

Kaz: Oh no. Babe. So sorry.

Ellie: Sad news)-*:*

Jake: Feel bad for you babe.

Jen17: Oh Mel. That sucks.

Gary: Sorry for your loss.

Adam: Happened to me last Christmas. Crap isn't it?

Ellie: Anything we can do?

Mel: Thanks everyone.

Kaz: You ok?

Mel: Can't stop crying. BBM ME. PRIVATE CHAT NOW.

Teenage Kicks

Oh God. The worst thing ever has happened.
  No – two worst things. It's official. I'm pregnant. I found out yesterday. I don't know what to do.
  And then something even worse.
  Mad Gran died this morning.
  I can't take it in. She's always been there. I thought she'd go on forever.

When we were little we used to call her Granny Dreamboat because she was our favourite granny. Then she went all mad and forgetful and I was sad. But she was still there. And she listened to me. And it was like she understood. You know. I even told her about worrying I was pregnant.

It sounds awful, but it was easy talking to Mad Gran, she never remembered anything, but she never judged me either. I'm going to miss her.

I was going to tell Mum. But how can I now? She's so upset about Mad Gran and I know she's going to be upset about this too.

Why have I stuffed everything up?

September

Chapter Twenty-Five

'So, first day of big school,' said Gabriel with forced cheerfulness. Marianne could see what it was costing him. Steven, nervous in his new school uniform, two sizes too big for him, had barely eaten, despite Marianne's pleading.

'You'll be hungry by the end of the day,' she said.

Steven just shrugged and said, 'Can I go and get ready now?'

'Of course you can,' said Gabriel, and they watched him spring from the table like a race horse out of the stalls.

'He can't wait to leave, can he?' said Gabriel gloomily.

'Better that he's excited and positive,' said Marianne. 'Don't worry, I'm sure he'll be missing us before too long, and it's not as if he's on the other side of the planet.'

'It's far enough away,' said Gabriel with a sigh. 'God I'm going to miss him.'

'I know,' said Marianne, touching his arm, 'but we'll get used to him not being around. And he will enjoy it . . .'

'You're right,' said Gabriel. 'I just wish he could go there and still be with us.'

'Well, at least we'll have the twins to keep us on our toes for a few years yet,' smiled Marianne. 'Now come on, we need to get a move on.'

But even she felt a pang, as they watched Steven going round the house saying goodbye to things, and having one last run around the yard with Patch.

The car was jam-packed with Steven's things. Amazing that an eleven-year-old boy could have so much junk. He had two suitcases, a holdall carrying his football kit, several bags jammed with an indeterminable number of electronic toys, plus one or two books, and sweetly, his favourite teddy. Marianne hoped no one would tease him for including that. By the time they'd squeezed in with the twins and the dog, whom Steven had insisted should accompany them, there was very little room, and Gabriel grumped his way up the A49, claiming not to be able to see a thing in the background.

To both Marianne and Gabriel's surprise, Eve and Darren had opted not to come and see Steven on his first day, both of them having important business meetings to attend to. Eve had airily promised to make it up to Steven by taking him out to lunch at the weekend, and Marianne was hoping this wasn't a sign of what was to come. It would be infuriating if, after having made so much fuss to get Steven into the school, Eve didn't in the end make the effort to come and see him there.

Thanks to Steven's anxious insistence that they shouldn't be late, they arrived in plenty of time. They were greeted by friendly members of staff, in the imposing entrance to Middleminster's main hall.

'Hello, I'm Mr Andrews, Head of Boarding,' said a friendly young man, who was accompanied by his wife and baby. 'This is my wife, Lindy, and our baby, Sam. And you are?'

'Steven North,' said Steven shyly.

'Well, Steven, I'm sure you're going to have a great time here,' said Mr Andrews. 'Josh here will show you to your room and your mum and dad can get you settled in.'

They followed Josh, a lively fourteen-year-old who took them up a vast staircase and through sweeping corridors to the boarding area, chatting nineteen to the dozen, and pointing out points of interest such as the chapel and the haunted corridor where a grey lady apparently walked at night.

'You'll love it here, Steven,' he said as left them in Steven's room. 'When you've finished unpacking, you'll need to go back down to the main hall. In the meantime, if you need anything, just let me know.'

'Thanks,' said Steven, clearly in awe of the older boy, who seemed so at home in this alien world. He looked slightly overwhelmed, and Marianne wondered if he was having a little wobble.

'That sounds promising. I bet he's right and you'll have a lot of fun,' said Gabriel encouragingly. Marianne could have hugged him for being so enthusiastic.

'And it's a lot better than the boarding schools you read about in books,' said Marianne with a grin. The room which Steven was to share with three other boys, was cosy and modern, and felt warm and welcoming. Steven's roommates hadn't arrived yet, so they helped Steven unpack and then took him back to the hall where as instructed, all the new intake were being gathered together.

'Well, this is it,' said Gabriel, with a forced heartiness. 'We'll come and see you on Friday.'

'And if you need us for anything at all, you remember to ring, okay?' said Marianne.

'Okay,' said Steven. He was starting to look a little panicky as everyone else seemed to have found someone to chat to.

It was time they went. Gabriel ruffled his hair and then Steven threw his arms around his dad and gave him a big hug.

'What if I don't have any friends?' he whispered.

'Now you just listen to me,' said Gabriel firmly. 'It's not going to be the way it was. You're here with people who are like you and want to sing. You will be fine. Besides, think of all that sport you're going to play.'

He hugged his son tight, and stepped away. Marianne gave Steven a swift kiss, and was rewarded with a huge and deeply gratifying hug.

'It's a bit mad isn't it?' A small boy with freckles and curly red hair came sidling up to Steven. 'I don't know anyone else here, do you?'

'No,' said Steven.

'I'm Tommy Griffiths,' said the boy. 'Shall we stick together?'

'Yeah, that would be cool,' said Steven with evident relief.

'You see?' said Gabriel. 'You're going to have plenty of mates before long.'

'You will ring me tonight, won't you?' Steven said.

'Of course we will,' assured Gabriel, and then turned away. Marianne saw the tears and knew he was trying to prevent Steven from seeing them, so she said brightly, 'It will be Friday before you know it, and we'll be coming to get you.'

'Time to go,' said Gabriel, giving his son one last hug. Steven kissed the twins, and then after one last goodbye, they all walked back to the car.

'You okay?' said Marianne, reaching over to Gabriel as they got in the car.

'Just about,' said Gabriel. 'But it's going to take a lot of getting used to.'

It was already busy in the café when Pippa pushed the door open. She found Cat sitting in a corner staring blankly at a cup of coffee, seemingly oblivious to the chatter of young mums with buggies and pensioners around her. Poor, poor thing. Pippa had rung Cat as soon as she'd heard the bad news. She could only imagine how Cat was feeling.

246

She came over and gave Cat a big hug.

'How are you, hon?' she said. 'I'm so sorry.'

'Rubbish,' said Cat. 'I can't stop crying. I'm a totally soggy mess. Noel must be getting really fed up with me.'

'I'm sure he isn't,' said Pippa. She looked around the café. There seemed to be several women having coffee with their mums this morning. Maybe this had been a bad idea.

'Sorry,' she said. 'Is this too public for you? We could always go back to mine.'

'No it's okay,' said Cat with a wan smile. 'I can't stand being at home at the moment. I feel like all four walls are closing in on me. I'll probably go for a walk in the hills after this, just to clear my mind a bit.'

'I prescribe chocolate and cake,' said Pippa, 'and put your purse away. I'm paying.'

She went up to the counter, where Vera was serving a very yummy mummy the skinniest of skinny lattes.

'What can I do for you today, Pippa?' she said.

'Two hot chocolates, with whipped cream and two of those blueberry muffins, which I know first-hand are delicious,' said Pippa.

'Are you with Cat?' said Vera. 'I heard about her mum. What a rotten thing. I didn't like to say anything when she came in, but tell her Albert and me are thinking of her.'

'I will,' said Pippa. 'Thanks.'

She got back to the table, and passed the message on.

'Oh that's really sweet of her,' said Cat. 'Now I feel all teary again. It's so nice living here. In London no one in my local caff would have even known my name.'

She wiped the tears away.

'It's so stupid,' she said. 'It's not as though Mum was even like herself over the last few years. And yet I feel so bereft.'

'It's not stupid,' said Pippa. 'It's natural. This is your mum

247

we're talking about. Of course you're going to feel it. When's the funeral?'

'We're going to the undertaker's tomorrow, to sort out a date,' said Cat, looking sombre. 'I'm dreading it.'

'How are the kids?' Pippa asked. 'It must be hard on them, losing their gran.'

'It is,' said Cat. 'With James it's hard to tell; all I get is monosyllabic grunting. But Mel's taken it very badly, and. Paige is being terribly melodramatic and weeping at the drop of a hat. Ruby's cried a bit, but I'm not quite sure she gets it.'

'It's bound to take time,' said Pippa.

'I know,' said Cat. 'I'm sure we'll be fine in the end. And at least Mum isn't suffering anymore.'

She sat up straighter, clearly making an effort to pull herself together.

'Anyway, enough of my gloom and doom. How are things with you?'

Taking her cue from Cat, Pippa turned her conversation towards the campaign.

'Sorry,' said Cat looking stricken. 'I haven't been much help lately.'

'Don't even think about it,' said Pippa. 'I've been speaking a lot to a guy called Richard La Fontaine, who Michael Nicholas put me in touch with. He works for a private investment firm but says they have a strong ethical strand and they think the Sunshine Trust is a good fit for their business. He's looking into ways he can invest at the moment.'

'That's fantastic,' said Cat.

'It's a great help,' said Pippa, 'but it's only a start. So I've organised a demonstration for next week, and my petition's up to over 10,000 signatures.'

'That's good going,' said Cat. 'Well done.'

'It's a good distraction, frankly,' said Pippa. 'And you know me, I like to keep busy.'

'Things at home no better, then?' said Cat with sympathy.

While not going into too much detail, Pippa had let slip that things weren't that fabulous at the moment.

'Better, I think,' said Pippa cautiously. 'We had a great family day out the other week, and it felt like old times. The doctor did say it would take a long time. We just have to be patient. I'm pleased today, I've actually managed to get Dan out of the house, and he's helping out in the hay barn.'

'Well that's something,' said Cat. 'You must be exhausted, after all the stuff you've been through. I found it tiring looking after Mum, and she wasn't even living with me. I don't know how you do it, and stay so calm.'

'I'm not really sure I am that calm,' said Pippa. 'I keep worrying about what happens if the campaign fails and Lucy loses her respite. Or what if Dan never gets any better than this . . .'

'Shame you can't get away for a bit,' said Cat.

'Not a chance,' said Pippa.

'Time for another girlie night out instead?' said Cat. 'I know Marianne's feeling a bit low now Steven's started school.'

'Now that,' said Pippa, 'is an excellent idea.'

Cat and Noel returned from the funeral directors feeling a bit shell-shocked. There had been so many things to consider, from the type of coffin they wanted (Cat had been tempted to go for bright pink, a colour Louise had had a penchant for in her later years, but thought better of it), to the headstone, which couldn't actually be put up for six months until the earth settled on the grave. Who knew that?

They had at least sorted out the order of service, which

would be held at the local parish church, St Olave's, with the local vicar, Andrew Lawton, presiding. He hadn't known Louise, but had welcomed the Tinsalls into the parish when they'd first arrived in Hope Christmas, and Cat got on well with him. When he'd popped round to see them a couple of nights earlier, Cat had liked the fact that he hadn't tried to put her off with platitudes, understanding immediately how she was suffering.

'What about the eulogy?' he'd asked. 'Do you feel up to doing it?'

'I don't think I'm brave enough,' Cat admitted. 'I'll ask my Auntie Eileen.'

'That's okay, you know,' Andrew said. 'Most people find it's too much.'

She'd been grateful for his understanding, and knew he'd lead the service with empathy and kindness. It was one less thing to worry about, as she woke up every day to the realisation that her world had changed forever.

Cat felt punch drunk, as if everything was in perpetual slow motion. She would think to herself every morning, when she got up, and looked out of her window onto the serene Shropshire hills, *Mum's dead*, but it didn't feel real. She said the words, but they were meaningless. It just didn't seem possible that the world was still turning and Mum wasn't in it. She knew she was being illogical, but that was how she felt. Horrible as all the last few years had been, she still felt the loss of her mother immensely. And probably always would.

They walked back into the house, into yet another fight. Mel had been left in charge, but things seemed to be a tad out of control.

'Will you get your lazy butt off that PlayStation, and come and help me with tea,' Mel was shouting at James. 'You're the famous cook!'

James was doing his usual infuriating *I'm a teenage boy in a world of my own* routine and ignoring her completely. Paige in the meantime was cutting up bits of paper on the living room floor for no apparent purpose, while Ruby, despite specific instructions not to, had got the pet hamster out and was letting it run all over the floor.

'What the hell is going on?' said Noel as Ruby let out a shriek, 'Hammy's got lost under the sofa!' while Mel took the earphones from James' head and poured water over him.

'Mel!' said Cat. 'That is enough. Apologise to your brother.'

'He should apologise to me,' said Mel sulkily.

'I don't think so,' said Cat. 'You're not the one with a wet head.'

'You always take his side!' said Mel and stormed out of the room, slamming the door so loudly, the whole house shook.

'Great,' said Cat.

'Mummy, Mummy, what about Hammy?' Ruby was clinging to Cat hysterically.

'Well, let's just carefully move the sofa back,' said Cat. As she did so the hamster shot out and across the floor. In a swift and sudden movement, Noel dived down and grabbed it triumphantly, only to yelp out loud when Hammy decided to bite his finger.

'Little bugger,' said Noel, sucking his finger. 'Now where's he gone?'

'There,' said Cat, in time to see Hammy squeeze through a gap in the floorboards.

'That'll be where the mice are getting in, then,' said Noel.

Ruby was still wailing, 'But Hammy! How are we going to get him back?'

'I know,' said Cat, 'why don't we leave the cage here with his food, and he'll come back when he's hungry.'

That had worked in the past, so with any luck Hammy wouldn't be lost for too long. It was enough to calm Ruby down at least. She and Noel made Paige clear up the mess on the floor, and James, spotting the way the wind was going, quickly got up to get the dinner on. 'I really *was* going to do it,' he said.

'Yeah, and the rest,' said Cat. Time to go and tackle Mel. It was unlike her to be quite so rotten to James. Cat resolved to be kind. Mel was clearly so upset about Louise, there was no point giving her a hard time.

'Can I come in?' She knocked on the door.

'Sure.' Mel was lying staring up at the ceiling looking so utterly miserable, Cat's telling off dried up on her tongue.

'Oh sweetheart,' she said. 'Are you okay? Is this about Granny?'

'Sort of,' said Mel through tearstained cheeks, 'but there's something else.'

Cat suddenly had a very very bad feeling.

'I'm really really sorry, Mum,' she said, 'but I'm pregnant.'

Chapter Twenty-Six

'You're what?' Cat sat down on the bed with a thump. 'But I thought . . . you said . . . haven't you been having your periods?'

The shock reverberated through her. She'd known all along something was wrong, but had ignored her instincts.

Mel sat, twisting the duvet she was holding on to for grim death.

'Well, yes, that's why I didn't realise,' she said. 'I did a test and it was negative, and then I kept having sort of periods, so I thought . . .'

Her voice trailed off miserably, but Cat was so furious, she was beyond caring.

Pregnant, pregnant, *pregnant*. At sixteen. All the signs were there and she'd missed it. What kind of mother was she? Anger at herself impelled Cat to bombard Mel with questions. 'Who's the father? When's it due? Have you seen a doctor?' and eventually, 'Mel, after everything I've taught you, how could you be so bloody stupid!'

Cat's emotions were a jumbled-up mess. She wanted badly to give Mel a hug and say it would be all right, but she was so angry she couldn't bring herself to. All she could see was Mel's future going down the drain. It was so unnecessary and stupid, she could have wept.

'I knew you wouldn't understand!' flared Mel. 'You never

do. You never listen. You're not interested in me. Why should you care if I get pregnant?'

'Of course I care!' said Cat. 'But you're very young. You have your whole life ahead of you. This isn't what we wanted for you.'

'Well, sorry to be such a disappointment!'

'Mel, I didn't say that–' said Cat, but Mel was picking up a bag and angrily throwing things into it, whilst crying big gulping tears.

'What do you think you're doing?' said Cat.

'Going to Karen's,' said Mel. 'At least her mum listens to me.'

'What – you mean Karen's mum knew? That's just terrific!' said Cat. 'Does the whole of Hope Christmas know too?'

'No, no one bloody does!' said Mel. 'But at least Karen's mum understands, which is more than you do.'

'Mel . . .' said Cat again, but Mel had barged past her and down the stairs. Dully, Cat heard the familiar sound of the front door slamming. She sat wearily back on Mel's bed, staring at the familiar teen bedroom with its pictures of various bands that Mel had liked over the years, the shelves still full of fluffy animals that Mel refused to give up. Her fluffy slippers lay discarded by the door – she'd evidently forgotten to pack them as she'd been in such a hurry, and her dressing gown still hung on the door. For all her aspirations to be grown up, this still felt like the room of a little girl. Her little girl, who was in terrible trouble and she'd turned her away. Ashamed of herself and bitterly guilty, Cat burst into hot angry tears.

Which is how Noel found her, sometime later.

'What on earth's going on?' he said. 'Where's Mel? And why are you crying?'

'Oh Noel,' said Cat, bursting into tears, 'Mel's pregnant.'

Noel turned ashen.

'Fuck. Fuck,' he sat down next to Cat, clearly in as much of a state of shock as she was.

'Fuck,' he said again.

'Are you going to say anything else?' said Cat, giving him a weak grin.

'I'm just – I don't know what to say – stunned, I guess,' said Noel. 'How? Who? When?'

'I don't know,' said Cat. 'I didn't deal with it very well. Mel's gone to stay at Karen's. Everything's such a mess – and it's all my fault.'

Noel put his arm around her. 'Don't be daft,' he said. 'How do you figure that out?'

'I should have guessed – I think I did really,' said Cat, 'but then with Mum and everything . . . I feel like such a failure.'

'If you're a failure, then so am I,' said Noel. 'We both made her, you know.'

He elbowed her gently.

'Come on, Cat, don't be so hard on yourself. We need to face this together. She's probably upset and angry with herself as much as you.'

'But I was so horrible to her,' said Cat. 'I couldn't bring myself to be sympathetic. The poor kid must be feeling terrible. It's just that . . .'

Her voice trailed off again. Noel kissed her on the top of the head. 'You're thinking about the baby again aren't you?'

Despite her misery, Cat felt a surge of gratitude for Noel's immediate empathy. She was so glad she was married to him, that she wasn't facing any of this alone.

'It's been such a shit year,' she said.

'Ah well,' said Noel, giving her a hug, 'then things can only get better, can't they?'

* * *

255

'So how far gone is she?' said Pippa struggling with three drinks through the packed bar at the Hopesay Arms. Michael's band The Dark Angels were playing, so the place was busy with very cheerful bikers, which wasn't ideal, but when Cat had called an emergency girls' night out, Pippa and Marianne had both responded with alacrity.

'A night out will do us all good,' Pippa said. 'God knows, I need one.'

Organising the demo had taken up all of her time in the last week, and with Dan having retreated back into a surly silence, she guiltily felt she needed to get away from home for a bit.

'I don't even know,' said Cat. She looked washed-out and pale, not her usual smart self. 'How crap is that? The signs were all there; rebellion, sneaking off, moodiness, never knowing where she was or what she was doing. Christ, Marianne, she was even sick at your barbie. But when I asked her, she kept denying it. She's a bloody convincing liar, I can tell you that. And she seemed to be still having periods . . . so I thought I was imagining things. And what with Mum and everything . . .' her voice trailed off. 'I'm sorry, I couldn't sound more miserable if I tried. This is supposed to be a cheering ourselves up kind of evening, isn't it?'

'Don't be so hard on yourself,' said Marianne, with sympathy. 'You have had an awful lot to deal with.'

'Have you thought what you'll do?' said Pippa.

'No idea,' said Cat. 'Mel's taken herself off to her friend Karen's house and is refusing to come home. I have to say I'm not impressed with Karen's mum, who seems to think Mel has come from such a dysfunctional family, she needs taking under her wing. I don't even know if she's going to be at the funeral.'

'When is the funeral?' said Marianne. 'I'd like to come if I may.'

'Next Tuesday at two p.m., two days before Pippa's demo,' said Cat. 'Would you? That would be wonderful if you could.'

'I'd like to come too,' said Pippa. Cat had been such a support to her with the campaign, it was the least she could do.

'Oh stop it, girls, you're making me well up again,' said Cat.

'By the way,' said Pippa thoughtfully, 'is the Karen that Mel is friends with Karen Darling?'

'Yes, why, do you know her?'

Marianne rolled her eyes. 'Pippa grew up here, haven't you worked out by now that she knows everyone?'

'I know her mum, Gina,' said Pippa. 'She's a single mum who treats Karen like she's a grown-up. I'm surprised Karen's not the one who's pregnant. By all accounts Gina had her on the pill by the time she was thirteen.'

'Crikey. I've led a sheltered life,' said Cat.

'I'll have a word with her if you like,' said Pippa. 'Gina means well, and I'm sure the last thing she'd want is to keep Mel away from you. She's a huge softie, and probably thinks you've been cruel to her.'

'Mel probably thinks I *have* been cruel to her,' said Cat with a sigh. 'I suppose I could have been more understanding.'

'I don't think many mums would be that thrilled when their sixteen-year-old daughter announces she's pregnant,' said Marianne. 'I know I wouldn't be.'

'And yet, I probably would be,' said Pippa wistfully, 'because I know it's never going to happen.'

She shook herself. She didn't often allow herself to look ahead to Lucy's future. The day to day was so tiring she couldn't bear to project into the future, to think what that might bring. But one day, Lucy would be grown up. What would happen to her then?

'Sorry, that probably wasn't helpful.'

'Actually,' said Cat, 'it was. You've given me a different perspective. I can't say I'm thrilled Mel's pregnant, but I suppose in one way I'm lucky she can get pregnant. But still. It looks like I'm going to be a granny at forty-two. Help!'

'You will be the most glamorous granny in town,' said Marianne.

'I'll drink to that,' said Pippa.

'That's something to be proud of, I suppose,' said Cat.

Marianne was having a bad day. She was exhausted and slightly depressed by the double whammy that her job share partner had just handed her notice in, and Mrs Garratt wanted her in for an urgent meeting.

'Ah Marianne, thank you for popping in,' Mrs Garratt said, as Marianne came tentatively into her study. She was sitting behind her desk, looking officious and anything but supportive. 'As you know, Jane is leaving us. Which leaves me with something of a dilemma.'

Marianne had a feeling she knew what was coming next, but she played dumb.

'Which is?'

'I know in the past that we've been generous in allowing people such as yourself to have a part-time teaching role, but Jane leaving has opened up an opportunity. And I feel, and the governors feel, for the sake of the school and the children it would be better to have a full-time teacher in that role. We don't really want another part-timer teaching half the week.'

'So how does this affect me?' asked Marianne flatly. Other than making an urgent phone call to her union.

'Well of course, we don't want to lose a teacher of your calibre,' Mrs Garratt said smoothly, and Marianne had the absurd thought that if she opened her mouth she would show the desperately huge fangs of a wolf. 'So of course, you can keep working part-time for us, if you so wish. But I'm afraid I won't be able to offer you a class of your own after Christmas. You can help out in a floating capacity, parachuting in where you're needed. Unless, of course, you want to return to full-time teaching?'

The question hung between them, though Marianne knew that Mrs Garratt was damned sure she knew the response to that one.

'I'll have to think about it,' said Marianne.

It was all she could think to say, and all she could think about for the rest of the day. But as she packed up for the day she felt overwhelmed with misery. She loved her job; loved having her own class. The thought of losing that wasn't at all appealing. But she loved the twins too, and she was struggling as it was to juggle the competing demands of home and work. Maybe it was time to throw in the towel and call it a day.

'You should follow your heart.'

'I'm sorry?' Marianne was so engrossed in her thoughts she'd run straight into Michael Nicholas, looking as smoulderingly gorgeous as ever. What on earth was he doing here?

'I've come for a governors meeting,' he said, as if reading her mind. 'I think you're a great teacher, and you'll be missed if you go, but you need to do what's right for you and your family. And only you can know that.'

'Oh, er, well, thanks,' said Marianne, wondering how he knew exactly what she was thinking.

'Call it my special gift,' he said, winking at her, as he opened the door to let her out. 'I'm sure you'll make the right decision.'

'I hope you're right,' she said, and set off for home.

She was so late back, Gabriel was in earlier than her for once, and she found him playing with the twins in the lounge. They were giggling their heads off while he tickled them, letting them jump all over him.

'How did it go?' he said.

Marianne pulled a face.

'How would you feel about me giving up work for a bit?' she said. 'I think that's the only proper choice I've got.'

The twins came toddling over to her, to grab her legs, saying 'Mama, Mama!' which was most gratifying as they still hadn't progressed to 'Dada!' and were stubbornly pursuing their own private language. Marianne would have worried about it, had it not been clear that their hearing was perfectly good, and had she not had a very sensible and sane health visitor, who told her it was quite common for twins not to speak much before they were two. 'They've got each other,' she'd said, 'why would they want to talk to anyone else?'

'Why indeed?' laughed Marianne, feeling much better that she hadn't produced two 'backward' babies, as her mother had so sweetly put it.

'Oh, well, whatever you want to do,' said Gabriel vaguely.

'Earth to Gabe,' said Marianne. 'I'm talking about giving up work here. Don't you have a stronger opinion than that?'

'Sorry,' said Gabriel, 'I've got a lot on my mind. Seriously. I don't mind what you do, so long as it's what you want.'

'I think I want to take a break,' said Marianne. 'That bloody head is making it so difficult for me to–'

Gabriel was looking distracted again.

'What's up?' said Marianne, as she knelt down and scooped the twins in her arms.

'Why do you think something's up?' said Gabriel.

'Oh, the look on your face, the fact that you are trying really hard to be cheerful, when clearly you're not, the fact that you're paying no notice to a word I'm saying,' said Marianne. 'Go on, what's Eve done now?'

'Why did you think this has to be about Eve?' said Gabriel.

'Doh,' said Marianne. 'Because she is the only person who gets under your skin like this. Come on, help me get these two monkeys to bed, and we can talk about it then.'

'So, go on then, what's the problem?' said Marianne, as she leant over the bath and tested the water with her elbow. The twins were running around in nappies on the landing. Luckily they hadn't worked out how to undo the stair gate yet, but it would be a job catching them to get them into the bath.

'It's this weekend,' said Gabriel. 'It seems that Eve has promised to take Steven to some show in London, and she forgot that it was our weekend to have him.'

'Oh,' said Marianne. 'Well, can we swap weekends?'

'Apparently not,' said Gabriel. 'Darren booked tickets for the football the following weekend.'

'But I thought you were taking him to that match?' said Marianne.

'Me too,' said Gabriel.

'What does Steven say?' said Marianne.

'He was really apologetic when I spoke to him tonight,' said Gabriel, 'I guess he's in an awkward position.'

'He certainly is,' said Marianne. 'Come on, it's only two weekends. We just have to make sure it doesn't happen again.'

'That might be harder than we think,' said Gabriel with a sigh. 'Eve is a law unto herself, you know that.'

'I know,' said Marianne. 'But we have rights too, and so does Steven. It will be okay, you'll see.'

She gave him a kiss and then went to catch the twins, who despite their protests, loved going in the bath. It was fun bathing them with Gabriel, as he didn't often have the opportunity to help out, and he'd cheered up considerably by the time the twins were in bed. Until the phone rang and Steven was in tears, because he felt he'd let his dad down. Listening to Gabriel speaking to him soothingly to calm him down, reassuring him that it wasn't his fault, and it didn't matter, Marianne felt she had never loved him more. But she was also anxious. Eve was stirring things up again, and that could only be bad news.

Chapter Twenty-Seven

The funeral cars deposited the Tinsalls outside Hope Christmas church. They were all there, even Mel, who, after Noel had gone round and pleaded with her, had sulkily returned home the previous day. Cat and Mel had been avoiding each other ever since, Cat being unwilling to start another argument, but at least she was here.

Andrew Lawton gave Cat an encouraging smile as he greeted the family at the church door. Then they stood in line behind the coffin, with Auntie Eileen and Angela bringing up the rear. It was a cold miserable day, but the threatened rain had held off for now. As the organ music started, Cat stiffened her spine, and followed the coffin into the church in a daze.

Gratifyingly, the church was packed. Many of Louise's friends from London had faithfully trekked all the way up on the train, and Cat's own friends – some from her school days who remembered sitting round Louise's kitchen table in their youth and several who didn't even know Mum but had come to support her. She was touched and startled to see Len, her moody director, in the congregation, sitting next to Anna, her agent. Susan Challoner was sitting with a slightly confused looking Alfie, and even Michael Nicholas had turned up.

The family filed in and sat down in the front pew. Cat

found herself wanting to look anywhere but at Mum's coffin, with its simple wreath of lilies from her and Noel, lilies having been Louise's favourite flower, and the larger wreath of yellow roses and carnations picked out by the children, because Ruby said it should be cheerful. Cat didn't want to look at the coffin. Didn't want to admit this was actually happening.

The service was a blur. She was vaguely aware of Auntie Eileen recalling the fun times they'd had before Mum got ill, and her stoicism when she realised what was happening to her. Andrew Lawton gave a moving tribute and talked of the strength both she and Louise had displayed when her illness took hold for good. Strength? Cat didn't think she'd been strong – she had just about held it together for the years when Louise was in the home. There was nothing else she could have done.

It was only at the end, when they sang *Jerusalem,* Mum's favourite hymn, that Cat felt her composure was slipping. She looked across at Paige, who was weeping hysterically in Auntie Eileen's arms. Noel squeezed her hand and she could feel his emotion – he had been very fond of his mother-in-law. Noel's mother Angela was hugging Ruby hard, and James wiped a surreptitious tear away from his eye. But it was Mel who defeated her. Tears streamed down her face, as she sobbed her heart out. Without pausing to think how she'd react, Cat pulled her daughter into her arms, and they both wept together.

'It's okay, sweetheart,' she said, 'everything will be okay.' It seemed like the right thing to say. Cat only wished she could believe it were true.

'God, Tom Brooker's actually done us proud,' said Marianne, as she stood on the steps of the Sunshine Trust posing for a group photo with Cat, Pippa and all the mums taking part in the demo, plus lots of the kids who attended the centre.

Not only were Shropshire TV there, thanks to Tom Brooker's impassioned piece in *The Times* the previous weekend, the story had made the nationals. As soon as the photos were over, Pippa and the woman who ran the Sunshine Trust were being besieged by an army of TV and print reporters alike. The story was much bigger than they could have imagined.

'And even Len Franklin's interested,' said Cat. 'Turns out, he's really good mates with Antoine Lavière.' (A famous award-winning chef, well known for his passionate support of children's charities.) 'Thanks to Len, Antoine's going to give us a donation and is offering to compere our charity auction.'

'Wow, that's brilliant,' said Marianne. 'I feel rather pathetic; I've contributed bugger all to this.'

'Don't be daft,' said Cat. 'You've done loads, plus you give Pippa regular support, and you're here aren't you? Demos wouldn't be any good without demonstrators.'

Pippa had started up a chant of 'What do we want? Respite care! When do we want it? Now!' for the benefit of the TV cameras, so Marianne and Cat joined in enthusiastically.

'I hope this makes a difference,' said Marianne. 'I can't see how Pippa will manage if it doesn't.'

'Me too,' said Cat. 'At least we've got people's interest. That's a good start.'

The demo was beginning to die down a bit, and the twins were beginning to play up, so Marianne dashed over to Pippa. 'Do you mind if I head off now? The twins are getting a bit grumpy.'

'No worries,' said Pippa, giving her a hug. 'Thanks so much for coming.'

Marianne put the twins in the car and got in and drove

home. As she pulled up into the farmyard, she caught a glimpse of someone in the lane.

'Oh hi, Mel,' she said, recognising Cat's daughter.

Mel's face was blotchy and red as if she'd been crying.

'Are you okay?'

'I'm fine,' said Mel. But she so patently wasn't, Marianne said, 'You look like you could do with a cup of tea and a chat.'

Mel looked as if she was going to say no, and then her resolve crumbled.

'Come on and sit down,' said Marianne, taking her into the kitchen. 'Can I get you a cup of tea?'

'Could I have hot chocolate?'

Mel looked so young and vulnerable. Too young to be a mum. Poor poor thing.

'You do know your mother is worried sick about you, don't you?' Marianne said carefully, as she sat down at the table.

Cat had told her only that morning that although Mel had come home for the funeral, she was still determinedly camping out at Karen's.

'I'm at my wit's end,' Cat had said. 'I thought yesterday I'd made a breakthrough, but she went straight back to Karen's afterwards. I just don't know what to do.'

'No she's not, she doesn't care,' said Mel.

'Of course she cares,' said Marianne. 'She's your mum. It's her job. She's just had a lot on her plate, and no mum wants her teenage daughter to be pregnant.'

'Well it's not like I planned it,' said Mel defiantly.

'So go on, then. Spill the beans. What happened?' said Marianne.

It was like a floodgate opening. Mel poured the whole story out, how Andy had chased after her, how she'd been frightened of losing him, and now, 'He doesn't want to know,' she wailed. 'I've just been to see him, and he keeps saying he doesn't even know if the baby is his. How can he say that?'

'Because he's a bastard?' said Marianne.

'I thought he loved me,' wailed Mel.

'And you wouldn't be the first,' said Marianne. 'Have you thought about not having it?'

'It's too late for that,' said Mel. 'Karen's mum took me to the doctor's last week and I'm nearly twenty weeks. I couldn't get rid of it now. And I'm not sure I want to anyway.'

'Do your parents know any of this?' said Marianne.

'No, I haven't told them,' said Mel. 'I don't think they'd understand. And I'm worried what Dad might do to Andy.'

'Oh come on, Mel, this isn't the dark ages,' laughed Marianne. 'I really think you should tell them what you've told me. They're your parents and they want to help, even if it doesn't seem like it right now. You should go home. It's not fair on your mum or your dad.'

'I'll think about it,' said Mel.

'And Mel,' Marianne added, 'it's not right. You shouldn't be seeing the doctor with Karen's mum. This may not be what your mum wants, but I'm damn sure she'd want to take you to the doctor herself.'

Pippa got in from the demonstration, feeling a huge sense of satisfaction. She had begun to feel a little bit of hope, that maybe they would actually do this. Maybe they *could* save the respite services. She'd deliberately left the boys at home with Dan. They did so much for their little sister on a daily basis, Pippa felt they needed a break. She walked into the lounge where she expected to find them where she'd left them, watching the cricket, but they weren't there.

'Hullo, anyone in?' She wheeled Lucy into the lounge

and helped her into her special chair. 'Things are looking up, Luce. We might just be able to keep the Sunshine Trust respite services after all.'

Lucy clicked her approval.

That's good, she typed. I'd hate to have to spend every weekend here.

Pippa laughed. Lucy's sense of humour was what kept her going some days.

The house was deadly quiet, and Pippa felt a sudden sense of foreboding. Where was everyone? She went upstairs calling for the boys, and Dan, to no avail. She went back into the lounge, and turned on the telly for Lucy.

'I'm just popping outside for a minute, sweetie,' she said. Maybe Dan had taken the boys out to play footie or something. Although he had barely kicked a ball since his accident, so it wasn't terribly likely. Pippa went out into the courtyard. The Land Rover was still there. No sign of anyone. Odd. She walked across the courtyard, and wandered towards the barn at the far end, shouting the boys' names. Barney, their dog, ran out barking wildly. He seemed determined to show her something, so she followed him to the barn door. She opened the door, and peered into the gloom.

'Mum, is that you?' Nathan peered over the hayloft. He looked pale and frightened, his dark hair even more messed up than usual. George followed quickly behind, covered in straw, and they flew down the ladder and fell into her arms, talking nineteen to the dozen.

'Dad went ballistic because the TV remote didn't work, then he told Nate off when he tried to help. So I said that wasn't fair, and then he really shouted at us,' said George.

'It was horrible,' said Nathan, 'he told us to get out or else. I thought he was going to hit us, so we ran off and hid.'

'Is Dad going to be okay?' said George, and she could see the tear streaks he'd tried to wipe away from his face. 'He really frightened me.'

'Oh boys,' said Pippa, holding them close and kissing them hard. 'I don't know. I just don't know.' She could have lied she supposed, but what was the point? The boys could see things were as bad as they could possibly be. Lying to them would mean they couldn't trust her, and they needed to be able to right now. She crouched down and looked them both in the eyes. 'The thing is, Daddy's really not well. You must understand this isn't his fault, none of it. He doesn't want to frighten you, he just can't help it.'

She kissed and hugged them both again.

'Now go inside, and get yourselves and Lucy ice cream. I'm going to find Dad and sort this out once and for all.'

It didn't take long to find Dan, because she knew exactly where he'd be. He was sitting at the edge of their meadow, staring at the stream. It was the place they'd picnicked all of their married lives, the place where, fifteen years ago, he'd asked her to marry him. And she'd said yes, her knight in shining armour. The one person she'd known she could always rely on. And now she could rely on him no longer.

'Hi,' she said.

'Hi,' Dan turned his face away from her. She went and sat down next to him.

'You know we can't go on like this, don't you?' she said, reaching over to touch his hand.

'I know,' Dan croaked, turning to face her, his face wet with tears.

'You have to understand,' said Pippa. 'The children come first. They have to.'

'I know,' said Dan again.

'Today . . .'

'I could have hurt the boys,' whispered Dan. 'I didn't

269

want to, but I could have. It's this black rage. It comes from nowhere and I can't control it.'

'You need help,' said Pippa. 'And I can't give you that help and manage the children, especially Lucy.'

'Oh Pippa, what's happened to us?' said Dan.

'I don't know,' said Pippa sadly, and held his hands. For the first time, she couldn't bring herself to say it.

'We're not going to get through this, are we?' Dan looked exhausted and wrung out.

'I don't know. . .' replied Pippa helplessly.

'I'll move back in with Mum and Dad,' said Dan.

'That seems best,' said Pippa. She pulled him close to her, wanting him to stay, knowing she had to let him go, feeling her heart being wrenched in two.

It wasn't going to get better. Not this time. Not ever.

Mel

FACEBOOK status So fucked
Jake: So it's true then?
Jen17: ??
Ellie: You ok?
Nick: Slag
Kaz: Oh so grown up Nick. Leave her alone
Mel: It's okay Kaz. Piss off Nick. You know fuck all about it.
Nick: Oh get over yourself.
Mel: You get over yourself.
Nick: You're still a fat pregnant slag.
Mel: OK, blocking you.
Kaz: You okay?
Mel: Not really.

Teenage Kicks

So now it's official. EVERYONE knows. I've had a lot of crap on FB and BBM, but they can go screw themselves. I know I'm not a slag. Even if the Boy thinks I am. It was only ever him. I know that even if no one else does.

Best Mate's been brilliant. She's letting me crash at hers. I can't face being home.

271

Dad came round and begged me to come back for Mad Gran's funeral. He cried. Said they both missed me.

So I went and it was sad, and I cried and cried. And it was okay with Mum for a bit. But then I remembered the stuff she'd said, so I knew I couldn't stay there.

So now I'm in limbo. At Best Mate's house. Going to school, studying for AS levels, like they're going to matter.

Half the year aren't talking to me. The teachers keep on at me to go to counselling, but I don't go.

And the Boy is badmouthing me. Telling everyone that I've been putting it out there. That the baby's not his. Why is he being like this? I thought he loved me.

I went to see him and he laughed at me. I guess it really is over.

I went to see one of Mum's mates after. She told me I should go home.

Maybe I should.

I feel so scared and alone.

I just don't know what to do.

Part Four

A Merry Little Christmas

October

Chapter Twenty-Eight

Pippa was giving another interview on phone to the papers, this time talking about the effects that government spending cuts were having on local disability services. There were so many people suffering, so many people worse off than her. Knowing she was helping them was the only way she kept going. She blinked back tears as the interview ended and she put the phone down and stared at the kitchen, once the heart and soul of her home. She and Dan had spent so much time in this kitchen together, sharing tea and sympathy, love and laughter. The kitchen hadn't changed: still with the familiar range, the cosiness, the knick-knacks on the shelves. But it all seemed so empty without Dan.

Pippa had got used to him being around all the time since his accident, and even before that he'd been in and out all day long. Now she barely saw him. At least he was back working on the farm, which was something, but he did his best to avoid her, spending more time with Gabriel and Marianne than he did at home. She knew from Dan's mum that he had finally started therapy, and she was happy to drop the children with him, knowing his mum was there to supervise.

The boys had been reluctant to go at first, but they missed their dad too, and seeing him cry and break down in front of them had persuaded them to give him another chance.

It broke Pippa's heart that it had come to this; her loving, caring Dan, and his own children were afraid of him. Their once-happy family was broken and fractured. She didn't know if it would ever be mended again.

This was no good.

'Pull yourself together, Pippa,' she said. 'Focus.'

She started to look at the seating arrangements for the charity ball. Cat had been able to persuade Antoine Lavière to be the compere for the charity auction, and had also been generous with prizes, giving away signed copies of her latest book and DVD, and offering another prize of a day on set with her for her next series, whatever that was.

Marianne, in the meantime, had reluctantly joined forces with Diana Carew and they'd both been busy working on all the local businesses and had come up with two weekend retreats at a couple of local hotels, a spa day for two and a year's free membership at a local gym. Not only that, she'd managed to persuade Eve's rich boyfriend Darren to use some of the charity funds in his office to pay for the champagne reception.

In the blind charity auction, Vera and Albert had managed to get hold of a signed copy of the England rugby team's photo and a signed Team GB flag for sporting fans, along with several bottles of very decent and old malt whisky from the firm Albert's brother worked in, a day racing at Silverstone, and some rather lovely prints from a local artist, Ivy Theakston. They were apparently still 'working on a few more sources', as Vera earnestly put it. The tables had nearly all sold now and it was beginning to look like a fun evening. As promised, Michael Nicholas' band, The Dark Angels, were going to play on the night. Pippa had enjoyed hearing them play at the Hopesay Arms. They'd certainly make the evening go with a swing.

And she'd had a couple of really useful meetings with

Richard La Fontaine, the businessman Michael had introduced her to, who was friendly and interested and seemed genuinely willing to help. She was hoping that he could persuade his company to look at seriously investing in the Sunshine Trust, as it was something he felt very strongly about.

'I have a special needs daughter too,' he had told her on their first meeting at Michael's bar, where he'd insisted on paying for lunch. 'I know how tough it is.'

He hadn't volunteered any more information, but she'd felt an immediate connection with him, and found herself looking forward to their next meeting. He was like a breath of fresh air, breathing new life into her world, and she found herself momentarily fantasising about him. She felt guilty for thinking about another man, with Dan away from home, but it was nice to fantasise about living a different kind of existence, with someone else, and without the daily drudgery and hardship of her actual life. A tear spilt down her cheek. How could she think like that? She scolded herself. She loved Lucy and the boys. She still loved Dan. She would always love Dan. But sometimes she wished beyond anything for her life to be very different.

'Hey Mazza!' Marianne laughed as she opened the door and her irrepressible younger brother bounced in, flinging his arms around her. He was the only person who had ever called her that. En route with Marcus to the Lake District, he'd suddenly called up and said they were passing and were she and Gabriel free? As it happened, it was a weekend that Steven was spending with Eve and Gabriel was busy tupping the ewes so he wasn't going to be around much. Marianne had seen precious little of her brother since coming up to Hope Christmas four years ago, so she was delighted to see him now.

'Come on in,' she said. 'Look Daisy, Harry; here are Uncle Matt and Uncle Marcus come to see us. And, when you're older I'll explain why you have two uncles.'

'Oi, less of that, sis,' said Matt, playfully punching her.

'Sorry, couldn't resist,' said Marianne.

The twins, who had just turned two, were still quite shy of strangers, so peered at their two strange uncles from between their mother's legs.

'Crikey, they've grown,' said Matt.

'Yeah, well, if you will only deign to visit once in a blue moon,' said Marianne, 'it's not like I haven't asked you before.'

'You know I'm busy,' pleaded her brother. 'Anyway, you're not much better. You've not been to London since Christmas.'

'True,' said Marianne, 'but you could have come on holiday with us. We did invite you.'

'And have Mum asking me every five minutes when I'm getting married? Yeah, right.'

'You could always tell her you *are* getting married,' said Marianne mischievously.

'Don't,' shuddered Matt. 'We've just been through all that with Marcus' family. I'm not sure I could *ever* cope with telling Mum.'

Marianne laughed. 'So you're not going to join us for Christmas then? We're having open house if you're interested.'

'Hmm, maybe we'll have a rain check on that,' said Matt. Although Marcus said wistfully, 'I've always fancied Christmas in the country. Does it ever snow?'

'Quite often,' said Marianne. 'And it is lovely up here. There's a nativity on Christmas Eve at the chapel in the local manor house, organised by my good self, and there's a tree in the square and carols at midnight. I love it.'

'It sounds like heaven,' said Marcus. 'You know we *could*

always stay in a local hotel, so that things don't get awkward. What do you think, Matt?'

'Oh go on,' said Marianne, 'we'd love to have you.'

'Okay,' said Matt, after Marcus had threatened to leave him if they didn't come, 'you're on.'

'Brill,' said Marianne. 'You won't regret it.'

'Regret what?' said Gabriel, who'd just come in from work.

'Christmas here,' said Marianne. 'Matt and Marcus are going to come too, isn't that nice?'

'Oh, right,' said Gabriel. 'So, hang on, that's you, me, your mum and dad, the twins, Steven, my mum and dad, and now these two. That's eleven. And wasn't your Auntie Mags coming too? Do you think you can cope with that many?'

'Auntie Mags had other arrangements, thankfully,' said Marianne, 'but really I don't mind how many people come. It's our first proper Christmas in our family home, and I want it to be perfect.'

Cat was also deeply into Christmas, but not planning her own. She was caught up in a whirl of PR to publicise both the book and TV programme of *Cat's Country Christmas*, now available at all good bookshops. The online recipes she'd released for Christmas cake and pudding were going down a storm apparently. There had been so much buzz about this book, as well as more interest in James, who'd finally produced (or rather Cat had produced for him) *Top Tips for Hungry Teens 2*, that she was run off her feet writing articles, doing blog posts, and even being whisked down to London for the odd interview. It was so manic, Cat had had relatively little time to think about anything; not about Mum, or Mel, or the baby she herself had lost, which she supposed was a good thing. If she thought too much about things, Cat reflected, she might just snap in two.

Everyone else seemed to be dealing with Mel's pregnancy so much better than her. Noel, to her amazement, apart from showing a very natural tendency to want to kill the still as-yet-unnamed dad, seemed to be taking it in his stride.

'The deed's done now,' he pointed out (far too reasonably for Cat), 'there's no point crying over spilt milk, we need to think about what happens next.'

Given that Mel had refused point blank to discuss an abortion, and it was probably too late anyway, Cat knew Noel was right, but she felt so churned up about it all she couldn't bring herself to agree with him, and instead buried her head in the sand, wishing this was happening to some other family. She was even ignoring the inevitable tittle tattle in the red tops about her failings as a mother.

James in the meantime was disregarding the whole thing, clearly mortified that his sister was 'up the duff' as he so elegantly put it, while Paige was already fantasising about being an auntie (not the response Cat was hoping for), and Ruby insisted on asking if Mel was going to dump the baby in the dustbin, like in the Jacqueline Wilson book.

The only person who seemed as upset about the whole thing as Cat was, was Noel's mum, Angela. Although that didn't help much. They'd moved a long way in the last few years from Angela being Granny Nightmare, but she was bristling with a disapproval that she'd clearly been holding back at the funeral. Angela was very correct, and would never dream of airing the family's dirty laundry in public, but she had been more forthright on the phone to Noel and he'd put the phone down on her several times.

'Mum, will you just leave it!' Noel had said sharply at the end of their last conversation. 'Mel's our daughter and we're still proud of her, whatever happens.'

Cat felt slightly ashamed that Noel was prepared to stand

up for Mel, and she wasn't. She wished she could support her daughter more, but she just couldn't.

The trouble was, and she had difficulty admitting this to herself, a nasty weaselly, selfish part of her was jealous of Mel. Jealous of her youth, beauty, her future (now royally screwed up) and yes, her fertility. Logically, Cat knew that there would be no more babies for her and Noel. They were too old, she hadn't the energy, and it wouldn't be right. And she'd accepted it, really she had, but seeing her daughter's pregnancy unfold before her was like adding salt to the wound. Cat couldn't help feeling jealous and angry. She fought against it, and would never have admitted it to anyone, but there it was. She was a lousy selfish mother, and now in place of the loving, sharing mother/daughter relationship she'd always longed for, there was bitterness and suspicion. Now more than ever, with Louise's death, Cat missed the sort of relationship she and Mel could have had. Mel never confided in her anymore, choosing to spend as much time as possible at Karen's house. It was breaking Cat's heart, but she only had herself to blame.

Chapter Twenty-Nine

'I thought you'd said no to helping with the nativity this year,' said Gabriel, as he walked into the kitchen to find Marianne knee deep in piles of Christmas carols and nativity plays. It was a cold autumnal night, and he'd been out checking on the newly pregnant ewes. The twins were in bed, and Steven was at Eve's so they had the evening to themselves.

'Yes, well that was before the entire Parish Council begged me to do it,' said Marianne, 'apparently Diana has been making noises about getting involved again, but Michael Nicholas, who's the Chair at the moment, has tactfully asked her if she'll arrange a charity carol concert at Hopesay Manor instead. Mrs Garratt had suggested again that Ali Strickland take it on, as a way to get her more involved in the community. So guess who drew the short straw?'

Marianne had finally made her decision and handed in her notice. Ali Strickland already looked like the cat had got the cream, the last thing she wanted to do was let her take over the nativity as well.

'Lucky old you,' said Gabriel. 'I suppose that means you've no time to cuddle up with your old man on the sofa this evening?'

'Give me ten minutes,' said Marianne. 'I'm nearly done for now. I just like making things a little different each time.

Do you know, I'd love one year to have a real donkey and a real baby.'

'One, they say never work with children and animals,' said Gabriel, 'and two, Hopesay chapel's not that big.'

'True,' said Marianne. Ever since she'd organised her first Hope Christmas nativity four years ago, it had been held on Christmas Eve in Hopesay Manor chapel, which probably wasn't the best place to introduce animals. Or a baby for that matter. It was freezing.

'We could always make it bigger,' said Marianne, 'our audience is growing, and the chapel is really tiny. I wonder if Michael would let us use one of the barns.'

'Yeah, and get Mel Tinsall to play Mary, while you're about it,' said Gabriel mischievously.

'I don't think Cat would ever forgive me if I did that,' said Marianne, 'she's really not at all happy about being a granny.'

'Can't say I blame her,' said Gabriel. 'Thank God we only have one girl to worry about.'

'Don't be so sexist. Who's to say Steven won't get a girl pregnant?' said Marianne. Although, the thought of Steven being old enough to even kiss a girl seemed quite preposterous enough at the moment. She couldn't ever imagine him being able to father babies.

'Don't,' shuddered Gabriel.

They sat in front of the roaring fire, drinking wine and watching the flames dance. It was a rare event, them having time together of an evening, just the two of them, sitting together cosily, warm and safe in each other's arms.

'We're so lucky, aren't we?' said Marianne, cuddling up to him some more.

'I'll say,' said Gabriel, kissing the top of her head. 'If only Steven were here all the time, life would be perfect.'

Marianne squeezed his hand. 'At least he's coming home

283

this weekend,' she said. 'And before you know it, it will be Christmas, and he'll be home for a lovely long time.'

'That's something to look forward to I suppose,' said Gabriel.

'Too right it is. I can't wait,' said Marianne. 'It will be lovely to have everyone here.'

'Provided you don't take on any more waifs and strays,' laughed Gabriel. 'We're going to run out of room.'

'It'll be fine if we extend our table through to the conservatory,' said Marianne, 'Mum and Dad can have the spare room, your mum and dad can go home. Marcus and Matt are staying at the Hopesay Arms. There'll be plenty of room for everyone. It will be fun.'

'I do hope you're right,' said Gabriel.

'I'm always right,' said Marianne. 'This is going to be a great Christmas. I can feel it in my waters.'

Cat was in Shrewsbury, Christmas shopping. Normally she liked to get some done by October, but this year, what with losing Louise, and the shock of Mel's pregnancy, she'd lost her shopping mojo and was really behind. So she'd taken advantage of a rare day off to sneak out and start perusing.

She mooched about idly for a bit. The shops were full of people like her, hesitant, not quite sure what to get, and not yet desperate enough to buy anything at random. It was a frustrating process; she didn't quite feel ready yet to commit herself to any particular purchase. Should she really get Noel a day out racing cars? Or would he prefer her to spend her money more wisely? And which PlayStation game was it that James wanted? Was it Death and Destruction 3 or had the fourth one come out? James inconveniently didn't write Christmas lists anymore, so she was supposed to guess by telepathy what he wanted. Which was why last year she had bought him a PlayStation game that was apparently a year out of date, and a football kit which was two seasons old. How she was supposed to work such things out, she had no idea. Paige's list on the other hand was deeply materialistic and consisted mainly of make-up and items of clothing from Hollister and Jack Wills, while Ruby had started writing hers on the first day of September and added to it on a daily basis. Her list was now so long that Cat was beginning to think she'd need to take out a second mortgage to pay for it.

Mel hadn't written a list. She had turned up one day out of the blue, stating baldly that she thought she'd better come home. After a day-long shouting match between Mel and her parents, in which Mel had finally admitted Andy Pilsdon was the father of her baby, leading Noel to leap in the car driving round Hope Christmas looking for him (and fortunately not succeeding), things had calmed down.

But now they were coexisting in a state of mutually ignoring one another, which was even worse. Apart from taking Mel to her ante-natal checkups, the baby was scarcely mentioned. Mel was going to school as if nothing had altered at all, and apart from her burgeoning shape, it would have been quite possible for Cat to have thought she'd dreamt the whole thing. Mel was even working quite hard, but Cat still had to tread on eggshells round her. One day Cat hoped they might start to have some kind of reasonable adult relationship, but it certainly wasn't going to be any day soon.

'You could always make the first move,' a voice behind her said.

'I'm sorry?' said Cat. She turned round to see Michael Nicholas, laden down with shopping bags. He looked terribly incongruous in Sainsbury's. He wasn't the sort of person you imagined doing the weekly shop.

'With your daughter,' he said. 'You're the grown-up, she needs you.'

Cat felt herself bristle at the unwanted interference.

'I know, you think it has nothing to do with me. But I'm still right,' said Michael.

It had been on the tip of her tongue to say it. How did he do that exactly? Just like his uncle Ralph, Michael had the uncanny knack of honing in what you were thinking.

And she was miffed that he felt the need to give her advice. What did he know about it? But then she stopped herself. He was probably only trying to help and God knew, she needed help.

Instead of biting his head off, Cat said shamefacedly, 'I know. I wish I could be better about it, but I feel so messed up. I just don't know how to react. I know I'm not being a great mum at the moment.'

'Talk to her, Cat,' urged Michael. 'It can't hurt, and who knows, it might even help.'

'Is Dad ever going to be well enough to come home?' Nathan's question took Pippa by surprise. The boys had seemed to adapt readily to the new arrangements – partly, she realised with a pang, because they had grown so wary of their dad.

'I don't know,' said Pippa, 'I really hope so. You do know it's not Dad's fault he's changed, don't you?'

'I know,' said Nathan, his face screwing up. 'I wish he was the way he used to be. I wish the accident hadn't happened.'

'Me too,' said Pippa, hugging her son fiercely. 'But it did happen and we just have to make the best of it. Dad still loves all three of you, that hasn't changed. We just need to give him time, and it will be okay, you'll see.'

But even as she said it, she felt her shoulders sag. Dan did seem a little better, it was true, but he was nowhere near ready enough to come home, and Pippa missed him every day. Getting the kids sorted, taking Lucy out, managing the day to day was getting harder and harder to do. Even Lucy's cheerful determination was no help. Pippa could feel herself sinking under the weight of her problems. She'd lost weight, and every time she looked in the mirror and saw the pale waiflike figure she'd become, she didn't recognise herself. If it hadn't been for Gabe and Marianne, and the support her parents were giving her, she didn't think she'd be able to cope.

At the end of the year it was looking like Lucy's respite care package would finally be over. Pippa's campaign had done nothing to stop it. Despite the widespread interest, no one had come forward to help in the way that Pippa had hoped. Much to her disappointment, Richard La Fontaine had so far not come up with the goods. He was still in discussions with people in his firm, but she was losing hope that he would be able to help after all. Her last chance was to drum up interest was at the Snow Ball in a few weeks' time, otherwise she was going to have to admit defeat. It was going to take a miracle to save the respite services. And miracles didn't happen in real life.

'Mum! Phone for you,' Nathan handed her the phone, shaking her out of her gloom.

'Is that Pippa Holliday?' An unfamiliar voice was on the other end of the line.

'Yes,' said Pippa, 'can I help?'

'My name's Aaron Jones and I'm a production assistant for Red Crews Production.'

'And?'

'And I believe you're running the campaign to keep the Sunshine Trust open?'

'Yes that's right,' said Pippa. 'Much good we're doing though.'

'We've just had the green light to go ahead with a

documentary about it. I wondered if you'd like to be interviewed for the programme?'

'I suppose so,' said Pippa. 'But it's really the work of the centre I want to highlight, and how they help families like mine. It's not about me.'

'And how do they help you?'

'First off, we get a weekend off every fortnight – although thanks to the cuts it's now down to one a month, and soon it will be gone altogether – which allows us to spend time with our two sons and gives me a break.'

'And why do you need the break?'

'My daughter has cystic fibrosis and needs constant care,' explained Pippa. 'I adore her, of course I do, but looking after Lucy 24/7 is exhausting, so the respite care is vital. What's so short sighted is that they're taking these services away without realising how much more it would cost to pay for the likes of me being hospitalised with nervous breakdowns. The respite care keeps me sane.'

'And your husband? How does he feel about it?'

Pippa paused, not sure what to say.

'He's not with us at the moment,' she said, 'but he fully supports the work the centre do.'

'May I speak with him?'

'I'd have to check,' said Pippa, thinking it was probably the last thing Dan wanted.

Having gone through a few more questions, the production assistant promised to ring back with a date for the TV interview.

'We'd like to interview you at home and film you with Lucy and the boys, if that's okay?'

'That's fine,' agreed Pippa, who was thrilled that at last the TV was going ahead. Maybe someone would see it, and come to their aid. She sincerely hoped so.

She rang Dan as soon as she'd got off the phone to check he had no objections.

'None at all,' he said, 'so long as they don't interview me.'

Pippa laughed. That was more like the old Dan, who was notoriously shy.

'It's all right, we don't have to mention you at all if you like,' said Pippa. 'I told them you didn't live here.'

There was a pause, and Pippa suddenly realised she'd said the wrong thing.

'I mean, I know it's not permanent,' she gabbled, 'I just didn't know what to say.'

'It's fine,' Dan said and changed the subject. 'Shall I take the boys to football on Saturday?'

'Yes, that would be great, thanks.'

Pippa put the phone down with a heavy heart. 'That would be great, thanks.' She mimicked herself. Of course it wasn't great. It was utter pants was what it was – to politely arrange for her estranged husband to come and pick up their children at the weekend. She'd never ever imagined that it would happen to her. And now it had.

Chapter Thirty

'Of course you can use the old stables at Hopesay Manor,' Michael said to Marianne, when she rang up to ask. 'I think that's an excellent idea. We don't unfortunately have any donkeys on the estate, but I'm sure we can find a calf or two.'

'It's okay. Don't laugh, but I think I've sourced a donkey,' said Marianne. 'It turns out Diana Carew is a patron of a donkey sanctuary over in Hope Sadler. Now all we need is a newborn baby and it will be really authentic.'

It crossed her mind that Gabriel might have a point. If she wasn't casting children for this nativity, it would have been perfect to have Mel Tinsall in the starring role.

'Well, good luck with that,' said Michael.

Marianne got off the phone and whooped with delight. 'Hurrah,' she said to the twins, 'I think this year, the nativity is going to be bigger and better than ever.'

With the help of Miss Woods, Marianne had come up with a new script, making the nativity story more relevant to the modern day, by depicting Mary and Joseph as illegal immigrants.

Marianne had still insisted on traditional carols though. Part of her brief, when she'd taken over the nativity when she first came to Hope Christmas, had been to keep it traditional, and Marianne had enjoyed using a different

variety of Christmas carols to achieve that effect. She liked
the challenge of keeping it fresh each year, but not making
people feel they were seeing the same show every time.

Noel had said he'd help light up the barn with fairy
lights, and she was hoping for a really magical evening.
Now all she had to do was get on and cast it. She usually
set about doing that on a Sunday afternoon in the middle
of November. And normally, she gave Steven a part. His
voice was so beautiful it seemed criminal not to include
him. This year, though . . . Marianne hesitated. She'd just
have to arrange the first rehearsal for a weekend that Steven
was home. That is, if Eve and Darren could ever manage
to organise things so that she and Gabriel got a weekend
with Steven at home. At first she'd thought Gabriel was
being paranoid, but now she wasn't sure. Of the six weeks
that Steven had been at school, she and Gabriel had only
managed to have him at home for two. Thankfully, he'd
been keen to come home for half term this weekend, otherwise she wasn't sure she'd have been able to answer for
Gabriel's behaviour . . .

'Can I go trick or treating? Thanks, Mum, you're the best.'
Paige flew in and out, before Cat had had time to say no.

'It's okay,' Paige called back after her, 'Anna and I are
going with Nathan, George and Steven.'

'That's okay then,' muttered Cat. Great. Now Ruby was
bound to demand to go. It was a cold brisk October night,
and the last thing Cat fancied doing was traipsing round
Hope Christmas demanding sweets with menaces.

Sure enough, Ruby appeared five minutes later in a ghost
costume, complete with Scream mask. How had she created
such a ghoulish child? She'd discovered her earlier, making
a 'witch's stew' that apparently contained eyeballs, and
entrails. All Cat had been sure of was that her spaghetti

supply had been depleted and she was going to have to buy ketchup next time she went shopping.

'Can Molly come too?'

'Sure,' said Cat, bracing herself to go out in the cold. 'But we're only going to people we know.'

'And can she stay for a sleepover?'

'Oh go on,' said Cat, 'if her mum doesn't mind.'

Noel poked his head into the kitchen.

'Oh, you're going trick or treating. Great. Have fun.'

'As if,' said Cat. 'What are you going to do?'

'James and I have a date with the footie,' said Noel. 'See you later.'

'And Mel?'

'Upstairs,' said Noel.

'Surprised, not,' said Cat, wondering if she should go up, but then chickening out. She didn't have the energy to have a fight with Mel, which is why she hadn't followed Michael's advice and tried to chat to her yet. Which was cowardly, but easier. And sometimes the easy option was all you had time for.

The streets of Hope Christmas seemed full of mothers on the same mission as her. She passed several mums she knew exchanging sympathetic glances, complete with over-excited, hyper children in devilish masks, witches' costumes and several skeletons.

By the time they'd exhausted most of the people they knew, Ruby and Molly were nearly satisfied with their sugar rush. (Memo to self, get them to brush their teeth really really well.) Cat's feet were killing her, and she just wanted to collapse with a glass of wine. The thought of football not being that enticing, and seeing that Marianne had a pumpkin lit in her house, Cat decided to make one last call there.

'Hi, did you know Paige was here?' Marianne welcomed her in.

'No, I didn't,' said Cat, then checked her phone, 'oh yes, she does appear to have texted me.'

'Can you stay for a drink?'

'That sounds like an excellent idea,' Cat said. 'Girls, do you want to stay for a bit?'

'Yes, please.' Ruby amazingly was still spotting sweets to stuff in her bag, and the pair of them took themselves off to Marianne's lounge to stuff their faces some more.

'How's it going?' said Marianne, opening a bottle.

Cat pulled a face.

'Oh the usual. Mel's still not speaking to me, I'm pretty furious with her. Same old, same old.'

'Oh I am sorry,' said Marianne. 'It must be such a huge strain on you and Noel.'

'The worst thing is,' Cat admitted, 'that I want to be supportive, but all I keep thinking is, how could she have been so stupid? And as for that bloody Andy Pilsdon, I could kill him. He doesn't seem to want to take any responsibility. Noel went round and had a serious chat with him, and he pretty much said the baby wasn't his.'

'Oh God that's awful,' said Marianne. 'Poor Mel.'

'I know,' said Cat. 'I wish she'd talked to me about it. I always wanted us to be close, and now we're miles apart.'

'I'm sure the rest of us would feel the same, Cat,' said Marianne. 'Don't be so hard on yourself.'

'But I am such a horrible person,' said Cat. 'I'm actually jealous of her. I'm never going to have another baby, and my daughter is having one. What kind of monster does that make me?'

'You're not a monster,' said Marianne. 'You've had a really tough time. I don't think you should beat yourself up. Come on, let's have a party to cheer you up.'

'A party for two?' said Cat. 'Where's Gabe?'

'Out for a drink with Dan,' said Marianne. 'Tell you what,

I'll ring Pippa. She's bound to ring soon to ask when the boys are coming home.'

Pippa came around straight away.

'Lucy and I were just settling down to watch *X Factor*, weren't we, Lucy?' said Pippa, as they came into the kitchen.

Lucy giggled.

Mum fancies Simon Cowell, she typed.

'That is so untrue,' protested Pippa.

You said he was hot, Lucy shot back.

'You can watch it with Ruby and Molly,' said Cat, 'they're next door.'

Ruby had an instinctive way with Lucy. At her old school in London there had been several special needs kids, so Ruby took differences in her stride and seemed to be able to communicate with Lucy in a way that Cat could only marvel at. She didn't think she'd been that tolerant as a child.

Paige heard the magic words *X Factor* and was down the stairs in a flash.

'Come on, Lucy,' she said, and she pushed her next door.

Cat, Marianne and Pippa sat in the kitchen and put the world to rights. Cat felt the upset and strain of the last few months slip away as she sipped her drink happily. Despite all the misery of her life at the moment, she was so glad she'd come to Hope Christmas; so glad she'd made these friends.

'Right, I think I'd really better be off,' Pippa declared, putting down her glass. 'Otherwise I'm going to push Lucy in the gutter.' She got up rather unsteadily and tripped over her feet, knocking straight into Cat. The pair of them ended up on the floor in a giggling heap.

'Oh dear, Marianne, what have you done to me?' laughed Pippa. 'I think I may have had a little too much to drink.'

'A little,' snorted Cat. 'I think you were matching me glass for glass, and I've had A LOT.'

Pippa tried to get herself up, and fell back laughing. By now she and Cat were helpless with laughter, and when Marianne tried to get them both up, and fell on top of them, Pippa thought she might never ever stop. She was laughing so hard it hurt. Suddenly everything came out in a rush, the misery of the last few months, not being with Dan, and the worry about Lucy. Her laughter turned to tears, and soon she was sobbing in Marianne's arms.

'Gi– ir–irls,' she sobbed, 'I don't know what I'd do without you. You're the best. I love you sooo much.'

'Uh oh,' said Cat, 'I think it's time we got you to bed.'

'Maybe a coffee, first,' said Marianne, extricating herself from Pippa's hug with difficulty. 'When Gabe gets back, I'll get him to walk you home.'

That set Pippa off again. 'Oh Gabe, and you, you're so fantastic, I don't know what I'd do without you.'

'I know, we're brilliant,' grinned Marianne, 'and you, my darling, are very drunk. Come, on, let's get some coffee down your neck. Gabe should be here soon.'

At that moment the key turned in the lock, and Gabe came in, saying, 'Well, I still think the defender was useless, letting that last goal in.'

Oh shit. Pippa sobered up the instant Dan walked through the door. He couldn't see her like this. She stood up and rushed out of the door, muttering something about going to the loo, where she frantically washed her face down, and hoped that the red blotches wouldn't be too noticeable.

If they were, Gabriel was discreetly ignoring them. 'I don't know, I go out for a quiet night and come back to a den of iniquity,' he was laughing with Marianne, when she came back into the room.

Dan was hovering awkwardly in the background.

'I should go,' he said, 'I don't want to disturb anything.'

'Oh don't be daft,' Marianne said, 'we were just having coffee, and then Pippa was going to take the kids home. I was going to ask Gabriel to escort her up the lane, but why don't you instead?'

'There's no need–' said Pippa, who'd just come back from the loo.

'That's fine,' said Dan simultaneously.

Oh God, this was awkward. Pippa had barely spent a moment alone with Dan since he'd moved out. She felt all at sea, wondering what he was thinking, but excited by the thought of spending some – any – time with him at all.

'Are you sure?' Pippa looked at Dan, feeling absurdly shy.

'Of course,' said Dan, and gave her his lovely wrinkled reassuring smile. Her heart did a little fillip and suddenly she felt eighteen again. It was that look which had floored her on their first meeting. He'd grinned at her across a dance floor, and she'd wanted to know more about the gorgeous dark-haired guy in the corner. Pippa's heart was hammering very loudly as she started to get ready to go.

'Right, I'll gather the troops.' Pippa could feel herself blushing and busied about shouting up at the boys, going to get Lucy out of the lounge, to hide her discomfiture.

It took ten minutes to get everyone ready, and after a flurry of goodbyes it was just Pippa and the children with Dan going home together, for the first time in several weeks. It was as though nothing had changed. The boys were delighted to see their dad, and he chased them up the road laughing and joking about, while Lucy had lit up when he'd come in the room.

When they got to the house, Dan looked all set to go, but the boys were disappointed, dragging him to show him their latest Wii scores, and Pippa said, 'Come on, stay for a quick drink. At the very least come and put Lucy to bed with me. You'd like that, wouldn't you, sweetheart?'

What do you think? typed Lucy, clicking with happiness, and the look of surprised delight on Dan's face made Pippa grateful that she'd asked.

By the time Lucy was settled, and the boys had been finally chased off the computer and Wii, it was gone eleven.

'I should go,' said Dan.

Taking a deep breath, Pippa said, 'Do you have to?'

Dan came closer towards her, and she could feel herself just wanting to fall into his arms.

'Would you like me to stay?' he said.

'More than anything,' she said. 'I've missed you.'

'I've missed you too,' he said taking her into his arms. She felt the weeks of heartache and loneliness melt away.

'Stay,' she said. 'This is where you belong.'

Mel

FACEBOOK status Fat. Bored. Fed up
Jen17: You're the one who got pregnant
Mel: Don't remind me Jen. Am trying to forget it.
Ellie: what's it like?
Mel: crap. I'm always going to be fat. And no one will ever love me.
Jake: Aw babe. I love you.
Mel: Thanks babe. But you don't count. xxxooxxx
Kaz: Do you want to come round?
Mel: Too much homework.
Adam: You're still doing homework?
Mel: I didn't lose my brain when I got pregnant.

Teenage Kicks

I'm getting quite scared now.

The doctor says I'm twenty-six weeks. That's well over halfway.

And the baby's kicking all the time. Soon it's going to be born, and I'll need to make some big decisions.

I wish I could talk to Mum about it. But there's no chance of that.

I realise I've been completely stupid.

The Boy isn't going to come riding round on a white charger to whisk me and the sprog away into the sunset. And TBH, I don't know whether I want him to.

He knows I'm pregnant and he hasn't come near me. He still won't admit the baby's his. Even when Dad went round and confronted him.

Mum warned me about guys like him. And I had to be the idiot who fell for his lines. I feel so stupid.

The thing is I've messed up. Big time. But I've started to work things out. I want to carry on with my education. I want to have a future. And I think I've figured a way to do it . . .

November

Chapter Thirty-One

'Right, let's have a go at the first scene, shall we? See what we're all made of.' Marianne had gathered her group of hopeful actors and actresses together in the village hall, which as usual, was freezing. You'd have thought when they rebuilt after the flood four years previously, someone might have managed to put in a modern heating system. But no, the boiler seemed perpetually on the blink. Every year, when she started rehearsing, Marianne swore she'd try and get it sorted out for the next year, and every year she forgot.

She was trying the children out in different combinations to work out who would get which parts. She always tried to be scrupulously fair, never picking the same girl for Mary twice, making sure that not all the angels had to have fair hair, using Steven's talents whilst ensuring that he didn't always get a pivotal role. It was an exhausting but necessary part of the job, but despite her best efforts, inevitably at least one mother would be unhappy and find something to complain about.

Which was why this year, she was torn. She felt Ruby Tinsall would make a lively and sparky Mary, judging by the verbal exchange she'd just had with Toby Davies, who was trying out for Joseph. To her amusement, Ruby had even improvised her own lines. But Ruby was only in Year 4, and Ruth Patterson in Year 6 had been angling for Mary for the past two years.

Ruth's mum was a notorious whinger. In the past Marianne might have been prepared to stick her neck out, but with the commitments she now had at home, she didn't think she had the energy for a full-on fight with Danielle Patterson, Ruth's mum. If she chose Ruby, she'd also be accused of favouritism, as everyone knew she was friends with Cat. So to counter such claims, the fact that she knew Ruby's mum would actually go against Ruby.

'Any thoughts so far?' Pippa slid into a seat behind her, as they watched Nathan and George and three other boys vying for roles as shepherds. Steven, who had come home for the weekend especially for the rehearsal, refused point blank to try out for a shepherd, so Marianne was thinking of casting him as wise man, as there was a rather haunting solo she had in mind for him to sing. Then she remembered that Ruth Patterson's brother Josh had also signed up for a wise man. Bugger. She'd probably need to give Steven something else to do. It was depressingly true what they said about squeaky wheels . . .

'Well, I'd love to cast Ruby as Mary, but I think she'll have to wait for next year,' said Marianne, 'otherwise I'll never hear the end of it from Danielle.'

'That's a shame,' said Pippa, 'I think Ruby would be a fun Mary.'

'I do too,' said Marianne, 'although I'm not sure Diana Carew would approve of Mary having fun . . .'

They both laughed at the thought of Diana's horror of things not being presented in a manner she thought appropriate.

'That's great, kids,' said Marianne, calling them all to order. 'I think I've got enough to decide who's going to play which part. Don't worry, there will be a part for everyone, and remember girls, just because only one of you can be Mary, doesn't mean I don't think you're all fabulous!'

The children laughed; it was part of Marianne's pep talk every year to tell them they were fabulous. She went round the group handing out scripts, and carol sheets.

'Next week, I'll put up cast lists, and we'll start going through the carols, but in the meantime you can all look through these to familiarise yourself with the words. See you all next time.'

There was a scrabble for the door, and the children poured out in an excited rabble to meet their patiently waiting parents.

'How are things, by the way?' Marianne said to Pippa when the last child was accounted for. She hadn't seen Pippa since Halloween, and had been wondering ever since how things with her and Dan had gone.

Pippa blushed.

'What do you mean?'

'Well, Dan walked you home the other night. What happened?'

'Nothing,' said Pippa, blushing some more.

'Nothing? I'm deeply disappointed,' said Marianne.

'Oh all right,' said Pippa, 'he came back.'

'And?'

'And, he stayed the night,' said Pippa, 'but we both agreed we'd take it slowly for now. So much has happened, and Dan's still struggling with his temper. We just thought we'd ease back into things gently.'

'I'm so pleased for you,' said Marianne giving Pippa a hug.

'Me too,' said Pippa, 'me too.'

'So how do you find it, managing Lucy at home?' the interviewer said from one of Pippa's comfy armchairs, while she sat self-consciously on the sofa.

'Well, fortunately, living in an old farmhouse, we've got

302

a lot of space,' said Pippa, 'and we've been able to adapt the house to Lucy's needs as she gets older. But it's increasingly difficult managing her physically as she gets bigger and stronger. I have very little to spare for my two sons, which is why the support from the Sunshine Trust is so fantastic. Without the respite care package I'd have gone under years ago.'

'And your husband?'

'Is a great support,' said Pippa quickly, 'but I really don't want to talk about him – this is about the Sunshine Trust and what it does for families like ours.'

'So it's been a strain on your marriage having Lucy?'

'No!' said Pippa quickly, 'not at all. Dan couldn't have been more supportive and is a wonderful father to Lucy.'

'But?'

'But nothing,' said Pippa.

'But he's not here,' said the interviewer, 'have you separated?'

'Whether we have or have not,' said Pippa getting really riled, 'is none of your business and has nothing to do with Lucy. Look, I really don't want to talk about this stuff. I agreed to do an interview about the Sunshine Trust, not about my personal life.'

'Sure, sure,' the interviewer said smoothly. 'I was just trying to get the back story.'

'The back story is that without the Sunshine Trust this family would have fallen apart,' said Pippa. 'And for families like ours it provides an invaluable service, and allows us to cope with the challenges life presents us with. Plus Lucy loves going there, and she benefits from having time away from us too. It's a win-win situation, which is why we're all so devastated about losing the service.'

'That's great,' said the interviewer. 'Thanks Pippa, we've got a lot of material we can use there. Now would it be all right to film you looking after Lucy? And some shots with Lucy at the Sunshine Trust would be good.'

'Yes, that would be fine,' said Pippa. She looked at her watch. It was two o'clock. 'Lucy comes home in an hour, but I can show you all the adaptations we've had to make to the house if you like.'

There followed another hour of Pippa being trailed round the house with the film crew, stopping and repeating answers to questions over and over until the director was happy with everything. By the time Lucy arrived home Pippa had had enough, but Lucy seemed thrilled to be the centre of attention so Pippa obligingly wheeled her in and out of the lounge several times, got her in and out of her chair, pretended to get Lucy ready for bed at least five times, and finally showed the difficulties of cooking tea when Lucy suddenly demanded the toilet.

I'm going to be famous, typed Lucy when they'd finished. Typically, she'd laughed through the whole thing, so Pippa hoped they'd have some positive footage of living with a child like Lucy. As she'd said to the interviewer, there was much to be positive about, 'And the Sunshine Trust helps us all stay that way,' she told him. 'It's our lifeline.'

The boys arrived home in the middle of it all with Marianne, who had helpfully picked them up from school, and cheerily took part in background shots, and spoke enthusiastically and eloquently about the impact of having Lucy in their lives. When Nathan answered the question, 'Do you sometimes wish Lucy wasn't in your family?' with a perplexed, 'But Lucy's special and it wouldn't be the same without her,' and George stoutly responded 'No, why would I?' Pippa felt herself well up. She'd always worried that the boys had missed out because of having Lucy as a sister. What a relief that *they* didn't see it that way.

Eventually the crew left, and Pippa had to go about

actually making them tea, and actually putting Lucy to bed, before sitting down with both boys and giving them a cuddle on the sofa.

'Thanks guys,' she said, 'you were great. I couldn't have asked for two more perfect sons.'

They wriggled out of her hug with a, 'Yuk, Mu–um!' each, and then Nathan said, 'Is Dad going to stay over again?'

'Maybe,' said Pippa. 'Would you like him to?'

'So long as he doesn't get angry again,' said Nathan.

'Well he's working on that,' said Pippa. 'So let's take each day as it comes, shall we? And who knows, maybe we'll be back to normal soon.'

Ha. Normal? As if she'd ever known what that meant.

Cat came into the house from two days away in London, talking about her next book and the next series of *Cat's Country Kitchen*, with both her publishers and the TV company. She'd had more long lunches than she'd been used to for a while and a couple of late-night sessions with her agent, chewing the fat about her home situation. It had done her good to get away; given her some perspective on the situation. Anna, her agent, who had been there, done that, a decade ago with her own rebellious teens, had been a fount of sage advice.

'You're going to have to talk to her,' she said. 'However she appears to you, Mel's a teenage girl in a lot of trouble. She needs her mum, and she needs your support. I know it's not what you wanted for her, but like it or not, it's happening, and the sooner you all face up to it, the better.'

'I know,' said Cat. 'It's just so hard when you're living with it all the time. Thanks though; it's done me good to get away.'

'And something else to think about, I hope,' said Anna.

305

'I think it's great they want to do another series of *Cat's Country Kitchen* in the spring, and the sales from *Cat's Country Christmas* are really encouraging. Especially in this difficult economic climate.'

'True,' said Cat, 'at least that's one area of my life that I'm not making a balls-up of.'

As she opened the door, she was nearly bowled over by Ruby.

'Mummy!' she said giving Cat a boisterously huge hug. 'It's so unfair, Mrs North hasn't made me Mary, and everyone said I was better than Ruth Patterson. And Ruth doesn't know anything about having babies, whereas I know *all about them.*'

Ouch. Another downside of having a pregnant teen daughter – making your eight-year-old grow up far too quickly.

'I heard that, runt,' said Mel crossly as she came down the stairs. She had suddenly ballooned out, and she was so obviously pregnant now, Cat couldn't believe she'd ever missed it. All those damn baggy jumpers Mel had been living in had clearly helped her cover up a lot.

'Please don't call your sister runt,' said Cat automatically, and Mel bristled. Great start.

'You okay?' said Cat.

'Why wouldn't I be?' snapped Mel.

'No reason,' said Cat, 'just asking.'

She put her bag down and followed Mel into the kitchen, where James was cooking a chicken madras and Noel was pouring himself a glass of wine.

'Hello,' she said giving him a kiss and a hug. 'I've missed you.'

'Me too,' said Noel, giving her a kiss on the lips.

She stood enveloped in his arms, for several long and lovely minutes. It was wonderful to be home.

'Parents, please,' said Paige who was sitting flicking through a magazine at the kitchen table. 'Can't you get a room or something?'

'I'm allowed to snog my wife in my own home,' said Noel, mock-seriously. 'Besides there is no guarantee of privacy anywhere in this house, so getting a room isn't an option.'

'Would you like a cup of tea, Mum?' Mel said.

'That would be great,' Cat said, hoping it was a peace offering. 'I'll just go and dump my stuff upstairs and then come down and catch up with you all.'

Five minutes later, Mel knocked on her door with the tea.

'Thanks, love,' said Cat. She went to hug her daughter, and was relieved to see she didn't flinch away. 'Mel, sweetheart, can we have a chat?'

'Only if you're not going to have a go,' said Mel.

'I'm not going to have a go,' said Cat. 'I was just going to say . . . we need to start thinking about when the baby comes. And you're bursting out of your clothes. So I was wondering, do you fancy a shopping trip? Just you and me. How about it?'

'I suppose,' said Mel, noncommittal.

'Great,' said Cat. 'Let's go on Saturday. No time like the present.'

'Fine,' said Mel, 'now can I go and do my homework?'

'Sure, of course,' said Cat with a sigh.

It wasn't much, but it was a start. One day at a time, Cat said to herself. One day at a time.

Chapter Thirty-Two

'I can't believe we've only got two weeks left until the ball,' said Pippa, who was poring over seating plans in Cat's lounge. It felt incredibly cosy on a winter's day with the fire burning in the grate. It was also exceptionally tidy, reminding Pippa she'd have to have a go at hers when she got home.

'How on earth do you keep it so tidy?' she asked.

'It's not normally like this,' said Cat. 'The cleaner's just been. Right, now where were we? There are still a few tables not totally filled, aren't there? Shall we do a quick email via the PTA at school? There are bound to be one or two people hiding in the woodwork.'

'Good idea,' said Pippa. 'And I'll leave some more fliers with Vera. She's really good at selling tickets. It's funny to think what a mouse she was before she met Albert. She never used to say boo to a goose.'

'Do you think Dan will still come?' said Cat, who had heard Pippa cursing about uneven numbers all morning.

Pippa shrugged. She hadn't yet got round to broaching the subject. Everything still felt raw and new between them.

'I really hope so,' she said. 'He's certainly more like himself than he was a couple of months ago, but I'm not sure how ready he is to come and socialise in the real world. It was never his favourite thing before.'

'And how are you two getting on?'

'It's better,' said Pippa. 'He comes round most days now, and helps me with Lucy. But we're both still a bit wary, so we're taking it slowly. He's stayed over once or twice, but he doesn't seem to want to rush things, which is probably a good thing. How about you? What are things like in your house?'

'Also slightly better,' said Cat. 'I'm planning a baby shopping trip with Mel, to try and bond with her a bit more. But to be honest, I'm dreading it. Going to buy baby clothes for my new grandchild was something I imagined doing in ten years' time, when I'm thoroughly delighted about it; not now when I've only just said goodbye to the last chance I'm going to have of having my own baby. It just feels wrong and too soon, and I can't get as excited about it as I'd like to.'

'That is fair enough,' said Pippa. 'Despite what I said to you about Lucy, if I was in a more regular situation, I think I'd feel the same.'

'The trouble is, whether I like it or not, this baby is on its way,' said Cat. 'So I guess I'd better get used to the idea of being a granny.'

'What does Noel think?'

'Well, as you can imagine he's not exactly thrilled that his eldest daughter is "up the duff" at the tender age of sixteen. But he's put on a much better face than me. He keeps going all gooey about baby pictures. I swear he's having some kind of weird male hormonal response to it all. Maybe it's because I lost our baby earlier in the year – his body's gone into hunter-gatherer mode, and now he's got a grandchild to look forward to, he's gone doubly protective.'

Pippa laughed. 'Sorry,' she said, 'it's probably not funny.'

'Not terribly,' said Cat, 'but there's only so much gloom a girl can take. You do have to laugh, otherwise you end up in the gutter slitting your wrists.'

'And that would never do,' said Pippa, laughing harder.

'No it wouldn't,' said Cat, grinning herself.

'That really is an excellent way of looking at life,' said Pippa. 'There's nothing to be done about the crap things in our lives, so we may as well try and enjoy the rest of it.'

'So let's make this ball a night to remember,' said Cat.

'I'll drink to that,' said Pippa, raising her cup of tea.

The shops were heaving. Christmas shopping was well underway, and Cat had already got a headache from hearing *Simply having a wonderful Christmas time* for the millionth time as she and Mel negotiated their way around the Shrewsbury shops. She felt quite nostalgic walking into Mothercare.

'It doesn't seem that long ago I was buying maternity clothes for you,' she said wistfully, as she picked up a baggy top that she thought might suit Mel.

'Why do you always have to rub it in?'

'What?' said Cat. 'What on earth did I do now?'

'I know you think I'm too young to be a mum,' said Mel. 'But you really don't have to go on about it.'

'That's not what I meant—' said Cat, but Mel had stormed out of the shop adding, 'And that top's gross. It's okay for old women like you, but I'm sixteen. Just because I'm pregnant doesn't mean to say I have to look sad and ugly.'

Ouch, hit your mother where it hurts, why don't you? Cat felt that familiar twinge of jealousy. Oh to be young and pretty again, like Mel, even if she was pregnant. She caught a glimpse of herself in the shop mirror. Her fair hair was looking flat and uninteresting, and she was dressed in unflattering jeans and a baggy jumper and fleece. She looked frumpy, fat and middle-aged. God she was turning into a wreck, while Mel looked beautiful. It didn't seem quite fair.

310

'Mel!' said Cat, chasing after her, 'come back. Come on, sit down and let's start again. I didn't mean anything by what I said. I was just remembering how excited I was when I first bought maternity clothes.'

'Well I'm hardly excited, am I?' said Mel. 'I don't want to be pregnant, remember?'

Resisting the temptation to say, And whose fault is that, do you think? Cat sat down with her daughter and said, 'Look sweetie, I know this isn't ideal. And it's not what Dad and I wanted for you, but this baby is coming, so we'd all better get used to it.'

'I don't want to get used to it,' grumbled Mel. 'I want to be out with my mates having fun, like I used to. Not cooped-up indoors, feeling miserable.'

'You don't have to be stuck inside all the time,' said Cat. 'Come on, there are some pretty Christmas dresses we could get you if you want. Just because you're pregnant you don't have to cut yourself off from the rest of the world, you know.'

That elicited a small smile.

'Better,' said Cat. 'Come on, let's have a look at these dresses and then we'll start looking at baby stuff.'

Half an hour later, they emerged with bags full of maternity clothes that Mel considered were halfway decent to wear, and a ridiculous number of babygros.

'Mum, calm down,' said Mel, laughing as Cat had been unable to resist more and more sweet designs.

'I can't help it,' said Cat. 'I used to love buying babygros for all of you, there's something so perfect about a tiny baby in a sweet little romper suit.'

'Barf,' said Mel. 'I didn't realise you were so sentimental. It's only a babygro.'

'You wait,' said Cat, 'when you hold that baby in your arms, and look at it in that sweet little babygro, your heart will melt.'

311

'No it won't,' said Mel, 'because I'm not going to keep it.'

'What?' said Cat.

'You heard me,' said Mel. 'I am not going to fall in love with this baby, because as far as I'm concerned it's just a little blip in my life. I'm going to have it, get it adopted, and move on, and go to uni and get a career like you want me to.'

'But—' Cat was staggered. She'd only just got her head round the idea of being a grandmother, now Mel threw this at her. 'Don't be daft, Mel, Dad and I will help you look after it.'

'Yeah, like that's what you really want to do,' said Mel. 'I can't get rid of the baby any other way. It's the perfect solution. I thought you'd be pleased.'

'The cathedral looks rather lovely at night, doesn't it?' said Marianne, as she and Gabriel slipped into the pews of Middleminster Cathedral, ready for the evensong service. It was the first time they'd been able to get over to a service since Steven started school, and he'd been really keen for them to attend. The cathedral was a medieval building with later additions, with a glorious rose window to rival York's and a staggeringly high nave. It was lit with candles for evensong, and coming in out of a cold frosty night, it felt welcoming and special. Marianne wasn't terribly churchy, but she found something comforting about the old church traditions, and hearing choir boys at evensong was one of those traditions which she found especially uplifting.

She and Gabriel had arrived early so that they could sit near the front and get a good view of Steven. It hadn't been his turn with them this weekend, but as he had a very small solo, Gabriel had promised they'd be there. And after all the weekends that Eve and Darren had monopolised Steven, it was the least they could do. They'd come without the twins, who were round at Jean and David's, and both she and Gabriel were really looking forward to hearing Steven sing.

'Oh, I didn't imagine you'd be coming too.' Marianne looked up, and to her dismay, saw Eve and Darren bearing down on them.

'We did say to Stevie that he probably only needed us to come along,' Eve continued. 'It's a bit over the top if we're all here, don't you think?'

'Steven asked us to come and so we're here,' said Gabriel with a deliberately level voice, but Marianne could see him practically grinding his teeth in rage. 'And as we haven't had Steven for the last two weekends, we really wanted to come and see him.' He was clearly furious with Eve, and rightly so. She had grabbed more than her share of Steven's weekends, and it was becoming a thorny issue.

Marianne grabbed hold of Gabriel's hand and squeezed it. Honestly, that woman was the limit. To think she used to feel sorry for her.

'Well now we're all here, do you mind if we join you?' said Darren, in forced hearty tones.

It seemed rude and somewhat inappropriate in church to tell them what they actually thought, so Marianne and Gabriel moved further up the pew to allow Eve and Darren to sit with them.

'We normally sit here of course,' said Darren.

'You've been before?' said Marianne in surprise. 'I thought this was the first time Steven had had a solo.'

'Oh it is,' said Eve, 'but we want to support him at every opportunity, so we've been making a point of coming every week.'

'Have you now,' said Gabriel between gritted teeth.

'Shhh,' said Marianne, 'I think it's about to start.'

The choir and the vicar had begun to process down

313

the cathedral aisle and make their way up to the High Altar. Steven was among them, looking swamped by his choir gown, but his face lit up when he saw Gabriel, and Marianne felt a warm glow. Good, he hadn't forgotten them, despite Eve's apparent best efforts to prise him away from them.

The service itself was beautiful, and Steven's solo was enchanting. Every note seemed to hang in the air and soar up to the rafters of the beautiful old building. Marianne surreptitiously wiped a tear away, and saw Gabriel doing the same. What was it about kids and singing? It was that purity somehow that ripped into your soul, and made you remember what it was like to be young and free and innocent. Eve and Darren were all over Steven once the service was over, and Gabriel and Marianne scarcely had a moment to say well done to him before he was whisked away back to school with his class.

'He's thriving so much at that school,' said Eve. 'I think it's the best thing we ever did for him. He was so full of it yesterday when we took him out for lunch.'

'I thought you were having him for the whole weekend,' frowned Gabriel.

'Oh yes, we were,' Eve said quickly, 'but then Darren had a business dinner he couldn't get out of, and he needed me there, so unfortunately we had to bring Steven back to school early. Unavoidable I'm afraid. Steven understood. And we'll see him next week.'

'No, I think it's our turn next week,' said Gabriel. 'You've had him for two weeks running.'

'Oh,' Eve's demeanour drooped. 'You're right of course. But I'm sure you wouldn't mind if we dropped in and took Steven out for a quick bite to eat at lunchtime?'

'Eve,' said Gabriel firmly. 'We have an arrangement, it's much better to stick to it.'

'Yes, that's right, darling,' said Darren, 'and I think I've got a golf thing next Saturday anyway.'

There was something about the way he said it, which made Marianne wonder if all was well in paradise. It was as if he wasn't all that keen to have Steven all the time. Maybe Eve was pushing for it more because of her guilt, but Darren would have been happy with less contact.

'Well that's settled, then,' said Marianne brightly. 'We'll see Steven next weekend, and you'll have him the weekend after. And then we can all meet up again at the Christmas concert. Won't that be nice?'

She hoped that no one noticed her sarcasm, but luckily both Eve and Darren were so caught up in themselves it seemed to have passed them by.

'Do you think we all need to come?' began Darren.

'Well if it's difficult for you and Eve,' said Gabriel, 'please don't worry, as we're happy to be there for Steven.'

There was a pregnant pause and Eve said brightly, 'And of course, so are we, but it's difficult in the week, when we both need to be in London. It's so tricky for us both to get away . . .'

'No worries,' said Gabriel, 'we're here, and it's *so* much easier for us.'

Marianne dug him in the ribs, but he carried on remorselessly, 'After all, my work doesn't really take me away from the family ever, does it, Marianne?'

'Never,' grinned Marianne. 'Come on, we need to get back to the twins.'

'Honestly,' said Gabriel as they got back in the car. 'I know we've just been to church, but I've never felt more like murdering someone.'

'I know,' said Marianne. 'Still, never mind, we won. We get Steven next weekend.'

'We did, didn't we?' said Gabriel with a grin.

Chapter Thirty-Three

'Do you think Mel was serious about giving the baby up?' Noel had been staggered when Cat told him the news.

'I don't know,' said Cat. 'She seemed pretty determined. I suppose it is the sensible thing to do . . .'

'But . . .?'

'I know we didn't want this, and I know we're getting ready to move on in our lives now and the last thing we need is a baby . . .'

Cat broke off again, trying to make sense of her feelings. Her anger with Mel had begun to ebb away, and now all she could see was her daughter in trouble, and a grandchild going to a stranger's home. And knowing she could have no more babies of her own somehow made it worse. Mel couldn't have found a better way to hurt her if she'd tried. Perhaps it was her own fault; if she hadn't pushed Mel away when she'd found out about the baby, if she could have brought herself to be more forgiving . . .

'Are you thinking what I'm thinking?' Noel gently laced his fingers over hers. 'Cat, this has been a tough year for you, losing the baby, then your mum, now Mel being pregnant.'

'It's hardly been easy for you, either,' said Cat. 'And I've probably been a bit of a drag, with one thing and another.'

'No you haven't,' said Noel kissing her. 'I've just been

316

thinking though. Maybe, we can turn this round, make a positive out of a negative.'

'What do you mean?'

'Well, neither of us wants Mel to ruin her life by having a baby, right?'

'No of course not,' said Cat. 'All I want is for her to have all the opportunities I did, not shut herself off from them so early on.'

'And you know I'd really love the thought of us having another baby?'

'Yes, you were rather keen on having a new baby,' said Cat. 'God alone knows why.'

'I like babies,' said Noel. 'And the thing is, *we* can't have another baby, and we'd have loved one. And Mel is having a baby she doesn't want. And it's too soon for her, so why don't we– ?'

The question hung in the air between them.

'What, look after the baby for her?'

'And let her continue her studies, do all the things she should be doing at her age,' said Noel. 'Come on, it's the perfect solution.'

'So long as you change your fair share of nappies,' said Cat.

'Scout's honour,' said Noel. 'See? Problem solved.'

'Oh lord,' said Cat. 'A baby in the house. Are we absolutely sure we're doing the right thing?'

'Of course we are,' said Noel, giving her a kiss. 'And it's the best thing for Mel and the baby.'

'I'm not sure Mel will be all that happy about it,' said Cat, wincing as she imagined Mel's response. 'She seems to think we don't want to help.'

'Well then,' said Noel, 'we need to persuade her we do, won't we?'

* * *

'Hi Steven,' Marianne came to greet him as Gabriel piled out of the car with several bags. He was only home for a weekend, but it looked like he was coming for a week.

'Sorry, he appears to have a lot of washing.'

'Don't they do it for you at school?' said Marianne.

'Yes, but it doesn't smell right,' said Steven. 'And I took some to Mum's and she made it smell all lavendery and old lady-ish. I like the way you make the washing smell, Marianne.'

'How does my washing smell?' laughed Marianne.

'Like home,' said Steven seriously, and she felt her heart melt instantly.

'You're not homesick are you?' said Gabriel anxiously.

'Not exactly,' said Steven, 'but it is nice to be back.'

He played around on the floor with the dog, as if to demonstrate.

'I mean, I do like school,' he said. 'It's great. I've got loads of mates now, and I like the singing. It was fab having a solo at evensong.'

'We thought you were pretty fab too,' said Marianne, giving Steven a cuddle.

'But it's cosy here,' said Steven. 'And I like it best of all the places I live.'

Gabriel smiled hugely and gave him a hug.

'Don't you feel cosy at your mum's?' Marianne said cautiously. She'd thought Steven had been happy to go to see Eve and Darren.

'Well it's okay,' said Steven slowly. 'It's just . . . it's all a bit tidy.'

'I hadn't realised you set such store by my slovenliness,' laughed Marianne.

'You know what I mean,' said Steven. 'Mum has white sofas. I'm terrified to sit on them in case I spill my Coke.'

Gabriel and Marianne both burst out laughing. Steven was always spilling things.

'Oh dear,' said Marianne. 'Well, never mind. I'm sure you have a lovely time when you're there.'

'Yes,' said Steven, but he didn't sound too sure, and Gabriel and Marianne exchanged glances.

'Is everything okay?' said Gabriel, 'with your mum I mean?'

'She's fine,' said Steven in a rush, and Marianne was taken again with his deep sense of loyalty to her. 'But Darren's – well, he's a bit mean to her. I don't like him very much.'

'But I thought he bought you loads of great presents,' said Gabriel. Marianne could feel he was resisting the urge to shout, 'Yes!'

'Only when he remembers,' said Steven. 'The rest of the time he seems to be on the phone and wants me to be quiet.'

'That's a shame,' said Marianne carefully. 'He's not mean to you is he?'

'No,' said Steven, 'he ignores me mostly. So that's okay. It's just that compared to here, it's boring.'

'Do you want to keep going over there then?' said Marianne. 'You don't have to if you don't want to.'

'Of course I do,' said Steven. 'I love seeing Mum. But coming here's better.'

'Thanks, Steven,' said Gabriel, looking touched. 'That means a lot.'

Steven smiled shyly, and Marianne grinned. Father and son were so alike. It was lovely to see them bonding again.

'Well this is exciting.' Pippa's mum and dad, Dan's parents, Dan, Pippa and the children were all gathered round the TV to watch the documentary about the Sunshine Trust which was just about to go out. 'I never thought I'd see my daughter on the telly,' Margaret said proudly.

'It's okay, Mum,' said Pippa. 'It's not like I'm going on *Britain's Got Talent*. This is purely a one-off. And I only did it to get interest in our campaign.'

The programme started with a panning-in view of the Sunshine Trust, and a hammily arranged shot of smiling children being welcomed by the staff at the home. 'For families like these,' the voiceover said, 'the Sunshine Trust offers a vital lifeline.' It then went on to describe three families in detail, showing each of them in their homes. Pippa was depicted baking, and declaring that 'Baking clears my head, and does me good, it's my default when I'm stressed.'

'And are you stressed much of the time?' said the interviewer.

'Constantly,' laughed Pippa on the TV.

Pippa squirmed. She sounded like some demented airhead who was desperate to palm off her daughter on the respite care team.

And it got worse. When it came to Pippa's big interview, she realised that her words had been twisted.

'Not only does Pippa have to care for Lucy,' the voiceover said, 'but recently, husband Dan has been feeling the strain and has moved out of the marital home.'

'I never said that!' protested Pippa, but then the interviewer was saying, 'So it's been a strain on your marriage having Lucy?'

'I really don't want to talk about this stuff,' TV Pippa was suddenly saying. 'Dan couldn't have been more supportive.'

'But he's not here,' said the interviewer tellingly, and the voiceover followed up with 'Just another casualty in the fight for support that all families with special needs children undergo, which is why the support of the Sunshine Trust is so vital.'

'I didn't say it like that,' said Pippa, 'I'm sure they didn't ask me those questions.'

'Probably makes for a better story,' said Margaret. 'You know what these TV folk are like. Don't worry about it.'

320

Pippa loved her mum very much, but sometimes she couldn't see what was under her nose.

No one else seemed to have noticed, so Pippa sat back and tried to relax and watch the rest of the programme, which fortunately didn't have any more surprises to throw at her, but she was left with a gnawing anxiety about what Dan was going to say. He'd been very quiet throughout. She hoped he hadn't taken it the wrong way.

But when it was over, and she was left alone with Dan and the children, he turned to her with a bitterness she'd never seen before.

'Well, you couldn't wait to put the knife in, could you?'

'Dan, they misrepresented me,' said Pippa. 'I didn't say those things.'

'Well, clearly you did, because you were on TV saying them.'

'What I meant was, I said them but in answer to different questions. They've joined it all up to fit a story they wanted to tell. I didn't breathe a word about you, honestly.'

'So how come they seemed to know all about my accident?'

'I have no idea,' said Pippa, 'but I swear I didn't tell them anything.'

'I don't believe you,' said Dan. 'Here I was thinking we were getting back on track, and I was even – how stupid of me – imagining I could move back in. But you've put a stop to all that.'

'Dan,' said Pippa.

'Dan nothing,' said Dan. 'You've let me down, Pippa. That's it. It's over.'

He got up and walked out of the house without a word. Pippa was left, standing speechless.

Mel

FACEBOOK status Well *that* went well.
Jen17: What?
Mel: Baby shopping with mum)-:
Jen17: Why
Mel: Cos I told her I'm going to give the baby up for adoption
Kaz: You can't do that!
Ellie: No!
Jen17: Are you mad?
Mel: I can. Why should I let this ruin my life? Andy's not letting it ruin his.
Kaz: But still . . .
Jen17: You should talk to him.
Mel: Tried, he doesn't want to know.
Ellie: Are you sure?
Mel: Sure
Kaz: But I wanted to be an auntie.
Mel: Shut up Kaz.

Teenage Kicks

I thought Mum was against the baby. But she's gone all weird.

She made me go baby shopping to 'bond' or

some shit. She bought half of Mothercare & got really soppy about babies. Shit.

Sounds like she's suddenly getting into being a granny.

Thing is, she's made me feel trapped. I don't want a baby now. I'm too young.

Every time it kicks and wriggles I want to scream. I don't want this now. I'm not ready. I've got to get away. Or give it away. Or do something.

So I've decided. I'm giving it up for adoption. It's the grown-up thing to do. And I told Mum. I thought she'd be pleased.

But she looked like I'd punched her in the stomach.

I can never do anything right.

December

Chapter Thirty-Four

'Fancy meeting you here,' Marianne grinned to Pippa, as she got out of the car with the twins in the farmyard of Batty Jack, the local turkey farmer who had earned his moniker by his obsession with the rare bat colony that had taken over one of his barns.

'I don't even know why I've come,' said Pippa, who looked pale and drawn. 'I have never felt less like celebrating Christmas. Dan's not going to be with us, Mum and Dad had a cruise booked months ago. It's going to be a sad lonely affair and I have no idea how I'm going to keep the children cheerful.'

'Oh no,' said Marianne, 'I thought you two were getting on better.'

'So did I,' said Pippa, 'but you saw that bloody programme, right?'

'Ah,' said Marianne, 'Dan thought . . .'

'That I'd deliberately been doing him down and blaming our marriage breakdown on his lack of support. I tried to tell him, but he walked out, and says it's over.'

'Oh Pippa, I'm so sorry,' said Marianne. 'Maybe if Gabe talked to him . . .'

'I really don't think it would make any difference,' said Pippa. 'Thanks anyway.'

'Why don't you come to us?' said Marianne, as they walked

across the incredibly muddy field with Batty Jack to inspect this year's crop of turkeys. 'I'm ordering a huge turkey anyway, and I've got a houseful. Better than being on your own.'

'Do you know, that would be bloody wonderful,' said Pippa. 'If you're sure . . .'

'Absolutely,' said Marianne. 'Come on, you're probably much better than me at this. Help me choose a turkey.'

'Well this one, here, see, I call her Hermione,' said Batty Jack, pointing out an enormous squat turkey, gobbling away. 'Beautiful isn't she? She's a nice strong bird, with no fat on her, and she'll be tasty and give you gorgeous white meat. And she'll be dripping with juice and blood and give you the best gravy in the world.

'Or here's my gorgeous Lizzie. Now she'll feed an army. You'll be eating turkey till the New Year. How many have you got for lunch, my lovely?'

'As of five minutes ago, fifteen,' said Marianne.

'Fifteen?' mouthed Pippa. 'Are you sure?'

'Positive,' said Marianne, enjoying the ghoulish showmanship with which Batty Jack demonstrated his prize turkeys. One year, she'd swear he'd even get out knives and start rubbing them together. She always found it astonishing that he could name every single one of his birds, and yet still relish the prospect of their demise.

'Six children, and nine adults, including five very hungry men.'

'And you'll be wanting plenty of extra for Boxing Day, I expect. Ah, then maybe you'll need my lovely Arietta. She's got a lovely pair of breasts on her – enough to keep any full-blooded male happy. However, steer clear of Miss Haversham over there. She's a bad-tempered old bird. I'm thinking of sending her down to the Hopesay Arms for their Christmas lunches. They still owe me money from last year.'

'What about you?' said Marianne. 'Which one have you got lined up for your Christmas lunch?'

'Oh bless you,' Batty Jack laughed. 'I couldn't eat 'em. I rear 'em and I can kill 'em, but I couldn't eat them. That would be like eating one of my friends. No, I'm a vegetarian. Me and the missus have nut roast on Christmas Day and then we're off to Barbados for a month, to get a bit of sunshine in.'

'Pippa,' said Marianne, 'we're in the wrong line of business.'

'Now, how does that look, do you think?' Cat was standing anxiously looking round the tables which were laid out for tonight's ball, as Pippa approached her, pushing Lucy. Knowing how snowed under Pippa was, she'd come over with Paige and Ruby to sort things out for the evening. Paige was a dab hand at folding napkins, and she and Ruby loved using the helium machine Cat had hired to blow up balloons. Ruby quickly made Lucy laugh by breathing into the machine and speaking with a helium voice. Each table had a red and white balloon display, and Cat had made up a hundred different table decorations with poinsettias, holly and ivy. There were stars hanging from the ceiling, and on the backcloths, which Cat had draped around the edges of the room. The effect was wonderfully Christmassy.

'Oh Cat, it looks fantastic!' said Pippa. 'Thanks so much. Look Lucy, isn't it pretty?'

Lucy's face lit up with pleasure, and she pointed at the balloons.

Can I have one? She typed.

'Here Lucy, have this one,' Ruby handed Lucy one of the balloons and tied it to her wheelchair. Lucy clapped with delight, and started to giggle. The giggling turned into a coughing fit.

'Hey, Lucy, you okay there?' said Pippa, giving her a pat on the back, and producing some water for her. Gradually the coughing died down.

'Is she all right?' said Cat.

'I hope so,' said Pippa. 'She's got the beginnings of a cold, and we always have to be careful at this time of year, as she's prone to chest infections. But you're feeling okay, aren't you, Luce?'

Lucy nodded and smiled again, giving a thumbs-up.

I wouldn't have missed this for anything, she typed.

'And we've got a lovely dress for you to wear tonight, haven't we?' said Pippa. 'Can't have anything less for the guest of honour.'

It had been agreed that Pippa would speak about Lucy and the other children who got help from the Sunshine Trust that night, and Pippa had been adamant that they should be allowed to attend. 'This is an evening about the children,' she'd argued. 'They shouldn't be locked out of sight.'

Cat had agreed, thinking it was a wonderfully inspiring idea, and when it had been mentioned to Michael, he'd arranged for a children's entertainer for the evening, free of charge.

'So are all yours coming tonight?' asked Cat.

'The boys said they wouldn't be seen dead at a ball,' admitted Pippa. 'So Dan's having them.'

'You haven't been able to persuade Dan to come then?'

'No,' said Pippa sadly. She mouthed over Lucy's head, 'Tell you later.'

Poor Pippa. Cat really felt for her. As if life hadn't handed her a tough enough deck of cards anyway. Why some people had so much rotten luck, she never knew. The past few months had taken its toll on her. She looked much too thin.

'Behind every cloud there's a silver lining,' said Michael Nicholas, appearing as if by magic behind her and nodding in Pippa's direction, while Pippa went off to oversee how the caterers were getting on. He was dressed in a black shirt and black jeans with cowboy boots, and carrying an electric guitar emblazoned with flames, ready for his set with the band.

'Do you think?' said Cat. 'I'm not sure Pippa feels like that at the moment. She really deserves some good luck.'

'You never know what's round the corner,' said Michael. 'Maybe Pippa's luck is about to turn.'

'I do hope so,' said Cat with feeling. 'I can't think of anyone who deserves it more.'

'This looks fantastic.' Marianne, radiant in a red satin dress, her dark curly hair piled up fetchingly on her head, dragged Gabriel over to Pippa, having had their obligatory couple photo as they'd entered the room. Pippa felt a pang. Time was when she and Dan would have been that happy together. Stop it, Pippa, she admonished herself sternly. You can't let it spoil the evening.

'Thanks,' said Pippa. 'I just hope it does what it's meant to do.'

'I'm sure it will.' Cat came and joined them. 'Pippa, shall I get people to start moving towards their tables? It's nearly eight o'clock and we need to get the auction going.'

Soon the evening was in full swing. The room was abuzz with the sound of laughter, and Antoine Lavière proved to be a dashing and urbane host, plus he was immensely good at getting money out of people.

'Do I only have £100 for the spa day at Congreve Hall? Only £100, surely you can dig a bit deeper than that,' he said, 'it's a bargain at twice the price. Come on, dig deep people, it's all for a good cause.' Sure enough, Antoine managed to get a further £200 out of a rather verbose chap sitting in the corner, who'd already gleefully bought signed copies of Cat's latest book and DVD. By the time he'd moved on to the second of the weekend retreats, the grand total was looking very healthy indeed. There were some fairly wealthy landowners in the area, and Antoine proved adept at winkling money out of them. Richard La Fontaine, who Pippa had noted arriving, but had yet to speak to, was being extremely generous. She felt extraordinarily tongue-tied at the thought of speaking to him, but she wasn't sure why.

The children were all being royally entertained in a side room by Michael's entertainer, and things couldn't be going better.

Pippa had opted not to drink tonight. She was going to have to drive Lucy home, and she wanted to be in control of herself. She was nervous as hell about her speech. Could she make a difference? Would anyone here be prepared to invest in the Sunshine Trust? Eventually, Antoine called for silence. 'Ladies and gentlemen, we've had a fun evening so far, and I promise you more fun on the way, but we're here tonight for one reason, and one reason only. Let me intro-duce the incredible, dynamic and inspiring Pippa Holliday, who's here to tell us what the point of this evening is all about.'

Pippa gulped as she went to stand in front of the micro-phone. She felt small and insignificant. If only Dan were with her. Normally when she'd done this kind of thing, he'd been at her side, and now she was doing this alone. And would be for the rest of her life. Deep breaths, Pippa, she said to herself, deep breaths. The kids still need you.

'Thank you so much for the kind and ridiculously over the top introduction,' said Pippa, 'I'm really none of the things Antoine called me. I'm just an ordinary mum. A mum who has a very special child. When Lucy was born, I confess at first I didn't know what to do –' (don't think of Dan, don't think of Dan) '– like all parents who have a special needs child, it's not what you expect, and you can feel all at sea. For years we fought a system which seemed almost determined to stand against us. And then we found the Sunshine Trust . . .'

Pippa went on to talk about the way having respite care had transformed their lives, and those of others. 'And it's not just me and my family who get help. Anita Thompson, over in that corner, has care for her son Timothy, Sufira Ali gets help twice a month for Suleiman, and I know that Jeanie Martin couldn't manage if her two autistic children, Sammi and John, didn't get a break every week. We all need the Sunshine Trust. It transforms our lives and helps us cope. So please. I know these are difficult times, I know money is tight, but tonight, please dig deep for this vital service and help the children like Lucy, and Timothy, Sammi and John get the support they so badly need.'

Pippa went to sit down with applause ringing in her ears. She was shaking like a leaf. She hoped she'd said enough to make a difference.

'That was brilliant,' said Cat, giving her a hug.

'Well done,' said Gabe, kissing her on the cheek.

'Thanks,' said Pippa, 'I just hope it helps.'

Pippa's speech had certainly made an impact. The bidding in the auction was brisker and people were spending money faster than she could have imagined. The evening was a success beyond her wildest reckoning. If only Dan was there, everything would have been perfect.

'You've met Richard La Fontaine, I think.' Michael Nicholas came over while the coffee was being served and people were beginning to drift off to other tables. 'Excuse me, I must go, the band are about to start playing.'

'Yes, of course,' said Pippa, getting up to greet him. 'Nice to meet you again.'

'Wonderful speech,' said Richard. He was tall and slim, with a lively smile, slightly greying hair which gave him a distinguished look, and vivid green eyes.

'Thank you,' said Pippa. 'I just spoke from the heart.'

'And it showed,' said Richard. 'Listen. I know I've not had much positive to say of late, but I brought some members of my board along tonight so they could see for themselves what you do. We like to get involved in ethical projects, and this is one close to my heart.'

'Oh?'

'I think I mentioned I have a daughter with special needs?' said Richard. 'We could have really benefited from some respite care. But we didn't have a Sunshine Trust in the area. I was away a lot on business, and my wife couldn't cope. We ended up splitting up, our daughter's in a care home, and I hardly see her. I think the work they do is vital, so I want to help if I can.'

'That would be fantastic,' said Pippa, overwhelmed. 'It's just the sort of good news we've been needing. Thank you so much.'

She headed back to her table feeling like punching the air. At last, something was going right. Suddenly, there was a commotion. 'Has anyone seen Pippa?' a voice was saying. It was Ruby, looking scared.

'Ruby, what's the matter?' said Pippa, suddenly gripped with fear.

'It's Lucy,' said Ruby, 'she's coughing really badly and it's like she can't breathe.'

Pippa raced towards the side room, where one of the helpers from the Sunshine Trust had got Lucy on an oxygen mask.

'Hospital?' said Pippa.

'The ambulance is on its way,' said the helper.

Pippa knelt down and held Lucy's hand, she looked very pale and was breathing in a horribly laboured way. Oh God, why hadn't she taken more notice of Lucy's cold? They'd both been so excited about this evening, she thought it would be all right. Stupid, stupid, stupid.

'It's okay, sweetie, help's coming,' she said, holding Lucy's hand tightly, hoping that the ambulance wouldn't be too late.

Chapter Thirty-Five

The journey to hospital, down windy dark country lanes, seemed endless. Pippa sat holding Lucy's hand, talking to her comfortingly as she had done so many times in the past. Her breathing had calmed down a bit since the paramedics had given her some Ventolin, but she looked pale and had a temperature. The paramedics had been efficient and friendly, instantly putting Pippa at her ease, and reassuring her that Lucy was in the best hands. Which she knew from experience to be true – she and Dan had done this hundreds of times after all. But this time she was doing it on her own. Never had she felt so lonely. She should text Dan and let him know what was going on, but it wasn't like he could do anything right now, and the boys were staying over, so there was no need for her to get back. Pippa had no idea what to do for the best. She'd never get used to this. Never.

The ambulance eventually pulled up at A&E, and the paramedics carefully took Lucy in, Pippa following, feeling slightly surreal in her ball gown and high heels. The lights of the hospital seemed far too bright after the darkness of the road, and Lucy squirmed a little in response to them. It being a Saturday night, this close to Christmas, A&E was full of drunks, and luckily the sister in charge saw fit to whisk them into a side room to give Lucy some privacy.

'Sorry, our children's department isn't staffed at this time of night,' she said. 'You really don't want to be out there with that rabble. Hell, *we* don't want to be out there with that rabble.'

Pippa laughed and sat down, expecting a very long wait. But to her surprise, a doctor came through almost instantly.

'Are you Lucy's mum?' he said holding out his hand. 'Dr Jenkins. I'm the on-call paediatrician.'

'Hi there,' said Pippa. 'I'm surprised we've never met before. We've been here rather often.'

'And this beautiful young lady must be Lucy,' said Dr Jenkins, giving Lucy a wide smile.

Lucy smiled weakly back, giving a faint thumbs-up.

'Have you been at a party?' said Dr Jenkins, expertly taking Lucy's temperature and blood pressure while putting her at her ease. 'That's a very pretty dress if I might say so.'

Lucy clicked approvingly, and Pippa could have hugged him.

'We've been at a charity ball,' said Pippa.

'And what happened?'

'I'd noticed she had a bit of a cough earlier on,' admitted Pippa, 'but it didn't seem to be bothering her much, and she really wanted to go to the ball. I think she might have got a bit overexcited, because the cough came on really suddenly again, and then she was struggling to breathe.'

'Well the good news is,' said Dr Jenkins, 'I think the Ventolin's worked. She's got a bit of a temperature though, so I think we should monitor that, and I'm going to give her some antibiotics. I'm afraid you're in for an overnight stay, but with any luck we'll have you home tomorrow.'

'Thanks,' said Pippa. 'That's a huge relief.'

'Right, I'll go and sort out getting a bed for this young lady,' Dr Jenkins said. 'I hope you won't be waiting too long.'

'It's okay,' said Pippa, 'we're used to it, aren't we Lucy?'

Lucy just shrugged her shoulders in a long-suffering gesture and then grinned at Pippa, in a way that tugged at her heart. She really was the most stoical of creatures, and never lost her ability to make Pippa laugh.

Pippa went out to request a glass of water and a straw for Lucy. She knew from previous experience that the casualty department wasn't well equipped with plastic cups for disabled children. The paediatric ward wasn't that much better. Normally Pippa carried everything she needed with her, but this time, she'd been in such a hurry it hadn't been possible.

She came back into the room, to hear voices and the sound of Lucy laughing. That lovely doctor must be back again.

'Hi,' she began and then 'Oh.'

Dan turned round to look at her.

'Dan,' she said, 'thanks for coming.'

'Where else would I be at a time like this?' he said.

'Have you heard from Pippa yet?' Cat asked Marianne, as they finished clearing the last of the tables away. Noel had taken the children home earlier, and Gabriel had gone to relieve his mum, who was babysitting the twins.

'Yes, she just texted me five minutes ago to say that Lucy's much better,' said Marianne. 'She's got to stay in overnight for observation, but she's going to be all right.'

'That's a relief,' said Cat. 'Poor thing. What a terrible worry for her. Do you know if anyone's told Dan yet?'

'Yes,' said Marianne. 'Gabriel texted him straight away. We both had a feeling Pippa might feel she shouldn't. Which is daft, of course.'

'I feel so bad,' said Cat. 'That bloody TV programme has caused a lot of trouble. I know they wanted an angle on their story, but I had no idea they were going to use Pippa and Dan's split to beef the story up. I'd only mentioned it in passing to the director because he was interested in Pippa's personal circumstances. I never said it was because of Lucy though.'

'It's not your fault,' said Marianne. 'And to be honest, I think Dan's overreacted. But he's had such a hard time, I suppose he could be forgiven for that.'

'Right, that's us done, I think,' said Cat. 'Michael, is it okay if we come back and do the rest in the morning?'

'Yes of course,' said Michael. 'Tell Pippa when you see her that it's been a great success, and she should be proud of herself.'

'Will do,' said Cat. 'I'm dying to know how much we raised. The auction was going great guns.'

'I think you'll find there's a huge amount of money sloshing around in the slush fund,' said Michael. 'And Richard La Fontaine has just told me Pippa's speech did the trick with his colleagues. He's just been given the go ahead to invest in the Sunshine Trust. So it looks like the respite care package has been saved.'

'That's wonderful,' said Cat. 'At last something to cheer Pippa up. Right, time to go. Lift, Marianne?'

'That would be great, thanks,' said Marianne. 'Gabriel took our car. I'll see you next week, Michael.'

'How's the nativity progressing?' said Michael.

'Oh, you know,' said Marianne. 'Dreadful rehearsal yesterday, but I'm sure it will be all right on the night.'

'I'm sure it will be brilliant,' said Cat. 'It always is. Ruby's certainly looking forward to it.'

'I so wish I'd made her Mary,' said Marianne, 'and sod Ruth Patterson's annoying mother. Ruth is the most irritating Mary we've ever had. She can't remember any of her lines, and having thought she could sing, it turns out she was miming to a version of *Mary's Boy Child* she'd got off YouTube, in the audition, and she can't sing at all. Little cow.'

'Oh well,' said Cat. 'I'm sure it will be fine.'

'That's what I keep telling myself,' grinned Marianne.

'What's on the agenda this morning?' said Noel, waking up with a yawn. He and Cat had sat up into the early hours dancing to Dire Straits and drinking far too much red wine. Cat could feel her head pounding. Oh God, to be twenty again and be able to get away with it.

'Nothing, I don't think. Ruby's got a party at three, but apart from that we're free agents.'

'Good,' said Noel, 'I'll go and get the Christmas tree.'

'About time too,' said Cat, 'I thought we were getting it last weekend.'

'Yeah, well you dragged me off to the hell that is Christmas shopping in Birmingham, remember,' said Noel. 'Besides, you know I like putting up the Christmas tree the week before.'

Cat laughed, and rolled over to go back to sleep for a bit. Oh the joy of having older children and the possibility of lie ins.

'Mum, Mum, Molly says she's going to see Santa tonight,' Ruby burst into their room in typically enthusiastic fashion.

'Oh, where's that then?' said Cat, thinking, bang goes my lie in. Ruby's enthusiastic outbursts left little room for relaxation. Once she'd gone out of the room, Cat would be so thoroughly woken up that she would have no chance of going back to sleep.

'At her house. SANTA WROTE HER A LETTER FROM HIS WEBSITE. Can you believe it?' Ruby was astounded. 'Why hasn't he written me a letter?'

'No! That's truly unbelievable,' Cat agreed. 'What did the letter say?'

'It said to look out for him at midnight tonight, because he will be doing the rounds pre-Christmas and if she's really really good, he'll land on her roof.'

'Is that so?' said Cat. 'And has she been really really good?'

'Well. No,' said Ruby. 'That's what's strange. She's drowned her brother's goldfish, she left her good school shoes out in the rain and her bedroom is really untidy. She couldn't have been more naughty.'

'Funny that,' said Cat glancing at Noel and trying to suppress a grin. 'Perhaps Santa's going to give her a week to make amends. LUCKILY, you haven't been such a naughty girl, so Santa will be coming to see you next week.'

'Oh, that's it,' said Ruby. 'Can I ring Molly back?'

'Of course,' said Cat, collapsing into giggles as Ruby skipped out. 'I take my hat off to Molly's mum. That is a really really good invention.'

Now thoroughly wide awake, she got up and went downstairs to make tea and toast, and think about tackling the decorations, which she'd got down from the attic the night before. Feeling a trifle weak, she let Paige and Ruby take over, and soon the house was looking wonkily festive.

'Right, who's coming to get the tree?' Noel appeared dressed in all-weather gear.

'We live in Shropshire, not the Arctic,' said Cat. 'I don't think it's even meant to snow today.'

'Best be prepared,' said Noel.

Mel had wandered in, looking bored and restless. She was getting really big now. Noel left with the other three, leaving Cat on her own with Mel.

'How are you feeling today?' said Cat. 'Any more Braxton Hicks?'

It was a bit early – Mel had still over six weeks to go, but she had been complaining of quite strong contractions.

'I'm fine,' snapped Mel.

'I only asked,' protested Cat. 'If it gets any worse, I really think we should ring the hospital.'

'Mum, I have six weeks to go,' said Mel. 'Nothing is going to happen.'

'I have done this myself, you know,' said Cat. 'And one thing I've learnt from having four babies is that nothing about childbirth is predictable. Ever.'

Mel rolled her eyes, and made to leave the room, but Cat stopped her.

'Look, maybe this isn't the right time to talk about it, but Dad and I have been talking. You really don't have to give the baby up. We'll look after it for you, of course we will. We'd love to, and you can go on to uni and do all the things you want to. Please think about it.'

'Oh for fuck's sake,' said Mel. 'I don't expect you to do the sackcloths and ashes routine. This is my screw-up, and I don't want this baby. So whatever you say, I'm giving it up for adoption.'

'Mel,' pleaded Cat, 'please think about this.'

'I've thought about nothing else for the last six months,' said Mel. 'If you don't stop going on at me I'm going to go and have the bloody thing in a gutter and give it away without you knowing anything about it.'

'Mel,' said Cat, 'don't be silly.'

But Mel had got herself all worked up. 'I've had enough. I'm leaving right now.' And with that, she got up and walked out of the house.

'Mel!' said Cat, but there was no reply. Just a door slammed in her face and the familiar feeling of failure.

Chapter Thirty-Six

'Hi, Karen, this is Mel's mum, is she with you? She's not? Right. Have you any idea where she might be? Okay, thanks.' Cat put the phone down and said to Noel, 'She's not with Karen, and Karen has no idea where she might be.'

'And you've tried her mobile?'

'Not picking up,' said Cat. 'She's been gone for hours, and it's getting dark. And the silly girl went out without a coat. I think we should go and look for her.'

'Where?' said Noel.

That was the problem of course, where to start.

Cat's phone rang.

'Karen? Has Mel been in touch?'

'No,' said Karen, 'but I've just remembered, she's been really upset about Andy recently, and I know she's tried to meet him in the hay barn in the farm where he works, but he won't see her.'

'Do you know which farm?'

'No, sorry.'

'Now what do we do?' said Cat putting the phone down.

'Didn't Marianne mention Andy works for Dan and Pippa?' Noel said.

'Of course,' said Cat, 'I can't believe I can have forgotten that. Come on, Noel, let's get over there.'

'Do you think we should ring first?' said Noel.

'Pippa's got enough on her plate,' said Cat. 'We'll just go over, look for Mel and come home.'

The temperature had really plummeted in the afternoon, so Cat decided to bring blankets and a couple of fleeces. She was glad she had done, because there was a fierce wind blowing by the time they got up to Pippa's. The farmhouse was in darkness when they arrived.

'Pippa must still be at the hospital,' said Cat. 'Come on, let's go round the back.'

They entered the farmyard, feeling like thieves. A security light flared on and they heard barking from one of the dogs.

'Mel, are you there?' Cat called, feeling a little foolish.

'Which one's the hay barn?' said Noel. 'There are so many buildings here.'

'Not this one,' said Cat, opening a door and hearing loud lowing. 'I think we've just found Pippa's cows.'

They explored all the buildings in the courtyard to no avail, and as they approached the one in the farthest corner, they heard a muffled moan.

'Mel!' Cat ran over to the barn door, pulled it open, and shone the torch she'd brought inside.

'Mum!' a pale and frightened looking Mel was leaning against a haystack, her face betraying her considerable discomfort. 'My waters have broken. I think I'm in labour.'

Shit. The baby was six weeks early.

Cat got her mobile to ring 999. Damn. No signal.

'Noel, can you get a signal on your phone?' said Cat. 'We need to call an ambulance.'

'What? You're joking,' said Noel.

'No, I'm not,' said Cat. 'Mel's in labour. We need an ambulance fast.'

'Shit,' said Noel. 'I can't get a signal.'

'Neither can I,' said Mel weakly. 'I tried to call you.'

She let out an ear-piercing shriek and Cat held her tightly.

'Come on sweetheart, try and breathe through it,' she said.

The contraction subsided and Mel leant against her mother in relief.

'Noel, go back to the lane and get the car,' said Cat. 'We'll have to take her to hospital ourselves.'

There was another bloodcurdling scream from Mel.

'Blimey, did I make that much noise when I was in labour?' said Cat.

'You certainly did,' said Noel. 'Right, I'll go and get the car.'

'Too late,' croaked Mel, 'I can't move. I think the baby's coming.'

Shit, shit, shit. Cat took a deep breath, 'Well then,' she said cheerfully, 'I'll have to deliver it, won't I? Noel, go and get help.'

Noel raced off, and Cat tried to get Mel more comfortable. She was shivering and clearly in a lot of pain. Thank God she'd brought warm clothes and a blanket.

'Come on,' she said, 'see if we can hold that baby off for a while.'

Another shriek from Mel made her realise that wasn't an option, so she swiftly arranged things, so that Mel was at least not lying in straw.

'Come on, Mel, pull your trousers off,' she said, 'otherwise the baby's going nowhere.'

'Mum!' shrieked Mel. 'This is so embarrassing.'

'Welcome to the world of childbirth,' said Cat. 'Now come on. Squat down, you may find it helps, and lean on me hard when the next contraction comes.'

With a supreme effort, Mel shouted, 'I can feel it coming, I want to push, noooow!'

'Bloody hell, Mel,' said Cat, 'I think they can hear you

on the other side of Hope Christmas. Come on, you're doing brilliantly.'

Mel smiled weakly, and Cat said with sudden excitement, 'I can see the head. One more push and you've done it.'

Mel let out another deafening scream, and with that, Cat's new grandchild shot into her waiting hands.

'Oh Mel,' Cat said, tears streaming down her face. 'You've got a beautiful baby girl.'

Tenderly she wrapped the baby in her coat, and passed her to Mel, who was also crying. 'Oh Mum, I'm so sorry for everything.'

'Nothing to be sorry about,' said Cat, who was crying too. 'Look at her, she's perfect. I've been a rubbish mum. I'm sorry I wasn't as supportive as I should have been.'

'I have been a bit of a cow,' said Mel.

'Yes, you have,' said Cat. 'But it's all right now. Everything's all right now. What are you going to call her?'

Mel smiled through her tears. 'Louise,' she said. 'What else?'

'Bloody hell, what's going on?' Pippa and Dan drove back into the farmyard with Lucy and the boys to see the floodlights blazing, two ambulances, and Mel Tinsall being escorted into one of them, while Cat, looking slightly stunned, was climbing into another, with a baby.

'I'm so sorry about this,' said Noel, coming over to them. 'We didn't have time to tell anyone, but Cat's just delivered Mel's baby in your barn.'

'Crikey,' said Pippa. 'Is everything all right?'

'I think so,' said Noel, as they watched the ambulances depart. 'I'm just off to the hospital now. Is Lucy okay?'

'Much better, thanks,' said Pippa. 'Congratulations.'

'Thanks,' said Noel, 'I feel a bit punch drunk actually. I can't quite take it in. I'm a granddad. Blimey.'

'Do you want to come in?' said Dan. 'Have a drink on us?'

'No, it's okay,' said Noel, 'I'd better get off.'

Dan and Pippa watched him go, and then got the children into the house.

Lucy was still tired, so they put her to bed, and then Pippa cooked tea for them all while Dan sat in the lounge watching footie with the boys. It felt restful and normal, and though Dan had said nothing to her in the hospital, she began to hope that maybe he was going to change his mind, and they could start all over again, particularly when they sat round the dinner table, bickering and joking as if nothing had changed. And yet, so much had . . .

But when they'd chased the boys off to bed, Dan got up to go.

'Oh,' said Pippa. 'I thought you might want to stay.'

'I don't think that's a good idea,' said Dan.

Suddenly, Pippa knew what was coming, but still she couldn't help herself from saying, 'Don't you? You're here, with us. Where you belong.'

'But that's it,' said Dan. 'I'm sorry. What I said to you last time was unforgiveable. I know it wasn't your fault that the programme made out that Lucy was the cause of us splitting up. But the trouble is, I've changed. I'm not the same person I was six months ago. I'm not sure I'm ever going to be the same again.'

'But that's okay,' said Pippa. 'We all have to adapt to you being different. Come on, we can get through this.'

'Oh Pippa, my lovely gorgeous optimistic Pippa.' Dan held her tightly and stroked her hair. 'I want to, more than anything but at the moment I don't think I can. I don't feel I belong here anymore. Everything's changed too much, and I don't think we can ever go back to the way we were.'

'Dan, please don't say that,' said Pippa, tears running down her cheeks. 'We can work it out.'

'No, sweetheart, this time I'm not sure we can,' said Dan. 'I'll continue to support you in every way, and I'll always be there for the boys and Lucy, but I think it's over. I'm sorry.'

He kissed her on the top of her head, and sadly picked up his coat and got up to go. Pippa didn't stop him. What was the point? Besides, in her heart she knew he was right. They'd both spent the last six months fighting it, but something had died the day of the accident, and now she had to acknowledge Dan was right. It looked as though her marriage was over for good.

She watched him drive out of the farmyard for the last time, and felt her heart break in two. It was over. Dan had left her, and life was never going to be the same.

'Oh Pippa, I'm so sorry,' said Marianne, giving Pippa a hug as she walked into the barn in the grounds of Hopesay Manor, where this year's nativity was going to be held. 'I'm really glad I asked you for Christmas now.'

'Me too,' said Pippa. 'But even though my heart is breaking, weirdly I think it's probably the right thing. That bloody accident changed everything. I'm not sure we could ever go back to being the way we were.'

'What's Dan going to do?' said Marianne.

'I don't know,' said Pippa. 'Stay with his parents for now, and then we need to think about the farm. I just want to get Christmas out of the way. And think about the future in January.'

'Are you going to be okay?' said Marianne.

'You know me,' said Pippa, 'I'm always okay, and I intend to make this Christmas as special as I can for the kids. Now, come on, what do you need me to do?'

'Pippa, you never cease to amaze me,' said Marianne. 'If you could help sort out the costumes, that would be fantastic. I've got to ring bloody Danielle Patterson. Ruth hasn't turned up.'

The next hour was spent in a flurry of activity, going over lines, making sure everyone knew what to do when, trying Danielle Patterson's number for the millionth time, Marianne eventually got through to her.

'Oh, sorry,' said Danielle, 'Ruth got invited to a party tonight, and can't make it. Didn't I say?'

'No, you didn't,' said Marianne between gritted teeth. She turned her phone off and said, 'Bugger, bugger, bugger! Now what are we going to do? We haven't got a Mary.'

Ruby put her hand up shyly.

'Please Mrs North,' she said, 'I've learnt all Mary's lines. Could I do it?'

Marianne hugged her. 'Of course you can, Ruby. Go on, quickly get changed out of your shepherd's costume and get ready to be Mary.'

As the crowds started to file in, she saw Cat, Noel, and the rest of the family come in, with Mel proudly showing off the baby, which gave Marianne a sudden idea . . .

The lights went out, and Steven walked to the front, looking nervous but assured as he sang the first few lines of The Angel Gabriel, before the lights came up on the cast in tableau around a kneeling Ruby, looking up at Toby Davies dressed as Gabriel.

This year, Marianne had opted to tell the story as simply as possible, and to give it a contemporary feeling, chosen to depict Mary and Joseph as illegal immigrants. Much of the action took place silently, with a background of music and carols propelling the story on. She had managed to get her donkey in, and Michael had produced a couple of calves, so the scene when Mary and Joseph arrived at the inn, with Mary on the donkey, felt wonderfully authentic. Although

Marianne was hoping against hope that none of the animals would disgrace themselves.

Joseph helped Mary off the donkey, and they settled down in the hay as the rest of the cast sang *Mary's Boy Child*.

The narrator read, 'And so Mary had her baby, and laid him in swaddling clothes and put him in a manger.'

With the pièce de résistance, Marianne smiled at Mel, as she swiftly passed Louise to her little sister. Ruby held her new niece in her arms, and carefully put her in the crib. There wasn't a dry eye in the house as thirty pure little voices piped up with *Away in a Manger*.

The shepherds and wise men duly came and adored the baby, but Marianne felt she would never top that moment.

'That was wonderful,' an emotional Cat flung her arms round Marianne at the end. 'Thank you so much.'

'My pleasure,' said Marianne. 'Thanks Mel, for letting us have your baby for five minutes. She is absolutely beautiful.'

'Thank you, Marianne,' said Mel shyly, holding the baby as if she'd been doing it forever.

'What are you going to do about school?' said Marianne.

'I've decided to stay on,' said Mel. 'Mum and Dad say they'll help with Louise, and then I'll see if I can still go to uni.'

'That's wonderful,' said Marianne. 'So you're not going to give her up after all.'

'I couldn't,' admitted Mel. 'Once she was here, I fell in love.'

'Babies have a way of doing that to you,' said Marianne.

'That was amazing, again,' Pippa came bounding over to see them all. 'What time do you want us tomorrow?'

'Say twelve?' said Marianne.

'Marianne,' Steven came up and tugged her shoulder, 'have we got room for one more?'

Eve was standing looking shamefaced beside him.

'Of course,' said Marianne. 'What about Darren?'

'We've split up,' said Eve. 'Turns out he wasn't very interested in Steven, and didn't like coming up here all the time. So . . .'

'You're going to be on your own for Christmas,' said Marianne. 'Of course you can come to us.'

'Sounds like you've got a houseful,' laughed Cat.

'Why don't you come too?' said Marianne. 'Thanks to Batty Jack, I've got the biggest turkey in Hope Christmas.'

'What, all of us?' said Cat.

'Come on, you probably don't want to be cooking Christmas dinner tomorrow with a newborn in the house, do you?'

'Actually, we've been so topsy-turvy this year,' admitted Cat, 'I haven't even got a proper turkey in. I was going to get a crown roast out of the freezer tonight.'

'Well that's settled then,' said Marianne. 'This Christmas is on me. And it's going to be the best ever.'

Mel

FACEBOOK status OMG I'm a MUM!!!! Louise Catherine Tinsall born 5pm 21 December 5bs 12 oz.

Jen17: WOW. Congratulations

Josh: Bloody hell. Well done.

Ellie: That's fab

Jen17: A baby at Christmas. That's so cute

Kaz: WHEN CAN I SEE HER???

Chas: Wow.

Mel: Thanks everyone. Can't believe how amazing it feels.

Andy: Congrats Mel. Happy Christmas.

Mel: You too. You can see her if you like.

Andy: And your dad won't kill me?

Mel: BBM ME PRIVATE CHATS NOW!!!!

Teenage Kicks

I had no idea it was going to be like this. From the moment I held the Babe I just knew I had to look after her and protect her. Even the Boy has been to see her. Apparently he's moving away soon. He says he'll keep in touch, but I don't think I believe him. I don't care anymore

*though. I've got Mum and Dad, and now Louise.
Everything I want in life is right here. She's the
best Christmas present ever.*

Epilogue

'Come on in,' said Gabriel as the Tinsalls squeezed themselves into the house, shaking the snow off their boots. Magically, they'd woken up to discover it had snowed in the night. 'Everyone's in the lounge.'

They divested themselves of boots and coats and followed Gabriel into the crowded lounge, dominated by an eight-foot-high Christmas tree in the corner, which was practically touching the ceiling, and seemingly dozens of people, talking animatedly.

'Mulled wine anyone?'

'Sounds perfect,' said Cat, happily accepting a glass.

'Marianne will be in in a minute,' said Gabriel, 'slight turkey crisis.'

'Does she need any help?' asked Cat.

'No, she does not,' retorted Marianne, emerging red-faced from the kitchen, sporting a Santa hat, and an apron saying Santa's Little Helper, over a sexy black cocktail dress. She looked stunning.

'Merry Christmas everyone. Let me introduce you to everyone.'

Marianne's mother nearly fainted when she finally met Cat. 'I love your recipes,' she said. 'I can't believe I've actually met you. You're even prettier than you are on the telly.'

'That's very nice of you,' said Cat, and proceeded to try and prove that really she was quite normal.

'This is my son, Matthew,' said Jenny, who was looking slightly flushed from one too many sherries, 'and his partner Marcus.'

'Mum!' Marianne nearly dropped her glass in shock.

'You knew?' Matthew was looking stunned and wide eyed.

'Of course I knew,' said Jenny. 'What, did you all think I was stupid or something?'

'Er no,' said Marcus, 'we're just a bit surprised.'

'You're a lovely boy, Marcus,' said Jenny raising her glass to him, 'so when are you going to make an honest man of my son? I do like a good wedding.'

After that bombshell nothing could possibly go wrong, Marianne felt. And so it proved. The room was buzzing with a sense of fun and excited chatter. Various of the children disappeared to Steven's room to watch TV, Paige had enthusiastically taken charge of the twins, Marcus and Matthew were talking football with Steven, Pippa was sitting in the corner with Lucy, pulling crackers, and telling each other jokes. Even Eve was unexpectedly getting on really well with Marianne's dad, while Noel, beer in hand, was busy extolling the virtues of being a granddad to Gabriel's parents.

'It's great,' he said, 'I hear the baby crying and I have no guilt whatsoever about not getting up in the night.'

'Funny that that isn't a granny reaction, isn't it?' Cat nudged him in the ribs.

Mel, shyly showing Louise off, was the centre of attention. And Louise was the perfect baby, waking up only to feed, and in between happily putting up with being passed round all the women in the room for a cuddle.

'Great mulled wine, Gabe,' said Cat.

'Your recipe, I believe,' said Gabriel, topping up her glass.

'Ah well, that will be why then,' blushed Cat. 'I can't believe I didn't recognise my own recipe!'

'Dinner is served,' said Marianne. 'We've extended the table from the kitchen into the conservatory, so we should all just about fit.'

In dribs and drabs, and after many dashes to the toilet from the children, everyone arrived at the table, which was laid for twenty-one. The children were down one end, and the adults at the other. Each place was set with a cracker, a party hat, and party poppers, which the children all let off noisily straight away. Louise didn't bat an eyelid, even then.

'Isn't that baby just the calmest baby you've ever seen?' said Pippa in awe.

'She has to be, living in our house. Isn't that right, Mel?' grinned Cat.

'Too right, Mum,' said Mel grinning back.

'Well, Batty Jack's done us proud this year,' said Gabriel as he carved the turkey. 'I bet he had no idea he was going to be providing for twenty-one. We certainly didn't, but we're very glad to have you!'

'You okay?' said Cat, as she squeezed in next to Pippa.

'I will be,' said Pippa with a determinedly cheerful grin. 'You know me, I'll survive.'

'And I know you've got an admirer,' said Cat with a grin.

'I don't know what you mean,' said Pippa, blushing.

'Richard La Fontaine seemed very interested in you after the ball,' said Cat, 'and he is not only rich, but good looking.'

'Is he?' said Pippa innocently. 'I really hadn't noticed.'

'Pull the other one,' said Cat. 'I've seen the way you look at him, when you don't think anyone's looking.'

Pippa blushed again.

'A girl can dream,' she said.

'And you deserve a dream to come true,' said Cat. 'Come the new year, it's going to be Project Find Pippa a Date.'

'I'll drink to that,' said Pippa and smiled.

'Time for crackers!' said Marianne, and they all joined arms around the table, and with 'A one, two, three, now!' pulled at the same time. As usual, half the crackers didn't work, but Louise, who was dozing in her car seat in the corner, barely even moved when one went off loudly in her ear.

'You don't think she could be deaf, do you?' said Noel doubtfully.

'I'm sure she's fine,' said Cat. 'Let's just be grateful she's asleep.'

The meal passed quickly in a haze of jollity and merriment. There was plenty to eat, plenty to drink and plenty of good cheer, just as there should be at Christmas. All too soon, the pudding had been eaten, plates pushed away, and the port was being cracked open. Gabriel stood up, tapped his glass, and called for quiet.

'I'd like to raise a glass to everyone here,' said Gabriel. 'Firstly, I'd like to thank you all for coming to share our Christmas with us. It wouldn't have been the same without you. And secondly, here's to surviving another year. I know it's been tough for some of us, but we've got here in one piece. So a very happy Christmas one and all.'

'Happy Christmas!' Everyone raised their glasses.

'Do you know, I think this Christmas has been the best ever,' said Noel.

'Oi, that's my line,' said Cat, digging him in the ribs.

'I think it's time we had some carols,' said Gabriel. 'Christmas isn't Christmas without carols. Anyone who fancies it come and join us in the lounge.'

Marianne sat down at the piano and started to play, while Steven sang the opening lines of *Once in Royal David's City*.

One by one everyone joined in, young and old united in memories for what had been lost, and for what had been gained. It was the most perfect moment of a perfect day.

Outside in the lane, a figure in black leather sat on his motorbike, listening to the sound of the carol fill the silent air. He smiled, turned on the engine and roared down the snowy lane and into Hope Christmas High Street, where he stopped briefly to speak to Miss Woods, out on her evening spin around the town.

'Happy Christmas,' Michael said.

'Happy Christmas, Michael,' she said. 'Are you off again, then?'

'Only for a while,' he said with a smile. He looked around him, at the sparkling Christmas lights which lit up the town, and the Christmas tree which dominated the town square.

'I'm sure I'll be needed before too long,' he said.

'I imagine you will,' she said. 'God speed for now.'

'And you Miss Woods, and you,' Michael said. Then he revved up the engine and sped off into the night. Soon all that could be seen of him was a small red dot in the distant hills.

Snow started to fall softly, and then more fiercely. And soon the tracks he'd made in the road were obliterated completely.

As if he'd never been there at all.

Acknowledgements

As usual, I'd like to thank a great many people.

To my long suffering editor, Claire Bord, I'd like to extend my gratitude for her patience and unswerving support when I was somewhat less then punctual in delivering the manuscript.

And to all the amazing staff at Avon Books, a huge thank you as ever for your enthusiasm on my behalf.

Thanks to my agent Dot Lumley, who has been a rock during a difficult period.

To the wonderful staff at Burway Books, thanks for all your support.

For help in research matters, I'd like to thank my amazing twin, Ginia Moffatt, and my lovely writing pal, Kate Harrison. And thanks to Ginia and my niece Beth Cole for being my first readers.

Huge thanks also to my daughters Alex and Katie, and Lorna Dicken for their fascinating insights into the world of the modern teenJ. I hope I've got it right.

For my wonderful mother, Ann Moffatt, who always turns up trumps, thank you is probably never going to be enough, but I'll say it anyway!

And this time, my biggest thanks have to go to my wonderful family: Dave, Katie, Alex, Christine and Steph, for helping me survive the ups and downs of everyday life.

Cheats Guide to Christmas

❄ Buy your Christmas presents in the January Sales. You know it makes sense.

❄ Invite helpful family members who will chip in, not interfere.

❄ Buy a plain fruit cake, slap on some Jusrol icing and a plastic Santa and pass it off as your own.

❄ If you're not feeding an army, get a turkey roll, rather than a whole turkey.

❄ If you'd rather socialise then cook, go out for dinner.

❄ If you can't afford to go out to dinner, buy it in, cheap.

❄ Wrap presents in stages so you're not leaving it till the last minute.

❄ Send people e greetings and save on stamps and wrist ache.

❄ If you HAVE to send cards, enlist those younger members of the family capable of wielding a pen to write them for you.

❄ If you HAVE to cook Christmas pudding, make this cheating one given below – it can be prepared two days before and is DELICIOUS.

* Prepare your veg early, blanch and freeze, so you're not slaving over the peeling when your guests arrive.

* Eat in the evening so you don't have to rise at dawn to put on your turkey.

* Shop online to avoid the crowds.

* Get the children to write Christmas lists in September so you have plenty of warning.

* Get the kids to decorate the tree and don't worry about how it looks.

* Forget about perfection and concentrate on fun.

* Try to get early nights before the big day.

* Decorate the table a few days before, shut the door and forget about it till Christmas Day.

* Minimise present buying by doing Secret Santa for the adults.

* Remember it's one day a year, and you don't want to waste time being stressed...

Economical Christmas Pudding

Cooking time 6-7 hours
you will need:

1 Ib seedless raisins
6oz chopped/shredded suet
4 oz sultanas
8oz brown sugar
8oz breadcrumbs
8oz apples (grated)
8oz flour
8oz carrots (grated)
2 level teaspoons

1 tablespoon marmalade
baking powder
1 teaspoon mixed
1tbs black treacle
spice
½ pint milk/ale
½ gratednutmeg
2 eggs

1 Wash & prepare fruit
2 Mix breadcrumbs with sieved flour, baking powder, spices,
   suet and sugar
3 Add apple & carrot and mix in raisin and sultanas
4 Mix together marmalade, treacle, milk and eggs
5 Add to dry ingredients and mix thoroughly to softly
   dropping consistency
6 Thoroughly grease two 1½ pint pudding basins and divide
   mixture equally between them
7 Place a round of greaseproof paper on top of each basin and
   cover with aluminium foil
8 Steam for 6-7 hours over gentle heat replenishing water as
   required (VERY IMPORTANT IF YOU DON'T WANT
   BOWL TO CRACK!)
9 Drain puddings well and store in cool dry larder

Do not make this pudding more then 2 weeks before required.
When ready to use steam for 2 hours.

Mel and Paige's guide to teen speak

Bad – Tough As in he's a bad boy (So not James, then? *Mum*)

Beef – Gossip (What Paige spends most of her time doing. *Mel*)

BF – Best Friend (Paige's changes every week. *Mel*)

BFF – Best Friend Forever (At least I have friends. *Paige*)

Douche – Idiot (Like my big sis? *Paige*. Shut up, Paige. *Mel*)

LOL – (Hint, Mum it doesn't mean LOTS OF LOVE. *Paige*) Laugh out loud

Frape – when someone takes over your Facebook page and writes rude stuff about you. (Yes, Paige? *Mel*)

Peng – Fit (As in that boy you fancy on the bus, Paige? *Mel* No. *Paige*)

Reem – Supreme, as in he's well reem (As in ALL of One Direction. *Paige*. Ugh. *Mel*)

Stack – trip over. Usually your own feet. (Mel does that A LOT. *Paige*)

Swaggerdon – Someone who thinks they're all that. (As in Mum. *Paige*. That's a good thing? *Mum*)

Read on for an extract from

LAST
CHRISTMAS

the prequel to A Merry Little Christmas

Prologue

Marianne sat back in the comfort of Luke's brand new BMW M5. Every inch of its sleek leather interior screamed luxury, while the latest technogizmos pronounced its top-of-the-range, worthy-of-praise-from-Jeremy-Clarkson status. She glanced at Luke, who oozed confidence with practised ease as he drove with one hand on the wheel. Marianne sighed happily . . .

'What?' he said, laughing at her.

'Just pinching myself,' she replied. 'I still can't believe all this is real.'

'You are daft,' said Luke grinning, before he accelerated into the wind.

It wasn't the first time she'd had to pinch herself since she and Luke had got together. His charm and looks had entranced her from the start, even though she had felt thoroughly out of his orbit. In fact, Luke was so far removed from the sort of man she tended to fall for, the strength of her feelings had taken her by surprise. But there was something mesmerising about the combination of hazel-brown eyes and fair hair, which swept back off a strong, classical-looking face.

Under normal circumstances Marianne would never have met someone like Luke, but, thanks to Marianne's two rich friends, Carly and Lisa, who still seemed to earn ridiculous amounts of money in the City, even with the credit crunch, she had found herself on a skiing trip during February half term. Her teacher's salary wouldn't usually have stretched to that, but at the last minute Carly had pulled out and generously donated her space to Marianne, who then spent a dizzyingly intoxicating week hitting the slopes and revelling in an après-ski environment she could hardly have imagined being part of in her normal life.

She'd met Luke on the first day when, overcome with nerves, she'd fallen flat on her back in front of a group of more experienced skiers. Their laughter hadn't been unkind, but Marianne was already feeling like a fish out of water in the company of these sophisticated beautiful people. She was so far removed from her own world, and they knew it. Now she felt that she'd proved herself for the ugly-duckling klutz she undoubtedly appeared to them.

Luke was the only one who hadn't laughed. Instead, he'd swept her up in those strong arms and offered to teach her to ski. Throughout that week he'd treated her with tenderness and affection, combined with infinite amounts of patience at her obvious lack of skiing ability. Marianne had been hugely grateful for his kindness. The fact that Luke was incredibly good looking, charming and clearly fancied the pants off her had also been a great help. He made her feel like a graceful swan, even though she knew the ugly duckling was hidden away somewhere, underneath the ski gear. Being with him was a magical, dazzling, life-changing experience.

Since then, Marianne felt like her feet hadn't touched the ground as Luke whisked her into a world so completely alien to her own. He took her to Henley for the Regatta, to Wimbledon for Finals Day, to Silverstone for the Grand Prix, for weekends away in the country at exquisite hotels

2

where she felt like a film star. Every day with Luke was an adventure, but today he had surpassed all her expectations.

He'd rung the previous night. 'Fancy a weekend at my parents' place in the country?' had been his opening gambit. Marianne's heart had leaped with anticipation. With Luke it was always feast or famine – he was either frantically busy at the weekends, or impulsively spiriting her off somewhere exciting. Which was wonderful but sometimes Marianne wished they could put their relationship on a bit more of an even footing.

Did this mean that finally he was going to introduce her to his family? He'd met her parents twice now. She'd been nervous as hell on both occasions, but Luke was his usual charming self, and professed himself delighted by Marianne's rather tame suburban home. Her parents had been charmed, and her mum, who was desperate for grand-children, had to be restrained on at least one occasion from asking outright when Luke was going to join the family.

Marianne had expected a reciprocal invitation, but so far it had been unforthcoming. Luke, it seemed, was happy to meet her family, but evasive about his own. She knew he'd got money, knew he worked for the family firm in property development – 'building eco towns' was how he put it – but, apart from that, the crumbs of information he'd scattered had been few and far between. Perhaps if she weren't so dazzled by his brightness, she would have asked more questions earlier. Besides, if he wanted to tell her things, she surmised, he would. She didn't want to pry.

They were driving through winding country lanes, the late summer sun warming the car and casting long shadows on fields ripe with corn and bursting with abundance. Cows wandered contentedly through fields, and birds sang in hedgerows. It was the countryside of her dreams. Of her imagination. As a child Marianne had been obsessed with

3

stories about children having adventures in the country-side: The Famous Five, Swallows and Amazons, the Lone Pine Club all seemed to lead much more exciting lives than she did in the dull North London suburb that she called home. Marianne's favourite television programmes, *The Waltons* and *Little House on the Prairie*, provided further confirmation that her ideal future involved a cosy country cottage, being married to a man who adored her, having several rosy-faced children and, of course, heaps of animals. Their square handkerchief of a garden not allowing for pets, Marianne had been determined to make up for that as an adult.

Growing up in a grey London street, Marianne had always felt stifled and hemmed in by the city. She was never happier than when she was out on a long country walk, breathing in the fresh air and feeling at the mercy of the elements. It had long been her dream to live somewhere like this.

'This is fabulous,' Marianne said. 'What a wonderful place to live.'

'It's okay, I suppose,' said Luke dismissively. 'But I get a bit bored being a country bumpkin.'

'Really?' Marianne was incredulous. She couldn't under-stand why anyone coming from here would ever think about leaving.

'Nearly there now,' said Luke, manoeuvring the car round an incredibly slow tractor, before putting his foot down and racing through the lanes at an exhilarating speed. The wind whipped back her hair and the sun shone bright on her back. It felt fantastic to be alive.

And then, suddenly, there it was. They came round a bend, and there before them, in the middle of a vast lawn – across which *peacocks* were wandering – was an imposing Tudor house, complete with two wings, Elizabethan towers, black and white timbering and pretty gables. Marianne felt her jaw drop. Finally she was seeing Hopesay Manor, home to the Nicholas family for generations, and where Marianne's future might lie.

'*This* is the family home?' she squeaked.

Luke glanced across at her in amusement.

'Didn't I say?'

'Not exactly,' said Marianne. She'd imagined Luke living in a huge house, of course. But she'd thought it would be a rockstar kind of house, with its own pool and tennis court in the back garden. But this, this was a mansion. Vast didn't quite cover it.

'Well, it's not technically where I grew up. My parents have a pad a bit closer to Hope Christmas. Hopesay belongs to my grandfather. Not that he's here much. Silly old sod still insists on globetrotting, even at his age. I don't think he's been back here for more than a day or two for years.'

Luke said this with unaccustomed savagery and Marianne was taken aback by his sudden vehemence.

'Don't you get on with your grandfather?'

Luke smiled. 'Oh, the old bugger's okay, I suppose. He's just a bit blinkered about the way the world works these days. Insists we have duties to our people, as he puts it. He likes to think we live in some bygone feudal age, when everyone doffs their cap to Sir. He can't see the world's changed.'

'What does he think about your eco towns then?'

'He doesn't know anything about them,' admitted Luke. 'I'm the only one interested in the business side of things in this family. My mum and dad are more into playing bridge and drinking G&Ts than anything else. They're pretty shortsighted too. I run the show in his absence. If he doesn't like the way I do things he should turn up at board meetings more.'

He swept the car into the circular gravel drive in front

of the house and they got out and crunched their way up the path to the house. The large oak door was about twelve foot high and looked immensely imposing. Marianne could just about make out an inscription carved in stone above the door. Something about being happy and owing it to God.

'What does it say?' she asked, squinting up to try and see better.

'Oh, nothing important.' Luke dismissed her question with a careless wave, and lifted the brass door knocker and banged it really hard. That, too, was unusual, Marianne noted, as it seemed to depict a man – or was it a man? – wearing some kind of long robe and crushing a serpent underneath his feet. Marianne wanted to ask but, put off by Luke's evident lack of interest in anything remotely connected to the house, she fell silent. Luke impatiently banged the knocker again, and eventually a rather dusty-looking retainer, who could have been any age from fifty to a hundred, came and opened the door.

'Ah, Mr Luke, sir,' he said. 'It's been a while.'

'Hello, Humphrey,' said Luke. 'This is my friend, Marianne.' Why doesn't he say girlfriend, Marianne thought, with a disappointed lurch of her heart. 'I just thought I'd show her round the old pad before we go to see the folks.'

Humphrey nodded, and disappeared somewhere into the bowels of the house, while Marianne stood and looked at the vast hallway in awe. Compared to the suburban London semi that she called home, this was massive. The hallway was panelled in dark oak, and pictures of people in old-fashioned dress lined the stairs, which swept upwards to an imposing landing above. The black and white tiled marble floor echoed as she walked on it. She felt fantastically overexposed in such a huge space. Marianne's stomach contracted. This was so different from where she grew up. How could she possibly ever fit in here? Surely now Luke had her on his home territory it was only a matter of time before he saw it too?

'Jeez, it's dark in here,' said Luke, and opened some shutters to let in the evening light. Motes danced in the beams cast by the setting sun, dazzling Marianne as she stood, silently drinking it in.

'Well, what do you think?' said Luke.

'It's fantastic,' murmured Marianne.

He drew her to him, and her heart thumped erratically as he kissed her on the lips. Marianne felt a familiar flutter in her stomach. She had never desired someone as strongly as she desired Luke. It terrified her how much she wanted him. Suppose he didn't want her as much?

'There's a four-poster in the master bedroom,' he said mischievously.

'We can't,' she protested. 'Not here.'

'There's no one here but us,' said Luke. 'Who's to know?'

'Er – your butler?' She went out with a man who had a butler? This felt so surreal. Any minute she was going to wake up.

'He won't say anything. Besides, he's as deaf as a post so you can be as noisy as you like,' said Luke, with a grin on his face that was impossible to resist.

He dragged her giggling by the hand up the stairs, pointing out various ancestors en route: 'The original Ralph Nicholas, went with Richard I to the Holy Land; Gabriel Nicholas, hid in the priest hole under Edward VI and lived to tell the tale; Ralph II saved Charles II at the battle of Worcester, nada, nada, nada . . .'

'How can you be so dismissive?' said Marianne. 'I mean, in my family the height of historical interest is the time when Great Aunt Maud stood next to George VI at Windsor Park. I come from a noble line of labourers and serfs. This is . . . just . . . incredible. I'd love to have this kind of ancestry.'

'You wouldn't if you knew my family,' said Luke, with a grimace. 'With power comes responsibility, manners maketh the man. We have a duty of care. We even have a Latin family motto, *Servimus liberi liberi quia diligimus*, which translates as: "Freely we serve, because we freely love". Having that shoved down your throat from birth is pretty stifling.'

'Oh,' exclaimed Marianne. They had come to the landing, and Luke flung open the window shutters to reveal a landscaped lawn complete with fountains, walled gardens and, in the background, a deer park. 'This is amazing. You're so lucky.'

'I *am* lucky – to have found you,' he said, and her heart skipped a sudden beat. *This* was why she was with him. For the way he looked at her as if she was the only woman in the world. For the way he made her feel so incredibly special. All her doubts and anxieties disappeared as Luke took her hand and knelt down. 'I wasn't going to do this now, but seeing you here looking so incredibly sexy, I can't resist.'

Oh my God, Marianne thought, was he going to . . .?

'Hang on, I've forgotten something . . .' Luke ran over to a set of curtains which was lying in a corner and unhooked a curtain ring. He came running back, fell back down on his knee, and said, 'Now, where were we?'

Marianne stood motionless as he kissed her hand, slipped the curtain ring onto her engagement finger, and said, 'Marianne Moore, will you marry me?'

'Yes,' she whispered. She didn't have to think for a second; this was what she'd wanted her whole life, to be with a man she loved and live in a wonderful place like this. 'Yes, of course I will.' And suddenly she was in his arms, and they were running through the house shrieking with delight.

A sudden slam of the door brought them both to their senses.

'What was that?' said Marianne.

A bell rang impatiently from the hall, and they ran to the banisters to look down.

A smallish, elderly, dapper man stood in the hallway looking rather cross.

'Grandfather?' Luke's face was a picture of shock and dismay.

'Luke, my boy, is that you?' the man said. 'I can see I haven't come home a moment too soon.'

Part One
I Gave You My Heart

Last Year

December 22

Sainsbury's was heaving. Catherine, already feeling hypo-critical that she was here at all, felt her heart sink as she saw the hordes of people ravaging through the super-market, frantically grabbing things from the shelves as if they were in the last-chance saloon and they might never have the chance to shop again. For God's sake, she felt like saying, as she saw people staggering past with trolleys full to the brim with hams and turkeys, mince pies and brandy butter, and the inevitable bottles of booze, it's not like we're all going to starve, is it? Then she berated herself. After all, *she* was here too, wasn't she?

But only for the necessary items, things she'd forgotten, like brandy butter and Christmas pud. Mum had prom-ised to make both, but uncharacteristically for her had forgotten, so Catherine was grumpily facing the seething hordes, all of whom looked as miserable as she felt. She wondered if she should give up and try and make them herself. It's what the bloody Happy Homemaker was always telling people to do.

No, Cat, she admonished herself. There were still pres-ents to wrap, a turkey to defrost, vegetables to prepare, a house to make ready for the guests (and one which would unscramble itself as fast as she tidied) – she *really* didn't have time to make a Christmas pudding. Not even that one from her Marguerite Patten cookbook, which could actually be made the day before. The Happy Homemaker could go stuff herself.

'That sounds like an eminently sensible idea to me.' A little old man in his seventies, wearing a smart gabardine coat, doffed his hat to her as he walked past with a basket under his arm.

'I beg your pardon?' Cat looked at the man in astonishment. She must have been wittering on to herself again. She had a bad habit of doing that in supermarkets.

'I was just observing that you could for once let yourself off the hook,' said the man. 'Christmas isn't all about perfection, you know.'

'Oh, but it is,' said Catherine, 'and this is going to be the most *perfect* Christmas ever.'

'Well, I certainly hope so,' said the man. 'I wish you a very happy and peaceful Christmas.' And with that he was gone, disappearing into the crowd while Catherine was left pondering how on earth a complete stranger seemed to know so much about her. How very, very odd.

Catherine took a deep breath and ploughed her trolley into the fray. Christmas muzak was pumping out, presumably to get her into the spirit of the thing. Not much chance of that, when she had felt all Christmassed out for months. Bugger off, she felt like shouting as a particularly cheesy version of 'Have Yourself a Merry Little Christmas' blared out. Look at all these people. Do any of them look bloody merry?

Christmas seemed to start earlier and earlier every year, and, now she had children in three different schools, Catherine had been obliged to sit through as many Christmas performances (one year she really was going to get Noel to come to one of these things if it killed her), which varied from the sweet but haphazard (her four-year-old's star turn as a donkey), through the completely incomprehensible (the seven and nine-year-olds' inclusive Nativity, which had somehow managed to encompass Diwali, Eid and Hanukkah – an impressive feat, she had to admit), to the minimalist and experimental concert put on at the secondary school her eleven-year-old had just started. One of the reasons Catherine had wanted a large family was so she could have the big family Christmas she'd always missed out on by being an only child. Catherine had always imagined that she'd love attending her children's carol concerts, not find them a huge chore. And no one told her how much work it would be preparing Christmas for a family of six, let alone all the hangers-on who always seemed to migrate her way, like so many homing pigeons, on Christmas Day.

'Next year, remind me to emigrate,' Catherine murmured to herself, as she propelled herself through the mince pie section. Bloody hell. Once upon a time people had bought (or most likely made) mince pies. Now Sainsbury's had a whole section devoted to them: luxury mince pies, mince pies with brandy, mince pies with sherry, deep-filled, fat-free, gluten-free, dairy-free, probably mince-free for all she knew. The world had gone mad.

'Me too.' The woman browsing the shelves next to her gave a wry laugh in sympathy. She looked at Catherine curiously. Oh God, no . . .

'Aren't you—?'

'Yes,' sighed Catherine, 'I'm afraid I am.'

'I'm such a huge fan,' said the woman. 'I keep *all* your recipes. I don't know what I'd do without your lemon tart.'

'Thanks so much,' said Catherine, guiltily hoping the woman wouldn't notice what she had in her shopping trolley, otherwise her cover as the provider of all things home-made was going to be well and truly blown. 'I'd love

15

to stop, really I would, but unfortunately I'm in a tearing hurry. Places to go, people to see. I'm sure you'll understand. Have a wonderful Christmas.'

Catherine felt terrible for rushing off. The poor woman had seemed nice and it was churlish of her to react like that. But couldn't she have five minutes' peace just to be herself and not the bloody awful persona who seemed to be taking over her life? She went to join one of the many huge queues that had built up as she'd wandered round the store, and caught sight of the latest version of *Happy Homes* by the tills. There she was resplendent in a Santa costume and hat (why, oh why, had she let herself be persuaded to do that shoot?), next to a headline that bore the legend, 'The Happy Homemaker's Guide to the Perfect Christmas.'

Any minute now someone in the queue was going to make the connection between the Happy Homemaker and the harassed woman standing behind them, and realise she was a big fat fraud. Catherine didn't think she could stand it. She glanced over at the serve yourself tills, where the queues looked even more horrendous, and people were indulging in supermarket rage as the computers overloaded and spat out incorrect answers or added up the bills wrong.

Catherine looked in her trolley. She had been in Sainsbury's for half an hour and all she had to show for it were two packets of mince pies, a bag of sugar, a Christmas pudding, and no brandy butter. At this rate she would be queuing for at least half an hour before she got served, by which time every sod in Sainsbury's would probably discover her alter ego.

16